Also by John Masters in Sphere Books:

NIGHTRUNNERS OF BENGAL
THE FIELD-MARSHAL'S MEMOIRS
FANDANGO ROCK
NOW, GOD BE THANKED

The
Himalayan Concerto

JOHN MASTERS

SPHERE BOOKS LIMITED
30/32 Gray's Inn Road, London WC1X 8JL

First published in Great Britain
by Michael Joseph Ltd 1976

Copyright © Bengal-Rockland 1976
First Sphere Books edition 1977
Reprinted 1980

To the 4th Gorkha Rifles
Heirs of the 4th Prince of Wales's Own Gorkha Rifles
All men of the Himalayas

TRADE
MARK

This book is sold subject to the condition that
it shall not, by way of trade or otherwise, be lent,
re-sold, hired out or otherwise circulated without
the publisher's prior consent in any form of
binding or cover other than that in which it is
published and without a similar condition
including this condition being imposed on the
subsequent purchaser.

Set in Linotype Times

Printed in Great Britain by
Hazell Watson and Viney Ltd
Aylesbury, Bucks

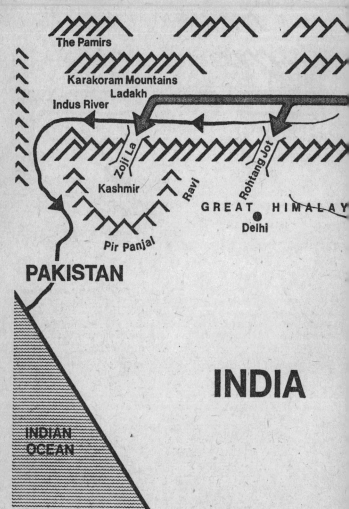

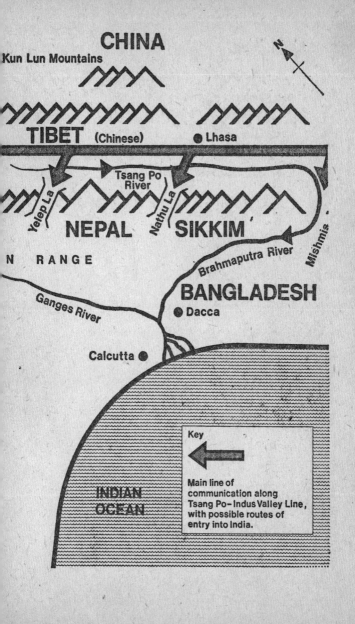

CHAPTER ONE

The pony stepped carefully down the rock-strewn path, the pony boy walking ten paces behind, his long hillman's stride effortlessly keeping pace. Rodney eased his weight forward, loosened the reins, and sighed with content. The sound of the Girwan torrent came muted to him up here, nearly six hundred feet above the gorge, adding a deep undertone to the soughing of the wind in the deodars and the rhythmic crunch of the pony's hooves. Straight ahead, looking down the V of the valley, the forested hills across the Liddar fell like a dense dark curtain from a pale blue sky, streaked with high, slow-moving cirrus clouds. Behind him a parapet of snow, glittering now in the direct rays of the late morning sun, blocked the upper end of the Girwan. Over his right shoulder, as he turned to look, Kolahoi towered in aloof splendour, veils of snow streaming away from its thrusting spires.

Turning again he saw that a lone rider had come into view below, struggling up towards him. Shading his eyes with his hand, he recognized the owner of the contracting service which had arranged this combination trek and fishing expedition for him. He waited for the slow-climbing horse to reach him.

The woman raised her hand in greeting and cried, 'Dr. Livingstone, I presume! Had a good trip?'

'Marvellous!' he answered. 'Terrific scenery, good weather ... and quite a few big browns.'

'Did my people look after you all right? I see you sent them on ahead today. I passed them about an hour ago.'

'They did me very well indeed.'

'But they couldn't make you really relax,' she said, smiling. 'You've been shaving! Every day?'

He nodded. 'I couldn't relax that far, Mrs. Sanders. What would my father the *pakka sahib* say? Her Majesty Our Queen?' He smiled, thinking that it wasn't a very good joke; the truth was the truth – that he couldn't relax the way most people could. He wished it were not so.

Kit Sanders swung her horse's head round to face down-hill. 'I needed some fresh air and thought I'd come out to meet you. It's not far to camp now.' She swept her hand round the immense vista. 'How do you like it? How does our Kashmir here compare to Sikkim and Darjeeling? I've never been down that end of the Himalayas.'

She was about forty, blonde, grey-eyed, big-bosomed, a little heavy of limb. The pony looked overloaded under her, though that was due rather to the smallness of the animal than to her largeness.

Rodney thought before answering. 'It's different. The mountains are bigger there, and that alters the scale of everything else – trees, rivers, people. Years ago I was trekking for six days round Kanchenjunga, and I had the top twenty thousand feet of it in view nearly all the time. Kolahoi up there isn't eighteen thousand in all, and we're a good many thousand above sea level, so there isn't so much sheer mass visible.'

'We're at about nine thousand here,' she said. She urged her pony into a walk, and Rodney followed. Both of them lapsed into a companionable silence. She had not lost her American accent in all these years, he thought, though her husband had been an Englishman. She was a pleasant woman and, more important for him, an efficient con-tractor. He thought back seven years to his trek above Darjeeling. It was higher country, but because it was farther south, it had felt richer, greener, more enclosed. Of course, once you came down off the high places, it *was* enclosed: the valley of the Teesta was pure rain forest, dense and teeming. Kashmir felt more remote, the light paler, the views generally farther. There was a breath of Central Asia in the air here, in the way the mountain shepherds, the *gujjars*, dressed; in the sight of a line of ponies, heavily laden, struggling up a distant pass, April snow flurries, suddenly hiding, as suddenly revealing . . . and he had been unhappier in Darjeeling, recognizing that his then-new marriage was already in trouble, unable to think how to improve it, his time of study of Indian music at an end, no idea how to use his new knowledge, no certainty that he had assimilated enough of its soul, outside the sheer technical facts. . . .

Some bars of a theme came into his head and for a few

minutes he followed them. That could be a nice intro-
ductory or bridge passage . . . but *from* what, *to* what. Besides, now that he had turned the passage well over, trans-
posed it into another key, and tried it again, he recognized
it: it was a bridge from his own first major work, the
Cotswold Suite, written immediately after he had got his
B.Mus. degree. A rather precious little bridge, really. . . .

Mrs. Sanders interrupted his thoughts. 'Composing again,
Mr. Bateman? I'm sorry to interrupt you, but, if you don't
mind a scramble, there's some excellent fishing down there.'
She reined in her pony and pointed down the steep hillside
toward the Girwan stream far below. 'See that narrow
place? You have to reach the stream before that – and then
probably wade quite a bit at this time of year, though the
real snow melt hasn't come down yet. There are a couple of
miles of alternating pools, rapids and narrows, till the
valley opens out above Arau.'

Rodney didn't waste time pondering. He'd come on this
trek to fish, as well as enjoy the mountains, and here was
some fishing. Tomorrow or the next day he'd have to face
the agony of composing. 'All right,' he said and began to
dismount, the pony boy running forward to hold the horse's
head as he did so.

'You'll find camp set up near the Arau rest house. You
can't miss it.'

He nodded, and took his telescopic rod and creel from
the pony boy who had been carrying them. 'Take it easy
going down there,' Mrs. Sanders called as he slipped over
the edge of the six-foot-wide bridle trail. 'There are no
hidden cliffs, but it's steep.'

He waved his rod and set off down the slope, passing
carefully from tree to giant tree till, looking back up the
hill, he could not see the path, nor even where it must be,
everything hidden by the trees. He went on down.

As Mrs. Sanders had warned him, he had to wade
through the first narrows, and the water was cold enough
to make his feet ache. But after that the river widened and
he strolled down the bank in sunlight, several yards back
from the water. After a few minutes he came to a silent,
swirling pool and stopped. He assembled the rod, opened
his fly case and leafed through the little felt pads . . . a
sunny day, early in the year, water very cold, but not yet

11

clouded by today's snow melt, fish probably rather sluggish . . . he selected a Peter Ross and tied it on carefully. Wet fly casting with this sort of rod wasn't the easiest thing in the world, nor could it ever be very well done, but it didn't need to be on a stream as narrow as this. The trees were well back from the water on this side; a brown cliff dropped sheer into the stream the other side. The pool was about fifteen feet wide and forty feet long. There ought to be some good fish in it . . . if he could wake them up.

He began to cast, settling the fly into the water near the head of the pool, and watching carefully as it swung across the current. When the line ran straight downstream without a bite, he flicked it back, let it curve in a bow behind him and gently bent his wrist forward. The fly settled exactly where he wanted, and sank without a ripple. He sighed. His hand had not lost its cunning. It would be pretty disgraceful if it had, he thought, after having a fly rod thrust into it at the age of four, and from seven on being an unofficial ghillie and instructor at his father's trout farm. He began to hum a theme from his opera, *Spitfire*, under his breath, casting steadily as he worked his way cautiously down the pool.

At the bottom he started back up, and stopped humming. He ought to be thinking of new themes, not congratulating himself on old ones. His *Himalayan Concerto* would never grow to be more than an idea, a bombastic idea at that, if he didn't work at it . . . try to find the natural music of these mountains and these rivers, and blend into that the singing of the men and women who lived here, the tunes that they played on their pipes as they sat on these great slopes, the sheep and goats spread below them across the tilted alps. Finding the tunes wasn't hard. Composing a great work from them was . . . hell.

Nothing here. He went on down through the next narrows to the next pool, and again began casting.

He didn't understand India, perhaps. Perhaps that was the reason he was finding it so damnably difficult to get started on a theme or even a movement of the new concerto. At the project's conception, a couple of months ago, he had thought that the composition would come easily. Why had he thought that, in the face of all his experience? Because it hadn't. Perhaps it was worse because he did not

12

understand Indreni; though it was fair to say that Indreni didn't understand him, either – or try to. But that was her problem. *She* wasn't trying to write a British symphony. She wasn't doing a thing, except sit back in England, with the children, withdrawn from nearly all contact with the real world, refusing to go back to India, hating England. God, why had they had the children?

The tip of the rod dipped and he felt a strong pull on the line. He saw the fish now, a brown of about a pound and a half, swimming strongly upstream, near the surface. There were several rocks and snags in the pool, and the telescopic rod didn't have the flexibility of an ordinary rod. He was using a nylon mono filament leader tapered to five pounds, so he'd have to be careful. He concentrated on the fish struggling against the pull of his line and the wavering bastion of the rod. Gently he walked forward and back, giving out line, taking it in. Slowly the trout came near the bank. He waded in, got his fingers under its gills, unhooked it, cracked its head against a stone, lined his creel with grass, damped it, and dropped the trout in. On, downstream.

Three fish, one of them a three-pounder, and four pools later, Rodney glanced at his watch. He whistled under his breath. With a fishing rod in his hand, and alone in this vastness, time had no meaning; but he acknowledged a little gnawing of hunger. He'd pack up and just walk downstream the rest of the way to Arau, however tempting the pools looked. After all, if he saw something particularly promising, he could always come back after lunch. He telescoped his rod, put away his reel in the fishing bag slung over his shoulder and started downstream, now on the right bank of the Girwan torrent, now on the left bank, as the fall of the cliffs dictated.

After a few minutes he thought he heard an alien sound, and stopped. The water rushed in his ears, the pines creaked, the needles sighed. Once more he heard it, this time more definite – a shout, a man's shout, formless and wordless as far as he could tell, though he did not know in what language it had been cast, if any. But it was not the shout of, say, a shepherd calling his dog. It was not the shout of a man calling to his wife to bring up his dinner. He began to run. It had been a cry of alarm.

13

He burst round a rocky outcrop and thought he saw, from the corner of his eye, some movement of grey figures among the trees across the river, but his attention was at once caught and held by the figure spreadeagled face down in the water directly in front of him, in a place where the torrent burst down and out between two great granite boulders, to form a boiling pool before breaking out under more rocks at the lower end. A man in a tweed jacket and corduroy trousers lay face down in this pool, his head jammed under one of the smaller rocks at the bottom end.

Rodney leaped forward, throwing aside rod and bag and creel, stumbling across the stones at the side of the river, climbed over a big rock and skidded down the lichen-covered far side into the pool. He gasped for breath as he plunged in up to his chest. The surging water tugged at his balance as he reached down for the man's collar. He caught it and pulled with all his strength. Suddenly the head came free, and Rodney held it above water, still fighting for his own balance. The man's eyes were closed, it was impossible to tell whether he was breathing or not . . . his face was violet, pale brown skin underneath, wide mouth, curved lips. Rodney slipped his hands under the other's armpits and began to drag him out of the pool. In a moment his foot slipped on the treacherous rounded stones under his boots, and he went under water, dragging the other down with him. Struggling for breath in the numbing cold he surfaced, the man still grasped firmly in his arms. He headed downstream, reached the shallows, and backed cautiously out over them, heaving the man after him. At last he reached the bank on the same side that he had started from and, shivering violently, collapsed beside the stranger.

Before he had properly regained his breath he struggled to his feet, turned the other on to his face and then, standing over him, caught him round the waist, and lifted him till he was a bow, his head and knees trailing. Rodney lifted, shook, shook again. The body in his hands heaved, retched, and a gout of water poured out of his mouth. 'That's it!' Rodney gasped. 'Get it all up!' He pulled again, and the man vomited more water. Twice more, and then Rodney lowered him, turned him over and knelt, placing his knees beside the other's chest. He pressed and relaxed

14

on the man's chest until his shaky, painful breathing settled into an almost regular rhythm. Twice the man turned his head slightly and threw up more of the water that had filled his lungs. His eyes opened and he muttered something. Rodney leaned down to hear. This time he heard the other's word: 'Geminus!'

Rodney leaned back. The man was temporarily out of his mind. A half smile was forming on the other's face, and now his eyes remained open. 'I feel awful,' he whispered.

'Don't move,' Rodney said. 'Can you breathe all right?'

'Yes.' The eyes closed. Rodney watched, anxious and puzzled. The man was about his own age, and dressed for fishing. In fact he thought he remembered seeing a good fly rod back there on the bank as he rushed into the water. But how had he got into this fix? No one in his right mind would have been trying to fish that particular piece of the river, or using it as a crossing place; but if he had been neither fishing nor crossing, how had he fallen in?

The stranger was shivering, and Rodney began to shiver again in sympathy. He said, 'How do you feel?'

'Still awful.'

'I know. But I want to get you to the edge of the trees, where I can find wood and light a fire.'

'I can walk that far, if you help.'

'I will. Here. . . .' He carefully pulled the other upright. The man reeled and if it had not been for Rodney's arm, would have fallen. His knees buckled and Rodney heaved him upright. 'Careful now . . . this way . . . hold tight on my shoulder. I've got you.' Step by step they crossed the uneven turf to the edge of the forest. Lowering his burden against a tree, saying, 'Rest there,' Rodney began to collect dried twigs. There were plenty for it had not rained for some time, and in five minutes he could use his lighter to start a fire. Ten minutes more again, and the twigs and small boughs were blazing cheerfully.

The stranger was leaning back against his tree, his eyes closed, his mouth drooping a little open, and – again – that strange half smile on his face. Rodney took a closer look at him. He was an Indian, at about six feet perhaps an inch or two taller than himself, also lighter and more slender. His hair, now dank, was long and black and straight; his hands were long – everything long, for the

15

face was narrow, the nose long, the fingers long on the fine-boned hands ... the sort of hands that people thought pianists and violinists had, instead of the stubby powerful ones, like his own, that they usually did.

'Now what?' the man said, his eyes open.

'Well . . .' Rodney paused. 'What happened?' he asked suddenly, remembering the thought, the hint of a vision he had had when he reached this place. Had he not seen pale grey or tan things, perhaps human beings? Could it have been two or three men running, disappearing into the forest?

'I fell in and hit my head,' the other said. 'I was trying to cross. Damned fool.' He spoke English perfectly, but the slight singsong intonation showed that he had not been educated in England itself; probably at some English-type public school out here, like the one in Darjeeling. And he may well have had a father who was English-educated. 'Here. Feel.'

Rodney felt gingerly where the other's hand led him. There was an open wound in the hair at the back of the man's head, and when he drew his hand back he saw blood on his fingers.

'I can't walk far yet,' the other said, 'but after some rest I could.'

'I could reach our camp in about half an hour,' Rodney said, 'and get Mrs. Sanders to send up a pony for you. I'll bring it up myself.'

The other shook his head, wincing. 'Can't get a horse up here from Arau. . . . Is Kit your contractor? You're in good hands.' He moved his head and winced again. 'Ow! That hurts . . . and I don't feel at all well, really. Excuse me.' He rolled to his knees, crawled a few paces away and vomited, this time food and drink. After a time he crawled back. 'I do apologize.'

'I wish I had my flask,' Rodney began, but the other waved a feeble hand. 'You need it more than I do, and you'd have to drink it all yourself. I don't touch the stuff. Whisky is the chain the British used to keep the educated Indian tied to their chariot wheels, my father said.' He smiled, a sweet smile spreading across his wide mouth, showing even white teeth.

16

He ought to start down to get help, Rodney thought; but he could not get that vision out of his mind. Would this fellow be safe if he left him here? But if there was danger, it meant that the man had lied about falling into the Girwan. Why? Why had he been crossing without his rod?

'My name's Chandra Gupta,' the other said, 'of an eminent Bengali family. I am a journalist and occasional writer. A poet, even. I ought to tackle the Great Indian Novel, but I never will. . . .' He was looking up, obviously expecting Rodney to introduce himself.

'Rodney Bateman,' he said.

'The composer? The *Ganges Symphony?*'

'Yes.' Rodney felt warm and gratified. His two 'River' symphonies, *No. 1, Severn,* and *No. 2, Ganges,* were quite well-known in the West, but he had written them in the western musical idiom, even the *Ganges,* and he had not expected. . . . The other interrupted his thoughts. 'Oah, we Bengalees are quite well educated, for black men.' He was laughing silently. He stopped, before Rodney could say anything, and said, 'You *are* Gemini, aren't you?'

Rodney said, 'Yes. June 12th.'

The other's half-mocking expression changed. He said softly, 'I knew the man who saved me was a Gemini. I said so, didn't I? But we are more. We are twins. My birthday is June 12th, 1942.'

'1942!' Rodney exclaimed, 'what an extraordinary . . .'

A man's voice interrupted him. 'I say . . .' Rodney turned to find himself looking into a pair of dark glasses set in a round red-brown face above a fierce R.A.F. type moustache. The newcomer removed his sunglasses, peered at Chandra Gupta, and said, 'Are you all right? You're soaked. You're both soaked!'

'This man – Mr. Chandra Gupta – fell in,' Rodney said. 'I was able to fish him out.'

'You look as if you could use a drink,' the new arrival said, and now Rodney saw that he was accompanied, at a short distance, by a Kashmiri servant carrying a creel, spare rod and other fishing equipment. The man felt in his pocket and pulled out a large silver flask. 'Black Knight,' he said proffering it. Rodney took a long pull while Gupta, smiling, held up one hand, palm outward.

The new arrival said, 'You should both get down to your

camps as soon as you can, and get into dry clothes. . . . By the way, I'm Nawal Contractor – Air Vice-Marshal. Are you the writer johnny?' he asked Chandra Gupta. Gupta nodded, 'Guilty.'

The Air Vice-Marshal sniffed, and Rodney got the impression that he didn't like writers in general and this one in particular; but he said grudgingly. 'You were pretty good on Krishna Menon.'

'*Menon and the Generals,*' Gupta murmured, 'I was too young, really. But that was when it happened, and I had no choice but to be twenty at the time.'

Gupta struggled to his feet, leaned against a tree for a long moment, then stood away. Rodney quickly stepped forward to support him. The long dark eyes turned to him, warm, and the voice whispered, barely audibly, 'Thank you, Geminus.' With Gupta leaning on Rodney's shoulder, they set off slowly down the river bank.

The Air Vice-Marshal's voice, calling from upstream behind them, was aggrieved. 'Hi, you chaps, one of you's leaving behind a telescopic rod and creel and fishing bag.'

Rodney turned. 'They're mine. Thanks. . . . What about yours, Gupta?'

Chandra Gupta looked around and said, 'It's gone. I had it in my hand when. . . . Forget it.'

The airman said, 'Wait a second. What's that, over there?' He walked along the bank and picked up a rod. 'Eight foot split cane. Feels like a Hardy.'

'That's mine,' Chandra Gupta said wearily. 'Could you possibly bring it down for me when you come? I'm really feeling a little done in.'

They started off again, down the bank of the Girwan torrent, the slope of the river gradually easing as they came out of the grip of Kolahoi's widespread arms.

The sun hung low over the western ridges as the old man carefully placed a bottle of whisky, three bottles of soda and three glasses on the folding table. Rodney sat facing west, the Air Marshal on his right, the red sunlight polishing his bald pate, and Kit Sanders on his left. Smoke rose from the cook tents a little down the rich green slope. In the tents for sleeping, men knelt blowing up inflatable mattresses and arranging sleeping bags and extra blankets,

18

for there would be a sharp frost in the spring night at this altitude.

The old man said, 'Does the presence require anything else?' His full beard was obviously dyed its rich orange-red with henna, and the gold *kulla* on his head was faded and a little tattered. The airman shook his head, 'Nothing, thank you, Akbar Khan.' The old man turned and strode silently away.

'Great old boy,' the airman murmured. 'You don't find servants like that any more. You're lucky, Kit.'

'He's not exactly a servant,' Mrs. Sanders said. 'More like a friend, and of course partner. I don't know what I'd have done without him.'

'But you were helping Mike to run the business for years before he ... for years, weren't you?'

She nodded, raising the glass that Rodney had filled for her. 'Yes, but I didn't know the intricacies – the parts that the *sahib log* don't usually see. Now I do . . .' She cocked an ear and seemed to be listening. Rodney heard a radio from the cook tent. It was giving out the news in Hindustani, and he too listened. The Chinese Government were lodging an official complaint about the treatment of their trade delegation in Nepal. Also in Nepal there had been an incident between Nepalese and Chinese troops somewhere along the northern border; details were lacking but would be broadcast as soon as known; it was not thought to be a serious matter. . . .

Rodney muttered, 'The Chinese are acting very aggressively these days, aren't they?'

The Air Marshal looked at him in surprise – 'You speak Hindustani?'

'After a fashion,' Rodney said, 'Hindi, really – and rather more Bengali. . . . I've come back to write a Himalayan Concerto.'

'Good show,' the airman said absently. He tapped the newspaper in his lap. 'How did this paper get here?'

'I flew it in this morning in the new Saab.'

The Air Marshal said, 'How you manage to land that Saab on the *marg* without pranging it, I don't know. It gives me the shakes just to watch you. If you were a man, I'd kidnap you and make you chief flying instructor to my command.'

19

'The Air Marshal is responsible for all our air forces in the far east,' Mrs. Sanders said. 'Assam, Arunachal Pradesh, all that. He's on leave . . . for this week, he's on leave from his wife, too.' She patted the Air Marshal's hand, laughing.

'She doesn't like fishing,' he growled, returning to his paper. After a while, as the others sat in aimless talk, he muttered, 'Ought to throw these bloody KAM leaders in jail, every one of them.'

'You'd have the biggest *hartal* you ever saw on your hands, if you did,' Mrs. Sanders said. 'And the K.P.P. might come out from underground, and then things would get violent, and not even the Sayyid could stop it. And you wouldn't like that, especially if the Pakistanis chose that moment to have another go at us.'

Rodney said, 'You sound like a newspaper headline, Mrs. Sanders – KAM and K.P.P. support SEATO, WAFFL nixes U.S. OGPU.'

She laughed. 'Do please call me Kit, Mr. Bateman. Everyone else does.'

'My name's Rodney.'

'Yes . . . KAM stands for Kashmir Azad Movement. It's a political party formed of Kashmiris who want to be independent both of India and Pakistan. The head of KAM is a wonderful man called Sayyid Ghulam Mohammed.'

'A *sayyid* is a descendant of the Prophet Mohammed through his daughter Fatima. I know that.' Rodney said.

'Yes. Well, our *sayyid* is a great landowner in the Vale, and also in Jammu. He's dedicated to non-violence. Gandhi was his hero. His KAM was made legal three years ago, because . . . '

'Because our politicians think it's a good safety valve,' the Air Marshal snorted. 'They're still a rotten lot of traitors, if you ask me.'

'Better than the K.P.P.,' Kit Sanders said. 'That's the Kashmir People's Party, which is illegal and therefore stays underground. They *do* believe in violence. Every now and then they blow up a police *thana,* or sabotage some government office. There have even been a couple of assassinations. No one knows just how many members K.P.P. has, or who the head of it is, because, as I said, it's underground.'

20

Akbar Khan appeared silently at her side and bent down to speak to her. She said, 'Akbar Khan says dinner will be ready in half an hour, and there's hot water available now for washing.'

'I washed and changed as soon as I got in,' Rodney said. 'I only hope my other clothes will be dry for tomorrow.'

'They'll be dry,' the Air Marshal said, waving his hand toward a roaring bonfire, whence sparks towered up into the twilight beyond the cook tent, 'perhaps a little browner than they were before.'

Rodney saw that his shirt, trousers and underclothes were spread out over empty cartons a few inches from the blaze. He stood up, glancing at his watch. 'I think I'll go and see how Gupta is.'

'He was asleep an hour ago,' Kit Sanders said anxiously. 'I don't think . . .'

'I won't wake him if he's still asleep,' Rodney reassured her, moving toward Gupta's tent.

Kit Sanders clucked over Gupta like a mother hen, he thought. She had obviously known him a long time and seemed to be a great admirer. At least, she had gone as pale about the chops as her ruddy complexion would allow when she saw Gupta limping slowly into camp, by then not needing Rodney's shoulder, but showing the strain of his experience in his face and the weary drag of his stride. She had run up. 'What's happened? Chandra, Chandra, my God, what's the matter, you look awful!'

'I'm feeling awful,' he had answered, still with his ghost of a smile, 'but not dead, or about to be, just yet.'

Then she had hurried back, shouting to his servants to come and undress him and get him to bed: she herself had run down to her own cooks and brought hot tea for him. . . .

Now, one of Gupta's men was squatting in the entrance to his tent, setting an electric battery lamp on the camp table inside. As Rodney came close, the strong yellowish light spread out through the open tent flap and he saw that Gupta was sitting up in the camp bed, smoking a cigarette, a dressing-gown thrown round his shoulders. The servant left, and from the entrance Rodney said, 'May I come in?'

'Geminus? Come in!' Gupta sat up higher in the bed and

reaching out, switched on a small transistor radio beside the lamp, turning the volume very low.

Rodney listened a moment and said, 'Manipuri, isn't it?'

'All India Radio, that's all I know. I wish I did know something about our music, but I don't, no more than any peasant or mechanic would.'

'You're a journalist. No one can know everything.'

Gupta looked up. 'I make a living as a journalist, and I've written a few books, as Contractor mentioned, but I'm not really a journalist. I'm a poet.'

'In English?'

'No. Bengali. My father was at Oxford – he was I.C.S. – but my education was St. Peter's, Darjeeling, and Calcutta University.'

'You speak English perfectly.'

'You'd know I was Indian, wouldn't you? Of course! Besides, I may speak English, but I think Bengali. My mother was very keen that I should use Bengali, and we always did in the house when I was a child.'

He sat back, closing his eyes. Rodney settled more comfortably into the canvas chair beside him. The aroma of Chandra's Turkish cigarette filled the tent. The radio was now playing recorded Indian classical music, a *rag* for *sarod*, *tabla* and *tamboura*. They were playing very well, and he thought he recognized the touch of Ram Dayal on the *sarod*. His eyes felt heavy and slowly closed. The yellow light bathed his eyelids. Down by the bonfire the Kashmiris were singing what sounded like a love song.

The *rag* ended. He sat up, rubbing his eyes. Chandra Gupta was smiling at him. The smile was subtle, the lips parted. A smile like that, on the face of any other man, would have meant a homosexual approach; but there was none here. He was sure of it, so sure that he put his hand out and let it rest on the bed, he didn't know why. Chandra's hand came down on his, and lay there, the fingers gripping lightly.

'Thank you, Geminus,' Gupta said. 'Again.'

Rodney turned over his hand and gently returned the other's pressure. Gupta looked down at his palm and said, 'You have the mark of Vishnu . . . here, see this line, and this? The sign of the male.'

'I am a man, I think,' Rodney said, smiling.

22

'So am I,' Gupta said, 'but look here . . .' He opened his left hand, palm up. 'See, the trident of Shiva, mark of the female. I like women and understand them. They understand me, too.' He looked again at Rodney's palm. 'And you, how do you live with women? A little obstinate sometimes? They are a mystery to you?'

'Often,' Rodney said: to his own surprise he found himself adding, 'My wife's about to divorce me. I don't understand what went wrong. Or why I asked her to marry me in the first place. Or why we had children when I, at least, knew it was not working out right. . . .'

Chandra smiled and released his hand. 'I don't know whether that will come out right . . . but you will, Geminus. There is the mark of genius in that hand. Geniuses are seldom altogether happy.'

Neither spoke for a long time. Rodney thought, this is very strange; I feel quite at ease, yet I am behaving as I have never done in my life, with man or woman.

He broke the silence by asking, 'Are you quite O.K. now?'

'Just about, though I have no right to be. My horoscope – the one the Brahmins made when I was born – said I'd never reach my thirty-seventh birthday, and that's to be this June. Well, you know that, don't you, because you'll be thirty-seven the same day. . . . I'll take two aspirins after dinner and get a good night's sleep. The bearer put a big plaster on the back of my head.'

'You're going to eat?'

'Good heavens, yes! I lost my breakfast and had no lunch. Besides, I have to have my daily tin of Campbell's tomato soup. I've had one every day since that pop painting came out.'

A bell was ringing from across the grass. Rodney looked out. It was dark, the night full of stars, shadowy figures moving between bright lamps, a white tablecloth spread over three boxes on the grass, Kit Sanders and the Air Marshal standing there, looking towards him.

'See you tomorrow,' he said.

'Are you going back to Srinagar?'

He nodded, 'I'm in one of Kit's houseboats on the Dal Lake. The Air Marshal's practically next door, I find.'

'I'm with another contractor this time. Kit'll give me hell

for it when she thinks I've recovered. May I come and see you?'

'Certainly.'

'Tomorrow? No, make it the day after. About noon?'

'Fine.' Rodney turned away, throwing 'Good night' over his shoulder.

'Good night.'

He walked slowly toward the lights. Had he seen men running away in the forest? If Gupta had been crossing the Girwan when he fell in, why did he not have his rod with him. Then, why would Gupta lie to him. He shrugged. God knew, and He wasn't telling.

'Tomato soup,' Kit Sanders said cheerfully, 'Trout, boily-roast chicken, caramel custard.'

He walked at Kit Sanders' side down the *marg*. He could see the light plane now, parked in the lee of a mud-walled barn at the west end, where the houses of the village began. Kit was saying, 'Chandra ought to be looked at by a doctor. That's a nasty bump he got on the back of his head – but he won't let me fly him out.'

'He'll be in Srinagar by tonight, anyway,' Rodney said.

'Yes,' she said grudgingly, 'I suppose so. . . . I ought to thank you for saving his life. We're all very fond of him.' Hastily she added, 'My husband was.'

'I don't think the Air Marshal's all that enthusiastic.'

'Nawal's very narrow-minded, especially for a Parsi and an airman. He always seems to be imitating a Colonel Blimp type of Britisher.'

'I don't suppose he's as – well – dumb, as he pretends.'

'Oh, I don't know. . . . Well, here we are. Will you untie those ropes there, and pull up those tent pegs?' They moved round the aircraft, loosening it from the bonds that had held it down during the night. Rodney peered through the Perspex into the cabin with its four seats, two in front and two behind. Kit slid into the pilot's seat. 'Are you sure you don't want to take any of your baggage in with you?' she called.

Rodney said, 'No. It can come down with the pony men and by car from Pahalgam.'

She nodded. 'Get in then . . . Safety strap . . .' She fiddled about and after a time pressed a button. At once the engine coughed, then caught. The propeller blade swung, steadied, and settled to a steady blur. 'Turbo prop,' she said, 'marvellous performance, considering. I need it for these mountains.'

'You learned to fly in Kashmir?'

'No way! I got my licence in 1959 while I was at Berkeley – University of California. Economics major.' She sat back, watching the needles of the dials in front of her. After a few minutes she moved the throttles and the little plane ambled out from its shelter on to the grass. She glanced at the smoke drifting away to the westward from the houses of the village, and gradually pushed the throttle wide. The compressor whined, the turbine roared, the wings shook and the whole plane vibrated as she held it against the brake. She released the brake and the plane lurched forward, rolling faster. The tail lifted. She held the nose down for several seconds more, then eased back on the controls. The Saab lifted easily, heading now for the dark rising mass of the Girwan forest. Unhurriedly, Kit swung the plane right in an ever-tightening circle, and settled on a course down the valley. She retracted the flaps and the plane began a gradual climb.

The majestical white spears of Kolahoi thrust up to Rodney's left. All round, as they climbed, other snow peaks rose like sentinels who had been asleep, or crouched behind the shelter of the lower forest-covered ridges. Almost at once he saw, below the wing, the huddled houses of a small town.

Kit Sanders saw him looking down and said, 'Pahalgam. You know – where the motor road ends ... or begins.'

They were barely a thousand feet above the ground as yet and Rodney could see the town quite clearly. 'It's full of people,' he said, 'there are thousands of them on the flat place by the river.'

She said, 'Can't be thousands – there aren't that many people in Pahalgam. Five hundred, perhaps.' She glanced down. 'But you're right! There must be well over a thousand down there. What on earth can ...? I remember! It's a KAM meeting. The Sayyid's speaking. It was in the paper I brought up yesterday. See the police cars on the outskirts?'

Rodney nodded. The Saab continued to climb, Pahalgam

now well behind them. With enough altitude gained to surmount the intervening ridges, Kit set course for Srinagar. Directly ahead the ice city of Nanga Parbat lay athwart the pale horizon.

'That's where I'm going,' she said, nodding, 'after I've dropped you.'

'Nanga Parbat?' he said, astonished.

'Wish I could, but it's in Pakistan. No. To a party I have in Gurais, directly below it as we look at it from here. Tourists weren't allowed up there till last year. The government's really getting less paranoiac.'

'Will you stay with that party?'

'No. I'll be back in Srinagar long before dark. I'll have lunch with them, leave the supplies and drugs they want, take out their mail, and be back in Srinagar before tea. See what we can do in the air age!'

Srinagar began to take shape ahead amid its lakes and the serpentine windings of the Jhelum. Villages proliferated in the rich fields. Convoys of heavy trucks raised dust along the road; more trucks and, in one place, tanks, were parked beside a wood.

'Army manoeuvres,' she said. 'And that village is Awantipura. That's the Sayyid's home.' She eased the throttle back and the stick forward. The Saab began to lose altitude, fast.

CHAPTER TWO

The houseboat was called *Dilkhusha III*. All the Sanders'
houseboats were called *Dilkhusha*, with only a number to
distinguish them, though they varied immensely in size
and luxuriousness. Some were floating palaces with three
double bedrooms – each with private bathroom – dining
room, sitting room, and verandah plus rooftop awning.
Some were single bedroom boats of the old-fashioned kind
with no plumbing, and no separate dining room. The rental
prices varied accordingly. *Dilkhusha III* had two bedrooms
and a large living room, with a dining alcove. In this room
Rodney had arranged for the installation of an upright
piano, and he sat there now, the morning after his return
from trek.

He played a few chords and then tried to bind together
some of the notes he had heard a few days back, of a
shepherd playing a pipe under a rock in a rain shower, into
a phrase which could serve as an introduction to some
grander melody. The simple tune haunted him – it was
catchy, pleasantly minor in its effect; but it was perhaps a
little cheap, a little tinny for use in what he hoped to make
a major work?

On the piano he began to transpose notes from their
places in the tune, putting them later, then earlier, sub-
stituting other notes altogether, looking absently out of the
window beside him as he worked.

Dilkhusha III was moored to the land on the west side
of the Dal Lake. To the south, the way he was looking,
houseboats lined the bank, the roofs bright under coloured
awnings, each boat attended by one or two of the small
punts called *shikaras,* as though the houseboats were ocean
liners and the *shikaras* tugs. The surface of the lake was
dotted with other *shikaras* where Kashmiri women, squatting in the very bows, pulled up weed from the lake bed to
feed the cattle that were kept in stalls on the land behind
the houseboats. Taxis and trucks passed soundlessly up
and down the road that skirted the eastern shore a quarter
of a mile away. Beyond the lake the Pir Panjal range made

a snowy backdrop to the houseboats and the bustling *shikaras* and hurrying cars, and the lotus blossoms, robbed from the last Maharajah's private gardens, that floated on the green surface of the water.

He realized that he was playing a theme from Beethoven's *Pastoral,* and swore under his breath. Those tunes, jolly and bucolically European, indeed specifically German, were quite unsuited for this particular rusticity . . . yet it would be a mistake for him to emphasize the exotic. To Europeans the Vale of Kashmir was Romance with a capital R; to the people who lived and worked here . . . it was where they lived and worked.

He saw a *shikara* approaching across the lake. It seemed to be heading for *Dilkhusha III,* and he glanced at his watch. Chandra Gupta had said he'd come at noon, but it was only half past ten. This must be someone else. He watched it idly. It wasn't a merchant peddling carpets or papier mâché ware or silk and *pashmina* and carved wood, for he could see no goods piled high on the *shikara*'s floor planks. It had one passenger, and was being poled by a single boatman. As it came closer he saw that the passenger was a woman; and a moment later he recognized her. He let his hands play a last sweeping run, up and down the keyboard, then carefully closed the piano, walked out on to the front verandah of the houseboat and stood there, waiting, his hands in his pockets. Ayesha Bakr had saved him from further composition for this morning, at any rate.

The *shikara* boy eased alongside and stepped off to moor his boat and hand out his passenger. She came up the steps. She was petite, with a heart-shaped face and small full lips, very dark red in her wheat-coloured skin. Her eyes were large, set close, and lightly rimmed with black eye-shadow or, Rodney thought, perhaps the traditional Indian *kohl.* She was wearing a green sari with a simple border of dark red flower patterns, and bare feet in sandals. From the corner of his eye Rodney saw Dost Mohammed, the butler, who came with the houseboat, watching from the servants' quarters on land; he knew that if he did not call for service, he would not be interrupted.

He held out his hand. 'Ayesha! You're looking beautiful, and younger than ever.'

28

'Because I'm on holiday,' she answered briskly. 'Two weeks' leave.'

'I don't know how the Home Department can survive without you.'

She swept past him into the sitting room, her sari swishing around her. At the piano she turned and for a moment Rodney thought she was going to hold out her arms and invite him to embrace her. She was very passionate, as a good many other men beside himself had been given the opportunity to learn for themselves, so the gossip went. She was also very clever, perhaps sometimes too clever for her own good. He had thought that what had passed between them was over; but the memory of it, and the possibility that she wanted to re-create those days of sexual fury made the flesh creep and harden in his loins.

But she said, 'I have another job for you.'

He felt his aroused lust disperse. He said, 'I have my own work to do.'

'You're composing a *Himalayan Concerto*, aren't you?'

'How did you know?'

'We have our methods.' She laughed. 'Don't look so glum. I can't force you to take it on, but it involves the Himalayas, so it shouldn't hinder your work. It might even help.'

He said, 'Sit down, Ayesha.' He sat on a chair facing her.

She said, 'Have you any reason to think this room is bugged?'

Startled, he said, 'I'm sure it isn't.'

'All right. . . . You did good work for us in 1972, Rodney. And again, though the job was quite different, in Calcutta in 1976.'

He nodded, thinking back. In 1972 he'd been trekking in the Darjeeling area, and worrying about his then-new marriage, when he'd realized that something strange was going on in that remote corner of India. He was meeting numbers of heavily laden coolies on paths that could only be useful to avoid police and frontier check posts. As much to take his mind off his marital problems as anything else, he had made a lot of observations, sometimes secretly, sometimes by night; and then gone to Darjeeling to report what he had learned.

Two days later the government in Delhi had sent up

Ayesha Bakr. She had interrogated him very sharply. A few weeks later, when he and his wife were about to leave India for further study in Singapore and Japan, Ayesha had asked him to meet her in Delhi. There she told him that his acumen and the observations he'd made had enabled her government to put a stop to the operations of a ring engaged in smuggling heroin, among other things; a ring whose operations also had undertones of military espionage and political intrigue – particularly in that hot corner where India, Nepal, Sikkim, and Chinese-controlled Tibet joined.

And then they'd started the affair, a wild ten days for which he could find no excuse for himself, as he was barely a year married, except that Indreni was already becoming hostile to him . . . or he to her. Did it matter which way round?

And then, three years ago, while spending six months teaching and studying at Calcutta University, Ayesha had come to him again, and asked him to get inside information about a group of Maoist student radicals. He hadn't liked the job, but had apparently unearthed what Ayesha's superiors wanted to know. But they had not renewed their love affair.

Now she said, 'We have a problem on our northern border, and frankly we have not been able to isolate it – to state it. There's a general sense of unease all along the Himalayas, from Arunachal Pradesh in the far east to Kashmir and Ladakh up this end. We guess, but don't know, that the root cause is the new situation in China, since Kan Tso Hang came to power. The new Central Committee seems to be pointing the country outwards, even to the extent of territorial expansion, to take the people's attention off their internal problems. We know the Russians are worried, and so are we. . . . The Chinese are making unnecessary charges and fomenting unnecessary incidents along the Nepal-Tibet border. Farther east they're building – it's almost finished – a jeepable road down towards the Mishmi country, that's the Luhit Division of Arunachal Pradesh. The political temperature's rising in all that area, and we assume that foreign bodies are in there, causing the unrest. At this end, the Chinese are up to something in Ladakh, but we don't know what, or why. Pakistan has

30

slightly increased its forces along our border with them in the plains, and considerably more in the mountain section, to the west and north of Kashmir. Kashmir itself, here where we are, worries us, too. There are several illegal radio transmitters operating here, and we can't find them. Two or three different ciphers are being used.'

'One of the ciphers would be for the K.P.P. to communicate with their agents in Pakistan,' Rodney said.

She looked up quickly. 'You're been looking into the K.P.P.?'

'No. I only learned about them recently.'

She nodded. 'But who are the other ciphers being read by? Russia? China? Traitors inside India itself. . . .? Have you ever heard the phrase *Azad Shadhinata?*'

Rodney shook his head slowly. ' "Free" in Urdu, then "Independence" in Bengali? No.'

'Keep your ears open for it. Our agents have heard it in odd places, particularly in Kashmir and Bangladesh, in circumstances where it might have been a password or slogan or recognition sign of some kind. If you hear it, follow the clue wherever it leads.'

'What has Bangladesh to do with the Himalayas?'

'We don't know . . . except that the northern border of Bangladesh is very close to Sikkim and Bhutan. It's only a very narrow strip of our territory there that connects Assam and Arunachal Pradesh with the rest of India.'

'I know,' Rodney said. He got up, went to the refrigerator and poured Ayesha a lemonade. For himself he opened a bottle of beer. A chill gust from the Pir Panjal swirled through the houseboat, making him shiver. 'What do you want me to do?' he asked.

'Travel along the Himalayas. Be inquisitive. Keep your ears and eyes open – the same thing you did in Darjeeling in '72. Look for the anomaly, the thing that isn't quite right, and follow it. We're not in a position to say, "such-and-such is going on, get us the details." The question we are asking ourselves – and you – is, *what* is going on?'

He thought, a large vague order. It wasn't at all like being invited to steal the secret formula, or blow up the arsenal. But the wind still blew cold. He said, 'I'm sorry, Ayesha, I don't want to get into any more of that kind of thing.'

She said, 'It might be dangerous.'

He did not answer. Whether she was taunting him or tempting him didn't matter; it wouldn't work, though the temptation, at least, was real. His father and grandfather had been soldiers and when he chose a career in music he had felt that he was in some sense shirking a dangerous duty. In recompense, all his life he had rather sought danger than avoided it; and found danger at least as effective a drug as marijuana.

She said, pleading, 'They're after me in the department to get results, Rodney. It's hard being a woman and a Muslim in that place. Bajwa hates me on both counts. He's my boss.' She rose, came to stand beside him, and said, 'I had another reason for coming to you.'

Rodney looked up. This time the invitation was unmistakable. Was she using her sex to get him to do what she wanted? If so, it wouldn't be the first time, nor he the first man to be manipulated. Anger rose in him and he jumped up, half shouting, 'Christ, Ayesha, I've just said I won't!' But his voice was thick with desire, and he knew it, and before the words were out of his mouth he knew he must have her, now, for she had aroused him to a barely suppressed trembling frenzy, as she used to in the old days. Her arms were round his neck, her soft belly was pressed against him, her pelvis was moving from side to side. Dost Mohammed and the other servants would know perfectly well what was going on . . . Chandra Gupta might come early . . . nothing mattered. She took his hand and led him towards the bedroom

As soon as they were there she leaned back against the door, sliding the bolt closed behind her. Then she held out her arms and pulled him into her embrace. For a few moments she writhed against him. Then she broke free, fumbling at the knot of her sari. The sari fell from her shoulders and her waist. She unfastened her *choli* and slid out of her underpants. She was on the bed, her arms again outstretched, her eyes glittering, her body moving in a slow, uneasy rhythm. Rodney's eyes fastened, mesmerized, on the bulging shaved curve of her Mount of Venus as she parted her legs, then the pink wet gleam of her lips. He could hardly get his clothes off, he felt so enormous, so removed. She whispered, 'Make it slow . . . all the way.'

32

Minutes later, he lay beside her, breathing deeply and evenly. It had not been slow – too many weeks had passed since he had had a woman and his physical hunger could not be held back; but she had made it longer afterwards, playing with him and herself, guiding him into and over her body, sighing and moaning, not softly.

She said, 'Oh Rodney, you're so good in bed. I can't understand why Indreni doesn't worship you.'

He said, 'I could say the same about Ali,' referring to the husband from whom she had long been separated.

After a while she whispered, 'Please do this job for me. And it really will help you with the concerto.'

She was right, he thought, his suppressed anger rising again. A man couldn't compose twenty-four hours a day, and here he was being asked to do just what he was in any case proposing to do – travel along the Himalayas, listening, looking, feeling. And given something to escape to when composing became too frustrating.

'All right,' he said.

She leaned over, her heavy breasts soft against him and whispered, 'Thank you.' Her lips sank on to his.

They were back in the living room. Her voice was business-like. 'As I told you, we sense, rather than know, that something is brewing along our northern border. One small specific incident might be a clue, or it might be totally unconnected.'

'What is that?'

'We had an agent here, a man who kept his eyes and ears open on our behalf, told us of anomalies, gossip, rumours. He vanished on November 10 last year – 1978. Here in Srinagar. Major Mike Sanders.'

He started. 'Kit's husband?'

'Yes. He was a British officer in the old Indian Army, but at Independence he decided to claim Indian citizenship. He was born in Bareilly, so he was an Indian citizen by birth. We couldn't prevent it. We didn't want to . . . He started this contracting business in '47, did well, and then our department realized that he'd be a most useful agent, especially among foreigners, as they would not realize that he was an Indian citizen, and would speak more freely in front of him in consequence.'

'When did he marry Kit?'

'Fifteen, sixteen years ago. She was an American tourist here, came with her parents, I believe. They stayed on one of Sanders' houseboats. She married Sanders within three weeks, and her parents went back to America without her. She was nearly twenty years younger than he, of course. As I say, though, his disappearance might be nothing to do with us. I want you to go to Nepal first.'

'I was planning to,' he said, feeling illogically aggrieved that he was being put to no inconvenience.

'After that, go where the scent leads. . . . You'll have to make your own travel arrangements. Don't come to the government for anything, except as you'd do if you were an ordinary tourist. Now, your drops. They're all camera shops. Here in Srinagar, it's Firoz Ali, on the Bund.'

'I know the place.'

'In Kathmandu, it's Harmukh Singh on New Road. Don't write anything down.'

'I'll remember.'

'At the drop, you always ask for Mr. P. S. Grewal. When you are handing in a report, address it to P. S. Grewal on the envelope. Nothing else. You can draw funds from the drops, any amount within reason. You'll have one private government contact other than me. That's Joseph Braganza, Deputy Secretary, Government of Jammu and Kashmir. He's I.A.S. I'll arrange for you to meet him socially, at a cocktail party – tonight, perhaps. Now, I have to go.'

He said, 'Wait a minute, I've been thinking. . . . If this business that I'm to investigate turns out to be serious, there'll be troop movements. Can you get the Russians to take satellite photographs for you, of specific areas?'

She said nothing for a moment, then – 'Yes,' and closed her lips.

'Well, I should ask for cover of passes along the Nepal-Tibet border, to see whether the Chinese are moving extra troops into that area. What other Russian help can you rely on? I know that you Indians talk about the Russian stick to beat the Chinese dog.'

'I'm not in the know there,' she said, 'but you could work it out for yourself.'

He gazed at her thoughtfully. She must know more than

she was willing to tell; but it wasn't important, yet. Later, he might have to press her.

Glancing at his watch he saw that it was a quarter to twelve. Chandra Gupta would be coming soon, if he was a punctual man. To Ayesha he said, 'Do you know a writer called Chandra Gupta? He's a Bengali.'

'I know him. He's not so much of a Bengali as his father, though, fortunately for him. He – Chandra – is quite well known for his books and poetry. And he often writes political columns for the Delhi *Independent*. Why?'

'I found him drowning in a pool in the Girwan stream above Arau the day before yesterday. He'd slipped and fallen in, bashing his head on a rock and knocking himself unconscious in the process. I fished him out. He seems a nice chap.'

'So Kit Sanders used to think,' she said, her full lips pressed together in a feline smile.

'Kit did seem very solicitous.'

'She's still in love with him, is what I hear. Mike knew about it, but he wasn't a jealous man. Is Chandra still out on trek?'

Rodney said, 'No. He's back in Srinagar. He's supposed to be coming here for a drink soon.'

Even as he spoke he heard a voice from the front calling, 'Rodney?' A pause, then again. Rodney got up, hearing the patter of feet on the gangplank that ran along outside the houseboat, and then Dost Mohammed's voice. 'The sahib is resting.'

Rodney went out and found Dost Mohammed on the front verandah and below, Chandra Gupta, seated alone in a small *shikara*. 'All right, Dost Mohammed,' he said, 'you may go.' The butler made salaam and returned quietly to his quarters.

'Did I wake you up?' Gupta said, mooring his *shikara* and running up the steps.

'Good heavens, no. I was just chatting with an old friend, Ayesha Bakr.'

Gupta cried, 'Oh, Ayesha's a darling,' just as Ayesha herself swept out on to the verandah, her sari rustling.

She made *namasti*, and bowed her head prettily to Gupta. 'Rodney told me he was expecting you. But I really must go. I'll be at Schweitzer's for the next fortnight, Chandra.

You can give me a cocktail or two some time, even if you do stick to tomato juice yourself.'

Ayesha's *shikara*, which had been waiting for her, moved out from the shade of willow trees that hung over the water a few yards beyond the servants' quarters. As Rodney handed her down into it she said, 'Thank you . . . and good luck.'

She sat back in the *shikara*'s cushioned and curtained alcove and the boatman at once poled off. She waved once, and blew him a kiss: then another *shikara* with three occupants, going in the opposite direction, passed in front of hers and hid her from him. When her *shikara* reappeared, she had pulled the side curtains forward and he could not see her.

Back in the living room, Chandra Gupta had a glass of fruit juice in one hand and was holding out a beer to him in the other. 'I took the liberty – hope you don't mind.' He looked round at the ornate furnishings and decorations and said, 'Standard Kashmir Gothic. I'm not in a Sanders boat, but you wouldn't know the difference. They're all the same, like pictures of Victorian drawing rooms, only with even more carved wood. Have you studied the chit book?'

Rodney shook his head. He was feeling more at ease. What did it matter if Chandra suspected the affair between himself and Ayesha?

Chandra said, 'There'll be one. Ask the bearer. Recommendations and not very subtle warnings, from long-dead sahibs, on crested regimental notepaper, browning and stained: *Sher Khan is an excellent cook, when he tries. He is often trying* . . . things like that.'

Rodney laughed, then asked. 'Are you quite recovered from your accident?'

'My head hurts a bit. I took the plaster off and am letting it heal its own way.'

There was a silence. Chandra seemed to be breathing the air, savouring it. Good God, could he detect the aura of recent concupiscence? Rodney said hastily, 'Ayesha said that your father was very Bengali, unfortunately – something like that. What did she mean?'

It was really impertinent on his part to be asking these questions of such a recent acquaintance, but he had wanted to break the silence in case Chandra talked about Ayesha;

and Chandra's manner was so warm that you felt you could ask him anything. Anyway, he wanted to know, for no reason that he could think of, except that he seemed to want to know everything about this Chandra Gupta.

'Bengali nationalism,' Chandra said briefly. 'My father thought that India needed a federal form of government, even confederated, to allow for regional pride and responsibility, and to overcome the problem that we have so many races, languages, religions. He wanted the regions of India to be semi-independent, each with its own language – and that applied especially to Bengal. Panditji – Nehru – didn't agree. Exit Mr. Hari Gupta, C.I.E., I.C.S. . . . . Will you play something for me, Geminus?'

'What sort of thing?' Rodney asked, feeling pleased.

'Something of yours, of course. Something of what you're working on now, if you care to.'

Rodney sat down at the piano and ran his fingers up and down the keyboard. Searching for notes for a minute or two, a light dancing tune came into his head. It was of the same sort as the lovesong the *gujjar* boy had played on his pipe above Astanmarg, but it was not that; this was faster, and in a major key, and it was a dancing tune. He swung into it, improvised, playing it straight with his right hand first, then finding the left-hand chords to go with it as he modulated, found variations.

He realized that Chandra was standing beside him, speaking in rhythmic Bengali.

'What's that?' he asked, still playing, but more softly.

'A poem I wrote a few years ago. It's about boys and girls, cowherds and their women, dancing.'

'So's this . . .' He swung into a final, dancing, leaping chorus, as Chandra began to speak again. They ended together.

Rodney sat back. 'That's amazing, that your poem and this little tune – which I've only just made up – should go together.'

'Don't forget we're Gemini.'

Rodney closed the piano. Chandra was feeling in the pocket of his tweed jacket, and saying, 'Geminus, I'd like you to have this. If it doesn't fit, I can get it altered . . . but I think it will.' In his open palm he held a gold signet ring, set with a heavy black opal. Into the opal was carved the figures of Gemini, the Twins – Castor and Pollux. Rodney saw that Chandra was wearing one exactly like it on his third finger.

Rodney took it wonderingly, and tried it on. It fitted the little finger on his left hand perfectly.

Gupta said, 'It belonged to my brother, my twin brother. He was shorter and stronger than me . . . killed in a car accident.'

Rodney looked at the ring, filled with mixed emotions. It was a very personal sort of present, he thought, implying an affection, or perhaps love, which had not been openly acknowledged.

'I shouldn't take it,' he said.

'Please . . . I'll be going. Are you planning to stay in Kashmir a while?'

'I don't know. If I go away, I'll come back. You can always reach me through Grindlay's, New Delhi – they'll forward my mail.'

'I move about a lot, too. I have a small house in Delhi. Here.' He saw Rodney's composing pad and wrote: *Chandra Gupta, 238 Narayan Road, New Delhi. Tel 494836.* 'There. We must keep in touch.'

He was halfway down the steps, waving, jumping into the little *shikara*. He paddled himself away, with one last look over his shoulder and a cheerful wave of the dripping paddle.

Rodney returned to the sitting room, looking at the ring on his finger. He shook his head, but found himself smiling. Chandra Gupta's friendliness was infectious.

A shadow appeared at the door leading over the plank to shore and the servant's quarters. He looked up. It was Akbar Khan, Kit Sanders' right-hand man, his hand touching his henna-dyed hair under the faded gold *kulla*. 'I am coming to see that the sahib has everything he wants.'

'Yes, Akbar Khan, thank you very much. Dost Mohammed is looking after me well.'

The old man continued in his halting, strongly accented English. 'You have not suffered any badness from before, in the river?'

'What? Oh, in the Girwan. Not a bit. Mr. Gupta's all right, too. He has just been calling.'

'I saw him. Then there is nothing more you wish?'

'Nothing, thanks. Oh, I'm going on a trip, I don't know for how long, but I'd like to keep the houseboat, at some sort of reduced rate, as long as you don't need it for another client. I want to leave the piano and some of my things here.'

'I will arrange it, certainly. It is early in the season. We will not need *Dilkhusha III* until June. Perhaps you will pay one quarter of the rent?'

'Certainly.'

'That is good. Can we make travel arrangements for you, sir? Book a flight, perhaps?'

'Yes, get me on the jet to Delhi tomorrow, please.'

'It is usually booked up several days ahead, sir, but we will secure the earliest reservation possible. I will talk to Travel Associates at once.'

He bowed himself out with another semi-military salute. Rodney stood looking after him, then turned to study the mirror-like calm of the Dal Lake. . . . Nepal. Time to pack when he got the reservation. And fix the onward flight to Kathmandu, and hotel accommodation there. He'd better go and talk to Travel Associates himself. It didn't look as though he'd have much leisure for brooding about his marriage . . . or for composing, in the immediate future. That was only putting off the day of reckoning but, for now, he felt better. He began to hum.

CHAPTER THREE

The 727 banked sharply and Rodney, looking out of a left-hand window, saw Kathmandu spread out below – huddled houses, white palaces, a few modern buildings, narrow streets, and here and there the glint of gold leaf on a temple tower. The city glittered like a jewel in the cupped palm of its valley, under a gigantic wall of mountains that lined the northern horizon. A disembodied voice announced, 'This is your pilot speaking. We are about to land at Kathmandu. Everest is near the centre of the range that can be seen from the left side of the aircraft. The near mountain is Lang-tang . . . beyond, the Ganesh Himal.' It was near noon and the sun poured down full on the panoply, transforming walls of ice to curtains of gold.

Cigarettes had already been extinguished and seat belts fastened. Rodney found himself rubbing the Gemini signet ring Chandra had given him, with the thumb of his right hand. From the moment he had first put it on, it had impressed itself on him as an emblem of good luck, or of someone's protection. Whose? God's? Ridiculous superstition, anyway. He quickly separated his hands, and tucked the left one under his thigh, out of temptation's way. The 727's hydraulic motors whined and the flaps purred out, the plane slowing noticeably in the air. The wheels came down with a thump, and the view shortened. Rodney settled back in his seat, watching fields and houses thicken, become bigger, race by faster under the wing . . . they were down.

Soon an Indian-made taxi was hurrying him toward the centre of the city, where the agency had reserved him a room in the new Bristol-Carlton. His room was small, over-furnished, and air-conditioned. The machine made an infernal purring, interrupted by occasional clanks. He switched it off and with difficulty managed to fling open the window and lean out. Late April was a good time to be in Kathmandu. The sun was hot, but the wind blew off the Himalayas and even in the early afternoon there was an edge to the breeze, so that all the people he saw in the

40

street below were wearing jackets, or were wrapped in woollen blankets. He unpacked slowly, washed, and went down to lunch.

It was late afternoon and he was sitting in an easy chair by the open window, reading the day's Calcutta *Statesman*, a copy of which had just been delivered to his room. Local news and gossip, lots of that . . . an article on the economic problems of Bangladesh: ever since he had arrived back in India that had been a recurring theme of all newspapers, and of much discussion . . . a report from the paper's Delhi correspondent about the intransigent attitude of Pakistan: that, too, was as recurrent as sunrise . . . a big headline, then a story about a new Chinese protest over incidents along the Tibet-Nepal border.

He read more carefully. The incidents were not described in detail – merely that shots were fired, no one was injured on the Nepalese side, the Chinese refusing to say whether they had suffered any casualties or not . . . a reprint of the Chinese communique – their patience was wearing thin under this continued provocation, which must be laid at the door of India, because Nepal was, as all the world knew, a mere puppet of India's unprincipled imperialist government.

On another page he found a leader on the same subject. The anonymous writer, presumably the editor, said that being patient was one thing, being humiliated was another. The Government of India must give full support to Nepalese independence, and it must not demean itself by further concessions to China. India must not forget the events of 1962; that was seventeen years ago, but the Chinese attack on India had been preceded by just such a barrage of false accusations and manufactured incidents as now seemed to be taking place in Nepal. Normally the writer would say that the United States of America was the last country which India should emulate in her foreign dealings, but in the case of China, India would do well to follow the precept of President Theodore Roosevelt – speak softly and carry a big stick.

Rodney threw the paper down. Below in the street someone was playing vilely on a broken guitar. He looked out and saw that it was a tall blond hippie youth, squatted in the gutter, a begging bowl in front of him. Nepalese and Indians passed by unheeding; now and then another hippie dropped a tiny coin into the bowl. Mutual back-scratching, he thought with a grim smile: I'll buy your pot, if you'll buy mine. He felt cooped up, with no view of the snow, and the sun and breeze stirring out there. He put his music notebook and pencil in his pocket and left the room.

The shops immediately round the Bristol-Carlton were, like the hotel, modern and banal. A couple of hundred yards away the street lost half its width; the paving became rutted and broken, the tarmac laid down twenty years before and never repaired; and the sound of car and truck and bus engines was overborne by the ever louder throb and hammer of people – voices of men arguing, women bickering and bargaining, vendors crying their wares, priests chanting from a temple somewhere out of sight but close by. Rodney stopped and took a deep breath. This was the bazaar; but there, visible above the corrugated iron roof of the spice-seller's shop in front of him, was the snowy mass of Langtang.

He pulled out his notebook and began to jot down the tune that was being chanted from the hidden temple. It was a montonous melody, the same note being held for long periods on end, then subtly changing. For the present all he could do was record it, for later study as to its structure and possible development.

At the next corner he found a narrow alley leading off to the left, followed it, and soon came to the temple. It was not large, its tower a bare forty feet high, built of dark red stone, heavily ornamented with carved figures. Going close he saw that they were, like those at Puri and Khajuraho, mainly erotic – here three doe-eyed, heavy hipped women pleasuring one man – there another standing, hip outflung, against an angle of the tower, for all the world like a harlot on a street corner in the West. Five priests, shaven headed, white robed, squatted in the small front courtyard, singing to the accompaniment of a long brass copper-tipped horn, and a pair of small drums. The singers were heavily painted on face and forehead with white and ochre designs.

Rodney leaned against the side of a fruit stall opposite them, listened, made an occasional note, and let himself become slowly absorbed into the place and the time. . . .

Till this moment he had still been in Kashmir: indeed, almost he had been in England, thinking like an Englishman: now he was in Nepal, not a Nepali, but knowing them, smelling them, breathing their air. After an hour he put away his notebook and took a circuitous route back to the hotel through the twilight, three times pressed to buy marijuana by young Nepalis in almost identical garb – leather jackets, and faded, flared, blue jeans. The barman's name was Machhindra, a small wrinkled man in his early fifties, with a good command of English, some of it clearly learned by youthful association with British soldiers. Rodney sat up to the bar on a high stool, a whisky and soda in his hand. An Indian honeymoon couple were staring silently into each other's eyes in one corner of the room, and in another three American businessmen were talking together about the stock market.

Rodney said, 'Do you ever get any Chinese in here, Machhindra?'

'Chinese, sir?' The barman nearly shook the black Nepalese-style cap off his head. 'Not bloody likely!'

'There are quite a lot of them in Kathmandu, though?'

'Many,' the barman said. 'At the embassy . . . engineers working on the Lhasa road. . . .'

'How's that coming along?'

'Finished. But it is often closed for landslides, avalanches, floods on the Sun Kosi. . . . We Nepalis don't want the bloody road. The British would have told the Ranas not to let the Chinese build it, but the Indians are weak.'

'They want to be friends with China, I suppose,' Rodney said, 'and China's a lot stronger than it was when the British ruled India.'

'That's fucking right,' the barman said, nodding agreeably. 'Another whisky, sir?'

Rodney nodded, pushing over his glass, but Machhindra was already pouring into a clean one. Rodney got out his pipe and began the ritual of filling and lighting it. In between puffs, he asked, 'When you say the Lhasa road is finished, you mean that people – travellers – can use it?'

'Yes, sir. But there are very few travellers. The Chinese give few permits to foreigners to go beyond Kodari, into Tibet. Most of the travellers are Chinese coming down here, or going back.'

43

'How do they travel?'

'There are trucks running from Lhasa – Chinese trucks, even buses. The Kuti La is usually closed in winter . . .' he wrinkled his crabapple face – 'I think it has just been opened for the season. Our trucks are not allowed to enter Tibet – they have to change their loads to Chinese trucks at Kodari – but the Chinese trucks come all the way into Kathmandu.'

'Where to? Where do Chinese travellers, people coming from Tibet, stay?'

Machhindra said, 'The Kosi Palace. It's a cheap hotel, off Mahendra Street, in the bazaar.'

'Close to the Vaishnavi temple, the small one?'

'That's it – not far from there . . . but be careful, sir, it's a bloody fleapit.'

Rodney blew out tobacco smoke, ruminating. Tomorrow he'd move in a little closer and see . . . see if there was anything to be seen.

The Kosi Palace was hard to find, for it was hidden down a side alley even narrower and darker and dirtier than the one that led to the Vaishnavi temple fifty yards away. On one side of the hotel was a cloth shop, its open front stacked to the ceiling with bolts of cheap cotton from Bombay mills. The proprietor, squatting inside, was just visible through a narrow gap in his fortifications. On the other side there was a small eating house, where large black kettles simmered over charcoal braziers, and pots full of rice and curried vegetables hung on chains just under the protection of the corrugated-iron roof; inside, half a dozen Nepali labourers and a white hippie ate eagerly, squatting over food spread on big green leaves, the floor stained with innumerable red splashes of betel juice.

Between these two crouched the Kosi Palace, behind a sign announcing a name in Nagri script, and a garish painting of a hotel that was presumably meant to be the Kosi Palace itself, but looked more like a half-stoned artist's vision of Gleneagles. Walking under this abstraction, Rodney found the front door open, and passed into a narrow, dark passage. At once a man's head poked out of a door beside him and said sharply in Nepali, *Kya chahinchha?*

44

Rodney spoke no Nepali but from the tone knew that he was being asked what was his business. He said, 'Do you speak English?'

'A little,' the man said. He came out. 'What you wanting?' He looked Rodney up and down and even in the dim light realized that he was no hippie. He said, 'Wanting nice room? Have girls, sometimes, if paying.'

Rodney smiled, shaking his head. 'No, thank you. I want to know if you have any traveller recently in from Tibet here.'

'Chinese not talking anyone,' the man said.

'Not a Chinese, if possible. An Indian, or a Nepali. A few do go to Tibet or even China, I hear, and I suppose, come back.'

'What you wanting for?' the man asked, his slanted eyes narrowing.

'I'm probably going to visit Tibet myself, soon. I have a permit and want to talk to someone who's been to Lhasa recently, and can give me practical advice – what to wear, how much things cost, where to stay, who are the people to see to arrange things . . . you understand? *Samajhlya?*' he finished, in Hindustani.

The man nodded, saying, 'Man here, but perhaps not wanting to talk anyone.'

Rodney already had a ten-rupee note in his hand. He pressed it into the other's palm and said, 'Which room?'

'That one . . . fourth. He is Mr. Jansingh Gharti.'

'Indian?'

'Now, I think. He was born Nepali. He works for Kapur and Katari, general merchants, Calcutta. I have seen his card.'

He disappeared back into his room, closing the door quietly. Rodney went to the fourth door and knocked. A voice said '*Ko ho?*'

'Mr. Jansingh?'

'*Fi-han*'; and then, in English, 'Who are you?'

'Rodney Bateman. May I speak to you a moment?'

From inside the room the sharp voice said, 'What about?'

'Travel in Tibet. Staying in Lhasa. I have a permit and . . .'

The door opened, and he was looking at a middle-aged man of about five foot eight with a dark face, pitted by smallpox. He had long dank black hair, on which he was wearing a dirty white Gandhi cap.

'Come in,' the man said.

A *charpoy* stood against one wall, and there were also two hard-backed cane-bottomed chairs, the cane split and fraying. Light filtered through one small window high up one wall, its glass fly-blown and stained. Jansingh sat down on the edge of the *charpoy,* swinging his bare feet, and indicated one of the chairs. Rodney sat cautiously, remembering Machhindra's warning. There were probably bedbugs, too.

Jansingh said, 'I came from Tibet two, three days ago.'

'From Lhasa?'

'Lhasa, yes. I am buyer for Kapur and Katari. General merchants. Import, export. Chinese give me permit. Don't allow me to take truck through. I can go myself, every month, talk to the commissar in Lhasa, get orders, find what he want from here, India, Bangladesh, everywhere, even U.S.A. Cheaper to ship goods to Lhasa from Calcutta than through Shanghai and the Gya Lam. Three thousand kilometres shorter, too!'

Rodney began to ask questions about life in Lhasa, which Jansingh appeared to answer readily enough, until, after a quarter of an hour he said suddenly, 'Why *you* going to Lhasa?'

'Compose music,' Rodney said, 'Study Tibetan music. I am a composer.'

'They give you permit for that?' Jansingh said incredulously.

Rodney said, 'I've applied, and they seem to be about to.'

Jansingh laughed derisively. 'They never give you permit! They just playing with you, trying to find out what you really want. . . . You English?' Rodney nodded. 'Then they surely never giving permit. Because they not going to let any British or American see what they got on the frontier – both sides.'

'What do you mean?'

Jansingh dropped his voice. 'They having troops up there – soldiers. Thousands, hidden where no one seeing them, in caves and villages off the road.'

Rodney interrupted. 'If you can't see them how do you know they're there?'

'I know,' Jansingh insisted impatiently. 'I see supplies going up from Lhasa, trucks enough to supply ten thousand men, but they only *show* five hundred, see? We get searched three, four times between Lhasa and the frontier. A Chinese man on the bus, maybe engineer on his way here, took out a camera. They beat him, smashed his camera, roped him up, put him on a truck right back to Lhasa. He probably chained to the wall in the Potala somewhere, or . . .' he made a motion of cutting his throat. 'Guards everywhere, sentries everywhere, roads being built, to the side, the west, going to another pass. Don't you tell anybody I tell you this, or they chain *me* in the Potala next time I go up there, see?'

'How long have you been visiting Tibet? When did you start?'

'Ten, no, thirteen years ago,' Jansingh said.

'And what you're seeing now is different from what it used to be like?'

Jansingh snorted. 'Different? Absolutely very different, even from last year.'

'Why are you telling me this, if you are frightened of what the Chinese might do to you?'

'I like English,' Jansingh said. 'English firms very good with me, very reliable, when I start with Kapur and Katari.' He leaned forward confidentially. 'I do not want you waste your time trying to get permit for Lhasa. Chinese won't give. And if you go, maybe won't come back, see?'

'What you have told me is hard to believe,' Rodney said thoughtfully. 'What would be their motive, their purpose? Why would they mass troops on the border of Nepal?'

'Perhaps they want to conquer Nepal,' Jansingh said. 'Take it into their house, out of India's, see? Listen, Mister Bateman, you know what I hear since I got here?'

'No. What?'

'There's a Chinese army deserter hiding in Kathmandu. An officer, a lieutenant, I heard, who ran away from the road, wearing Nepali clothes, passed the outposts, and escaped to here – Kathmandu.'

'Where is this deserter hiding?'

Jansingh shook his head emphatically. 'Not knowing anything about that . . . just told you what I heard . . . maybe not true, maybe yes.'

Rodney surveyed the other curiously. He probably did have an idea of where the deserter was hiding, but thought it might be dangerous to tell him more. Nor would a charitable donation help, for Jansingh, though poorly dressed and the very opposite of goodlooking, had nothing servile about his manner. Ten rupees would get him nowhere, nor a hundred.

'Thank you,' he said at last. 'I'll take note of your advice . . . though I must tell you that I would undergo almost any risks or hardships to get to Lhasa and spend enough time there to understand the roots and structure of Tibetan music.'

And that, he thought, as he fumbled his way down the dark passage and out of the hotel, was the absolute truth. The modern tragedy was that most of the extraordinary places in the world, once difficult of access for purely physical reasons, had now disappeared behind far more impenetrable barriers of national suspicion, security and xenophobia.

In his room, Rodney finished writing his report and then re-read it. The Chinese were planning an invasion of Nepal; or an invasion of India through Nepal; or they wanted it to be thought that they were, as a bluff to cover action elsewhere; or they were merely flexing their muscles, to intimidate Nepal and India. More information was vital, and he urged Ayesha to see that all the resources of her department were turned to getting it. He stressed the importance, also, of asking the Russians to take satellite photos along that border on a continuing basis. A single aerial photograph was sometimes useful; a series taken at regular intervals, of exactly the same place, invariably was.

He felt that he had already almost solved Ayesha's riddle. Of course he would try to run the Chinese deserter to earth and get confirmation from him, but the main work was done. He'd have to turn his energies to his music.

He added a postscript. 'Run a check on background and activities of Jansingh Gharti, buyer for Kapur and Katari, Calcutta.' Finding an envelope, he sealed the letter and addressed it to Mr. P. S. Grewal, put it in his pocket and went out once more into the street. He had already seen Harmukh Singh's shop on New Road, about two hundred

48

yards from his hotel, and now headed there, the sun low and the smoke of cooking fires filling the bazaar with a blue haze.

He walked into the camera shop and found two other customers in it, being attended by a young man in a light suit. The young man raised his head and called over his shoulder, 'Father!'

An older man wearing horn-rimmed glasses came out and Rodney said, 'Mr. Harmukh Singh?'

'Yes, sir. What can I do for you, sir?'

'I'd like to buy some colour film for my camera. It's a Kodak 120, and I want Kodacolor.'

'Colour prints?'

'Yes . . . and these are for processing.' He handed over the envelope. Harmukh Singh glanced down at the address, and slipped the envelope into his pocket. 'Certainly, sir. Your address is . . .?'

'Bristol-Carlton.'

'Very good, sir. How many rolls of Kodacolor, sir?'

'Oh, two will do.'

'Very good, sir. As you like colour prints, perhaps I could show you some prints from a new film that we have recently been able to buy in large quantities, at a very good price.' He led toward the side of the room, saying, 'It's Japanese, called Furuoka-Color. Perhaps you have not seen the remarkable results which . . .'

They were in the side room then, a large room hung with enlarged prints in colour and black and white, and a few advertising posters. Without changing his tone Mr. Harmukh Singh said, 'Anything else? Money?'

Rodney shook his head and said, 'There's probably a Chinese deserter hiding in Kathmandu; a lieutenant. Where would he be?'

'Excellent quality, as you see,' Harmukh said; and then, his voice low – 'Ask round the small Vaishnavi temple. Be careful.'

Rodney turned and led back into the main room, saying, 'I think I'll stick with Kodacolor for the time being.' The other customers had gone by then and as Harmukh Singh showed him out he said, 'You can give papers to my son, too . . . Thank you, sir. Any time, sir. . . .'

CHAPTER FOUR

Late the next morning Rodney was sitting on the stone steps outside the Vaishnavi temple, notebook in hand, leaning back against the whitewashed wall that surrounded the courtyard. He was jotting down the notations of the music emanating from the inside of the temple itself. It was livelier than yesterday's, and fitted comfortably into the sounds of the city – the voices, the clop of ponies' hooves, the cries of vendors, and the distant growl of truck engines. This was city music, he thought, not bucolic, very remote in its feel from the notes of the *gujjar* boy under his rock below Kolahoi. Perhaps these mountains were different; he ought to go into them, and find out. He glanced up to the north, for reassurance that the great chain which was to be the subject of his concerto, and of his present investigation, still stood in its appointed place.

A priest came out of the temple, barefoot, barechested, the Brahmin sacred thread hanging over one shoulder and across his chest. He squatted down at a brass tap on the inner wall near Rodney, hooked the sacred thread over his ear so that the lower end of the loop should not trail in the mud, and washed his hands, face and neck under the running water. Rodney watched, almost shivering, wondering how the man could stand the cold with so little outward show; for it was a chill day, the sun hidden and the wind bitter in the street.

When he had finished the priest looked up and caught Rodney's eye. Rodney smiled at him. The priest made a brief *namasti* in acknowledgement and then walked over. He was a man in his early thirties perhaps, a year or two younger than Rodney, his head shaven. He stood over Rodney looking down at the musically lined notebook.

'*Woh kya hai?*' – What's that? he asked in Hindustani.

Rodney answered in the same language. 'A book to write down the notes of music.' He was glad the priest was not a Nepali, for although many words were the same in Hindustani and Nepali he could not have held a conversation in the latter language: and he was looking for an opportunity to talk to someone connected with the temple.

He marked four ascending breves in the treble clef and sang them: then a semi-breve, minims, quavers, and semi-quavers, and chanted again, indicating the different lengths of the notes.

'And this?' the priest asked, putting his finger on the bass clef. Rodney marked again, and then sang first the treble part, then the bass.

'You are a musician?' the priest asked, squatting down facing him.

Rodney nodded. 'I am going to compose music that will, I hope, express the spirit of Himachal.'

'In your music or ours?'

'Both, I hope . . . not a mixture, a blend.'

The priest pulled thoughtfully at his ear. 'I have seen English and Americans here with tape recorders. Is not that simpler than this writing of the music? Though I have heard that in the past few years our Indian music is being written down, but in a simpler manner than this.'

Rodney said, 'A tape recorder helps in some ways, but it's not as easy to compose with one. At least not for me. You don't see the structure of the music. I was trained this way, though of course I sometimes use tape recorders.'

The priest said, 'You should go to the villages. What you were listening to here is sacred music, ancient Brahmin chants handed down from generation to generation . . . the songs of our forefathers, of our Indian gods, not of Himachal.'

'I think that the gods of India and Himachal cannot be separated,' Rodney said.

'Ah, an interesting thought. But, even if you study our temple music, and the music of the city – the street music, the dancers – you should go to the villages.'

'Any place in particular?'

'Any high valley will do . . . Jumla in the west . . . Namche Bazaar, where the Sherpas come from . . . Muktinath and Mustang . . . I visited all those places when I first came to Nepal fifteen years ago. There you will hear the music of Himachal.'

'Thank you, I'll try to get out. Kathmandu hardly seems Nepalese to me. There are so many foreigners.'

51

'That is correct. . . . It was good to talk to you. Would you like to see inside the temple?'

'Very much,' Rodney said, scrambling to his feet and putting away his notebook. The priest led across the courtyard. At the entrance to the temple he turned, looking down, obviously about to advise Rodney to take off his shoes, but Rodney had already got one off, and soon the other as well. He followed into the gloom. The sound of the chanting grew louder, accompanied by a low drone which he recognized as a *tamboura*. He had heard it from outside, but its timbre had been distorted by the stone walls and passages through which the sound had filtered, and he had thought it must be some other instrument.

He had been in many Hindu temples during his years of musical study in India and the bareness of the interior did not surprise him, still less the phallus of black stone, its knob decorated with orange powder and hung with garlands, more flowers scattered round the base; nor the silent darkness of alcoves, guarded by larger-than-life-size figures carved in the dim stone on either side, containing nothing – nothing, that is, which a man could touch with his hand or see with his eye; the inner mystery contained in those places could only be comprehended by the inner sense.

They passed the singers and the *tamboura* player, squatting in a circle in a corner, facing a blank wall. At another place, his guide shook out some red powder from a brass container and scattered it over the centre of a bare stone slab, murmuring a prayer in Sanskrit.

'Where do you priests live?' Rodney asked, as the priest straightened up.

'In the back parts of this temple,' the priest said. 'There are only six of us here and we do not need much . . . no beds, chairs, wardrobes, carpets. People bring us food. There is water from the tap outside.'

They were in the open then, in another courtyard behind the temple. The priest pointed to a cloister at the far side. Two men, presumably priests, were lying there asleep. What more did they need, indeed? Rodney thought. Food was brought to them on leaves, and they ate it; they drank from the tap; like everyone else they went in the dawn, brass *lotah* in hand, to relieve their bowels in the open spaces between the houses; they slept on the bare stone, in summer wrapped in their white cotton robe, in winter with an added blanket.

Rodney said, 'Pandit-ji, the Chinese say they are going to give me a pass to go to Lhasa and study Tibetan music there. Yet I have also been told that there is danger in going, and that I may be turned back at the frontier, even though I have a pass.'

The priest said, 'I have heard the same.'

Rodney said, 'I have talked with travellers recently come from Lhasa and they have told me what they know. But that is not much, and perhaps it is not accurate, for of course they are not permitted to see more than the Chinese wish them to see.'

'That is so.'

'I have also heard that there is a Chinese deserter, an officer, hiding in Kathmandu. It has been said that if he is indeed in Kathmandu, he would be somewhere near this temple. I don't know why they would say that.'

'We Vaishnavis have always given sanctuary to those who ask for it,' the priest said. His expression had not altered, but Rodney thought he was picking his words more carefully than before.

He said, 'Can you . . . would you . . . put me in touch with him? Under the strictest precautions for his safety, of course. I really must talk to someone who can tell me whether I am wise to go to Lhasa, whether I will be allowed to get there, what obstacles I will encounter if I do . . .'

The priest led back through the temple, saying nothing. Rodney followed, keeping close. At the little gap in the front wall where he had been sitting, near the brass tap, the priest made *namasti*, bowing slightly, and said, 'Nine o'clock tomorrow morning, here.'

'I shall need an interpreter,' Rodney said quickly, 'unless he speaks English or Hindustani.'

'I speak some Mandarin . . . enough,' the priest said, bowing again. He turned, and stalked away across the courtyard and into the temple.

Rodney swung quickly up the steps into the plastic grandeur of the Bristol-Carlton's lobby. He felt distinctly pleased with himself. The cloak-and-dagger business was coming along famously, and so was his collection of local music. The composing of the concerto from it would be a different matter. He stopped in mid-stride. Surely he knew that back crossing the lobby in front of him toward the lifts – the back of a man wearing a well-cut hacking jacket, and dark grey flannel trousers.

'Chandra!' he said, coming up behind the other.

Chandra Gupta turned, the smile already warming his mobile face. 'Geminus!' He flung open his arms, but then dropped them. 'Mustn't hug a *pakka sahib*,' he said grinning. 'So . . . your quest for music has brought you here. What have you heard so far?'

'Temple music, mostly. Some street stuff. I'm planning to go to a performance in a sort of office tonight. I don't suppose it'll be classical Nepali but it'll be something.'

'The curse of Indian music today is the cinema,' Chandra said. 'Nothing's been written for thirty years that wasn't designed for a sound track – and sounds like it. . . . I got a cable from my bloody editor right after I got back to my houseboat from visiting you that day. He wanted me to tell him – and our readers – what's going on in Nepal. Top priority, drop whatever else I was doing. And I had two more weeks of fishing planned, a week on the Sind and a week on the Kishenganga. Here, isn't it about time for a drink?'

'I could do with a beer,' Rodney admitted and they went together toward the bar. Machhindra greeted them with a wrinkled Mongolian smile. 'Morning, Mister Bateman. Morning, sir. One beer, one tomato juice. Right away.'

Rodney turned to Chandra – 'I thought you were a freelance for the *Independent*.'

'So I am, but the editor was very pressing. And when I got on the phone to complain, he waved large bundles of rupee notes before me – over the phone, of course. *And* I think a useful book could come out of this, too. What is the attitude of the Nepalese government towards China, deep down – and towards India? And the people? Have there been enough improvements made in social standards, enough political advances, for the country to withstand a determined effort by some outside power to, well, effectively destroy its independence? To what extent does the economy still depend on pay and pensions coming in from the Gorkha troops employed by us and the British?'

54

Rodney whistled. 'That's a tall order.'

Chandra sipped his juice. 'Not as big as it sounds, because all the problems are interrelated. But I can't afford to waste time. I have half a dozen interviews lined up for tomorrow. After a few days I'll probably have to go away and work out what the stuff I've got is pointing towards, then come back and dig deeper. Listen, I'm already late for an appointment with a politician . . . an opposition man, thought to be secretly in Chinese pay. It should be interesting.'

Rodney said, 'Yes. Why don't we have dinner together, before this concert?'

'All right. Let's make it at the Yak and Yeti. I've heard the food's good there. . . . Seven o'clock? Oh, and listen, if you want to find out about Nepali music – or Indian for that matter – get out in the villages. In the country, the mountains. With us, music is the people's thing, not the scholars', nor even the musicians'.'

'So I am learning,' Rodney murmured.

A few minutes before nine the next morning Rodney left the hotel, notebook and pencil in his pocket, and walked briskly toward the Vaishnavi temple. The music last night at the concert – if that was what the formless evening in the crowded back room of some government building should be called – had not been good. As Chandra had warned, the music was cheap and derivative, and smelled rankly of a Bombay film studio dedicated to churning out motion picture 'hits'. The dinner at the Yak and Yeti had redeemed the evening. The food was indeed good, the Russian proprietor amusing, and his own talk with Chandra most interesting. It was astounding how much Chandra had learned in the three or four interviews he had made since their meeting in the hotel lobby. Of course, he was a working journalist and wasn't coming to Nepal cold; he had been a presence in Indian politics, and in the news ever since he took up his profession.

At the outer wall of the temple, Rodney sat down on a step, produced his notebook, and began to annotate the chant coming from inside. Within a few minutes his acquaintance the priest strode out toward him, made *namasti*, and said in his clearly articulated Hindustani,

55

'Would you care to listen to the music inside? You will perhaps detect subtleties lost out here.'

'Certainly, thank you,' Rodney said, getting up. He followed the priest across the courtyard. At the temple door he took off his shoes, and was about to leave them there when the priest said, 'Carry them.'

They went on in semi-darkness; the chanting, unaccompanied today by any instrument, grew louder, then faded as the priest turned left, passed down a narrow passage, and again out into the open. He motioned to Rodney to put on his shoes. They crossed a small open space and at once went down an alley between tall brick walls, and into a door fifty paces into the alley. A flight of creaking and filthy wooden stairs led upwards; at the top, behind a battered door of unpainted walnut, in a room lit by a hurricane lantern set on the floor, no stick of furniture in the room, and no window, a man squatted on a pair of blankets, a wooden pillow behind his back.

'He will not give us his name,' the priest murmured. 'We call him The Lieutenant.'

The Lieutenant was about thirty, Rodney thought, a slightly built man with big eyes in a flat pale yellow face, a strong jaw and unusually long upper lip. His black hair was cut very short, almost shaven, and he was wearing a homespun woollen robe wrapped first round his waist to make a sort of skirt, and then the end thrown over his shoulders, like a Scottish Highlander's plaid. In a rope coiled round his waist was thrust a *kukri* in its sheath.

Rodney sank to his heels opposite the man and the priest followed suit, squatting between the two of them, to one side. Rodney produced five Nepalese ten-rupee notes and held them out. The Lieutenant's eyes glinted momentarily in the wavering light as he took the notes without speaking, and thrust them into the breast of his plaid.

Rodney said, 'I expect to be going to Lhasa soon, to study music. Will I be able to get there?'

The priest interpreted, haltingly. The Lieutenant spoke quickly, a few words. The priest turned to Rodney. 'Probably not. The soldiers at Kodari will not honour any permit the Chinese officials here might give you.'

'Why?'

More talk and finally the answer: 'Because there are big military preparations going on along the frontier. The army is responsible, so the general will not let the others, the commissars and politicians, spoil the plan.'

'What is the plan?'

'He does not know the great plan, of course. He is only a lieutenant. He knows that there are many, many soldiers up there, with guns and tanks, hiding in caves and up the side valleys on the Kuti La route to Kodari and Nepal. Also on other routes, which are being built or improved, to the west.'

'How many soldiers, in all, along the frontier?'

'Perhaps ten thousand, perhaps twenty thousand. And many more in Lhasa, who could reach the frontier in two or three days.'

Rodney surveyed the Lieutenant's impassive face. Ten thousand was a lot of men to put along a border as severe as that between Nepal and Tibet, where the easiest passes were sixteen thousand feet above sea level, and most much higher.

'What are the Chinese general's intentions?' he asked.

'He says he does not know. There was talk that the army has been ordered to conquer Nepal, so that Nepal will become part of China, or a protectorate . . . and the Indians and British will not be able to have Gorkha soldiers serving for them.'

That last would be quite a blow to both Britain and India, Rodney thought. The British Army didn't have many Gorkhas now, he knew, but there were some. The Indians, someone had told him, had over twenty thousand. They would be hard to replace, and India would miss them in any future confrontation with China. But the acquisition of Nepal would be of dubious value to China. It would not be a source of income, only a drain on China's resources, and a continuing source of friction with India. Yet every indication seemed to point towards China's intention to embark on so dangerous a course.

He asked, 'Why did the Lieutenant desert?'

'He says he is a university intellectual, forced into the army as an engineer. He was a Communist, originally, but became disillusioned some years ago. There is no hope of changing the Chinese regime from inside, he says. There is only escape, for those lucky enough to be given an opportunity.'

Rodney asked a few more questions, about specific areas and about the Lieutenant's own work, then said, 'That's all. Thank the Lieutenant very much.'

'He says, don't try to go to Lhasa. You will not pass the frontier, and you may not come back at all.'

'Why did they let some travellers through, a few days ago? I have heard that they did.'

'He says, it depends on who gave the travellers permits. There is a military headquarters in Lhasa, and if they give a permit, the soldiers on the frontier honour it . . . but not the permits from civil officials.'

'Thank him again.'

Out in the street the priest said, 'You must have a good memory. You did not make any notes.'

Rodney said, 'I'm not trying to remember anything, just find out what the conditions are,' but he realized that his questions had been too pointed not to arouse suspicion about his true motives. But what else could he do? He had to take some risks to find out, quickly, enough to indicate to Ayesha where more intensive investigations should be directed.

In his pocket he found the fifty rupees he had decided to pay the priest, and slipped it to him. 'Thank you,' the other said. 'It will be for incense . . . and perhaps flowers for the inner mystery.' He pointed down the street, the opposite direction to that by which they had come in. 'Go out that way. When you reach the lane at the end, turn right, then right again. You will soon reach the main street.'

Rodney nodded and walked away, the priest going in the opposite direction. The sun did not reach this narrow gut, and it smelled of human ordure and charcoal smoke. The Lieutenant had merely confirmed Jansingh's information. As a bonus he had learned that military permits were necessary; and thus that Jansingh Gharti, the buyer for a firm of general merchants, must have had one, but that could mean that . . .

A darker darkness in a doorway almost beside him caught the corner of his eye. He suddenly became aware of where he was – a deserted lane, sinister, noisome: two men in the doorway. He saw them clearly now, and they saw that he had seen. They slipped forward, swinging short black billies. Rodney broke into a run and dashed by them before they could quite reach him. The nearest swung his club, the blow bouncing off Rodney's right shoulder . . . rubber, he thought. Why the hell wasn't anyone about? He heard them panting behind . . . bare feet pad-pad-pad, barely audible in the dirt. A billy whistled and thudded onto his other shoulder. He saw a man ahead and gasped 'Help!' but the man took one terrified look, his eyes gleaming suddenly white, dived into a doorway, and vanished.

The thugs were too fast for him. It was no good running, presenting only his back and his head as unprotected targets to their billies. He ran on a few seconds, swung round a corner then turned, pressed back against the wall, and catapulted himself at his pursuers. His head hit one of them in the throat, as he lashed out with both fists into the man's stomach. The man gasped and went down. Rodney regained his balance and turned on the other, as a billy smashed into the side of his head. And again. Feebly Rodney swung at the man, but his eyes were going out of focus, his head filling with sound, his knees buckling. He collapsed into the dirt.

This was most strange, for he could hear and see his assailants, but feel nothing. He didn't think they were hitting him any more. One was kneeling over him, feeling in his pockets; the other, the one he'd knocked down, was on his feet, leaning forward, retching painfully. The searcher had got his wallet, was fingering swiftly through it . . . taking money . . . throwing it down . . . then the musical notebook, shaking it, stuffing it away inside his shirt . . . muttering something to the other man . . . a voice was calling from miles away . . . the men were gone.

Rodney lay a minute longer, motionless. He was not sure whether he could stand or not, and did not want to get up half way, then fall. Gingerly he tried his muscles, as he heard footsteps close, at first running, then slowing to a walk. His knees seemed to have regained something of their strength. He stood up groggily, putting out an arm to support himself against a house wall. He looked down at his clothes and began to dust them off. There was a man close, the man who had come running, probably the same whose call had disturbed the robbers. He was a burly young fellow, probably a labourer, now speaking to him in Nepali. Rodney stooped, picked up his wallet and looked through it. They'd taken his cash, about a hundred rupees, and the notebook, presumably imagining there might be more money concealed between the pages; but they'd left his credit card and the photos of his children. Surprising that they hadn't torn the Gemini ring off his finger while they were at it; that would fetch a lot more than a hundred rupees.

The labourer was speaking again, and Rodney said, in Hindi, 'I'm all right.'

The man pointed up the street, and Rodney thought, I suppose he saw them escaping that way. 'I don't know,' he said, 'I'm all right. Thank you.' The young man shrugged and went on his way. Rodney followed more slowly. He didn't know where he was, precisely, but it didn't matter. He'd find his way home somehow.

Two thugs – *goondas* in the usual Indian word – had attacked and robbed him. They had also stolen his notebook. Why? The obvious motive was robbery; but it was most unlikely that *goondas* would make a habit of lying in wait in a lane such as this, for its normal users would not be worth robbing. So the *goondas* had been tipped off. By whom? The Lieutenant was one candidate, since he must have been forewarned of the visit; the priest was another; and anyone whom either the Lieutenant or the priest might have told about the visit, or asked to help in arranging it made the third possibility an unknown but perhaps large quantity.

Suppose now that the motive was not robbery. The only sensible alternative was counter-espionage: it was intended that he should not pass on whatever he had learned from the Lieutenant. But in that case, why had they not killed him? They could have, probably; it was possible that the Nepali labourer had come into view and seen them before they could finish the job; but from his recollection, hazy from the blows on his head, they had had plenty of time. But then why hadn't they – presumably the Chinese secret service – killed the Lieutenant, and shut his mouth, long since? Perhaps they did not want to risk stirring up the Nepalese government by the murder of a foreigner – that would cause a big commotion; mugging one for a hundred chips – nothing at all. In logic, it was also possible that they had spared his life – and the Lieutenant's – because they *did* want his information to be passed on. But surely that didn't make sense; and in that case why had they taken his notebook, which for all they knew might contain coded notes on his conversation with the Lieutenant?

His head ached, not badly but steadily, and he was stirred by a vague unease. A few hours ago he had been congratulating himself on having it all sorted out, and had told Ayesha so. Now, he was queasily unsure. If his head had been his stomach, he would have thought that he was about to suffer an upheaval. Damn it, he was . . .

When he had finished writing his second report, and had addressed it to Mr. P. S. Grewal, he took it to Harmukh Singh's, handing it this time to the son. Then he returned to his room, found a spare musical notebook and spent an hour trying to remember tunes and themes he had already noted in Kashmir, and earlier in Kathmandu, that were now lost. Then he sat at the window, looking moodily out. He could not see the mountains from here, and whatever was going on, was going on up there.

After a time of fretting, he picked up the phone and spoke to reception. 'Is there any agency in Kathmandu that arranges treks?'

'Certainly, sir, two or three. We recommend Colonel Crowley.'

Rodney was about to ask the desk to get him Colonel Crowley when he paused, thought a moment, then said instead, 'Get me Mr. Chandra Gupta, please. Room 349, I think.'

When Chandra came on the line Rodney said, 'Rodney Bateman here, Chandra. I'm going trekking, starting to-morrow, if I can get an agency to fix me up in time. Do you want to come?'

'Taking my advice to get into the hills?' Chandra said. 'How long do you propose to be away?'

'About ten days, I thought. It depends whether the agency can fly us direct to a good trekking area.'

'Any idea where you want to go?'

'I was looking at the map earlier, after you had advised me to go to the mountains, and thought I'd like to go up one of the branches of the Gandaki – the Buria Gandaki, perhaps.'

'I don't know any of them – never been trekking in Nepal. Will there be fishing?'

'I'm sure. I'm going to take a rod.'

'Well . . .' There was a long pause; then, aloud, but clearly half to himself, 'I can cancel the appointment with the minister, he's nothing but an old windbag, anyway . . . and I have to go to the villages sooner or later to find out the difference between the government's official information, as given out in Kathmandu, and the reality. I'll come.'

'Good!' Rodney cried, 'that's great!' An unreasonable pleasure possessed him. 'I'll ring Crowley now and let you know as soon as I have the details fixed.'

'Don't forget to tell them I want a can of tomato soup for each day we're going to be out.'

CHAPTER FIVE

Rodney climbed slowly, the sweat dripping steadily into his eyes, though the air bit chill here at nearly twelve thousand feet above sea level, and snow lay in all the shaded corners. It was not long since he had been trekking in the Kashmir mountains, and he was in good condition; but this was the Nepal Himalaya, higher and more severe, where the jagged peaks rent a cloud-dotted sky and the stony path climbed in fierce zigzags. A thousand feet below, the forest began, sweeping down another three thousand feet to the deep trench of the Buria Gandaki. Far down there he could see villages, and the terraced fields where the Gorkha peasants wrung a hard living from the soil; above – rocks, and short grass, and a wind blowing down from the ice towers that leaned over the ragged little train of men crawling up towards them.

He stopped to mop his forehead, Chandra stopping beside him. The heavily laden porters passed slowly by, powerful necks bent to bear the strain of the eighty-pound loads which each man carried on a wide head band. 'This is bigger country than Kashmir,' Rodney said.

'Denser, too,' Chandra said.

Rodney had been thinking the same thing, and wondering whether it would be possible for any large bodies of men to pass through these tremendous gorges, or surmount those dazzling snow walls across the upper horizon. Or, having done what seemed the impossible, how they could fight or manoeuvre their way through the cultivation below there, and the close-packed villages of the middle ranges, and below again, the rain forest, the heavy jungles of the Terai. On the flight from Delhi to Kathmandu the Royal Nepal Airlines 727 had passed over the Terai; he had looked down on a thickly woven green carpet, and had wondered how anyone or anything could pass through it. He wondered again now, but with more reason for his speculation.

He started on again, at once picking up the rhythmic climbing pace. The breath came short and thin into his

63

lungs as the path continued to climb, easing higher along the valley side, aiming, he now saw, to pass above a rock face that seemed to drop sheer, in cliff and landslide, all the way down to the pale river, an impossible obstacle.

In a grassy alp the wildflowers streamed and glittered, and Chandra cried, 'Look . . . *naspati ka rajah!* He knelt beside a flower that seemed to be made of frozen cotton-wool, the spikes of a thistle-like flower just peering out of the frothy exterior. 'And here's a Himalayan blue poppy! By God, Geminus, we should pitch our camp here. What a place, what views! Looking south, it's easy to believe we can see Patna . . .'

'But we can't,' Rodney said, laughing, 'And there's no water here for me to wash my socks, which badly need it.'

'No appreciation of beauty, unless you receive it through the ear,' Chandra grumbled, starting up the mountain again.

'Nonsense,' Rodney gasped, following. 'Didn't you see – me giving – that Gorkha girl – the eye – in the last village – we camped in?'

'I did,' Chandra said, 'so did her father. He was sharpening his *kukri* as we left.'

They continued climbing. Half an hour later their path made one last zig and levelled out above the great cliff. There, under a grey boulder, sat an old man with a wispy beard such as Chinese sages used to wear, and a drooping white moustache. He climbed creakily to his feet and saluted. 'Subadar Manjang Gurung, sahib,' he said, 'Thar-teen Gorkha Rifle. *Pension ma gayo sun unis sau paintalis.*'

Chandra said, 'Went on pension in 1947. He must be eighty.'

The old man motioned to them to sit beside him, on some well-worn stones placed in the shelter of the big rock, for this place was obviously used by porters and travellers to rest after the long climb from either direction.

From the battered haversack slung over his shoulder, the old subadar produced a bottle of dark liquid and a tin mug. '*Raksi,*' he said, grinning a toothless grin.

'Rum,' Chandra said, 'probably about a hundred and fifty proof. Be careful, Rodney.'

Rodney poured a little rum into the mug, tilted his head and poured the spirit down his throat without letting the

rim of the mug touch his lips. He coughed and spluttered
and wiped his eye.

'*Shahbash!*' the old subadar cried, pouring more rum for
Chandra. Chandra shook his head and explained in Hindi
that he did not drink. The old subadar shook his head
sadly and emptied the mug himself. Smacking his lips and
setting the bottle down at his side he spoke to them now
in a rough-hewn Hindustani that he must have learned in
his army days. 'I had heard that two sahibs were coming
up.'

'How did you hear?' Rodney asked.

'Oh, they called up from Chisopani,' the old man said.
Chisopani was the name of the last village, where the pretty
girl had smiled at him; but it was ten miles back, nearly
four thousand feet down and out of sight round two or
three sharp bends of the Buria Gandaki.

Chandra explained. 'One man shouts from the village to
his son working a field a mile away, and high up, and he
to another, and so on.'

Rodney remembered then that he had heard thin cries,
that soon faded in the high air, as they were climbing out
of Chisopani. 'Where are the presences going?' the subadar
asked.

'We're just trekking,' Rodney said, 'We'd like to go on
up the valley as far as we can before we have to start back.'

'Up the Buria Gandaki?' the old man asked, nodding at
the river far below.

'Yes.'

'You can go up another two days' march above my
village, Dukseni Bazaar, which you can see down there.
Then they'll stop you.'

'Who will stop us?'

'The sentries. Ours. They don't let anyone go any closer
than that to the Tibet-desh border. The China-log would
shoot them.'

'Oh,' Chandra shook his head, and whistled in surprise.

Rodney said, 'Then perhaps we can go up one of the
side valleys.' He pointed ahead where steep walls of rock
and scattered pines curving down from the north-east
showed that another stream flowed into the Buria Gandaki
a couple of miles above Dukseni Bazaar.

The old subadar looked serious. 'Don't go there, sahib.

There are *yetis* up there. You'll never reach the *bhanjyang*.'

'A *bhanjyang* is a pass, like the Tibetan *la*,' Chandra said to him in an aside: then 'What *bhanjyang* is that, subadar sahib?'

'The Rasua Bhanjyang. It is high. The breath comes short, even to us Gorkhas, and there may still be much snow.'

'It leads into Tibet-desh?'

The old man nodded – 'Yes, but the *yetis* will kill and eat you before you could reach there. One of our boys, who went up there last autumn to look for a lost sheep, never came back.'

'Did you go up and search for him?'

'What would be the use? The *yetis* are too cunning. They are not stupid animals, you know.' He picked up the rum bottle and drank from it, without using the mug.

Chandra rose to his feet. 'We'll think about it. Is there a good place to set up our camp in your village, sahib?'

'There is. I told your head porter. . . . It is just above the last house, which is mine, by the river. The river water is good . . . there are no villages above Dukseni Bazaar. Go on down, sahib. I will come more slowly. My legs are not what they were when I outran three *wakhlis* above Razmak and took all their heads. Aiih, it is cold at my age. . . .' He picked up the bottle again as Chandra and Rodney waved their hands in salutation and swung with long steps down the path toward the village nestled in a little curve of the river three thousand feet below them.

'A bit of an old rumpot, I think,' Rodney said, grinning.

'Yes, but not addled. And fit enough to climb up three thousand feet to greet us. Abominable Snowmen on the Rasua Bhanjyang, eh? Very interesting, eh?'

'Very . . . I think we should investigate.'

'I wonder if our porters will come with us.'

'We could leave most of them behind, just take two or three volunteers with us. We could be back in Dukseni Bazaar in four days, five at the outside. We can afford a few extra days before we go back to Kathmandu, can't we?'

'Right. I'm sure we can get three porters to come with us, though it'll cost a few rupees extra.' They strode on faster down the stony trail, Rodney now singing a Gorkha tune the pretty girl of Chisopani had sung last night at the well.

They were singing again now, on the beaten earth outside the old subadar's house. The Buria Gandaki swung by close below, an icy breath and a subdued thunder in the darkness with a deeper diapason of heavy boulders shifting in the swift current, and now and then the glitter of white in the starlight as spears of spray were flung high above the surface of the water.

Chandra and Rodney sat side by side on wooden chairs, the subadar to Chandra's right. A rickety table had been set up before them, spread with a blanket, and furnished with a bottle of rum, several glasses, plates of curried goat and vegetables, and a pitcher of water for Chandra. Three other old men, all pensioners of Gorkha Rifle regiments, sat to right and left, mugs in hand, while forty or fifty other men, women and children, the entire population of the village as far as Rodney could see, squatted along the wall of the house and out in the open by the river bank. All were huddled in homespun blankets; for it was cold here, though they had come down to ten thousand feet from the point where the subadar had been waiting for them.

Four young men gyrated in lazy circles on the threshing floor, slowly swooping, slowly rising, two dressed in black and white and two dressed, as girls, in black and red. Two older men sang and beat on the small drums called *madals,* which they held on their laps where they sat cross-legged opposite the subadar, who was obviously the squire of Dukseni Bazaar. Rodney's pencil was in his hand, but the notebook lay open on the table beside his glass. The tune had not changed for twenty minutes, and what there was to note about it, he had done; also the subtle cross rhythms of the men with the *madals.* The subadar was asleep, the other old soldiers nodding or leaning over talking to each other.

'Himachal!' Chandra muttered softly. 'The Abode of Snow. If there was a full moon we'd see snow, up there. . . . Perhaps it's better that we can't, then we can imagine it all in our minds. India wouldn't be India without Himachal. It's a shield, and the soul that the shield protects, at the same time.'

67

'And if it's pierced?' Rodney said.

'India bleeds to death,' Chandra said. 'There will be new souls, new bodies, of course ... Bengal, Hindustan, the old Deccan, Mysore – death for one means life for others, just as if Great Britain were to die, Wales and Scotland would be born, or reborn ... and if the United States were to die – New England, the old Confederacy, new nations of the Pacific, of the Rockies. ... The Himalaya is the biggest range on earth, by far. It contains hundreds of peaks taller than any outside it. It's sixteen hundred miles long, from Nanga Parbat to Namcha Barwa. That's not as long as the Andes, but the main chain itself is two hundred miles wide, and it's protected to the south by lesser ranges – the Pir Panjal, the Sewaliks, and to the north by other chains nearly as high and even more difficult – the Kun Lun, the Karakoram ...'

'They are joined to the Himalayas, to the north?' Rodney asked.

Chandra said, 'No, they are separated from it by a remarkable transverse passage or corridor. Right behind the centre of the Himalayas, on the north side, in Tibet, two rivers rise close together at about fourteen thousand feet above sea level. One flows east and one flows west. The one flowing west is the Indus. It passes off the Tibetan plateau, through the area called Ladakh or Little Tibet. The frontier between India and Tibet there is undefined and disputed. Then it passes north of Kashmir, swings south round Nanga Parbat as though it were the end of a jetty and heads due south for the plains of Pakistan, and the sea near Karachi.

'The eastward flowing river is called the Tsang Po. It crosses the high Tibetan plateau near Lhasa, flows farther east, then swings south round Namcha Barwa and disappears into almost impassable gorges. There it is called the Dihang. Soon after it emerges into Arunachal Pradesh, which is part of India, it is called the Brahmaputra. In Bangladesh it joins the Ganges, and the joined rivers reach the sea in many channels, called the Sunderbunds, east of Calcutta. ...

'The valleys of those two rivers, where they are flowing in opposite directions on the other side of the Himalayas – up there' – he jerked his head toward the north – 'form the passage way, the corridor, I was talking about. People and goods can move along it. It's high country, used to be very primitive, and difficult, but the Chinese have made or improved roads all along that corridor . . . which also serves to separate the Himalayas from the northern ranges.'

'Which don't concern India,' Rodney said.

Chandra said, 'Not really. They matter to China and Russia, but not really to India.'

'How many passes are there through the Himalayas?' Rodney asked.

'Places where ibex, or skilled mountaineers, or *yetis* could pass – many. Places for traffic of any kind – few. There is an important way between Ladakh, north of the range, and Kashmir, south of it . . . the Zoji La. That's the main route the Indian Army uses to support troops facing the Chinese and Pakistanis in Ladakh and on the Upper Indus. Next, after a few difficult ones in Ravi, is the Rohtang Jot, which also has a motor road over it leading to Ladakh but across some very high intermediate passes. Then in Nepal there is the main Kathmandu-Lhasa road over the Kuti La. There are several other much harder passes, like this Rasua Bhanjyang we mean to look at. East again there is the Natu La leading from Sikkim into Tibet – that's the main route between India and Tibet for such trade as there is . . . a few more difficult ones leading down from Tibet into Bhutan, or the tribal territories farther east. I believe the Chinese are rumoured to be developing a route into Mishmi country, in the extreme east. Any farther east and you wouldn't be in India, but Burma.'

'The Zoji, the Rohtang, the Kuti, the Natu, the Mishmi,' Rodney murmured half to himself. 'Far west, west-centre, centre east-centre, far east.'

'What do you mean?' Chandra asked, cocking an eye at him.

He said, 'I was thinking – where India could be wounded. The Chinese seem to be feeling their oats.'

'Oh, they threaten and bluster,' Chandra said confidently, 'but they've got too many problems of their own to start anything foolish.' After a time of silence he looked at his water glass, in something like disgust and said, 'I sometimes wish I wasn't a teetotaller. On a night like this, in the Himalayas, I would like to be drinking rum with you quietly, each of us thinking our own thoughts, but shared because we are together here, and because we are Gemini.' He fell silent.

Rodney too did not speak for several minutes, half listening to the music and the drums, while his mind circled far, then returned to the place where he was. He said, 'I am thinking of my wife. I wish everything was all right between us, and that she was here with me.'

Chandra said, 'I am thinking of Kit Sanders.'

'Kit?' Rodney said, startled.

'We were lovers once, a few years ago. It began in the Himalayas . . . below Kolahoi on the upper Liddar as a matter of fact . . . in bliss and wild flowers and clean snow . . . and ended in a dirty place in the plains in the middle of the hot weather – just like any other torrent born in the mountains.'

'It is over?' Rodney said inquiringly. 'Kit seemed very upset over your accident.' He was glad that Chandra had told him of his own accord what Ayesha had passed on as a piece of malicious gossip.

Chandra nodded. 'She was getting too possessive. I am a bird . . . irresponsible and unreliable, if you like, but I can't be tied. I'll never marry. And Mike was getting suspicious.'

'I've heard that he was a ladies' man himself.'

'He was. He regularly visited a famous courtesan in the Srinagar bazaar, and enjoyed other favours, too. Kit found him in bed with a trek client once, a good-looking Australian widow. Kit only laughed.'

'She wasn't jealous?'

'Kit? Not a bit. Not of poor Mike, anyway. She watched *me* like a tigress while our affair was going on, though, so I suppose it depends on how closely her emotions are involved. But she and Mike got on very well together, on a certain level . . . very friendly, each made sensible concessions . . .'

One of the pensioners limped over, took the bottle of rum, filled Rodney's glass before he could stop him, and poured a goodly tot down his own throat. The intimacy between Chandra and Rodney was broken.

Chandra said, yawning, 'Do you believe in Abominable Snowmen, Geminus?'

'Perhaps we'll find out tomorrow.'

'Perhaps a *yeti* will swoop down on Dukseni Bazaar to-night, looking for food, or a bride.'

Rodney chuckled. 'That little minx over there's been eyeing us all evening. She wouldn't mind whether it was Abominable or Snowy, just as long as it was a Man. I'm going to creep off to bed. This has been great fun, but I'm tired, and we're starting early.'

I'll come with you. We'll have to wake the old boy . . . subadar sahib . . . *subadar sahib!*'

There was no path up the Rasua, and by the end of the second hour they had left the trees and once more come out onto open hillsides, alive with alpine wildflowers. Across the Buria Gandaki behind them the mountains rose in ever more savage profusion; ahead, the Rasua torrent hurried down from invisible rocks and crags up the long trench of its valley. The gradient had been steep up through the trees, but now it had eased, and Rodney and Chandra climbed side by side a hundred yards to the right of the stream. Their three porters were out of sight, still toiling up through the trees below.

After a time the sound of the stream became louder and, looking up, Rodney saw why – the valley floor tilted up at a much steeper angle for the next thousand feet. The whole slope was strewn with grey boulders and stippled with blue gentians and white anemones. The Rasua tumbled down the centre of this jumble over rocks and hanging moss and spreading lichen, part torrent, part a series of waterfalls. The two men bent their backs to the scramble, and did not speak, keeping their breaths for the climbing.

After three-quarters of an hour of hard effort Rodney reached the top of the steep section. Scrambling over a rock he found that he was looking up a long open alp, the Rasua stream winding across it toward him in big loops and bends. At the far end of the alp the slope again steepened, and there the mountainsides were dusted with white. As his eye swept higher, he saw that the snow lay thicker until, high up where the Rasua curved to the left and out of sight, it must have been a foot deep, and solid across the stream bed and up the sides, except where cliffs were too steep to hold it.

71

Then, as his eye returned to savour the calm of the alp, with its unmistakable geological evidence of once having been a lake bed, he saw movement at the far end, among big scattered boulders. He stared, feeling for the binoculars that hung around his neck. Finding them, he lifted them to his eyes. The far end of the alp sprang into focus in the circle of the view ... water, a loop of the stream soon after it came off a scree slope, two large boulders ... and three men, one of them bent over a tripod, another peering through a theodolite. Surveyors, obviously.

Chandra was tugging at his elbow. He lowered his binoculars, and turned, eager to show Chandra what he had seen; but Chandra's face was taut with absolute astonishment, his mouth dropped open, his finger to his lips in an imperative gesture of silence. He pointed. At first Rodney could see nothing among the tumbled rocks beside the stream, thirty or forty yards away, where his friend was indicating. Then he saw something, its colour orange-red and dark brown. Again he focused the binoculars. The thing was hairy. He felt shock like a heavy blow over the heart as the whole object took shape in the lenses. It was a creature, about man's height, covered in thick red-brown fur, lying on its side, asleep. The gorilla-like face, the skin almost black, was turned toward him, great lower canine tusks sticking up at each side of the out-thrust jaw.

'Yeti,' he whispered, as Chandra echoed the same word.

The creature's feet were larger than would have been expected from its height of about five foot nine or ten. One of the important scientific discoveries of the century had been entrusted, by chance, to them. What incredible luck! Beside him Chandra was kneeling, taking off his pack, getting out the long lens of his camera from a side pocket, clicking it into place. Then he rose carefully, and took two photographs. Rodney winced at each heavy clack of the single-lens reflex, but the *yeti* had not been awakened. Now even if it sprang to its feet and vanished, they would have a record of its existence.

Chandra put his mouth close to Rodney's ear and breathed, 'Let's go forward. I'll take a picture every five paces.'

We mustn't block its escape – up the alp, that way ...

When we've got to ten yards, I'll throw something to wake it, and it'll run off, and you'll get some good pictures.'

'I *hope* it'll run off. You've got a nerve, Geminus, for a meek musician. I've got twelve more pictures on the roll.'

Rodney rose carefully with Chandra at his side, and advanced step by step, moving with excruciating slowness, at every pace looking down to make sure that he did not turn a stone or slide on loose gravel. At five paces Chandra took another photograph; the clack of the lens again sounded very loud, but Rodney realized that the tempestuous Rasua was close, and its voice would drown other sounds. On, another five paces . . . another picture. On again . . . now they were no more than twenty yards from it. Chandra took another picture.

The sound of the Rasua was much less noticeable now. From the far end of the lake a human voice called out in a high pitched cry. The *yeti* awoke and sat up, and Chandra took another picture. It turned its head from side to side and stretched just like a human. Then it saw them. For a moment it stared, the heavy jaw dropping . . . it uttered an unearthly screeching roar as the camera clacked again by Rodney's ear. Turning, the *yeti* half scrambled, half ran up the alp beside the stream. Rodney broke into a run after it, yelling, 'Come on, Chandra!'

'Once it reaches the snow we'll be able to follow its tracks for ever,' Chandra cried; then they were both running.

Rodney remembered the surveyors. Perhaps they'd have arms. They must be warned not to shoot . . . that would be just what they might do when they saw the *yeti;* either they'd be terrified, or eager to get a unique trophy and brag and strut about it for years after – the Man who Bagged the *Yeti.* He began to shout as he ran, waving his arms, 'Don't shoot! *Fire mat karo!*' In front of them the *yeti* bounded along beside the stream, mostly half upright, but now and then shambling fast with its front paws touching the ground as they swung.

Rodney saw that one of the surveyors had heard the yells. Now all three of them turned, and seemed to freeze where they were. The *yeti* bounded on toward them, again screaming and roaring. The man with the theodolite stooped and picked up something at his feet . . . a rifle. Rodney yelled louder in agonized entreaty. 'Don't shoot!

Fire mat karo! Kuchh khattar nahin hai – there's no danger!' The other two men up there ran behind one of the huge boulders near where they had been working. The man with the rifle raised it.

'He's going to shoot at us!' Chandra gasped.

'No, the idiot's trying to get the *yeti.*'

A bullet smacked close over his head and he stopped. 'English,' he yelled, '*Angrezi! Fire mat karo!*'

'Get down, Rodney, for God's sake,' Chandra yelled, flinging himself down.

'I don't believe . . .' Another shot cracked by. Chandra cried, '*Down,* Geminus! Don't be so damned *pakka sahib!*' Rodney knelt unwillingly. One of the men at the far end of the alp was shouting in a language he did not understand. The *yeti* was still running, but had now turned to the left and was scrambling up the snow-powdered slope. Rodney sank down.

Chandra said, 'We've got to get out of here . . . if we can.'

'I'd like to know what the bloody hell they think they're doing!'

Chandra said, 'One of them's come out from behind the rocks and is coming this way, down the side of the valley. He has a gun . . . and he'll cut us off if we don't start back soon. Have you got a weapon?'

'Nothing.'

'Nor have I. Not here.'

Rodney controlled his rage. Chandra said, 'Get up when I do, but don't keep close . . . head for the stream. It's down a bit below the general level of the alp. Ready? Go!'

He jumped to his feet and began to run, racing back for five paces, then jinking sideways for four, always trying to keep the direction of his motion at a diagonal to the line of sight from the gunman to him. Two bullets smacked overhead and another, he thought, tugged at the material of his windjacket as it passed; then they were at the stream, hurling themselves over the two-foot bank of crumbled earth and face down into the swirling icy water.

Scrambling to their feet they began to hurry downstream at an awkward crouching trot. Humps in the valley floor, the banks of the stream, and the scattered boulders seemed to hide them effectively, at least enough to prevent the others from getting a good shot at them, until they were

74

near the lip of the steep drop. The voice of the Rasua changed from its whispering gurgle to a many-toned roar.

'That man's almost at the edge,' Chandra said, 'he's still running.' He crouched, peering downstream between the rocks. 'We can't get there ahead of him. We'll be sitting ducks when we arrive.'

Rodney raised his head and looked around. The gunman at the upper end of the alp might be able to see him, but his range was long now; in any case, he didn't fire. Rodney watched the running man reach the lip and turn as though to find a suitable spot in which to lie and ambush them as they came down the stream. But he didn't finish his turn; instead he crept forward another pace, two more, another – then knelt, peering down the steep slope below him. Slowly he raised his rifle as Chandra muttered, 'What's he seen? Another *yeti?*'

Rodney said, 'It must be our porters. Now's our chance. Run – this way!'

They sprang up together and raced across the valley toward the left side, where big boulders lay precariously on a steep slope two hundred yards from the stream. The man at the lip of the slope fired twice more, but the sound of the explosions showed that they had not been aimed toward Rodney and Chandra. Then he must have seen them, for five seconds later a bullet splattered against a stone behind them and splinters whined past Rodney's feet. Another shot ricocheted over their heads before they reached the rocks.

They knelt in shelter, gasping to recover their breath in the thin air, for they were now over fourteen thousand feet above sea level. 'How many of them, altogether?' Chandra asked.

'I've only see three. One ran down to the lip – that one. Two at the far end of the alp – one was shooting at us, the other may have a rifle, too – don't know.'

'Can you see what the man at the lip's doing?'

Rodney peered round the edge of the rock. The man was again looking down the hill. Once he half raised his rifle, then lowered it again, and turned to scan the rocks where Rodney and Chandra were. Rodney said, 'The porters probably thought the shots were a mistake, and kept coming on up. He was getting ready to fire at them again, but put his rifle down.'

'They turned back. I bet Tularam persuaded the others that discretion is the better part of valour. . . . I wish we'd got rifles.'

'Well, we don't, and we're going to have our work cut out to get out of here alive. Let's have a shot at getting on down. We're certainly not going to improve our situation by staying here and giving them time to organize a drive on us.'

Chandra said, 'We'll have to get farther away from the stream line. That man's still there. At the lip, on the far side.'

'So the others will come down this side, behind us, if they're going to come at all.'

'All the more reason to get farther over. Good God, Geminus, it's steep country, and there's no shelter once we get out of these rocks . . . except that the man at the lip won't be able to see us. We'll be over the ridge crest from him. But from behind . . .'

'Let's get going.'

They started moving cautiously down and across the steep slope among dirty snow patches and great lichen-spotted boulders. At every boulder Rodney kept a watch on the man at the lip, while Chandra searched back up the hill for signs of pursuit from that direction. In twenty minutes they had covered barely a quarter of a mile, but they had descended three hundred feet. Rodney said, 'Can't see the man at the lip any more. We're round the ridge.'

'Look out!' Chandra flung himself at him as a bullet exploded into the rock beside them. Rodney scrambled on his knees round the other side of the rock where he pressed himself against it, recovering his breath. His arm hurt where he had grazed it in his dive for cover, blood flowed from a long cut on his cheek, and his windjacket was torn. They were both soaked through, but did not feel the cold in the urgent press of danger.

'Two of them are on the backbone of the ridge behind us,' Chandra said. 'I saw one at the same moment he saw us.'

'We've got to run for it,' Rodney said. 'They're three, four hundred yards off now, but if we just wait here, they'll . . .'

'Wait!' Chandra pointed east along the line of the slope where they were sheltering. A tendril of mountain fog was creeping toward them, gradually blurring, hazing, then hiding the rocky landscape. Already the mountain line that had been white and dazzling sharp on the eastern horizon had vanished.

'Which gets here first?' Rodney muttered. Chandra peered round the rock and up the slope. 'They're moving . . . cautiously, but moving. They'll be here in six or seven minutes.'

The mist crept on with ghostly deliberation. Above, a rock clattered. 'Five minutes,' Chandra muttered. The mist surged forward, and he said, 'Ready! . . . Oh God, it's gone back.'

Rodney said, 'We can't wait. I'd rather die trying. At the word Go. One . . . two . . .'

The mist again lunged forward across the mountain. This time it did not fall back, but came on, and folded and hid them in its cloak. Shots cracked close as Rodney called 'Go!' and hurled himself down the slope. Then the mist hid everything, far and near. He could not see Chandra. Three minutes later, still running, his foot shot off a rock and he hurtled out in the grey murk, landing on his shoulder, his arm protecting his head from the full force of the blow. The mist swam, took on many colours, and went black.

The forest was dense here at a mere four thousand feet, and the sun struck hot on their faces. Rodney's bruises and cuts had partly healed, and his head still sometimes ached at night, but he was better; and he had had five days to think over the affair of the Rasua *yeti*. To Chandra, striding beside him, he said, 'I've come to the conclusion those surveyors must have been Chinese.'

'The old Subadar in Dukseni Bazaar hinted as much, when we told him. But I suppose they might have been bandits.'

'Up the Rasua? Who would they steal from? What would they be doing with theodolites and plane tables? No, it only makes sense if they were Nepalese on a secret mission, or Chinese . . . and I think the subadar would have known about any Nepalese up there. They'd have

77

had to come up through Dukseni Bazaar, for one thing. What we ran into was a Chinese party, probably military, surveying for defences, or perhaps for an attack route.'

'And the *yeti?*'

Rodney laughed sourly. 'My prize *yeti!* The paper that would have made us Fellows of the Royal Society! This part of my Himalayan experience will feature as the scherzo of the Concerto, a medieval practical joke – full of jolly violence and head cracking.'

'Bloody dangerous, really, Geminus. If that mist hadn't come up we'd have been added to the *yetis'* list of victims, and the subadar would have nodded his head, and said, I told them so, and knocked off another bottle of *raksi* in memory of us.'

Rodney laughed wholeheartedly then, for the first time since the incident. 'It was funny, though,' he said. 'We ought to have realized that no *yeti* would go to sleep within half a mile of those surveyors. I'd already seen them, up at the end. And when he ran, at first, when he was in a panic because he didn't know whether we had weapons or not, he was really running just like a terrified man, not at all like an ape.'

Chandra said, 'When we got close, before he woke up, I saw a circle round each leg, above the ankle. I couldn't think what it was, then, but it was where they'd sewn extra large feet on to the legs of the skin, to make his tracks gigantic . . . and there was probably another circle round his neck, where they'd sewn on the head . . .'

'He was there to frighten any villagers who might stray up, but he'd got bored, no one coming, day after day, so he dozed off . . .'

'So much for our Abominable Snowman!'

'Hey, don't think I don't believe in *yetis*. I do . . . Are you feeling all right now?' He looked anxiously at Rodney, as though he might have offended him.

Rodney said, 'Yes. I didn't have a nightmare last night. I've stopped trembling . . . look.' He held out his hand, and it was steady. 'I've been an idiot these last few days. I apologize.'

'Don't be a fool!' Chandra cried. 'While it was actually going on, you were incredible . . . the classic Englishman of legend, cool as a cucumber, decisive, brave. I was scared

78

to death, ready to shit my pants. There has to be a reaction, either way. When it was all over you realized how near you'd been to death, and I realized I had escaped scot free.'

Rodney nodded, without speaking. Now he and Chandra had shared more than the pleasures and toils of a Himalayan trek. They had faced death side by side, and neither had failed. They were truly Gemini, and the twin rings on their fingers were the sign of it. He knew that he had never forged so close a tie with anyone before, either man or woman; and never would; nor would this bond ever be broken, while they both lived.

Chandra said, 'We'll get to Nawakot tomorrow. I hope to God the plane arrives on time.'

'I'm sure it will. Crowley has a very good reputation. We'll have to make a report to the Tehsildar there, about what happened, before we fly out.'

He strode on for a time without speaking. Of course they'd have to make a report. But something else, a minor oddity, was nagging at his mind. It was not the sort of thing that would figure in their report, but . . .

He turned to Chandra. 'Most of the time, when we were trying to escape, we were fairly well separated, weren't we? At least, when we were in the open?'

Chandra said, 'Yes. We were huddled pretty close when we were in cover, in the rocks.'

'Yes . . . Thinking back over it all – and believe me, it's been on my mind pretty intensively – an impression remains with me that whoever was shooting at us was only shooting at one of us at a time.'

Chandra took a few minutes to think that one over, then said, 'Perhaps. But remember there was only one man shooting at us at a time – one man at the far end of the *marg*, then the man at the lip of the slope first, then the man up the ridge behind us. The shooter would always pick one of us at a time and concentrate on him, until he got into cover. Next time we appeared he'd take whoever presented the best target and stick with that one.'

'That's the only explanation,' Rodney said, feeling relieved. It had only been a small niggle, but he was glad to be rid of it. 'Come on,' he said. 'There'll be lukewarm beer in Nawakot, and a thrilling glass of *nimbu pani* for you.'

79

After seeing their kit safely stacked beside the Nawakot airstrip, Rodney and Chandra went back up into the village and asked the way to the Tehsildar's office. The Tehsildar was small, middle-aged, and sharp-eyed, faultlessly dressed in white. As they entered his office he placed a Nepalese cap on his bald head. He twiddled his thumbs, his face expressionless, as Chandra told him in rapid Hindi what they had seen and what had happened on their way to the Rasua Bhanjyang.

When he had finished, the Tehsildar said in the same language, but accented, 'Thank you, Shri Gupta. It is good of you to bring me this information.' He rose behind his desk, clearly ending the interview. Overhead the drone of a light aircraft engine sounded closer and louder.

Rodney and Chandra rose. Rodney said, 'What are you going to do about it, Tehsildar Sahib?'

The Tehsildar said, 'I will report the matter to the proper authorities in Kathmandu, in writing.'

'But . . .'

'That's our plane,' Chandra said, 'He won't wait more than ten minutes for us. Crowley warned us, remember.'

Rodney said, 'But can't you send people up to capture them, sahib? They can't be allowed to shoot at peaceful travellers . . .'

The Tehsildar said, 'That is your aeroplane, I think, sir.'

'But . . .'

The Tehsildar's composure broke. The corners of his mouth turned down and his eyes glowed with sudden anger. 'Nepal is small,' he snapped. 'Once our neighbour to the north was small, too – Tibet-desh. We respected each other, we kept ourselves to ourselves. Now our neighbour to the north is no small Tibet-desh, but large China. Perhaps if we annoy this new neighbour, our large neighbour to the south will protect us. Perhaps she will protect us as she protected Sikkim a few years ago, by swallowing us. Perhaps she will try to protect us – and be unable to. Perhaps she will not try – as she did nothing to protect Tibet-desh in 1950. We have to protect ourselves, in what ways small countries can. I have my orders, which are *not* in writing.'

'Come on, Rodney,' Chandra said, 'we'll have to run.'

CHAPTER SIX

Once off the ground the pilot, a young Nepalese who had served in the Indian Air Force, switched the little cabin radio to a news programme. 'Can you understand Hindi?' he asked Rodney as he banked the little plane over the houses of Nawakot and headed for Kathmandu.

Rodney nodded, and the pilot said, 'This is from Lhasa . . . mostly propaganda, but some of it's true. The Chinese tell us much that our own government has kept secret . . . things that are not on All India Radio, either. After this programme there's one in Nepali. In the evenings they even have programmes in Magarkura and Gurung-kura, the tribal languages of the people high up the valleys. They're blanketing the country.'

Rodney listened as he watched the giants of the Nepal Himalaya climb out of the haze to stand like a white-armoured host along the northern horizon. The plane droned steadily east and south, the doomsday voice blaring out of the radio . . . the scoundrelly Nepalese government would be held responsible for the indignities heaped upon respectable Chinese engineers and diplomats by its fascist servants. The villainous Nepalese government, lackeys of running dogs, should not think that it will find shelter behind the skirts of India; the valiant Chinese people showed India to be no more than a paper tiger in 1962 and were able and willing to do it again. In spite of its government's suppression of truth, the people of Nepal would learn what was being hidden from them – that the people of China had offered to build a hospital in every village of the country, at no cost to the good Nepalese . . .

'Except our independence,' the pilot said.

The radio voice became more indignant. . . . As if its behaviour in Nepal, and its continued suppression of the Naga people's legitimate aspirations in Arunachal Pradesh was not enough, the Indian lackey government was now murdering defenceless Mishmis of the same state in cold blood, sending in troops to kill and rape and burn with no more excuse than that the Mishmi people had sent a deputation to Delhi to ask for more self government. And in Madras, the people were starving, because . . .

The pilot said, 'This programme reaches most of Bengal, Assam, Bihar, and Bangladesh, too.'

Rodney yawned. He ought to be more interested, but he wasn't. His brain moved in slow gear, mulling, digesting, like a cow chewing the cud, as the peaks slid along to the left.

'Less than twenty minutes more,' the pilot said.

Were these Chinese threats no more than that, to gain bargaining positions, or were they the background of an invasion? One fact was sure; nothing could save Nepal, if China did indeed have intentions against her, except firm, powerful, and immediate action by India. The same had been true of Tibet, in 1950; but India had done nothing, preferring the dubious friendship of China to the obvious danger of inviting so large, aggressive, and revolutionary a country to her northern border.

There was a difference between the two cases . . . that wall of white, those endless buttresses of ice and snow, banners flying, that was the subject of his musical thoughts, and the heart of the mystery that Ayesha had given him to solve . . . the Himalayan Range, Himachal, the Abode of Snow – and of the Gods. Tibet was to the north of it, and the range was therefore a barrier between India and whoever held Tibet, while Nepal was to the south of it. If China took Nepal, she would have stepped, for the first time, out of the confines of Central Asia and the gigantic mountain ranges that made its boundaries, and descended into the basin of the Indian Ocean. The Indian Ocean washed the shores of Malaysia, Burma, India, Pakistan, all the countries of East Africa . . . and of the kingdoms and sheikdoms that produced eighty-five per cent of the world's oil.

The pilot said, 'Ten minutes. There's Kathmandu.' Rodney tightened his seat belt and turned to Chandra. 'You mentioned the Mishmis when we were talking about the Himalayas that night in Dukseni Bazaar. Who are they?'

'A tribe living on our side of the Himalayas in the extreme east of Arunchal Pradesh, beyond where the Dihang comes out of the gorges.'

'Do you thing it's true, what the Chinese radio was saying about them?'

'Probably. It'll be exaggerated, of course, but there'll be some truth in it – more than our Delhi bureaucrats will be willing to admit in public. I knew, when I passed through Delhi on my way here, that a Mishmi delegation had come to see the Prime Minister. I wanted to speak to them myself, but had promised to get on with this Nepal thing instead. Why don't you go there? All those frontier hill people are very interesting – primitive in some ways, quite the opposite in others. They've had to advance a thousand years in twenty.'

'I'll think about it,' Rodney said, 'I like Nepal, but there's so much else to see, to listen to. . . . Did you learn anything useful while we were out?'

'A great deal,' Chandra said enthusiastically. 'Those nights in the village were invaluable, to find out what is really happening, how the people really live.'

Good. I got a lot of music down, too. . . . You know, Chandra, I feel that the Chinese are playing some instrument, or better still, conducting an orchestra. The violins play a theme up in Ladakh – an Indian patrol gets shot up, an Indian plane is damaged by anti-aircraft fire, there are whining complaints, shrill threats. Then the violins become quiet, the theme is taken up, with variations, by the woodwind section, in Nepal. While we are attending to that, the brass starts a counterpoint, *piano*, seven hundred miles farther east again, in Arunachal Pradesh. My feeling is that it is not random noises we're listening to, but a composition.'

'And our generals and politicians have to guess what is going to be the theme of the last movement? A nice idea.'

'I'm sure they're listening,' Rodney said, 'but can they interpret? They're not musicians.'

Then they were down, bumping along the taxi track, unstowing their gear, crowding into the taxi which would take them to their hotel.

Soon after he reached his room, Rodney sat down to write a report destined for 'Mr. P. S. Grewal', but before he had written a word he put down his pen, staring at the wall, thinking – I can tell Ayesha what happened, what I saw –

83

but what does it mean? He had written in his last report that the Chinese were definitely planning some action against Nepal. Now he was not so sure. He did not want to make a fool of himself, still less to lead Ayesha and the Government of India in a wrong direction through hasty conclusions. After sitting for five minutes in the same brooding position he got up and went out. There might be something for him at Harmukh Singh's. If there was, he'd better study it before writing anything more.

At the camera shop, Harmukh Singh handed him an envelope, saying, 'The film you wanted specially processed in Calcutta, sir.' Rodney took it, returned to his hotel, locked the door of his room, and sat down to open the envelope.

Ayesha acknowledged his first report, sent off before going on trek. She was sorry he had been beaten and robbed, and must in future take more care of himself. She was also grateful for his advice on how and where to apportion the resources available to her department, but he would realize that such matters could not be decided on the impressions of one person alone, and that person perhaps unduly influenced by his immediate surroundings . . . (Quite right, Rodney admitted, acknowledging the edge of sarcasm; I must be more cautious in reaching my conclusions) . . . As to facts, rather than speculation and information of dubious reliability, Ayesha's letter continued, the Russians had been extremely co-operative over satellite photographs . . . (Naturally, Rodney thought: they want to know what the Chinese are up to just as much as the Indians do) . . . and the results were interesting, but also somewhat baffling.

The photos taken and flown to Delhi were of excellent quality, taken through the diamond-clear atmosphere of High Asia, where there was no pollution at all, and under microscopic examination could show objects no larger than a football. The photos revealed the presence of some Chinese troops along the Nepal-Tibet border, and there was some road building going on – but it was impossible that there were more than a thousand Chinese troops in all along that border. So where were the ten to fifteen thousand reported by Jansingh Gharti and the Chinese Lieutenant? Were they in barracks in Lhasa, where they

would not show on satellite photographs? Were they somewhere else along the southern frontiers of Tibet – farther
west, perhaps, which meant closer to Kashmir . . . or farther
east, which meant closer to Sikkim . . . or still farther east,
poised above Mishmiland? This problem, rather than that
suggested to her by Rodney in his last report, was occupy-
ing the attention of others in her department. For his part,
Rodney was free to do what he thought best, within the
terms of his original instructions; but she suggested that
fruitful results would be achieved if he continued his re-
searches in Nepal, this time endeavouring not to let the
trees blind him to the shape of the wood.

Jansingh Gharti had been investigated, as Rodney had
asked. It had been learned that he was born in Nepal in
1922, left to seek work in India in 1943, and in that year
joined the very respectable Calcutta firm of Kapur and
Katari as a messenger. He was now one of the firm's top
buyers and was highly regarded by its owners. It was true
that he had good connections with Chinese merchants and
officials in Tibet; but he also had excellent contacts in
Burma, Malaysia, Singapore, Indonesia, Sri Lanka,
Pakistan and Bangladesh.

The letter ended with a conventional expression of
sincerity.

Rodney read it again, then carefully burned it and the
envelope. Ayesha was very businesslike, in business. Come
to that, she was rather businesslike in sex, too . . . an unhappy woman, he suspected. But what did he know of
women?

She wanted him to stay in Nepal. The whereabouts of
the Chinese troops and Chinese intentions in general were
being investigated by 'others' in her department, by which
she meant her regular agents.

He took his pen and began his report on what he had
seen and heard since he went on trek. He made it brief
and factual, leaving Ayesha to draw her own conclusions;
and ended, 'I am considering what is wisest to do next.'
Sealing the letter in an envelope he took it at once down
to Harmukh Singh's, then headed for the bar of the hotel.

Now, what *was* the wisest thing to do? Every indication
pointed to Nepal. But his inner mind added, too much so.
He felt that he was being led by the nose and, like a re-

bellious horse, did not want to go. He raised his head and asked the barman a question.

'Mishmis, sir?' Machhindra said, pouring him a cold beer, 'I know Mishmis bloody well. I was butler on tea garden for English gentleman, garden manager, for two years. It was at Dambuk, where the Sesseri River comes out of the mountains where the Mishmis live.'

'What are they like – the Mishmis?'

'Very bloody wild men, sir. No clothes, most of them, poisoned arrows and spears, drinking *zo* – like beer, sir – out of bamboo mugs, painting faces. A few came down to work on the garden, but they never stayed long.'

'And the country?'

'In a moment, sir.'

Machhindra moved off to the far end of the bar, served another customer, and returned. 'Another beer, sir? . . . Big rivers come down on to the plain there, sir. That's flat, good rich land. But where the rivers come from—' He shook his head – 'nearly as big as up there—' he nodded north-eastward toward the invisible Everest '—thick jungle at first, for forty, fifty miles . . . then it gets very big, steep mountains, deep gorges, no roads, just footpaths. I went up once with the sahib. They were beginning to change, get civilized, like, but this Tondrup, he's making them go back to their old ways, the old clothes or no-clothes, ha ha, the old music and dancing. So they don't start to think they're Indians instead of Mishmis. You ought to go up, sir.' He shook his head in remembered wonder '. . . . and I think you'll get permission nowadays. I heard on All India Radio two weeks ago that the fighting with the Nagas was finished, so I suppose travel would not be restricted any more. They want tourist money, that's the bloody truth, sir.'

'Then there's been no trouble in Arunachal Pradesh itself?'

The barman shrugged. 'The Chinese say yes. The Indians say no . . . so how can they refuse permission?' He began to move off along the bar but Rodney said, 'One more thing, Machhindra. What sort of tribe or caste are the Ghartis?'

Machhindra looked up and down the bar and his wrinkled face closed in a comical expression of caution.

86

His voice when he spoke was low. 'Don't want to hurt anyone's fucking feelings, sir, but . . . be careful with a Gharti! When the Maharajah freed the slaves a lot of them – the slaves – took the name and caste of Gharti. They're called Shivbhagti Ghartis, but they're still casteless slaves to most of us. *I* wouldn't let my daughter marry one of them for a *lakh* of rupees.'

He bustled off in response to a call, and Rodney drank slowly from his tall glass. So the Ghartis, through the misfortune that some of them were descended from freed slaves, were scorned by the rest of the people. An unpleasant situation for them, and one liable to lead to a generalized bitterness. Jansingh didn't seem quite typical; but then, he might be a real Gharti, not a Shivbhagti.

His glass was empty and he stared into the bottom as though seeking a solution to the riddle there. Where were the Chinese troops? He felt uneasy, as though in the presence of a confidence trick. Nepal might be the focal point . . . but then again it might not. He could not tell what was going on in Arunachal Pradesh, or what might happen next, unless he went there and saw for himself. As the Government of India had apparently opened the area to travellers, there was no reason why he shouldn't go. And he knew he'd always be uneasy in his own mind until he did.

He returned to his room and began to pack. Then he rang the hotel manager, the travel agency, and finally Chandra Gupta. 'I'm going to Arunachal Pradesh.'

'Good! You'll hear some marvellous music. Don't lose your head. Some of those tribes were headhunters till quite recently. Some say they still are.'

'Thanks for the warning. I'm off tomorrow early.'

'Goodbye, then, till we meet again.'

CHAPTER SEVEN

Five coolies fought to gain possession of his suitcase as he stepped out on the platform at Tinsukia. Apparently there used to be train service on to Saikhoa Ghat, on the near bank of the Luhit River, but two weeks ago it had been suspended, without reason given. The weather was pleasant, the time near one o'clock in the afternoon, the sky a clear pale blue dotted with small clouds. The coolie who had been victorious in the battle stood waiting expectantly, the suitcase on his head.

'Hotel, sahib?' he enquired.

Rodney shook his head. 'Taxi.'

'This way, this way!'

He followed the coolie out of the building and to the side of a Hindustan taxi. This one looked in good condition: the driver was young, and perhaps a Gorkha – he had the Mongolian features, round head and ready grin.

'Where to, sir?' he asked.

Rodney said, 'Dambuk.'

The driver's brow furrowed. 'Dambuk? Up there?' – he pointed to the east.

Rodney nodded. 'Dambuk.'

The driver said, 'You having permit, sir?'

'No. I was told that travel was now free in all this area.'

'It was, for a little time, sir, but restrictions put back on, two days ago. Now you must see Special Officer, Dibrugarh, to get permission to go beyond the Luhit River.'

'Where's Dibrugarh?'

The taxi driver pointed west. The wrong direction, Rodney thought; and very like a waste of time to go there. Clearly something had happened or was happening in these north-eastern territories and, knowing the Indian bureaucracy's normal secretiveness and aversion from publicity, it was very unlikely that he would be given a permit.

'How far to the Luhit River?' he asked.

'Fifty kilometres. Hour and a half, is not good road.'

'Well, take me that far.'

The driver hesitated, and Rodney said, 'I'll get another taxi.'

Then the driver said, 'All right, sir, I take you. Perhaps rules changed again, permits not needed. Rules being changed every week here, since beginning of Naga troubles, years ago. . . . Perhaps you pay me something in advance? My rate one rupee fifty per kilometre, including return trip.'

Rodney handed over a hundred-rupee note. The driver tucked it away, quickly stowed the suitcase and started his engine. Rodney paid the baggage coolie and sat back.

The land passed – intense cultivation, small dense forest patches, rolling acres of tea bushes, broad water. The people walked upright, and seemed better fed than in other parts of India. More tea, and now he saw the derrick of an oil well. He dozed off as the car bumped eastward.

The car stopped and he awoke. They were at the bank of a great river, a ferry boat waiting at the foot of the ramp, the stream swirling deep green, two or three miles wide. Four cars were already on the little ferry steamer, with a score of foot passengers. Another car drove down as he watched, to stop at the ferry bridge where two policemen, both with rifles slung over their shoulders, leaned in, examined papers, then waved the car on.

'Luhit River – and permit still needed,' the taxi driver said gloomily. 'This is Saikhoa Ghat. Sadiya, where another Special Officer lives, far side. He could give permit.'

'Try it.'

They drove down and stopped as a policeman raised his hand. Without waiting for a demand the driver produced his pass, saying in Hindustani, 'Tilokbir Rana, licensed taxi driver, Tinsukia.' He handed over the folder.

The other policeman said brusquely to Rodney, 'Pass, permit!'

'What permit?' Rodney asked. He held out his hands, palms up and empty to indicate that he had no permit.

The policeman said, 'You must have a permit to go farther.'

'Who said so? I haven't seen any notice about that.'

The driver broke in. 'The sahib started travelling when there was no need for a permit. He was told that . . .'

'Can't help that. He has to have a permit now.'

The driver looked at Rodney, raising his shoulders in a gesture of helplessness. Rodney looked across the river at the distant houses of Sadiya. He said, 'I have to see the Special Officer in Sadiya. It's on secret government business.'

For a moment he thought he had one of the policemen worried, but the other cut in stolidly – 'Can't help that. Can't go over the river without a permit. Get back now, driver, you are blocking other cars.'

The driver backed and turned. 'Is there any other way to get to Dambuk?' Rodney asked.

'There is another small ferry, upstream, but there will be police there, too.'

'Back to Tinsukia,' Rodney said, 'But first stop by that eating house.'

'Tanduri chicken very good here, sir,' the driver said cheerfully. 'Also beer.'

The Ritz hotel in Tinsukia was a little better than the Kosi Palace in Kathmandu, where he had spoken with the Chinese Lieutenant – but not much; yet it was full, with many uniformed officers among its guests. It was almost dark by the time Rodney had installed himself, and had a wash and brush up to rid himself of the dust of his ride to Saikhoa Ghat and back.

He went out to look round Tinsukia. The streets bustled with life under glaring lights in the centre of the town, and round the station. The bazaar was crowded with men and women, again many of them in military or air force uniform. Rodney wandered slowly and aimlessly through the crowds, thinking. He wanted to get to Dambuk and beyond, into Mishmi territory; but he did not want to apply for a permit. He might have to, if there was no other way – but then he'd have the government bureaucracy aware of where he was going; and probably doing their best to control his movements, if they allowed him any freedom at all.

Music tinkled from a dim-lit alley and he started down to investigate; but after two or three steps he paused, leaned against one wall of the alley, and spent a few minutes just resting there, watching the people pass and, with more care, those who did not pass, but hung about.

The attack on him in Kathmandu, and the attempts of the *yeti*-surveyors to kill him on the Rasua were close in his mind. What danger could threaten him in this little railway junction among the tea gardens? Yet he must learn now to be careful, all the time.

Smells of cooking *ghi* and boiling sweetmeats drifted past, reminding him that he was hungry again. The men who argued and cajoled at the stalls were Indian soldiers from all over the sub-continent. The women who swirled through the bazaar, and those who ran the stalls, were of a different cast of features from Nepalese or Kashmiris, and more beautiful than either. They stood straight, and looked directly at him with unafraid curiosity. Their skin was pale brown and their eyes clear. Some wore silver ornaments at their breasts, that chinked in rhythm with their even strides, and those in time with the music of the invisible orchestra playing inside some house or room down this alley. Others of the women had deep baskets on their backs, which were filled with supplies; and they carried the baskets as easily as though the load were ten pounds instead of the seventy or eighty which some must have been. This was indeed a different India . . . a rich peninsula of tea gardens and oil wells, watered by the great river and its tributaries, thrust out into the farthest north-east recesses of India, surrounded by jungle covered mountains, and in them the headhunters, the naked men with blowpipes and bamboo helmets and poisoned arrows . . .

Time to quell the pangs of hunger; time to sit down and seriously tackle his problem – how to get to Dambuk without official permission. With money it could probably be done – anything could be; and he had plenty of that, at least for bribery on the petty scale indicated. He set off back towards his hotel.

As he entered the Ritz the clock in the shadowy hall was indicating eight o'clock. A smell of food wafted out of the open door to the dining-room on the right, and he turned in. Eat first and think later. He looked round for an empty table. There were nine tables in the room, all occupied, though at some there was only one diner. Then he recognized one of those lone men; it was not easy to forget the bald head, red face and aggressive moustache of Air Vice-Marshal Nawal Contractor. The airman, who was in shirt-sleeved uniform, looked up from his soup at the same instant, and after a momentary stare of astonishment got up, waved his hand and indicated the empty place opposite him.

Rodney moved over and sat down, after shaking hands. 'Get on with your soup, Air Vice-Marshal,' he said. 'It won't taste nice cold.'

'It tastes godawful hot,' the airman grumbled, 'and please call me Nawal. Air Vice-Marshal's too much of a mouthful for anyone. You're Rodney, aren't you?'

Rodney nodded and studied the menu: chicken soup, kofta curry with rice, and caramel custard. A waiter in unclean khaki trousers and shirt brought him the soup.

The Air Marshal said, 'What brings you here?'

'Music chasing,' Rodney said. 'I was in Kathmandu and heard there that the hill people in these parts – Nagas, Daflas, Abors, Mishmis, etcetera – have a distinctive music of their own.'

'Quite true,' the airman said, bending over his plate.

Rodney continued, 'They also told me in Kathmandu that there were no restrictions on travel up here now, but when I hired a taxi at the station and tried to get up to Dambuk, the police wouldn't let me on the ferry at Saikhoa Ghat.'

The airman said, 'Oh, is that true? Yes, I believe they did make some change in the rules a few days ago. Because of the new troubles, was the story, I think.'

'I suppose it doesn't affect you,' Rodney said. A wild thought entered his mind . . . suppose he could persuade Contractor to employ him as a servant? Call him an 'adviser'?

The Air Marshal interrupted his thoughts. 'To tell you the truth I don't usually know what the rules are on the ground at any time, because we fly over it all, from one of our airfields to another.'

'Are you flying up in that direction now?' Rodney asked, his mind off on another tack.

Contractor said, 'Yes. To Dambuk, as a matter of fact.'

Rodney was on the point of asking what he, a senior officer, was doing in this civilian hotel when the Air Marshal answered the unspoken question: 'My plane's on Chabua airfield now – it was the biggest American airbase for flying over the Hump in World War II. It's about five miles from here. I'm on an inspection tour of Air Force Establishments in my command. Chabua were going to put me up, but they have a case of spotted fever – cerebro-spinalmeningitis – and I agreed that I'd better keep away. My plane was handled by erks wearing gasmasks! . . . How did the rest of your stay in Kashmir go? Any more fishing?'

Rodney shook his head. 'I left immediately after returning from that trek. I'll probably be going back, though.'

'When you've . . . finished, in the east here?' the Air Marshal said. There was the hint of a pause before the word 'finished', and the hint of a conspiratorial look in his eye as he glanced across at Rodney. He believes, or knows, that I have some mission beyond listening to music, Rodney thought. His further wondering, as to what sort of a mission Nawal Contractor had imagined for him, was cut short by the Air Marshal saying, 'Would you like to come up with me in my plane?'

Rodney started. 'Yes,' he said, 'of course, I'd love it.'

'You'll be on your own once you get there,' the airman said warningly, 'but I imagine you can handle that.'

'Yes,' Rodney said, doubting it very much: but sure that at this moment he had to follow the lead and take what was being offered to him. Let tomorrow look after tomorrow.

'All right, then,' the Air Marshal said. 'Let's meet in the hall here at seven a.m.'

'Fine.'

At the Dambuk airfield, no more than a long earth runway made all-weather by perforated metal strips, and fit only for D.C.3s at the biggest, a beflagged staff car was waiting for the Air Marshal, who had piloted his own plane, an eight-seater of Russian make, up from Chabua.

He said, 'Do we have room for Mr. Bateman?'

'Certainly, sir,' said the flight lieutenant who had been sent down with the driver, and, saluting Rodney with great energy, showed him into the back seat beside Contractor. It was barely five minutes' drive to the crowded huts that were the bazaar of Dambuk.

Contractor said, 'I'm going on to the other side of town. Do you want to get off here?'

'This'll do fine,' Rodney said.

'Stop here,' the Air Marshal called to the driver. As the car slowed he turned and shook Rodney's hand. 'Good luck,' he said; and then in a low voice, which could not be heard in front, 'Give my best to Ayesha.'

Then Rodney was out in the street, his suitcase in hand, and the staff car was moving on in a swirl of dust, scattering the crowd as it went. As he stood, soldiers passed, and many saluted. He wondered why they did so until he realized that the first of them had seen him get out from the Air Marshal's car; and those later had seen the earlier one saluting, and had followed suit. He decided he had better take advantage of this atmosphere of respect while it lasted. He stopped a tall soldier with a havildar's three chevrons on his sleeve, and said in Hindustani, 'Can you tell me where there is a bus or truck service?'

The soldier saluted smartly and said, 'Certainly, sahib. Down that road, two hundred metres, is the bus station. There are buses back to Sadiya, and up to Ashalin, Asonli and Damro in the hills.' He seemed about to say something else, but didn't. Rodney thanked him and walked off in the direction indicated, carrying his suitcase. It wasn't hot at this comparatively early hour, but he was sweating when he found the bus station, unmistakable by reason of the four or five roadworn Tata diesel buses parked outside the open-ended building. Another Tata inside was in the process of loading passengers. In a dusty open space to one side half a dozen trucks were in various stages of being loaded or unloaded of crates, bags, sacks, kerosene oil cans, and timber.

Ashalin, Asonli and Damro, the soldier had said. He had not heard of any of them, but they must be in the Mishmi hills, and important to merit bus service. He watched as passengers boarded the bus inside the station. Everyone who got in, man, woman, and child, was showing some sort of a paper: obviously a permit for those who did not live in this area, or a proof of local residence for those who did. By now another bus was loading, and there too the passengers were showing papers; and this one's head-board showed that it was going back westward to Sadiya,

94

away from the Mishmi hills, but still east of the Luhit River.

Most of the people boarding the bus were the same types as he had seen in Tinsukia – the cheerful men whom the Air Marshal had told him were of the Khasi race, the pretty women who had carried their tea-gathering baskets into the bazaar to bring home their purchases; but here were others, too – well-muscled men with black hair cut in a bob, carrying slung swords in bamboo sheaths, wearing trousers or shorts, and shirt, with an indefinable air as though they had put on such garments for the first time this very morning; and one or two women, these shorter than the Khasis, heavy-breasted, walking pigeon-toed two paces behind their men, carrying bags woven of many bright colours slung over one shoulder on long woven straps of the same material – Mishmis.

He looked across at the trucks, thinking the truck drivers were probably less supervised. He walked over, put his bag in the shade of a truck and spoke to the driver, who was leaning into the engine under a raised hood. 'Will you take me to Ashalin, Asonli or Damro?'

The man straightened his back. 'Which?'

'Which is the farthest into the Mishmi country?'

'Asonli.'

'That's where I want to go.'

'Why?'

'I am a musician, and I want to study Mishmi music.' Looking closely at him, Rodney thought the driver might have Mishmi blood himself.

The man said, 'Do you have a permit?'

'No.'

'Why don't you get one?'

'They might not want to give me one. And they'd be following me round.' On an instinct, strengthened by his feeling that the driver was himself a Mishmi or attached in some way to their cause, he said, 'It is true that I am a musician, but I also want to find out what's happening in the Mishmi country, so that I can tell the truth to the rest of the world.'

'They're being killed, that's what is happening,' the driver said.

'Who by? Why?'

The other shrugged, and made to return to his work. Rodney said, 'Two hundred rupees to get me to Asonli.'

The driver, again bent under the raised hood, said in a muffled voice, 'Let's see it.'

Rodney pushed two hundred rupees under the hood. An oily hand took it, and vanished. The voice said, 'Here, five o'clock tomorrow morning. No suitcase.'

'May I leave it here?'

'No. Go to Nizamullah's Rest House. You'll have to pay double rent if you don't have a permit, but he won't tell the police.'

Rodney lay among the piled sacks of grain in the back of the truck as it groaned and swayed on upward to the north. It had been inspected at the edge of Dambuk. A little later the driver had stopped and told him, speaking from outside the truck into the piled sacks, that there would be one more inspection.

Now it must be coming, for the truck was slowing again. Again he heard the sharp Hindustani commands of the soldiers, felt the weight of them as they crawled about on top of the load, felt one or two sacks being moved for inspection; but that was all. He heard the order, *'Thik hai. Age chalo, bhai.'* It's all right. Go ahead, brother. The driver slipped his vehicle into gear and again started up the steep slope.

Rodney settled himself more comfortably, pushing a sack away from his face so that he could breathe more easily. Fumes from the exhaust seeped in through the groaning floorboards, and a cold draught eddied through the many crevices and cracks. It must be about seven o'clock in the morning. He wished there had been time to talk to the driver, or someone, about Asonli. Was there anyone in particular he should ask for? The driver must make regular trips up there, and must know people. Would he introduce Rodney? Was the place full of soldiers and police? Would he find sullen conspiracies, civil war, preparations to repel invasion – what?

The tyres screeched and he felt a violent braking effect. A dislodged crate fell over and pressed extra weight on his back. The truck ground to a stop and now he heard guttural voices shouting, and he recognized the driver's voice answering, apparently in the same language, which he could not understand. Then a cry, another, and dull thumping sounds. Feet trod on the sacks above him. The sacks were dragged aside. These people, whoever they were, were not carrying out a perfunctory search; they knew what they were looking for – him. The damned driver must have told them. But perhaps it had been someone else, for surely those cries just now had come from the driver, being beaten up.

In a few minutes the last sack was dragged off him and he heard an exclamation of triumph – 'Ah!' A hand was laid on the nape of his neck and he was dragged upright. He was about to say something when the man who had uncovered him tapped him twice on the mouth with the palm of his hand, and pushed him toward the back of the truck. He jumped down on to the road. Twenty Mishmis, all wearing only bamboo helmets and loin cloths, barefooted, all carrying bamboo-sheathed *dahs* and two modern rifles as well, surrounded the bus. The driver sat against a tree, holding his hand to the side of his face. All around was tall silent jungle, steep set among great mountains, and glowing with wild white orchids.

The Mishmi leader barked something at the driver, who got up painfully, came over and began to indicate certain sacks and crates. Those that he pointed out were dragged aside by the Mishmis, and collected on the grass verge of the road. When a dozen loads had been so collected, the leader rapped out another string of orders. The Mishmis seized the loads, humped them on to their backs and prepared to move off into the jungle. The leader pushed Rodney in the small of the back and snapped something. He did not need to know Mishimi to understand that he was being told – follow! As the trees closed in he glanced back, to have a last look at the scattered remains of the cargo, the abandoned truck, and the driver, now again seated against a tree, a hand still to his head.

In the next five hours Rodney thanked God a dozen times that the Mishmi raiders had saddled themselves with such heavy loads from the truck, for if they had been travelling light he would never have been able to keep up with them. As it was, they moved fast enought to bring the sweat out on him within five minutes, and keep his shirt wet and his face dripping all the time, except once when the party stopped in a heavily wooded ravine while three of the men, leaving their loads behind, went off on a scouting mission. The Mishmi leader spoke a few words to him at that time, probably in explanation of the halt, but he did not understand them. An explanation was hardly necessary, anyway. From the caution everyone was now showing it was obvious that the party was about to cross a route used by Indian Army patrols, or perhaps circumvent some standing jungle outpost set up in order to hamper the movement of just such raiding parties as this.

After forty-five minutes they moved on at the same relentless speed, up the long slopes under the canopies of the great trees, fast down the other side through green scrub jungle, once by a hamlet of four wooden huts where women working at pounding meal hardly looked up as they passed, three times fording fast-running streams where the icy stroke of the water told that these streams had not been born from the flanks of ordinary hills, but from the springs and snows of Himachal.

Without warning the distinctive clatter of a helicopter sprang up in the south, fast growing louder. The Mishmis flung themselves flat under the nearest tree. Rodney looked up, wondering where the chopper was, trying to scan the sky between the boughs far above. A heavy blow in the middle of his back hurled him to the ground. This Mishmi leader snarled a word at him and pressed him down, then grabbed his head and forced his face into the earth. The helicopter's roar grew deafening. It was a big one, he thought; probably troop-carrying . . . at least fifteen men, well-armed. They'd easily be able to deal with this band, who only had the two rifles between them. He hoped that the Indians would not see them. He had not had time or lesiure to assess his own position with the Mishmis, but he did not feel the pressure of danger or hostility. He was being taken to some Mishmi hide-out in the mountains. If he was to learn anything about what was going on in the farthest corner of India, now would be his opportunity. It struck him that precisely that might be the purpose of the raid, and of his kidnapping.

The helicopter blatted away. They waited five more

minutes, then at a word from the leader rose again, and proceeded on their way.

Half an hour later, Rodney, walking near the front of the column, saw a person ahead . . . it was a bare-breasted woman. Then, behind her he saw more women, and a few men lolling by trees. When he was no more than twenty paces off, he recognized that he was approaching a rough circle of a dozen or more huts. The huts were made of boughs and leaves. They had no hard edges in their shapes, but flowed round the boles of the trees or against the face of the rock outcrops among which they were set, by a small steep-falling stream.

The leader of the band called a few words and the party stopped. A young man in Mishmi costume – that is, naked except for the loin cloth and slung *dah,* stepped out of one of the huts. He came forward, right hand raised: he and the leader of the band embraced. The leader stepped aside and indicated Rodney. The newcomer said, in English, 'We received the message that you were English, and wanted to know about my people. But our means of communication are too primitive – yet – to send your name.'

'Rodney Bateman,' Rodney said.

The other held out his hand. 'I am Tondrup,' He waited, looking expectant, and Rodney realized that he should have heard the name.

He said apologetically, 'I am a musician, Mr. Tondrup . . .'

'Just Tondrup.'

'. . . I haven't been back in India long, nor read the papers much. I only heard that the Mishmis were trying to achieve a greater independence, and thought I ought to find out more. You can't believe everything you read in the papers, although I do write articles for English newspapers sometimes.'

'It's what *doesn't* appear in the papers that is the worst,' Tondrup said grimly. 'You have heard the truth, or part of it. I am the leader of the Abor and Mishmi Independence Party. We also work with the Naga leaders. Their country is across the valley of the Dihang, to the south, round Kohima. They have been fighting the Indians for years.'

He spoke excellent English, and seemed to be about thirty. He was wearing a short cotton front flap over his

99

loin cloth, and a wrist watch. His hair was cut short and parted in the middle, not worn in the heavy bob that was one of the Mishmi trademarks. He was taller and paler than the other men. He said now, 'We'll put you into a hut, and when you've had a rest I will tell you about our movement, and what you can do to help us. What paper do you write for?'

'The *Daily Telegraph Magazine*,' Rodney said. It was true, as the magazine had once published a piece of his about the influence of Indian music on hard rock: but he didn't think it advisable to go into such detail with the intense looking young Mishmi chief.

Tondrup turned and walked away, beckoning Rodney to follow.

Ten minutes later Rodney found himself installed in one of the huts, at that moment unoccupied, though homespun blankets, and pots and pans on bamboo shelves, showed that other people did live in it. A Mishmi woman brought him a plate of cooked rice, with vegetables already mixed in it, and one of the distinctive cut bamboo sections full of home-brewed beer. He sat in the doorway of the hut, eating, drinking, wondering.

Going backward in time, the Indian helicopter had been looking for the raiding party, or perhaps for this jungle hide-out. When it flew over, they couldn't have been more than a mile and a half away from here. So the Indians had some idea where Tondrup's 'capital' was, and in the near future would probably stage an operation against it; for in dealing with guerilla bands the most important step seemed to be to disrupt the guerillas' lives and means of communication, forcing continuous moves so that no one knew from day to day where the headquarters was, where supplies and ammunition were to be picked up.

Supplies . . . the raiders had taken a lot of supplies out of the truck, for an obvious reason – they needed the stuff. They knew that the truck was coming, what sort of a load it carried, and that he was in it. How? Probably because the driver had told them. How? Jungle telegraph. The jungle began right outside Dambuk and they'd had time. . . . That was why the Mishmis had beaten up the driver a little – to clear him of complicity when the Indian authorities came to investigate the hold-up. And the news of himself,

100

and what he wanted to learn about had been passed the same way; and Tondrup had decided to let him come. So here he was, looking at a headquarters that would probably vanish within twenty-four hours; otherwise Tondrup would not have let him see it, but met him somewhere in the jungle, talked to him and sent him back. . . .

He found himself yawning. He went back deep into the hut, borrowed a blanket to roll under his head for a pillow, curled up, and went to sleep.

When he awoke it was four o'clock, with a hint of chill under the trees. Two Mishmi men were asleep in the hut near him, and he thought he recognized them as having been in the raiding party. He got up, and went out to the stream to wash his face and have a drink.

As he came back Tondrup appeared and walked beside him. 'We will not be here much longer.'

'I guessed that,' Rodney said.

The other nodded. 'The Indians have been closing in for a long time, but our people have given them so many wrong leads, and we and our friends have been able to set up so many diversions, that it has taken them six months to get so close that we must move.'

'When you say your friends, whom do you mean?'

Tondrup pointed. They had come to the north end of the encampment, the farthest from the stream, and there Rodney saw two men in the shapeless clothes and Mao Tse Tung caps of Communist China. One was explaining the working of a light rocket launcher to a circle of five Mishmi men: the other was taking apart what looked like a small portable radio set, for the benefit of five absorbed Mishmi women, all bare-breasted.

'Chinese?' he asked.

Tondrup nodded. 'China has built a road southward from Shumdo on their Gya Lam, the Tibet-China road, to our frontier north of here. As far as there, that road will already take trucks . . . and tanks. From the frontier south, they and we have made a jeepable track for twenty miles, but we don't use it now. It is too easy a target for the Indian Air Force. It is for the future.'

'Do you want to set up an independent communist state in the mountains here?' Rodney asked.

'Independent, yes!' Tondrup said vehemently. 'We have our culture – we have nothing against the Indians, but they are interfering with us. We need more autonomy, and if they won't give it to us we must have independence – we and the Abors and the Daflas and all the other peoples along the Himalayas.'

'Do you think you can survive economically, without India?'

'With some help from China, yes. We don't need much. I do not think we will be communist for long, though.' He shrugged.

'That is the price the Chinese are asking for their help?'

Tondrup did not answer. He said, 'We cannot look too far to the future. We have to do what we have to do. The Chinese are helping us directly and, what is more important for us, their presence and their interest is preventing the Indians from using all the force they could, and would perhaps like to. They must be careful, because they understand that if they act more strongly against us, China will help us more strongly, and more openly. . . . We will be eating soon. Then we go to bed. No lights, no singing, after dusk. But tomorrow afternoon we will have a little celebration for all the food we captured today, and to show you how a free people should be able to live in their own land.'

CHAPTER EIGHT

The encampment came to life shortly before first light and
Rodney left the hut to stand outside, savouring the freshness of dawn in the high jungle. Birds began to call harshly
on the feathery tops of the trees. Men slipped by in the
monochrome light, some carrying firearms, all the universal
dah. Women went to the stream and came back with full
water pots on their heads. The light grew, pale green now
in the east, turning yellow, until he looked out over a
heaving, falling ocean of jungle, the ground beneath the
trees swelling in great curves and now, for the first time,
he saw between two northern hills, the icy glitter of morning snow. Up there was the northern boundary, and beyond,
Tibet, and the road that linked China with Tibet; and
through Tibet, with Nepal; and past Tibet, with Kashmir.

As full daylight spread rapidly across the sky cooking
fires were lit, and soon the smell of food permeated the
open spaces, but all the wood was dry, and no telltale
smoke drifted out through the open lattice work of the huts'
walls. The two Chinese he had seen yesterday were eating a
little apart at the edge of the encampment, and Rodney,
seeing Tondrup, went up to him and asked, 'May I talk to
the Chinese? Do they speak Hindustani?'

'No. But the tall one speaks English. They both speak
Mishmi very well. Go ahead.'

Rodney walked over, thinking that the Chinese must
have been maturing their plans for this area – whatever
they were – for a considerable time. The Mishmi tongue
could not be mastered overnight.

He sat down beside the Chinese and said, 'Tondrup has
said I may speak to you.'

They went on eating, using their chopsticks delicately on
the nameless titbits in their bowls. The tall one said, 'You
are the English imperialist?'

'That was my father, Colonel Bateman,' he said, smiling,
but their faces remained stony. He realized he had been
foolish to expect Chinese revolutionary cadres to

103

appreciate his humour. 'I am a musician,' he said, 'a composer.'

'Ah. Why have you come here? To spy on the Mishmi people in their struggle for freedom against the Indian aggressors?'

Rodney felt an almost irresistible urge to add – 'who are the running dogs of British and American capitalist imperialism' – but managed to restrain himself. He said, 'I was brought here, by force, though I did want to come, as a matter of fact. I want to understand Mishmi music, and you can't understand a people's music unless you know something about their culture – how they live, what they want out of life.'

'They are fighting for their freedom against the Indian aggressors,' the tall Chinese repeated, 'and the People's Republic of China is helping them.'

'What are you doing for them, if you don't mind telling me?'

'We are servants of the People's Republic and we are proud of what we are doing for the Mishmi and Abor people. All the world should know that the Mishmi and Abor peoples are being befriended by the People's Republic of China in their struggle for freedom against the Indian aggressors. . . . I am a weapons expert. We have brought with us anti-tank rockets, modern light machine guns, anti-personnel grenades, and anti-tank mines. Soon our leaders will send ground-to-air missiles that can be carried by one man, that are radar controlled and can destroy the largest enemy bomber or helicopter . . . from the jungle. We are teaching selected Mishmis how to care for and use these weapons. When the time is ripe we will send in many, many weapons, and the Mishmis will defeat the Indians.'

'What about leaders, generals?'

The tall Chinese looked at him sharply. 'Tondrup is the leader. Some others have gone to China to study Chairman Kan's doctrines there, and when they return they will help Tondrup.'

I bet, Rodney thought; help him with a stab in the back, while they take over the movement. 'And the other, your friend?' he asked.

'He is a communications expert. He is teaching the

people – particularly the women – how to use radios and repair them.'

Rodney thought the time was ripe to try a little gamble. He said, 'The papers in India have been full of stories that China has sent a large army to the area north of here. Is that true?'

The tall man said, 'I know nothing of the movements of our armies, and if I did I would not tell you.'

Rodney persisted. 'But you must know whether your country intends to send in troops to help the Mishmi in their struggle.'

The tall man said, 'We will do what is necessary as we have shown in Korea and Tibet. If an army is necessary, it will be ready, and it will come.'

He stood up abruptly and carried his bowl away, followed by his companion, who had not said a word the whole time.

The encampment looked like something William Blake might have painted if he had lived in the Mishmi hills. A dozen men, their faces painted with whorls and diagonal designs, danced in a circle in the centre, their heavy helmets of bamboo decorated with parrots' feathers nodding and shaking as they plunged forward, jerked their heads back, down again. In their right hands they shook long spears in time with the fierce rhythm of the dance. There was no music but a solitary drum, being beaten with relentless energy by another Mishmi. The dancers sang as they gyrated, an almost tuneless chant that defied Rodney's attempts to memorize it. It was late afternoon, the sun near setting, the shadows long across the clearing.

Tondrup, squatting beside him, said, 'This is a very old dance.'

'Everyone's completely absorbed in it,' Rodney said. 'I've been watching their faces.'

'They are simple people. No one here, except me, has ever been out of our hills except to Dambuk, and then only two or three of them, and for the inside of a day. There are many dangers in civilization, especially for such people as ours.'

'That's very true,' Rodney said. Tondrup sounded a little apologetic, as though embarrassed by the image his people were creating with this war dance; and perhaps afraid that Rodney would return with the message that the Mishmis were no more than savages. He was right, Rodney thought, but it depended on what you meant by the word 'savage', and whether you thought it a good thing or a bad thing that people should live in such simplicity. He had not seen a book or a piece of paper since he reached the encampment; there was nothing that could be called comfort; and obviously for centuries the main occupation of these people had been war, yet he could not think of them as savages. That word he would like to reserve for those who, having had greater opportunities, and been given wider visions, had ruined the earth for themselves and their descendants and all the other living things with which they shared the globe.

The sound of the singing grew louder and other men, not formally dancing nor formally painted, joined in. Rodney looked apprehensively up at the sky and round at the silent walls of the jungle. If a troop-carrying helicopter or, worse, a gunship appeared, he would not be given an opportunity to explain what he was doing in the middle of this Mishmi celebration. But Tondrup didn't seem to care; and the Chinese were here, sitting apart as always, but smiling and clapping their hands in time with the music.

The dance ended with no warning. As the sun set a dozen women hurried out, as though eager to get in their dance before twilight. They began to sing and gyrate. Their dance was quite different from the men's, and seemed to represent the work of raising a girl child, teaching her their own skills, and at last handing her over to a suitor. Some of the women were very young, he thought, perhaps no more than twelve or thirteen, but all were sturdy and full-bosomed, their faces a golden bronze, their long hair tied back in plaits with coloured wool, the plaits now swirling around as they gyrated, now falling into the valleys between their ample breasts, as they bent their heads. They shuffled and thumped, their strong widespread toes kneading the soft earth.

This was a much better tune. It was in a minor key, going up the scale, then halfway down again, ending in a series of simple slow trills. He thought he'd remember it, if he associated it with the wooden flute-like instrument that was playing it. The flute player was the other side of the dancers from him, but another man, next to Tondrup, had a similar flute in his hand. When Rodney said, 'Could I borrow that flute for a moment?', Tondrup took it and handed it over.

Rodney tried it out, blowing softly, until he found what notes it produced. Then he began to play it properly, in unison with the man providing the accompaniment for the dancers. The Mishmis heard him, and crowded round, clapping. Rodney walked round the dancers, playing as he went, and sat down beside the other flautist. For a time they played in unison. Then Rodney began to play a counterpoint to the theme. The flute player turned his head, looking in puzzlement. Tondrup was behind him. 'There's no harmony in our music,' he said in Rodney's ear, 'but go on. They hear it.'

Rodney saw in the Mishmis' faces, as he played, that they did not know what he was doing, but that they liked it. He continued to improvise for another quarter of an hour, through another tune, then the flute player blew a sudden rising wail, and the dance ended as suddenly as the men's had – the women simply stopping where they were, in mid step.

'You ought to stay longer and teach the musicians that,' Tondrup said. 'Rather, teach all our people. We have no professional musicians. All the men can play the flute.'

'And the women?'

'Music making is not for women, except to sing. Oh, things like that will change one day. Why force it? It's not important.'

'I ought to go back,' Rodney said. 'I don't know whether anyone in Dambuk knows I've managed to get up here, but they probably do. They must have informants.'

'We'll take you back tonight.'

'To Dambuk?'

'We can't get you there. To somewhere on the Dambuk-Asonli road, where the first truck down in the morning will pick you up. . . . I hope you feel that we have treated you well.'

'Certainly. The kidnapping was a bit of a shock at first, but I know it was necessary. You've treated me very kindly.'

107

Tondrup said, 'We want you to tell the truth about us and our struggle when you get out. Have it published in your magazine. We only want to be free to live our own lives in our own way. We don't want to be governed from Delhi, which is what has happened to Sikkim, and will happen to Nepal.'

'You really believe that?'

'If they think they can annex Nepal without causing war with China, they will do so,' Tondrup said grimly.

Rodney waited a moment then said, 'Have you ever heard the phrase *Azad Shadhinata?*'

He watched the Mishmi leader narrowly as he spoke, looking for a change of expression, some hint that he had touched a chord or hit a nerve. But Tondrup's frown was simple perplexity, as he said, 'I don't know what it means. *Azad* is 'free', isn't it?'

Rodney decided to press his question more closely. 'Do you have a code word for the eventual rising you plan to make against India to achieve your independence?'

This time Tondrup did start. 'How did you know . . .? Oh, the Indians told you that we had one.'

Rodney shook his head. 'No. I just guessed there might be one. There usually is.'

And you thought it might be *Azad Shadhinata?*'

'Possibly.'

'Well, it is not. . . . You are right, we do have such a code word, but it is secret. It is a Mishmi phrase known to all our people. The Indians know – or guess – that we have such a phrase, but they don't know what it is. They have been trying to find out for a long time. You had better rest now. You will have to do some hard walking soon, in the dark.'

The party was much smaller this time, only three Mishmis, one of them armed with a Chinese sub-machine gun, to escort him. The pace was just as fast, too, for the absence of loads compensated for the darkness. When he had fallen three times, the last time uttering an involuntary cry that could have been heard fifty yards away, his guides slowed the pace, realizing that he did not know the trail as they did, and probably could not see as well in the diffused starlight under the high canopy of the jungle.

Four hours they went, never resting, stopping a few times while the Mishmis stood motionless, listening with intentness that was like a physical tension. After a minute, each time, they made a small change of direction and loped on.

At midnight they stopped. The leader pointed to the right front, shook his head, moved his hand in a gesture of negation. This had all been rehearsed by Tondrup before their departure, so that the guides could communicate at least the simplest directives and warnings to Rodney. This sign meant – danger in that direction. Then the leader did the same, pointing to the left front – danger in that direction, too. Pointing straight ahead he nodded two or three times, and held up all the fingers of his right hand, displaying them five times. Five times five equalled twenty-five, and each finger indicated a distance of ten paces: in that direction, at two hundred and fifty paces, was the mountain road, recently built by the Indian Army, linking Dambuk and Asonli.

Without another word or gesture the Mishmis vanished, leaving Rodney alone. He faced the front again. It would be fatally easy to forget or lose the direction they had pointed out to him; and the result would be fatal, in fact. He picked out a constellation of three bright stars close together, noting that it was just to the right of the direction he should take, and started forward.

The ground dropped away rapidly, and he fell once on the steep slope, fetching up hard against the bole of a tree. He lay breathless, listening, trying to contol his gasping efforts to regain his breath. Nothing moved, there was no sound except the gentle soughing of a small breeze through the tree tops. He stood up carefully, and looked for his constellation, but could not find it. He moved on until he could see another patch of sky, found his star mark, and began to move faster.

Five minutes later, when he thought he must be getting close, a bullet cracked past his head, followed immediately by a short burst from an automatic weapon. Ahead he could see red and orange stabs of flame under the trees. He threw himself to the ground, shouting, 'English! *Angrezi, angrezi*!' His answer was another burst of automatic fire that ripped through the bushes above him on the slope, scattering twigs and leaves over him. Dimly ahead he saw movement. Something whirred overhead and landed with a thump beside him. He pressed himself closer to the earth and the grenade exploded ten feet away, most of the blast caught in the great tree which the grenade had rolled behind, steel splinters whining low past his head.

'Don't shoot!' he yelled at the top of his voice, *'Fire mat kara! Angrezi hun!'*

He expected another burst from the automatic, but there was a half minute's silence. Then he thought he heard a muttering from ahead there, where the firing had come from. A voice called in Hindi, 'How many of you are there?'

'One. I am alone.'

Another long silence; they didn't believe him. The N.C.O. was debating with his men whether to throw a few more grenades, then charge, or accept his statement. At last – 'Come forward, one man only, hands up.'

He rose slowly, shouting, 'I am standing up . . . my hands are up . . . I am coming towards you . . .'

He walked slowly forward. Before he had gone twenty paces he found himself on the hard pale surface of the road that he had been looking for. Darker shadows lined the far side. He stopped, saying, 'I am not armed.'

'Forward, come off the road,' a voice commanded.

He went forward again. At the edge of the farther trees he almost walked into the muzzle of a sub-machine gun held by a sepoy in camouflage uniform and shapeless jungle hat. He made out other forms to the right and left, nine or ten in all.

'Who are you?' the nearest soldier asked.

'Rodney Bateman. English. The Mishmis captured me from a lorry, two days ago. They brought me back close to here and let me free.'

A long silence. Then, 'Tie up his hands. We'll take him back to the post. The captain-sahib will be down in the morning, when it's light.'

The Brigadier sat behind a desk in a wooden hut in the military enclave, obviously recently built, close to the north of Dambuk. A wooden plaque on the desk announced that he was Brigadier K. P. Gunturkala Vr.C. He was thin and clean shaven, very dark skinned, and spoke English

110

without the trace of an accent or inflection. A tall young captain stood at his side. On the verandah outside, the escort, of a *naik* and three men, who had brought Rodney down from Mishmiland, waited, seated on benches.

The Brigadier said, 'You have a passport to prove your identity?'

'Yes. It's in my suitcase. I can get it if . . .'

'Later,' the Brigadier waved a hand. 'Let me start at the beginning. You say you don't have a permit. How did you get over the Luhit, then?'

Rodney said, 'I'd prefer not to say. It might involve others beside myself.'

The captain interrupted, 'Sir, I think he was flown into Dambuk by Air Vice-Marshal Contractor.'

'The Air Marshal?' the Brigadier said in astonishment. 'Good God! How do you know?'

'I was at the airfield waiting for the ration plane to come in, and saw the Air Vice-Marshal's light plane land. This man – Mr. Bateman – passed close by me, with the Air Vice-Marshal, on their way to his staff car.'

'They were talking? I mean, Mr. Bateman wasn't a prisoner?'

'No, sir. They seemed friendly.'

The Brigadier turned to Rodney. 'Is this true?'

He nodded. The Brigadier said to himself, 'Now why on earth would Nawal do that?' Aloud – 'Do you know how this came about?'

Rodney said, 'I'm afraid I don't. Honestly. I had been stopped by the police at Saikhoa Ghat, and had returned to Tinsukia. There I ran into the Air Marshal, whom I had met in Kashmir just recently, and he offered to fly me in. Of course I accepted. It is very important to me that I hear the local music of all the Himalayan peoples, including the Mishmis and Abors, and . . .'

'I know, you explained,' the Brigadier interrupted. 'This place is becoming a madhouse. First you, and now I've been asked to let in a writer who says he has to tell the people of India what it's really like in the Mishmi villages.'

Rodney said, 'A reporter? Is his name Chandra Gupta?'

The Brigadier looked up, again startled, 'Yes, why?'

'I know him.'

'He's well known. I've read a couple of his books, and

111

I see his articles in the *Independent* when I'm in Delhi. But if I let him go up, he'll report how we are needlessly antagonizing the kindly Mishmis . . . or he'll get his throat cut by the kindly Mishmis. If I don't let him in, some blighter in the Lok Sabha will ask why the army is allowed to keep their brutal acts secret from the taxpayers.'

'I think he's a good chap,' Rodney said. 'I've talked with him quite a bit. We went trekking together in Nepal, as a matter of fact. He's not anti-Army. Nor am I.'

The Brigadier held out a cigarette case. 'Do you smoke? Wish I didn't. . . . What did you learn up there, that might be useful to me?'

Rodney said, 'Nothing you don't know already, I'm sure. Some hearsay.'

'Did you meet Tondrup?'

'Yes. I liked him.'

'So do I, what I've heard of him, though I wish he wouldn't put out all these statements about our torturing Mishmis. We haven't tortured anyone, though we've shot a few. He calls it repression, we call it maintaining law and order. We can't have government offices burned and policemen murdered. . . . I wish he wouldn't let himself be deluded by the Chinese, though. They've sent in a few weapons and some instructors, we know, and they've built that road to the frontier, and they've got Tondrup to make a trace farther southward, ready for The Day. But I'm damned sure they – the Chinese – won't lift a finger to help the Mishmis when The Day comes.'

'Tondrup thinks they will.'

'Of course, but it's strategic nonsense. The difficulties of keeping Mishmis and Abor territory linked with China are tremendous – out of all proportion to the possible re-turn. Nepal or Sikkim now, they're different propositions. Where do you think Tondrup's headquarters are?'

'Close to where you think they are. A search helicopter went close over us the day I was captured.'

'So Tondrup will be moving. . . . I wish I could make out what the Chinese are up to. The Mishmis don't bother me at all. We've got a long job here, to persuade all these hill people that somehow they've got to work out their destiny with us – not with China, or even in absolute in-dependence – that's impossible, in this day and age, if only for economic reasons. . . . But the Chinese! As I said, what they are doing makes no strategic sense, yet the evidence is there.'

'Are you moving more troops to this area to face that threat?' Rodney asked.

Brigadier Gunturkala said, 'The Chief says . . .' He looked up sharply. 'It's none of your business what the Chief says, is it? Only the music. I'll call Nawal Contractor, if I can get hold of him. And speak to Chandra Gupta – he's an Indian citizen and his opinion is worth something, but my guess is that you'll be going to Itanagar as a prisoner, and will remain one until all this is satisfactorily explained. Meanwhile, we'll do our best to make you comfortable. Will you give me your word as an officer that you won't try to escape . . . but, of couse, you're not an officer.'

'No,' Rodney said, smiling, 'but my father was – Royal Vindhya Horse. And my grandfather – 44th Bengal Lancers, and . . .'

'Good God, I was in the R.V.H.! Your father left years before I joined, of course, but his portrait's in our mess, and the silver salver he presented. Why didn't I make the connection? You come and live in my headquarters' mess till we have this sorted out. Tilak, fetch his suitcase from . . .'

'Nizamullah's Rest House.'

So far so good, Rodney thought, standing up. He wasn't out of the wood yet, but he felt optimistic. Then, in a day or two, to Delhi to report to Ayesha. He felt a familiar heaviness in his loins at the memory of her body as she had lain naked before him on the houseboat's bed.

CHAPTER NINE

The Boeing 737 glided down into the pall of smog hanging over the Vale. The encircling ring of ice peaks blurred and disappeared. Rodney closed his eyes and rested his head in his hands. He was to call her as soon as he got in. The message had an exciting, urgent ring to it . . . Ayesha . . . Ayesha . . .

As soon as he had cleared his baggage he telephoned her at Schweitzer's Hotel. Her voice sounded strange, and he thought that she was suppressing some emotion. 'Come to Room 648 here,' she said. 'No, it's not mine.'

'I'll be over in an hour and a half,' he said, 'I have to dump my bags at the houseboat and clean up a bit.'

'Leave them in the hall here and get another taxi later,' she said. The receiver clicked. Rodney smiled inwardly. She was in a hell of a hurry. Outside, he fought off half a dozen taxi drivers, and to the seventh said, 'Schweitzer's Hotel, please.'

Schweitzer's was large, modern, air conditioned throughout, and in every way but one indistinguishable from a thousand other hotels of its type. Its distinction lay in the view across the Maidan to the snow wall of the Pir Panjal. Room 648 was on the sixth floor, and there was a hotel servant polishing shoes at the end of the passage as Rodney stepped out of the lift, found the room, and knocked.

The door was opened at once from inside, and he went in. She was there. He went toward her, hands outstretched – 'Ayesha!'

She stepped quickly away, turned to face him, and snapped, 'What have you got to say for yourself?' Her voice was high and hard, her hands clenched beside her, her face blazing, her eyes glittering like points of obsidian.

Rodney set his jaw, wiping desire and tenderness from his mind. The room smelled of pipe tobacco, there were men's hairbrushes on the dressing table, a man's jacket over the back of a chair.

'My room is next door,' Ayesha said impatiently, 'this is – never mind whose. Answer my questions.'

'What have I got to say for myself about what?' he asked, feeling suddenly weary. 'About the British High Commissioner having to get me out of military custody? Brigadier Gunturkala told me he had intervened on my behalf, but frankly I didn't believe it.'

She said, 'He did, in a way, because I went and told him privately that we would be grateful if he would ask for your release. . . . I had to get Bajwa's permission to do that. Bajwa doesn't think I ought to have employed you in the first place. Bajwa's been trying to get rid of me since I was posted to his department, and now you've given him another knife to stab me with, when the time's ripe. He's right about one thing though. I should never have employed you!'

Rodney said, 'Mind if I sit down?' He sank into an easy chair before she could answer.

She stormed on, 'We've kept it out of the papers so far and will probably be able to continue to do so, but there have been so many accusations of lax security inside the government that the Prime Minister has been at Bajwa, and Bajwa is not going to let the axe fall on *him*. A sacrificial goat will be found before anything like that happens, and it is not hard to see who that will be!'

'Chandra Gupta was up there,' Rodney said. 'He knows I was, too, because we met in Brigadier Gunturkala's mess. He might publish something.'

'He won't say anything about you,' she said. 'We asked the army to let him into the Luhit Division if they could. But our price for doing Chandra that favour was the right to censor his copy. He depends too much on us to get on the wrong side of us.'

Rodney said, 'Air Marshal Contractor got me to Dambuk in the first place, and when I was released from military custody, he flew me down to Calcutta in his own plane. I don't know why. *He* doesn't trust Chandra. He hinted to me on the flight out that there was something fishy about him, and warned me to watch my step with him. Said Chandra had a brother who was killed in fishy circumstances.'

'That was Chandra's twin,' Ayesha said impatiently. 'He was involved with some revolutionary nonsense when he was in Calcutta University – but Chandra never was.'

115

'Does Contractor know I'm working for you?' Rodney asked.

She shook her head. 'No, he might have guessed, if he ever saw us together. He's one of the few people who have a good idea of what my real job is. He was in air intelligence before he got his present command.'

She flung herself into a chair opposite Rodney, and lit a cigarette. She said, 'Now, what in *hell* were you doing in Arunachal Pradesh?' The words were sharp, but her voice had changed and was softer, almost resigned.

Rodney said, 'You told me originally that my first problem was to find out what the problem was. In the past three weeks I have been grasping at the inkling of an idea. It led me to Mishmiland. I had to see for myself, feel for myself, breathe the air, the literal air, and also the atmosphere, what people are feeling, inside themselves, along the Himalayas . . . here, Nepal, Arunachal Pradesh.'

'What have your learned?'

'Not learned – felt, heard. . . . Someone is orchestrating happenings. A left-hand bass note or chord is sounded here in Kashmir, or in Ladakh. The next chord is played in the middle of the keyboard – Nepal. The next, in musical progression, ought to be right-hand, treble. And it is – beyond the Luhit. Now I expect the next one to come back to the left-hand. Something will happen here.'

'Back to Kashmir?' she said. She was looking at him with surprise more than anger now.

He shrugged. 'I was speaking musically – making a musical allegory. Perhaps I am wrong. Perhaps I hear music where there is none.'

She said, 'Something *is* happening in this area, though we are not letting anything out about it. Satellite photos show the Chinese building a new airfield on the Ladakh front . . . and the road along the Indus valley seems to be more heavily used, but that may be because they seem to be reopening some of the turquoise mines there. There also seem to be some new military installations, but we can't tell what, and they're not big. We haven't got enough to make any firm deductions. . . . Things are happening with Pakistan, too. There have been incidents along the Line of Actual Control here in Kashmir – a few shots fired, a round or two of artillery, some mortar bombing, troop movements, changes in routines that haven't changed for months. . . . What do you think the Chinese are going to do in Nepal?'

He said, 'I don't know. The *yeti*-surveyors prove they're up to something . . . but that, and the complaints in Kathmandu, and the hate barrage on the radio, could all be orchestration. Same with the Chinese instructors with Tondrup.' He recounted what he had seen while with the Mishmi leader.

She said, 'What do you think about Chinese intentions there?'

'It's damned difficult country,' he said, 'but Tondrup is convinced they're going to help him when the moment comes . . . help in a big way, militarily. Gunturkala, at least, does not agree, but he and his superiors obviously have to be ready – which ties down a lot of troops and aircraft.'

'And you?'

'I don't think I've heard the true major theme yet . . . or, for that matter, the main counter theme. What I have heard rings too minor, too decorative, in my mind. There are notes that have not been struck yet. Look—' he continued earnestly, leaning forward: it was damnably difficult to make a non-musician understand the realness of what he had felt, '—you asked me to find out what the problem is. If I had to make a final report to you today, I would say that the problem is this: where are the Chinese going to make their decisive move? Through the east, centre, or west of the Himalayas? And what will be their purpose? To aid Pakistan in some confrontation with you? To embarrass India, and through India, Russia? To get a good bargaining position for some other, outside negotiation or ploy? To spread the revolution? To reach the Indian Ocean? I don't know the answer to these questions, but I am becoming pretty sure that those *are* the questions. Some of them would be less hard to answer if I knew the real intentions of the Government of India. Do you intend to make an opportunity to take over Nepal, as many up there believe? If so, the Chinese preparations may not be aggressive at all, but defensive.'

'What my government has in mind is none of your business,' she snapped, angry again. 'We have no intentions of overturning anyone's freedom or independence.'

117

'Tell them that in Sikkim and Bhutan,' he said.

'We took Sikkim and Bhutan into the Union for the same reason that Pakistan took Hunza and Nagar into their country immediately afterwards,' she said, 'because they are anachronisms, anomalies. We can't have little semi-independent feudal kingdoms sitting on our vital frontiers.'

She sat back, stubbed out her cigarette and lit another. She did not speak for a time, staring moodily at him, her face wreathed in blue smoke, a frown creasing her forehead. At length she said, 'You are a strange man, Rodney. You don't learn by the ordinary senses, certainly not ordinary observation or ordinary logic. You may be right, or you may be talking metaphysical nonsense.' She sat up. 'In any case, you are to stay in Kashmir now, and continue your investigations here. And do not go anywhere in this area where a permit is required without getting my approval first. Do you understand?' Her manner eased a little as she ended. 'You did say the next chord would be here, didn't you?'

'Yes, I did,' he said, 'and I do understand your words. But I'm not going to accept your orders.' He felt tired, and frustrated. Majestic music sounded in his ears, music he had not written, or heard before; he was trying to make sense out of it, to give it shape and form, while Ayesha spoiled his concentration with her yapping. He got up and headed for the door. 'I'm resigning, now. You can tell Bajwa that he was right, Bateman's no good . . . and put your ham-handed agents on to listening for the music of the Himalayas.'

He had the door knob in his hand. Ayesha was on her feet, and hands out. 'Rodney, please . . .'

He went out. God damn her! He had been thinking of her for three days and nights, and not only sexually. Now she had spoiled everything, the sex, the tenderness, and his growing involvement with the mystery being prepared in the Himalayas. Now what the hell could he do?

After dinner he sat on the front patio of *Dilkhusha III*. He had not touched the piano since coming back, had not even lifted the lid to see whether it was still in tune. He'd do some practising tomorrow, or the day after, when he had freed his mind from Ayesha's mystery, that other Himalayan Concerto, with its unexpected notes, its shepherd melodies, its sudden staccato outbursts. He had said that China was the orchestrator. But was that true? Suppose that the Nepalese, with Indian encouragement, had in fact been needling the Chinese along that border? And the same here. Suppose the Indians had been needling the Pakistanis in Kashmir, the Chinese in Ladakh? Then India would be the orchestrator, the composer . . . and Ayesha would not tell him. She might not even know, for high as she was, she was not at the very top. She was in fact at just the right height to be used in a top level deception plan, the implication for the person to be deceived being 'If Ayesha Bakr thinks so-and-so is the truth, then it must be.'

He heard the soft chunk of a paddle, the rhythmic drip of water. The moon had not risen, the sky blazed with stars, the surface of the lake was sprinkled with gold, deep blue shadows lay athwart the bank under the chenars on the distant shore. Yellow lights shone from houseboats moored along the near bank on both sides of *Dilkhusha III*. The evening was warm, and he was wearing no jacket over his thin flannel shirt.

He saw the *shikara* approaching, the canopy swaying, some decorations on it catching the starlight. It came close and he made out the boatman at the back, paddling slowly, the boat gliding on. It turned awkwardly at his steps and he heard a door open in the servants' quarters behind him. Dost Mohammed had heard the quiet strokes of the paddle and come out to investigate. Immediately below Rodney, the boatman turned up his face and Rodney saw that it was Ayesha. She said in a low voice, 'Rodney . . . come for a ride in the *shikara* with me.'

He heard Dost Mohammed return into the servants' quarters, a door shutting. He said, 'What do you want?'

'We can talk about it.'

He stayed, leaning over the wooden rail, looking down into her face from a few feet distance. The heart-shaped outline was soft, the small full mouth very dark, the eyes large and liquid, far different from the daggers that they had been in the hotel room. He thought, she will try to talk me back into the job; and she will succeed, because I can't get the theme out of my head.

Without a word he stepped down into the *shikara* and

119

she paddled it out on the lake with a few strong strokes. He saw from the name plate on the front canopy that it was called *Light of Love, Full Spring Cushions*. 'I hired it, self drive,' she said from behind him. He heard a laugh in her voice and knew she had got over her anger; it was not a personal thing against him, but caused by her fight for her job, her position in the government, and her ambitions.

He said, 'Let me paddle.'

'You can paddle us back,' she said. The *shikara* glided on farther from the shores toward the middle of the lake. From a houseboat someone was playing a radio very loud, Indian film music.

She said, 'I've been ill. I got some sick leave in extension of my ordinary leave.'

He said, 'I was surprised to learn that you were still in Kashmir.'

'I have only just recovered. Perhaps I haven't, yet. I am sorry for what I said. . . . You can go where you want, when you want. Tell me first, please, though.'

'I'll try.'

'I have to go back to Delhi tomorrow. This is our only night, our only time together.'

He said nothing. She paddled on. Five minutes later, when they were far from any shore, alone in a still, pale undimensional shimmer of light, floating as it seemed to him in a velvet void, he heard her bring up the paddle, shake the drops off it and lay it on the deck. Then she slipped through the canopy and knelt over him, her mouth wet and sucking, her hands reaching for his trousers, undoing, touching, stroking, her breath coming in shorter and shorter gasps. He broke his mouth free from hers and said, 'All right, I'll come back . . . I am back . . .'

Her loins were full and streaming and even as he caressed her he wondered, could she have got into this state if she was only 'cajoling' him for her duty's sake? Did she really love him? Perhaps she was the sort of woman who could do and be both. He'd have to think it through some day – another time, another place. She let out her breath in a long quavering moan as he entered her.

CHAPTER TEN

Joseph Braganza, I.A.S., Deputy Secretary to the Government of Jammu and Kashmir, was tall and urbane with thick smooth hair and practically no trace of his Portuguese heritage in his delicate features; he looked pure South Indian, the skin thin and dark, white teeth, fine bones. Rodney was sitting with him, late, in the study of his comfortable house off the Bund, a pale glass of whisky and soda beside him.

Braganza said, 'There are rumours that the Pakistanis are going to attack.'

'Here, in Kashmir?'

Braganza said, 'That's one version. In another, the Punjab is favoured as the area for attack.'

'Do you believe any of it?'

'Frankly, no – not as far as Kashmir is concerned, at any rate. We have a good intelligence set-up here in J & K, and if the Paks were really going to mount an offensive, some of their supporters here would know about it, and would be making preparations to join in, as a fifth column.'

'The KAM?'

'No, they're non-violent. The old Sayyid would not be told anything about such plans, because he wouldn't co-operate, which is fortunate for us. In one way or another the KAM involves nearly every Muslim in Kashmir, which means over ninety per cent of the population. If they were ever unified, or the Sayyid started to preach violent opposition or guerilla warfare, we'd be in trouble. No, we have the much easier job of keeping an eye on the K.P.P. – a finger, to test the pulse, is better – and there's been no change in the pulse rate.'

'That's the party Zulfikr Shah is the head of?'

'We are almost certain. He's high up in it, anyway. We know that.'

'How do the K.P.P. get their orders, or information, from whoever are their masters in Pakistan? Is it the Pakistan government? Or is it an external branch of the party, in Pakistan? The Party isn't confined to Kashmir, I suppose?'

'Dear me no. Many Pakistanis join the K.P.P. because they believe in it . . . some used to live here before Partition, some have relatives here, or are of Kashmiri descent. Some have no connection. You asked me how they communicate. A few messages are passed by word of mouth. A sympathizer will be given a message in Teheran, when on his way to visit India, or for that matter in New York, at the U.N. He will drop it to the K.P.P. contact in Srinagar when he gets here. But that is slow and a bit chancy. The major method is concealed radios – two-way, illegal, of course – and ciphers.'

'You can't locate the radios?'

'No. We often get close but then they are moved.'

'And ciphers? How many ciphers are there? Have you broken any?'

'There are three, used in messages to different destinations, as far as we have been able to get directional beams on the incoming signals. We are near breaking one cipher. Our people are just about positive that it's the one used by the K.P.P. here to communicate with Pakistan – their headquarters there, though, as we have just been discussing, we don't know who in Pakistan actually pulls the strings.'

'One cipher nearly broken,' Rodney said, half aloud. He sipped his whisky, thinking. 'What do you need to break it?'

'I don't know. I'm not a cipher expert. Just more time, I suppose.'

'I'm not an expert, either, but it strikes me that if you were to cause some rumour to be started – say about troop movements, something so important that the K.P.P. would feel it urgent to get the news out at once . . . and have the rumour very definite – such and such a division is going to concentrate at such and such a place by such and such a date, and General XYZ has been appointed to command it . . . rumours have an extraordinary way of being passed word for word . . . there's at least a sporting chance that within a few hours or a day at most you'd pick up a cipher message of the right length which might enable you to break the cipher, because you'd know what the message was.'

Braganza whistled softly – 'It's an idea. . . . Would the information, the rumour, have to be true?'

Rodney said slowly, 'I think there would have to be some action of the sort indicated in the rumour, or there'd be no sense of urgency. The K.P.P. would feel they could afford to wait and see whether it was true. And, also, if nothing happened to bear out the rumour, they might realize they'd been hoaxed, and why, and change their cipher.'

'H'mm. Let me speak to the Army Commander about this.'

'Do it right away, I think. I don't know how much time we have. . . . When does the monsoon break here?'

'We don't get it badly here, but there are rains from late June through September . . . and in the rest of northern India, along the Himalayas, rather earlier than that.'

Rodney finished his drink. 'I think I'd better be going. . . . Can you give me an introduction to the Sayyid?'

'Yes, of course. I know him well. A great gentleman and scholar, even if our government does frown on him and his activities. I'll call him tomorrow morning.'

Ten o'clock, and he had been practising for an hour and a half. The great lake basked in golden sun, a slow breeze stirred the chenars. A small boy and a small girl were importuning him from a *shikara* to buy lotus blossoms. The open air was beckoning, but he should either practise, or compose, or think. About Major Mike Sanders, for instance. He closed the piano lid and pressed a bell by the door. A moment later Dost Mohammed stalked in, adjusting the *kulla* and turban on his head. 'You called, sir?'

'Yes. Sit down. This firm which owns this houseboat and the other *Dilkhushas,* and organizes treks and fishing, was founded by Major Sanders, wasn't it?'

'Yes, sir.'

'Were you with him then?'

'Not at the beginning, sir. I was only a *chokra* then. I became a *shikara* boy for him two years later, in 1951. He appointed me to *Dilkhusha III* in 1965, when the previous manager, who was my uncle, died.'

'What happened to him?'

'Major Sanders? He disappeared.'

'Tell me.'

'It was last year, sir. November. I do not remember the exact date. He had arranged to fly to Delhi to talk to some suppliers, and see government officials about opening up tourism to areas here that had been closed to visitors for a long time on account of security reasons. He lived on a houseboat, you know, *Dilkhusha VII* . . . where Mrs. Sanders lives now. On the day he was to go to Delhi, Akbar Khan brought his car – Major Sanders' – to the taxi stand across the lake, there, by the big lone chenar . . .'

'Wait a minute. Akbar Khan's the head man of the whole business, under Mrs. Sanders?'

'*With* Mrs. Sanders now, sir. She made him a partner after the Major disappeared.'

'I understand. Go on.'

'That day in November the *shikara* boy took the Major across to his car. Akbar Khan drove him off, through the city – you have to drive through the city to get to the airport from the Dal Lake, sir,'

'I know.'

'In the bazaar Major Sanders told Akbar Khan to stop, and wait for him, as he had some business to transact. He got out and walked away. Akbar Khan waited.'

'There was no one else in the car? Just the two of them?'

'That is what Akbar Khan said,' Dost Mohammed replied. 'You understand, sir, that I was not present personally. I was here. This houseboat was not occupied, and I worked on polishing the woodwork in here all that day.'

'All right. Go on.'

'Akbar Khan said he waited until it would have been too late to catch the aeroplane, then he went into the bazaar, where he had seen Major Sanders go, asking people whether they had seen him. No one had seen anything. More than an hour had passed, and . . .'

'Is it a tough part of the city?'

'Sir? I do not quite . . .'

'Tough, dangerous, full of *badmashes*.'

'I see. Yes, it is, rather, sir. . . . No one had seen anything.'

'Or said they hadn't.'

'Akbar Khan telephoned Mrs. Sanders, asking for instructions. Mrs. Sanders told him to do nothing, as the Major was able to look after himself.'

Rodney examined the swarthy face opposite. Dost Mohammed's heavy black moustache was drooping and he looked a little unhappy, his eyes wandering. He said, 'Why wouldn't she report to the police at once?'

The bearer looked even more unhappy, and began to mumble, 'I don't know, sir' – when Rodney interrupted. 'Was Major Sanders in the habit of sneaking off . . . disappearing . . . for a few hours, or days, to visit some lady, perhaps? Is that the whores' quarter of Srinagar?'

'There are whores everywhere in Srinagar,' the bearer said with dignity. 'But yes, there are some well-known courtesans in the area where the Major disappeared – very expensive, too, also.'

Rodney said, 'Had the Major left himself plenty of time to catch the plane?'

Dost Mohammed said, 'Yes, sir. He had told Madam that he had some business in Srinagar. He left his houseboat nearly three hours before the plane was due to leave.'

'And the car trip would take three-quarters of an hour, plus an hour for airport formalities. . . . So he left himself an hour or so for his business. When was a report made to the police?'

'Two days later, sir. Mrs. Sanders had, I believe, telephoned the hotel in Delhi where Major Sanders was due to stay, and Akbar Khan had made further inquiries, on his own, you understand, in some of the, *hrrm*, houses where the Major might have visited. But he had not. He had disappeared.'

'He has not been seen since? No trace? Nothing of his turned up?'

'Nothing, sir.'

Rodney sat thinking, then said, 'Thank you, Dost Mohammed.'

He sat on after the bearer had left, his shoulders hunched. Sanders was in the habit of visiting a Kashmiri courtesan, enough for his head man, Akbar Khan, to know about it, probably in detail: and the lesser staff, such as Dost Mohammed, to have a good idea. On the other hand, Sanders was a secret agent of India . . . so when he visited

125

ladies of no virtue, it might be for purposes of fornication or it might be to do with his secret service. He was an agent of India, which was predominantly Hindu. Kashmir was over ninety per cent Muslim, and considerable numbers of the people resented Indian rule. Therefore some Muslim fanatic, a member of the K.P.P. for instance, might have discovered Sanders' secret trade, and had him murdered. But, just because Sanders was a secret agent, one must be careful not to invest all his activities with political or secret service overtones. He might have been murdered for a gold watch, or cash, or for jealousy, or for business reasons. He might have committed suicide, or skipped, to get away from Kit, financial troubles, prosecution of some kind . . . better find out whether Sanders Ltd was, or had been, near bankruptcy, though it seemed very unlikely, from external appearances.

'Anyone at home?' The American voice echoed cheerfully through the open front door. Rodney got up and went out on the front patio. Kit Sanders was there, expertly steering a small *shikara* alongside his steps, then running up toward him. 'May I come in?' Her big face was ruddy with exertion, her skin damp with perspiration.

'Of course.' He stepped aside and she walked past him and flopped into a chair. 'Paddling a *shikara* is harder work than it looks, if you try to hurry.'

'A beer? A drink?'

'No, thanks . . . I came over to ask whether you were thinking of another trek. I don't want to send out my best men with other clients if you plan to go out again. The fishing's excellent up the Sind now, or would you like to try for *mahseer* in the Wular Lake?'

Rodney looked out at the water, and the shimmering mountains beyond. He'd like nothing better – but his work, his composition . . . he ought to keep himself hard at that now. That or Ayesha's riddle. Or both. Were they interwoven?

'I don't think I can,' he said at last. 'Not for a bit, at any rate.'

'All right, but take today off anyway. I'm going to fly some provisions into Chistakatha Sar. A party's trekking in there tomorrow and I want to be certain the provisions

126

are there for them. Tomorrow might be bad flying weather, today's perfect. Like to come with me?'

Rodney didn't hesitate. 'I'd love to.'

'Great. Get into something warm. Take a sweater and a wind-jacket, at least. We'll have a picnic lunch up there.'

'Give me five minutes.'

The Dornier seaplane roared down the weed-cleared water runway of Anchar Lake into the breeze, Kit's hand pushed forward on the throttle, the stick held forward. She eased it back and the seaplane stepped up on to its floats. A few seconds later she eased back again and the floats broke free from the surface tension of the water and the Dornier roared on up into the blue sky, lake and gardens and houseboats and circling chenars swinging down and back.

It was a five-seater, Kit and Rodney sitting side by side in front, the seats for three behind now stacked with boxes and sacks of provisions, a crate of beer and three bottles of whisky. The engine steadied its note as Kit eased back on the throttle, the propeller blades hummed in resonance, making a whirling disc of light in the sun. All about the mountains rose as the plane climbed.

Kit leaned over and said, 'Chistakatha Sar is about seventy miles, north by west' – she indicated the bearing on the compass in front of her, 343° – 'It's under the south slope of Hari Parbat, at about fifteen thousand five hundred feet, the other side of the Kishenganga . . . I hope all the ice has melted off it.'

'So do I,' Rodney said fervently.

She laughed, and placed a hand over his. 'Don't worry. Aunt Kit won't lose you. How could I face the British Academy of Music if I did?'

They were at twelve thousand feet now, thirteen . . . the view was staggering, the Vale of Kashmir spreading wider and farther below, streams curving and bending across its flat lands, fields of flowers, groves of trees, lakes large and small . . . and all round, the mountains, ice and snow covered, climbing as the Dornier climbed. And dominating all else, seizing the attention and holding it fast so that after a while nothing else mattered, or even existed – straight ahead, the sun full on it, an enormous fortress of ice spread across the world, its battlements thrusting higher and higher into the sky ...

'Nanga Parbat,' Kit said, 'Twenty-six thousand, six hundred and sixty feet ... the grave of thirty-one mountaineers, from Mummery in eighteen ninety-five to the British of nineteen fifty ... the most dangerous mountain on earth.'

Rodney stared at the great mass, his attention intensely concentrated, for he felt that with enough effort he could carry its image with him for the rest of his life.

A shadow flashed by on the starboard side and a powerful roar filled the cabin and was instantly gone. The Dornier trembled in air for a few seconds before settling down again.

'Damn him,' Kit muttered. 'What the hell ...?'

The jet fighter wheeled tightly straight ahead and the markings on its wing became clear in the sun – 'Pak!' Kit muttered, 'what's he doing here? We're well short of the LAC.'

'Isn't this Indian-held territory?' Rodney asked, feeling an unpleasant emptiness at the pit of his stomach and a dryness in his mouth. The Dornier would be a flaming wreck any moment if the Pakistani pilot's intentions were hostile.

'That's what I was saying – the Line of Actual Control's over there, beyond the Kishenganga at this point.'

The jet had completed its turn and was diving down from above and behind them. A pair of rockets whooshed past and flared on down toward the distant earth. 'My God!' Kit muttered, throwing the seaplane into a sidespin, 'they've gone mad!' The Phantom dived past, pulling up sharply, with another thunderclap of sound. 'We're going to end up as another "incident",' Kit said grimly. 'I'm sorry, Rodney.' She turned her head, watching the Phantom as it positioned itself in the eye of the sun. She jerked the stick over and back when the Phantom was at the same distance it had fired the pair of rockets before; but this time it did not fire. Six smaller rockets flamed like shooting stars across the horizon directly in front of the Dornier.

Rodney, twisting his head round, cried, 'It's another fighter ... two more ... they're firing at the Pakistani!'

'Indian Air Force Migs!' Kit cried. 'God, I was praying

128

they'd pick up the intrusion in time to save us!' She mopped her brow with a handkerchief pulled from the pocket of her slacks. 'Do you want to go back?' ·

Rodney looked round the empty bowl of the sky. The three fighters had disappeared, leaving twisted vapour trails. He could hear no sound of their engines, or of firing. He said, 'Let's finish what we've begun.'

'Good for you!' She steadied the Dornier on its old course. 'I know there have been incidents along the LAC on the ground over there' – she pointed to the north west – 'but I didn't expect anything in the air. And even on the ground, I don't know why the Pakistanis are bothering. I wouldn't think that advancing farther up the Kishenganga would help them at all. It's nothing but a great trench, ending in a dead world.'

Rodney looked down, watching the earth slide by . . . the land gradually rising until they passed over some peaks, snow scattered, with barely a thousand feet to spare; then the ridges dropped down sharp and long to a winding river before rising again. 'The Kishenganga,' Kit murmured, 'and that's Hari Parbat.' She indicated the peak the Dornier was heading for. 'Now look straight below the highest point of it . . . a little to the left . . . that's Chista-katha Sar.'

The lake seemed to be about two miles long, irregular in shape, its general axis north-west to south-east. Kit banked the seaplane, and flew along the line of the lake a thousand feet up and almost over the southern rim. 'See any ice?' she asked.

Rodney stared, saw some irregular white lumps and pointed. 'Up there, on the far side.'

'The wind's pushed the broken floes over that side,' she said, 'and it's still blowing . . . cross wind landing. Safety belt good and tight? OK. Relax.' She started a gradual turn to the left, banking gently, continued sweeping round in a long slow circle till she was back at the south end, again flying north-west, the mass of Hari Parbat close to the right, the lake, milky green with melted snow and ice, straight ahead. She eased the throttle back and wound down the flaps. The Dornier bucked and slowed in air. 'Crabbing badly,' she muttered, 'the wind must be twenty knots . . . dead cross.' She pointed the seaplane's nose farther into the wind. It continued descending, crabbing through the air ... down ... down ... close below Rodney saw a black bear bounding across a rocky slope ... a moment later, another one, confused, staring up, running in a tight circle ... large boulders, stones, snow dazzling white ... the water, very shallow. The floats cut the surface and water arched up in great plumes to either side. Kit kicked the rudder left again, and held the nose up as she pulled the throttle back a little more. The floats sank in and the Dornier lurched, slowed heavily, the water plumes subsiding. The roar of the engine came louder as Kit threw open her window and leaned out, moving the plane forward in diagonals, first fifty yards half left, then fifty yards half right.

'Good work,' Rodney said.

'I told you Aunt Kit was a good pilot,' she said, laughing, 'Or are you a male chauvinist pig, and believe women should just be stewardesses, good only for having their bottoms pinched? "I'm Kit, fly me!" '

They had reached the far end of the lake, and she said, 'I have to get my feet wet now, up to the timber line.'

She opened the door beside her, stepped down on to the float and threw a small anchor overboard. Then she began to take off her shoes, slacks, and shirt, thrusting them back into the cabin. After a moment's reflection she called up, 'What the hell – I like swimming in ice water' – and took off her bra and underpants.

Rodney said, 'Do you mind if I join you? I trust there'll be some refreshment afterwards?'

'Curry puffs and whisky,' she called. She stood a moment naked on the float. Rodney, struggling out of his own shirt, thought, she's a damned good-looking woman, blonde hair, rather darker in the pubic triangle, full breasts, white-skinned except at the face and neck; she was not one for sunbathing, obviously ... the body and thighs perhaps a little heavy for modern tastes, not slender enough through the hips; Juno rather than Diana ... the clear grey eyes were laughing at him as she stepped into the water, to her waist, and screamed 'Oh God, it's cold!' She threw herself into a frantic crawl, found the anchor rope and began to pull the seaplane toward shore.

In a moment Rodney joined her, gasping in his turn as

the water, so recently ice, bit into his flesh. 'This'll do,' she said. 'Any further and we might hole a float if the wind gets up. Pass me out the things from inside.' She busied herself with securing the plane while Rodney got his first load. In twenty minutes they had transferred the loads to the shore and stacked them under a rock. 'All waterproof,' Kit said. 'And now we're two hundred pounds lighter for take-off . . . not to mention the fuel we've used.' She turned and ran out over the grey granitic sand between the scattered rocks, and again hurled herself into the water. Rodney, watching her flailing arms and kicking legs, felt the sun warm on his naked body, his legs nearly numb and suffering from a thousand pinpricks, But there was no help for it . . . probably good for him, too, in the end. He dived after her, swimming madly to try to keep out the inward thrusting augers of cold.

They sat by the shore, on a rock that was almost too hot to his naked skin. 'I can't believe we're at fifteen thousand feet,' he said.

'Fifteen thousand, three hundred and eighty-six,' she said. 'We're in perfect shelter just here. And the view . . .' She waved a hand southward over the dark trench of the Kishenganga, where the shallow bowl of Kashmir stretched to a remote rim of ice.

She handed him a curry puff. He already had a paper cup of whisky laced with lake water in his hand. The movement of her arm was a little mannered, graceful rather than natural, emphasizing the stretched pectoral muscle and uplifted breast on that side. He caught himself examining her body as she turned away again, staring out over the view, knees hunched, arms around them.

After a moment she said, 'Like the view?' She turned toward him, dropping her arms and parting her knees a little.

'You're very handsome,' he said.

'A big broad,' she said, smiling. 'Do you like them smaller?'

'I don't go by size,' he said. He should reach out and touch her. She'd lean forward and her breast would be cupped in his hand. The sun beat down, the snow fiercely reflected its beam from the wall of Hari Parbat behind them, there was not another soul within God knew how many miles. She might be able to tell him something more about her husband. It was possible that Mike Sanders had heard the music that he, Rodney, was striving to identify and codify, and had died for it.

She said, 'Ayesha is a small woman, isn't she?' Her smile, and the pose of her naked legs, was provocative.

Rodney said, 'Yes, I suppose so.' So Kit suspected or knew of his affair with Ayesha. Did she instruct her houseboat staffs to render her weekly reports on the love-makings of all her clients? Or was it generally known? They had certainly not taken any trouble to conceal it back in 1972.

She said, 'She had an affair with Chandra Gupta once, you know.'

'I didn't know.'

'She's still jealous because he was the one who broke it off. Hell hath no fury etcetera. Besides, Chandra's such a marvellous man. Any woman would hate to lose him.'

'When was this?'

She wrinkled her brow and pursed her lips, like a little girl calculating – 'Oh, the last part of 1971. It was in Delhi, not here.'

Rodney munched his curry puff. So Chandra had been Ayesha's lover just before his own affair with her. Was it possible that she had taken up with him just to make Chandra jealous? If so, it certainly hadn't worked. But it was another odd coincidence, another semi-mystical fact of their Gemini relationship.

He said, 'I keep running into Chandra. I sometimes wonder if he isn't doing a Sherlock Holmes, or Saint, on the side.'

'Other people have wondered that,' she said. 'The government let him into places they won't let any other journalist into. And it isn't as though he were always friendly or subservient to them in his reports. Do you really think he's a . . . well, secret agent?'

She had moved her position again, and her eyes were large on his, one full breast touching his shoulder and one thigh drawn up to part her loins. Information by seduction, Rodney thought; it's the oldest, and still probably the best method . . . if only he had any information. But Kit, if anyone, was the one who knew something; and it would be no good him trying to seduce her. She might give him sex – to all appearances would – but not information.

He said, 'I honestly don't know, Kit. . . . How did you come to meet your husband?'

'Don't you know? I thought everyone in Kashmir knew. My parents took me on a world tour in 1963, to get me away from a boyfriend I'd met at Berkeley – that's the University of California. They thought he was a dangerous commie, so when we got to Kashmir I let Mike seduce me. He was quite an expert at that, in those days. And it must have been good, because he married me.'

'When were you at the University?'

Her eyes narrowed slightly. 'I graduated in 1962. Economics major.'

'Did you like it?'

'Yes, I liked it. I learned to fly. I broke away from my parents' stuffy circle and their stuffier outlook. I got laid – for the first time, believe me.'

1958 to 1962, Rodney thought. That was about the time of the Berkeley campus riots, the beginning of the blow-up in American universities; and she had been there. She might well have been radicalized as well as laid.

He said, 'Where can one hire killers in Srinagar?'

She stared a long moment, her face – so close – at first marking astonishment, then something else – fear, anger, both. That would be natural enough. A woman who was showing a man her private charms, and inviting him to enjoy them, had a right to be angry if he changed the subject so abruptly and, to tell the truth, so offensively. Her breast was no longer touching him, and she had closed her thighs.

She answered him at last, 'I really don't know, Mr. Bateman. I have never put a contract on anyone, though I have been tempted. I am now.'

'Don't be angry,' he said, reaching out his hand. Her thought, that she might seduce him, for whatever purpose, had passed. He could touch her now and there would be no further result.

Her manner softened again. 'Why do you want to know?'

'I was wondering what happened to your husband. I was asking Dost Mohammed this morning. It's not idle curiosity. We may be going on trek again, you and I. I hope

133

we do. We meet socially. You are very kind to me. I need to know exactly how to handle the subject with you, and with other people.'

She said, 'He vanished. That's all. I suppose it's possible that he was murdered, but I somehow feel it's unlikely. And not a trace of him, or of any evidence, has turned up, in six months. Mike was an important person in Kashmir. The police put their best people on the investigation. Rewards were offered. Surely something would have turned up . . . somebody would have talked . . . but nothing . . . We must be getting back, Rodney.'

She stood up and walked out into the lake towards the seaplane. Rodney thought, I must get an opportunity to interrogate Akbar Khan.

Sayyid Ghulam Mohammed's house was big and sprawling, set back a hundred yards from the main road where the military trucks roared and grumbled day and night on their way to and from the Banihal Pass and India proper. Women and girls peeped out of upper storey windows, the barns were stacked with grain, the stables with horses and donkeys. The Sayyid himself was tall, white-robed, with a white beard and an expression of immense calm and authority. Rodney sat opposite him in a booklined study, looking out on an inner courtyard where two women were working at the well.

Rodney said, 'I think Mr. Braganza told you about me, sir?'

The old Sayyid inclined his head. 'He did. He said you were a composer and musician.'

'I am writing a concerto about the Himalaya, and the people who live in it. Kashmir is at one end of the range. I would like to learn something about Kashmiri people, and of course, more about Kashmiri music.'

The Sayyid surveyed him steadily, through square gold-rimmed glasses. 'There is a concert of Kashmiri music in the Nishat Bagh tomorrow evening. I am the patron. Would you care to attend?'

'Very much.'

'I shall see that you get a good place. . . . What can I tell you about my people? Our history? Our religion? Our culture – other than musical?'

134

'I've read up on most of that, sir, as far as one can in the time I've had. I wanted to ask you about the Kashmir Azad Movement.'

The Sayyid's majestic gaze sharpened. 'I am the leader of that party. I have been in British jails and Indian jails for my beliefs.'

'What are they, sir?'

The Sayyid paused, looking out of the window, then said, 'Kashmiris are not Pakistanis or Indians. We are a separate and distinct people with our own culture, our own language, our own music. We have the most beautiful country in the world, and the world should be free to enjoy it – but the control of it, its troubles and benefits, belong to us – Kashmiris. Our independence should be guaranteed by both Pakistan and India, who should also help and advise us over such matters as posts and telegraphs. We do not wish to have any dealings with other countries except for trade and tourism.'

'Something like Andorra, then,' Rodney said.

The Sayyid nodded in agreement. 'That would serve as a model. Andorra is technically under the sovereignty of both France and Spain, but in reality governs itself in all internal matters.'

'Do you think India would ever agree to such a plan – or Pakistan, if it succeeds in pushing the Indians out?'

The Sayyid said, 'It will come. Perhaps not in my lifetime.'

'Do you think the K.P.P. will help you achieve your aim?'

'They are a violent organization,' the Sayyid said, his voice rising. 'And they are controlled by Pakistan. Their only aim is to unite Kashmir with Pakistan.'

'Do you know Zulfikr Shah, sir?'

This time the old eyes were definitely wary behind the gold rims. 'I have met him,' he said.

Rodney saw that the Sayyid was not going to say that Zulfikr Shah was the leader of the K.P.P.; perhaps he wasn't. He said, 'You have talked about India and Pakistan, sir. But other powers are involved. What do you think are the intentions of Russia and China towards Kashmir?'

The Sayyid said, 'Russia does not touch our territory anywhere. During the British time, the Wakhan panhandle of Afghanistan, along the upper Oxus, was established as a buffer so that the Russian and British empires should not physically confront each other at any point. China is a different matter. When Kashmir is reconstituted as a single state it will include Gilgit, Hunza, Nagar and part of Ladakh. Some of those areas do have a border with China, although in very high and difficult country.'

'What would you do about protecting yourself against the Chinese?' Rodney asked.

The Sayyid shook his white beard and seemed to be speaking almost to himself. 'They would surely not attempt . . . the mountains are so great . . . the country so harsh, so barren . . . What would they gain, except the enmity of Pakistan, India and Russia . . . and of our own people?' To Rodney he said, 'Why should we not be friends with China?'

'No reason, sir. But China might not want to be friends with you. That's what India learned in 1962.'

'It is possible. I think that with both India and Pakistan guaranteeing our independence, China would not interfere.'

Rodney said, 'Have you heard the phrase *Azad Shadhinata*?'

The Sayyid said, ' "Free Independence", but in two languages? No, I have not.'

Rodney rose to his feet, 'Thank you, sir. You have been most kind. I hope I will see you at the concert.'

'Yes, yes.'

'Please don't get up. I can see myself out, and I told my taxi to wait.'

He went out across the courtyard, to find a dozen men and women squatting patiently in the dust beside the outer gate. 'What are they waiting for?' he asked the driver.

'To see the Sayyid,' the driver said. 'To touch his feet . . . ask his blessing . . . but just to see him would be enough. He is a descendant of the Prophet, and he is Ghulam Mohammed, a Kashmiri. We love him, sir.'

The taxi tore through the crowded village street at high speed, the horn blaring continually, dogs, cows, women and children rushing for safety before it. At the main road the driver had to wait for a gap in a line of heavy military trucks, and tanks on long transporters, all heading west toward Srinagar.

'A lot of military traffic this afternoon,' Rodney remarked.

The driver turned his head and spoke in a lowered voice. 'Yes, sir. . . . People saying, the 2nd Corps has been ordered to go to Lundarwan immediately . . . that's to the north, only forty miles beyond Srinagar. The Pakistanis must be preparing to attack there . . .'

'Sounds bad,' Rodney said cautiously.

'It must be,' the driver said. 'General Jalawar Singh Dhillon has been ordered up from Delhi to take command of the operations. He was called the Fire Eater of Dacca in '71.'

'H'm,' Rodney said.

CHAPTER ELEVEN

It was mid morning, and Rodney was sitting patiently on a chair in the corridor outside a door marked *Joseph Braganza I.A.S., Deputy Secretary,* in the sprawling offices of the Jammu and Kashmir Government. He held his passport and a folded document in his hand. The document was a long-winded application for permission to reside in Kashmir for longer than the period normally allowed to foreigners, and he had thought it best to prepare it as the justification for this visit, which Braganza had arranged by telephone late last night. Two other men and a woman waited in front of him, and a *chuprassi* in a tattered coat squatted on the floor immediately outside the door.

A man came out. The *chuprassi* rose, ushered the next man in, and closed the door behind him. Listening carefully as he pretended to doze, Rodney could hear no more than a subdued buzz from inside. And Braganza would have made sure that his office, of all those in the building, was certainly not bugged.

Twenty-five minutes later his turn came. He walked in, the door closed behind him. He held out the papers. Braganza glanced at them, and wrote across the application – *Refused at this time. Apply again closer to the expiration of present tourist permit,* with his initials and the date. Then he said, 'Your idea worked. The army got on to it at once.'

'I know,' Rodney said.

'A radio transmitter from somewhere inside Srinagar transmitted a cipher message at 3 a.m., of just the length we were looking for. We sent it on the scrambler to Delhi, where our cipher department is, and they broke it by five o'clock. By then we could send them another message, from another radio, but in the same cipher, which we'd picked up in the interval. Our people down there deciphered it. . . . Tomorrow, a consignment of six two-way UHF radios is being sent up in a single case, to the usual consignee.'

'Is that what the message said, "the usual consignee"?'

'Yes. The case is being shipped from Pathankot. That's the railhead for Kashmir.'

Rodney thought a moment. 'Does it say what freight company is transporting the case? Or how the radios are getting to Pathankot?'

Braganza shook his head. 'One thing's important to us – will the lorry driver know what's in the case, which will presumably be only a part of his load?'

Rodney said slowly, 'I think not. That would simply add to the number of people in the know – and so to the danger. This is a normal operation, remember – one of many, by which arms, radios, printing presses perhaps, have been sent up. There must be a routine . . . goods are shipped to 'the usual consignee' in Srinagar, from any part of India. They would probably be sent by rail, consigned to some trucking company in Pathankot, which would take delivery from the railway, and bring them on by road . . . over the Banihal Pass, presumably.'

Braganza nodded. 'There's no other way, for us, except via the Rohtang Jot all the way up to Ladakh and back here over the Zoji La . . . some five hundred miles and five high passes instead of one hundred miles and an all-weather tunnel under the Banihal. All right, I agree that the driver will probably not know what's in the case. We could search all lorries coming up at some check point on the road.'

'Then we'll find out who's eventually supposed to get the radios – because he won't collect the case. And we'll give away the fact that we've broken the cipher. We have to be more subtle. . . . Let me think a moment.'

'Not too long,' Braganza said. 'It shouldn't take me long to give you a residence permit, still less to refuse it.'

Rodney said, 'Can we examine all lorry loads tomorrow, at some point? Six radio sets are going to be of a certain size and weight. On some pretext, at some place, we should stop all traffic, and examine the loads, but cursorily.'

'The Banihal Pass,' Braganza said, 'The troop movements that everyone's heard about, and the Pakistani threat that was the reason for them – those are good causes.'

'Good!'

'We'll close the Banihal tunnel and make all traffic go over the top, on the old road over the pass itself, which

139

will probably start a rumour that we're preparing the tunnel for demolition, something dramatic like that, to keep their minds off what we're actually doing, which is . . .'

'Look at the crates, only. Don't open any. Note the consignees of anything that looks suspicious, but do it in an inconspicuous way. Radio those names to your security people here, so that they can put a watch on them, and eventually see who comes to pick up the goods. I have a feeling that the consignee is going to be a warehouse or agency. If this is a regularly used routine they would have to use some place which in any case is going to receive quite a volume of miscellaneous consignments – so suspicions would not be aroused as they would be if, say, Zulfikr Shah was regularly receiving crates from India. The consignee might be notified ahead of time, or a day or two later, by separate letter or cable, that invoice number so and so should be delivered to Mr. XZY, on demand, and charges guaranteed by the sender, or he might have paid in advance . . .'

'Suppose it is Zulfikr who eventually picks up the radios, do you think we should arrest him?' Braganza asked.

Rodney said, 'I can't answer for your department. But if you do, all you'll get is a piece of the K.P.P., I think. I'm after something bigger and, speaking for myself, I don't want the K.P.P. disturbed. I want the members pinpointed, identified, known – so that when the decisive moment comes . . .'

'*Azad Shadhinata*,' Braganza said quietly.

Rodney looked up. 'Any idea what it denotes – or to whom?'

Braganza shook his head. After a while he said, 'I agree. The K.P.P. could be a damnable nuisance to us here in J & K, but the other matter is obviously more important. We'll leave the K.P.P. as the live bait that might lead us – you – to the big shark.'

Rodney said, 'I'd like to go up to the Banihal tomorrow.'

Braganza said, 'It's a little dangerous, but I suppose you know what you're doing. Be outside Nedou's Hotel at five-thirty a.m. tomorrow. A Tata diesel lorry with a Sikh driver will pick you up. Inside there'll be four of my men, in police uniform. They all speak some English. They'll be the ones to do the actual examination of the lorry loads.

Ordinary police are going up there as well. We'll stop all traffic through the Banihal tunnel at eight a.m., without any advance warning, in case someone gets frightened and has the consignment held at Pathankot. . . . My people will be in position on the pass by seven thirty a.m. There are a few old barrack-type hutments there. You yourself should keep out of sight. There will be a two-way radio, and an operator to use it. . . .'

Rodney sat on a folding chair inside the bleak hutment that had once housed police or soldiers, sipping excessively sweet artificially flavoured lemonade from a dirty glass. Peering through the cracks in a window that Braganza's men had boarded up with cardboard only five minutes before, he saw the first heavy lorries grinding up the pass in both directions, from where they had been diverted from the tunnel that bored through the Pir Panjal two thousand feet below. Half a dozen uniformed police under a sub-inspector began to check the trucks on the pass, a hundred yards away, and it was impossible for him to tell, by sight alone, which of them were real police and which were Braganza's operatives. But it was only the security men who were examining the insides of the trucks; the regular police halted the vehicles, directed them to parking places on the verges, and waved them on down into the Vale or into Jammu when the inspections were over.

By ten o'clock a strong wind was chasing mist tendrils fast and low over the short grass of the pass. To the north thickening clouds hid the great peaks of the true Himalaya; across the Vale, Nanga Parbat, the naked god, had hidden his giant stature in dense white veiling. The view over Jammu to the south was large, hazily fading toward the plains where India and Pakistan met, their armies facing each other suspiciously across a tenuous armistice line. Rodney sighed moodily: they were all such nice people, why the hell couldn't they live in peace together? But they might, with a great deal more reason, ask the same question of England and Germany, and all the western nations.

One of the police was coming up the slope towards him – walking with the sense of purpose proper to a man about to attend to the demands of nature.

'It's the sub-inspector, sir,' the operator sitting at the radio in the corner behind Rodney said.

The inspector came in, flicking an imaginary speck of dust off the black leather off his revolver belt. 'One suspicious, Mr. Bateman,' he said. 'Consigned to Itma-ud-Daulah . . . he has a radio and TV shop in the bazaar.'

'Probably not him, then – this will be genuine,' Rodney said. 'But you'll be reporting it to Srinagar?'

The inspector nodded and, pausing by the radio table, wrote a brief message and handed it to the operator. Then he went on through the back door and out to the latrine. Five minutes later Rodney watched him striding back down to the road.

Two more hours passed. One by one police came in to eat there rations, squatting on the floor, drink water from their waterbottles, go out to the latrine, smoke a *bidi,* then return to the pass below. The clouds grew denser and the light weaker. At half past twelve, with a tremendous crash, a bolt of lightning stabbed into the vitals of the rocks across the pass. The electrical storm built up in intensity.

In the middle of it, running up through driving spouting rain, lightning searing the eyeballs, thunder booming like a demented giant's drums around them, the earth shaking and the hut rocking, the window coverings blown in as though by cannon blasts, the sub-inspector arrived.

He leaned back against the door, water pouring from his uniform and the peak of his cap. He swore a moment, then, 'Two more lots, Mr. Bateman. One consigned to Muzaffar Khan's Warehouse, the other to General Storage, Private, Ltd . . .' He dashed water from his sleeves, and wrote another message.

After waiting five minutes looking at the storm from the doorway, he said 'I suppose I must go back' – opened the door, and ran out.

At four the storm was gone, the sky an evil blue from horizon to horizon, Nanga Parbat aglitter to the north. The radio operator began to take down an incoming message. He handed it to Rodney. It was from Braganza to the inspector – *Pathankot reports last lorry to pass check point there will reach you at 1630. At 1700 redirect traffic through tunnel, close your post and return to base here.*

Itma-ud-Daulah's consignment checked out – commercial radio sets only, for general sale.

Rodney said, 'Signal for the inspector to come up, please.'

The operator shouted and waved from the door of the hut. The inspector acknowledged the signal with a wave, but did not come up for another five minutes. When he arrived he said, 'Nothing more, and not likely now. The first arrivals will have had time to telephone back to Pathankot about the inspection, if any of the drivers are in the know, which I doubt. At any rate, they will want to be in Srinagar and have their loads disposed of by dark.'

Rodney handed him the message. He read it, and said, 'Good. I'll tell the sergeant at the tunnel mouth by walkie talkie.'

An hour later, just as the police were closing down the inspection post on the pass and the last trucks were rolling south into Jammu and north into the Vale, another message began to arrive on the radio. The operator showed it to the inspector as he came in through the door. Rodney read it beside him – *Muzaffar Khan's consignment being picked up by J & K government vehicle maintenance depot manager – consists of engine parts and tools for instructional purposes. General Store Private consignment not picked up yet, establishment under surveillance.*

'Very discreet surveillance, I hope,' Rodney said, 'otherwise we may end up having to confiscate six UHF sets, with no more real knowledge than we had this morning – except that we'll have lost the ability to read their cipher, because they'll change it.'

Soon, with everything stowed, the police already gone, Braganza's security men dozing in the back of their truck under the tightly drawn and fastened canopy, they were heading back for Srinagar. The radio was set up and in operation: if Braganza had anything important to tell Rodney, he could still do so. But really it was his show now, not Rodney's. Rodney made himself as comfortable as he could in the lurching truck, a metal frame bar biting into his back, and closed his eyes ... music; an age-old tune, women's voices coming from a far part of a big house; the Sayyid's? The old man was a patriarch, with probably three or four junior wives, but the first, of his own age, as mistress of the house and all the rest ... children, servants,

143

land, scholarship, wisdom . . . a functional harmony, formed and practised under these Himalayan skies. . . . He must build that into his Concerto. Yet there had always been sounds of war, too – people trying to force through the passes, in one direction or the other, seeking trade, love, dominion . . . perhaps only excitement.

The radio operator handed him a message. The sub-inspector shone a flashlight beam on the flimsy paper: *General Storage visited by three men in past half-hour, in private cars – ownership of cars now being traced through registration bureau.*

Braganza pushed the whisky bottle across the table towards him. Rodney poured and drank. It had been a long day. The curtains were drawn and a wood fire burned aromatically in the grate. From upstairs he heard the echoing sounds of children calling, a woman scolding – nothing angry, just a young family being firmly put to bed.

Braganza said, 'Two of these cars belonged to merchants who were picking up other goods – not the crate with the radios. The one which took the crate away – together with other boxes labelled as X-ray equipment – belonged to Dr. K. M. Jaffar. And that is very interesting. Jaffar is a radiologist, and a good one. He has a big practice and he does much work for the J & K Government, and for our Army and Air Force up here. He is a pillar of the pro-Indian community in the Vale.'

'But he's a Muslim?'

'Oh yes, a Shiah, which is fairly rare. We thought that was what made him pro-Indian – there's no fascination like sectarian fanaticism and plenty of Shiah Muslims would rather have Christians or Buddhists, or for that matter communists, rule over them, than Sunni Muslims. . . . Jaffar does a lot of work free, in the villages and for the *gujjars*, but he also makes a lot of money. He's best known for his politics, though – as I said, he's strongly for the Indian connection. We took a good look at him five, six years ago – nothing suspicious, just on general principle. We found nothing. I have a feeling that if we arrested him and searched his house and office now though, we would unearth a great deal – lists of members, cipher books, plans . . .'

144

Rodney said, 'Please don't, Mr. Braganza. Assume that he's the real head of the K.P.P. in Kashmir and Zulfikr Shah is just a sort of dummy, set up for you to watch. Assume, too, that if Dr. Jaffar has taken so much trouble to conceal his tracks, and be active on the Indian side up to now, it's because he has a big job to do at some future date – *Azad Shadhinata*. I suggest that he should not be put under surveillance, not inside Kashmir at any rate. If he leaves Kashmir that would be a different matter. It would be very instructive to know whom he contacted, because outside contacts would point towards, perhaps even indicate, the people who are in the long run controlling the K.P.P.'

'They're in the Pakistan government,' Braganza said.

'Perhaps,' Rodney said, 'perhaps not. Even if they are, it would be valuable to know just *who* in Pakistan is to give the K.P.P. its orders – and far more valuable if it were someone outside Pakistan. Before I head for *Dilkhusha III* and some sleep, can you tell me whom one would go to in Srinagar if one wanted to put out a contract?'

'A contract? Oh, I see – make an offer he couldn't refuse? Well, that's the C.I.D.'s department, but I can find out for you. Do you feel that you're in danger, yourself?'

Rodney shrugged. 'Yes, in a way. Illogically. But not from murderers. . . . I loved the concert of Kashmiri music, by the way. I sat next to the Sayyid.'

'So my informers tell me,' Braganza said drily.

'He's a great man. Far more dangerous to you than the K.P.P. if he should start preaching violence.'

'We'd have to put him back in jail in that case.'

'That wouldn't help – the violence would be continued, probably increased, by his followers without his personal authority to control it. . . . I think I'd better see Zulfikr Shah, their dummy head man, some time and try to assess him.'

'I'll have a mutual friend introduce you.'

As the *shikara* drew up to the lighted houseboat Rodney thought he saw movement inside. The servants must be getting ready for his return. As the bow reached the steps the living room door flung open and a figure bounded out

145

on the front patio. It was silhouetted against the light from inside, but it didn't need the voice, calling 'Welcome home, Geminus,' for Rodney to know it was Chandra Gupta.

Chandra handed him a glass of beer as he stepped out on the landing deck. 'I heard your boy's paddles from halfway across the lake. Take this – it's cold.'

Rodney climbed stiffly up the steps and into the houseboat. He raised his glass to his friend and asked, 'How did you get here? You were just going up to see the Mishmis.'

'That was a week ago,' Chandra cried, '*Independent* reporters have to keep on the ball, the go, the hop. . . . I was in and out of Arunachal Pradesh in three days.'

'Did you see Tondrup?'

'No. He refused to contact me, or let me contact him, because I am an Indian. What did you find out from him, or is it an exclusive, for your Concerto?'

'There's nothing secret about it. It's . . .'

'Tell me later – tomorrow, while we're fishing the Sind. I've got a car coming for me at four a.m. We'll spend three or four days out, and you can tell me about Tondrup. I can use it for a book – too late for my story. I filed that from Dambuk, after the army censors had been at it with their scissors. Damned military seem to think it's a stain on India's escutcheon, or theirs, if one Mishmi makes a rude noise at one of our politicians.'

Rodney said, 'I'd love to get in a little fishing. I don't know how long I can stay out, though.'

'Come back any time,' Chandra said. 'God knows how long my bloody editor will leave me in peace, either. Gather we rosebuds while we may. Have you eaten?'

'Yes.'

'Then get to bed. We'd better warn your butler, what's his name, Dost Mohammed, to get everything ready and call you early, Rodney dear, for you're to be queen of the Sind. Do I sound a little hilarious?'

Rodney laughed, 'Have you been having a few in the bar at Nedou's? I thought you were teetotal.'

Chandra said, 'I am . . . I have done better than that. I have got into Kashmir without Kit Sanders knowing!'

'Kit?' Rodney said in surprise, 'Is she . . .?'

Chandra said, his manner more serious and his voice lower, 'I told you we'd had an affair. Well, to me it was an

146

affair. To her, I was the only person she had ever loved, or would. . . . I had opened her eyes to real love. How on earth do you get out of a thing like that?'

'You can't,' Rodney said grimly, 'except by adding brutality to thoughtlessness. I can say that because I've done the same myself.'

'I knew it must have happened to you, too. Anyway, I did manage to cool her off, make her see that though I liked and admired her, which I did and do – the big stuff was off. She said she'd accept it, but she didn't. She doesn't. I hate being alone with her – oh no, no rape, nothing like that, just those big eyes, the sadness, the way she looks at me, hidden hunger, hidden reproach. I use other contractors when I come to Kashmir, but she always gets to know I'm up, sooner or later – usually sooner.'

He jumped up and clasped Rodney round the shoulders. 'No secrets between Gemini, eh? Now you know what a cad I am, we needn't hide anything from each other. You want a leetle boy, I get, vairy cheap, vairy clean. . . . May I call your *shikara* to take me back?' He went out, laughing.

CHAPTER TWELVE

Rodney sat in an accustomed place, in a wicker chair on the front patio of the houseboat, looking down the Dal Lake toward the snows of the Pir Panjal. There'd be trout for dinner tonight; as there had been trout last night and trout every night on his short fishing trek. Tomorrow he'd damn well insist on a nice Irish stew, or a Kashmir curry with *chupattis*. He wondered whether Chandra, in his hotel room at Nedou's, was feeling the same. Perhaps he'd call him and suggest that he come to dinner . . . or for a tomato juice cocktail, at least. But they'd been very much in each other's pockets for several days now. It had been tremendous fun, but he'd better not lean on the poor chap too much. They each had their own lives to live.

What had he learned in Kashmir, since he had been summoned up here by Ayesha? That the country seemed placid enough, in spite of the attempts of the K.P.P. to upset it; yet the placidity was not that of a firm set rock or a stone house, but more like a rock balanced, or a pile of dry wood. Let the right lever come – a push to topple the rock, a match to light the wood – and there was tremendous potential for action, change, violence. The K.P.P. didn't seem to possess any such lever, or have any real idea how to get one, in spite of their secret radios, caches of arms and explosives, and what Braganza had told him about their plans for sabotage and assassination. Hence Zulfikr Shah's surly uncommunicative attitude during their interview today.

Rodney had not expected much – after all, the K.P.P. was illegal, and Zulfikr wasn't going to tell someone introduced to him through the Indian governmental machine much about the organization of which he was rumoured to be a leading light. But Rodney had expected a certain cockiness, an aggressiveness such as one might meet in an I.R.A. Provisionals' leader; there had been none, only the rather dejected surliness.

The KAM was passive, under the leadership of the man

the whole country seemed to worship – Sayyid Ghulam Mohammed.

The Chinese to the north were, according to bazaar rumour, firing a few shots, building a new road, enlarging an airfield. From his own observation he knew that Indian Army troops were moving in the Vale, but there was no sense of flow, all in one direction. They seemed to be marching one way today and countermarching the other way the next; in fact he was sure that he had seen a column of tanks on transporters going up the Sind Valley, towards Ladakh one day, while they were fishing, and the same column coming back down the next. The bazaars, and hence his houseboat servants, were more full of talk about the 2nd Corps and the fire-eating General Dhillon, concentrated by now close to Lundarwan, ready for – what? And cross the mountains from Lundarwan, in the lower Kishenganga, were the Pakistanis massing too? And if so, for what? As a precaution against an Indian move, or to initiate a move of their own?

He drummed his fingers impatiently on the wooden railing for a minute, then got up, walked into the living room, threw back the lid of the piano and began to play. It was the middle section of the first movement of his own *Ganges Symphony*, angry confused music which the programme writers equated with the great river's passage through the gorges of the outer Himalayas above Hardwar; but that had not been his thought when he wrote it – only to transmit a sense of the loss of purpose, of frustrated self-searching, which he had been experiencing at the time.

He'd go and see for himself. That was the only way. He'd probably finish up in someone's jail, as he had in Arunachal Pradesh, but he had learned a lot there. He dropped the piano lid, picked up the telephone and dialled Kit Sanders' number. She answered herself. 'Kit? Rodney Bateman here. Can you come round? I'm thinking of making a trip . . . a trek.'

'I hear you've just come back from one,' the disembodied voice said. 'With Chandra. Why didn't you let me arrange it?'

Rodney said, 'Chandra already had it laid on, when he came here to ask me to go with him.'

'Where do you want to go now?'

'I'd like to discuss it with you. Will you bring maps — towards the Kishenganga.'

'I'll come round. Could you give me some tea?'

A quarter of an hour later her *shikara* glided up, paddled by two *shikara* boys. She jumped out and ran up the front steps as Dost Mohammed crossed the side gangplank from the servant's quarters bringing tea and toast. He bowed himself out, and she sat down. 'Now – where do you want to go?'

Rodney said, 'Did you bring the maps?'

'I only have the quarter-inch one. The government haven't allowed the printing of the large-scale ones again yet.' She took a folded map out of the small briefcase she had brought, opened it, and spread it on the table. He examined it . . . there was Lundarwan, on a trail of some kind from the Vale over to the Kishenganga.

He said, 'I've learned that the fishing's very good in the Kishenganga.'

She said, 'It is, everywhere.'

'Especially lower down, someone told me.'

'That's usually true,' she said, 'but the Line of Actual Control crosses the Kishenganga between Dhakki, which we hold, and Dudhnial, which the Paks hold.'

'I'd like to get as far down river as possible.'

She said, 'Lundarwan itself is open – or it used to be. I don't know now, since all these rumours of the army concentrating there . . . but the path is closed a mile or two beyond. You can go to Dhakki, that's all.'

'And if I tried to fish downstream from Dhakki, what would happen?'

'You'd be stopped – or shot – first by Indian outposts and then, if you managed to sneak past them, by Pakistani outposts.'

Rodney bent over the map. There was a motorable road as far as a place called Darugmal. There it forked, one branch going to Lundarwan, which had now become a dead end; the other to a village called Kharhom, and thence over the intervening range and down to the Kishenganga river at Dhakki.

He looked up. 'Suppose I drove to some point between Darugmal and Lundarwan, and from there went on foot, cross country or through Balhom here?' He pointed out a village marked a few miles to the north of Lundarwan.

Kit Sanders glanced down and said. 'You'd have to go over the top of this mountain – it's called the Balhom Tiger locally.'

'Thirteen thousand and ninety feet,' Rodney said, 'not very high.'

'But also forbidden territory,' she said. 'I don't want any of my men shot by the army, and I don't want my contractor's licence lifted, either.'

'I'm going alone,' he said. 'I like trekking, Kashmir style, with all the comforts, but I also like to do it the hard way sometimes, and be with myself, backpacking. Can you supply me with dehydrated foods?'

She nodded, but said, 'I'll be held responsible. Why don't you just go to Dhakki, and keep out of trouble and possible danger?'

He said, 'I am not a combatant, there's no war been declared, and I intend to fish where I want to, and if India or Pakistan don't like it, they can throw me in jail.'

She sighed. 'All right. I'll just say you told me you were going to Dhakki. How much food do you want?'

'Seven days. Mixed. You know what I'll need. And a car to take me beyond Darugmal.'

'When?'

'Tomorrow.'

'Can't do it in time. The day after tomorrow.'

'All right. May I keep this map?'

She poured herself a second cup of tea and thoughtfully chewed on a second piece of toast, looking at him with a frown.

She said, 'You're a fool, but I suppose I have to help. I know that country fairly well, and I can give you some advice. . . . When you get to Darugmal don't take the road to Lundarwan, but turn right on the road to Kharhom and Dhakki. Two miles out a long ridge crosses that road, and leads to the top of the Balhom Tiger – the mountain's shaped something like a crouching animal. It's called the Kharhom ridge and it's wooded all the way till near the very top. It passes well to the east of Balhom village, which is down in the valley, off the ridge. The crest of the Balhom Tiger has been held by an Indian Army post since the Line

151

of Actual Control was moved a year ago. So, about a mile before you reach the crest, cut across the east face of the ridge and work round the crest that way. Eventually you'll hit another ridge, which drops due north down into the Kishenganga on the Pakistani side of the LAC. That's a six-thousand foot drop by the way, and severe . . . your best plan is to pass over that ridge and work down the bed of the little stream to the west of it – it's called the Namkula. That's steep too, but more even. People who were here before Partition tell me there's very good fishing where the Namkula flows into the Kishenganga. That route ought to get you through *our* army's posts, but I can't tell you anything about the Pakistanis', or how often they patrol the river. Personally, I think you're nuts . . . but my mother did tell me about mad dogs and Englishmen. Mike had his crazy moments, too.'

She picked up her briefcase and went out, pausing at the door to say, 'Take care of yourself, Rodney. For the sake of my business reputation.'

He went out to the patio and stood watching till her *shikara* was well up the lake. Then he telephoned Braganza. He did not give his name when the secretary put him through, but said, 'You remember we were talking about contracts?'

Braganza said, 'Yes.'

'I suggest you have all the likely contractors examined very closely about their movements on November 10 last year. And look for any increase in wealth after that date.'

Braganza was silent for a time, then the remote voice said, 'I see. Have you any idea who might have done the hiring?'

'I have one or two. The K.P.P. for instance.'

'We thought of that at the time. But they don't hire people. They do such jobs themselves, using their own members, and usually bungle it. Still, we'll bear it in mind. Anyone else?'

'The closest – a possibility.'

'We looked into that at the time, too. But I'll have my people check it again.'

Rodney hung up. They clearly hadn't given much attention to possible personal reasons for Mike Sanders' disappearance; when a secret agent vanishes one doesn't

152

normally think first of his marital affairs or financial problems, but perhaps one should.

He picked up the telephone and dialled again. 'Chandra? Come out to dinner. I want to talk to you.'

Chandra's voice sounded sleepy at the other end: perhaps he'd been napping. 'Sorry, old boy, can't. Nose on honourable grindstone for slave-driving editor. Besides, you'll be eating trout and they're coming out of my ears already.'

'I'm sorry . . . I'm going to fish the lower Kishenganga.'

'How low?'

'About Dudhnial.'

He heard the whistle at the other end. 'You'll end up in Rawalpindi jail, or in front of a Pak firing squad. How on earth are you going to get there?'

'Kit told me a way . . . up the Kharhom ridge to a mile short of the summit of the Balhom Tiger, then east round the face, then down the Namkula.'

'Dangerous, Geminus.'

'I don't care. I'm going to fish the lower Kishenganga whatever your bloody bureaucracy says.'

'Spoken like a true Bara Sahib . . . I don't think you'll like that Pak jail, you know.'

'I won't mind at all. I could hear their music, and in a few days, they'd have to let me go.'

'Perhaps. Who else knows you're going on this expedition?'

'Kit – no one else. And don't you tell anyone.'

'I won't. Good luck. You'll need it.'

He waited beside the dusty road until the car had turned and driven back, the driver giving him a last puzzled look and a wave as he went. When the car was no longer visible he shouldered his heavy pack, to which was strapped his sixteen-inch-long fishing rod, and set off into the scattered pine trees covering the slope. He could not see the top of the mountain, for he was too close under it here, and also the trees obscured the ridge line. He followed the broad back of the mountain upward, pausing now and then to check the direction on his compass. The ridge was taking him, as Kit had said, due north.

Eleven o'clock in the morning, nothing and no one to

see, the sun hot on his back, the pine needles crunching under his boots. He ought to be within a mile of the summit of the Balhom Tiger within five or six hours . . . say by five o'clock. Then he ought to use the last hour or two of daylight getting a good visual picture of the mountain – for, from up there, five hundred feet higher than he was now, and the trees thinner or even non-existent, he would be able to see forward. Then, after dark, he'd cross the eastward face, aiming to pass at least a quarter of a mile below the summit. The Indian picquet on top would not hear him at that distance even if he were to set a few loose stones rolling; and they wouldn't see him, for it was a new moon. By starlight alone he'd have to find the Namkula stream, work down it, and before daybreak hole up somewhere to rest for a few hours before going on down to the Kishenganga. Once he was anywhere near the river it ought to be quite plain whether the Pakistanis were or were not preparing for a major operation in the area.

He checked that the cork of his waterbottle was tightly fastened, adjusted the pack straps more comfortably on his back, and again bent to the climb. The ridge rose steadily, and sweat began to darken his shirt. His pack was heavy, for beside gym shoes and a change of clothing he carried a sleeping bag, a light-weight cooking pot, and seven day's dehydrated food. In addition to the pack he carried a light haversack on one side and his fishing creel on the other. From time to time he stopped, mopped his brow, and turned so that as he rested, the pack supported against a tree, he could look southward between the tall stems of the pines across the Vale. In that direction nothing dominated the horizon the way Nanga Parbat did towards the north; but to the south-east, as he climbed, the white fangs of Kolahoi steadily rose higher against the distant serrated wall of the Nun Kun range.

One o'clock . . . three o'clock . . . four . . . The big deciduous trees had died out far back, and now the pines were thinning. He could see a little ahead where they ended: beyond, the ridge rose in scattered bushes and alpine scrub towards a bare rounded summit. He thought he detected there some hardness in the shape, as of a man-made wall or concreted roof. It was about a mile and a half away. He went on more cautiously until, moving over to

154

the right side of the ridge, he found a nest of tumbled rocks and low rhododendron bushes, the buds ready to burst. From there he could see the summit ridge and also along the eastern slope, the one he intended to traverse after dark in order to by-pass the Indian Army post on the summit.

He took off his pack, stowed it under a rock, and settled down to survey the landscape before him with the utmost care, trying to remember every detail of it: the slope he would cross and how it changed; the footing – rock and scrub here, a stretch of scree directly beneath the summit, falling away to the east; more rock beyond; the compass bearings he would follow; the time it would take to reach the northward-falling ridge. Then he ate a bar of chocolate, and prepared himself for a nap.

He sprang awake, a small crack loud in his ear as his arm broke a dead twig of rhododendron beside him . . . twilight creeping up from the valley, but not here yet, the sun gone. What had awakened him? He put on his pack, then lay flat, peering up the ridge in the direction of the Indian summit post. No sign of movement there. He searched methodically down the ridge with his eyes, until the scree slopes blurred and faded in the darkness of the lower earth: nothing there.

The second time, being wide awake, he heard the strange sound clearly – strange because it did not belong on this silent mountain, where now the last tinge of red from the sun, set half an hour ago, had vanished, leaving the earth cold and the rocks grey. Again he heard the clink of steel on stone, and it came from behind him. He crawled quickly round the tumbled rocks, not caring now about any look-outs in the summit post, for they were too far and it had become too dark for them to see. Lying still he peered south. Almost at once he caught the edge of a movement and his eyes focused . . . a man in the grey homespun cloth called *mazri*, wearing a khaki beret, was coming up the hill. He could see nothing below the waist, but on his shoulder the man was carrying two long bars of wood wound in canvas. What the hell was that? He was about fifty yards away, moving slowly upwards through the scattered limits of the pines. His hair was long, black, bobbed. Rodney

155

picked up another man to the first one's right, another to his left; those were carrying weapons; he recognized a rifle and a sub-machine gun.

Crouching, he began to run across the slope, as he had originally planned. The darkness was suddenly almost total, and he stumbled and fell among bushes and over stones large and small; but even as he ran he knew he was covering distance painfully slowly, for he was tired, and the heavy pack, which he had not found insupportable during the day's long climb, weighed him down now that he was running for his life, and robbed the strength from his thigh muscles.

There was a light out there to his right, far below in the valleys; a light to his left, too, up in the summit post. When he reached the scree section that he had so carefully studied from his hiding place earlier, he ran across it, two hundred yards of stones all clinking and clashing under his boots, starting innumerable small rock slides. At the far side, where the stones gave way to short turf, he stopped, kneeling, and listening intently. If the men in *mazri* were still coming, he'd hear them on the scree. He counted the seconds, trying to hold his breathing silent . . . ten . . . twenty . . . forty-five . . . a minute . . . minute and a half . . . he heard the sound of stones moving, no clink of metal now, but stones susurrating down the steep as men's weight set them moving.

He rose heavily and ran on, north across the face of the slope. The light in the valley seemed to be in the same place – it must be a long way off; the light in the summit post had vanished – it must be obscured by the slope, or perhaps it only showed toward the south and east; behind – he could not tell He stumbled on through the rocks that he had seen and studied. He had cursed the darkness, and the absence of a moon, but now, moving among these huge granite boulders he thanked God for them, for in moonlight his pursuers could not have failed to see him, now and then outlined like a black moth against a pale face of granite.

Yet, what were they doing? When he listened to them back there on the scree they had seemed to be coming on steadily, as though driving sheep . . . he had felt then that if they wanted they could have been upon him much sooner, and afterwards could have come up fast on him, doing twice his pace across the mountain, and shot or stabbed or bayoneted him without any trouble. That bobbed hair and hawklike face he had seen belonged to a Pathan. A man of the Himalayas, but from beyond the peaceful vales and rills and trout-filled rivers of Kashmir; a man from what his father called the North-west Frontier, or simply, The Frontier, as though it were the only one in the world. . . . Pathans were Pakistanis. What were Pakistanis doing here, on the Indian side of the LAC?

He reached the ridge line that fell north down that six-thousand foot slope Kit had told him of, to the Kishenganga, and worked on round to drop into the trench of the Namkula. Perhaps here he'd shake off the silent, loping pursuers; perhaps they would think he had continued on down the ridge. Perhaps . . .

Forms rose up round him and pounced. He sank to the ground under three, four men. A pair of strong hands was at his throat and he began to struggle with frantic desperation for his life. 'Quiet! Shhh!' a voice hissed in his ear. "Friends!'

He relaxed his struggle for a moment, to test the meaning of the words he thought he had heard. The grip on his throat relaxed as much. He muttered 'Who are you?'

The voice said again, 'Friends.' Rodney realized that one of the men was kneeling over him, pressing his face to his and whispering in his ear. 'Let me up,' he said.

'Quiet,' the voice reiterated, but the grip on his throat dropped away, and hands helped him up. He heard faint sounds and breathing and in the starlight made out more men coming from the direction he himself had come, to join his assailants. They were all muttering to each other in a guttural language which he did not understand; but he understood clearly that his sense of being herded was literally true; the men behind him had driven him neatly into the arms of the men waiting in the Namkula, who had obviously been expecting him to come this way, and no other. A mystery here, but no time to solve it now.

Another voice spoke close to him. 'Who are you?'

'Rodney Bateman, British subject. I was . . .'

'I'm Lieutenant Nawazish Malik, Guides. Are you hurt?'

'A bit sore . . . no, not hurt.'

157

'We have to move on now, on down this stream.'

Rodney recovered something of his wits, and said, 'What are you holding me for? You are in Indian-controlled territory...'

The lieutenant said, 'Please, no arguments, Mr. Bateman. I have my orders.' He spoke a few words in the guttural language, and unseen hands took the pack from Rodney's back. The lieutenant said, 'We will be moving fast, and you will have a hard time keeping up, even without the pack. These are Black Mountain Khattaks, and they speak only Pushtu, except that we taught them all to say Quiet, and Friend. . . . We'll start now. Keep close behind me and my orderly will be behind you.'

'With a gun in the middle of my back?' Rodney said.

'A knife,' the lieutenant whispered. 'There are Indian patrols on this mountain tonight, too, looking for you.'

They started moving. The stream's course was steep and long and their movements fast but careful. Every ten or fifteen minutes the party, which seemed to be about twelve in all, stopped and listened; but Rodney only heard the soughing of the wind in the trees, which had replaced the bare rock and short grass soon after they started – and once the cry of an owl. As they went on, hour after hour, never seeming to tire, his legs grew heavier and heavier. He gritted his teeth and forced himself on. He would not let them think of him as a weakling. He would not give them the chance to use the strange object the first man he had seen was carrying; and which now, in the starlight, he realized was a stretcher. A stretcher, he repeated to himself . . . so they had orders to bring him in, wounded or not; but not kill him. The whole affair was odd, more than odd, it was . . . He stumbled and all but fell, saving himself at the last moment by catching a tree trunk. He leaned against it, breathing heavily.

The lieutenant stopped and turned. 'Tired?'

'No,' he said, 'go on.'

'We'll rest here till dawn. The next bit's too tricky to attempt in the dark.'

'Why? Where are we going?'

'This area is not Indian-controlled, as you said. It's No Man's Land. But the Indians have been patrolling it heavily for a week now – especially tonight, when they were looking for you – and if we go on down the Namkula we are likely to run into them. So I propose to turn west across the mountain here. Then we will reach the Kishenganga below or at Dudhnial, our outpost and supporting base.'

'You're going to do that in daylight?'

'We have to. Anyway, my men are Khattaks, they can beat any Indian on a hill.'

The young man's voice was full of pride, and Rodney forbore to say what was in his mind: that the Indian Army's Gorkhas and Dogras were also mountain men. If it came to a confrontation the outcome would rest on the particular circumstances of the case, and the leadership displayed.

He found a comfortable-seeming spot and gathered pine needles to make a bed. A Khattak brought his pack and he lay down, the pack as his pillow, and waited for sleep to come. The stars blazed above: the giant firs stood like a darker army about him in the night. The air was balmy, for they must have already come down four thousand feet or more. He thought he heard the roar of the Kishenganga in its bed below, but decided that it must be his imagination, or the wind through the branches. The Khattaks were lying against trees, here and there one standing motionless, weapon at his side looking out. Sleep came.

It was near eleven o'clock in the morning, just twenty-four hours after Rodney had started up the Kharhom ridge, when the lieutenant, peering down the slope under a shading hand said triumphantly, 'We're safe! That's our supporting base.' He pointed down, across the blackened stumps of an ancient forest fire. Rodney saw an encampment, small tents by the river, men moving about. The Khattaks crowded round, laughing. They were fine looking men, mostly tall and all lean and hard. One was older, with a grizzled moustache and three chevrons on his sleeve; the rest young and, except for the long bobbed black hair, clean shaven. They wore leather sandals on their feet, with no socks, carried their ammunition in a leather cross belt with pouches, and appeared to be otherwise unencumbered except for a water bottle and a little waist bag which, as he had seen during a dawn halt, contained dates.

Rodney had asked then, 'You said you were Guides. That's a regiment, isn't it?'

The lieutenant had said, 'I'm Guides, seconded to the Indus Scouts. These are all Scouts.' His voice was full of the same pride that had filled it earlier when he spoke of his men's ability on the mountain.

Now he came up, smiling. 'We'll go down now, and you can have a real rest . . . until I have to send you on to headquarters.'

'When will that be?' Rodney asked.

'Tomorrow. Tonight, we'll eat, drink – water only for my men, they're good Muslims – but I happen to have some whisky and when Allah isn't looking, I take a little. You will like some?'

'I certainly will,' Rodney said.

'Let's go, then.'

He lay on the air mattress in the little tent, looking out at the clearing. There was the roar of water in his ears – the Kishenganga, below the bank behind his tent. There were people squatting over against the trees, smoking, passing cigarettes from hand to hand – the Khattaks. There was no table, as there had been at the subadar's village in Nepal, but there were half a dozen rough stools made from the lumber lying about the valley floor, and a couple of sawn-off tree stumps, and the lieutenant and his havildar sitting on them, talking. Beyond, cooks were bent over a fire, making *chupattis* of unleavened bread, and he smelled the savoury smell of grilling meat, where a sheep was turning on a spit.

He had crossed the mountain, and been arrested, and slept. Now . . . how had it happened? A Pakistani patrol, searching the Indian side of the Balhom Tiger for signs of the rumoured Indian build-up near Lundarwan had run into him by chance? Balls! It had been a carefully planned operation, whose only object was to capture him, Rodney Bateman. That would also explain why the Khattaks had been taught to say *Quiet* and *Friend* in English. If they were expecting to capture Indian soldiers, they would have spoken their own Urdu, for everyone in both armies understood the words *Chup raho!* and *Dost!* . . . One corollary of the facts so far was that the Pakistanis must have known his plans, in detail. But beside himself only two people had known them – Kit Sanders and Chandra Gupta. It was possible that others might have guessed or inferred or worked out for themselves the routes by which he might go, *if* they knew that he intended to reach the Kishenganga between Dudhnial and Dhakki. Still, the odds were heavy that only Kit or Chandra could have given the Pakistanis the information. And Lieutenant Nawazish had said that Indian patrols were on the mountain, too, looking for him. So the Indians knew of his plan. And still only Kit or Chandra could have told them.

There was an interesting corollary to the first set of facts: assuming that Kit or Chandra had told the Pakistanis, how had the information been passed in the time available? And, in both cases – why, what was the object?

And how did the Pakistanis know that the Indians had patrols out after him?

The lieutenant came to the tent, and peered in, kneeling on one knee. 'Had a good sleep?'

'Yes. I feel much better.'

Good. Come and have some lamb *pilao.* And that whisky I promised you. And afterwards, a Khattak dance.'

A great fire crackled and spat, its heart glowing red and gold, its ashy fringes grey, here and there brown logs dancing with flame. Rodney's head swam a little from the heat of the fire, the food with which he had hungrily stuffed himself, and the copious draughts of whisky he was sharing with Lieutenant Nawazish Malik.

The lieutenant's face was flushed and his eyes sparkling. He held up his mug and cried. 'To a Pakistani Kashmir!'

Rodney raised his mug. 'Can I say, to a Kashmiri Kashmir?'

'Good chap,' the lieutenant beamed, drinking. 'What's the difference? They're all Muslims. We'll turn the Indians out soon . . .' He lowered his voice. 'This year!'

The old havildar said a word or two in the harsh guttural language which the lieutenant had told him was Pushtu, the language of all the tribes who inhabited the mountains west of the Indus. The lieutenant said, 'My havildar understands some English, but doesn't speak it. He thinks I'm giving away military secrets . . . but what's it matter? The

Indians know we're going to get Kashmir back, when we want to, and they can't stop us . . . not next time.'

Two Khattaks stepped out, one with a small drum and the other with a wooden pipe. 'Dol and sarnai,' the lieutenant said.

The sarnai resembled a chanter, and was very like the wooden pipes Rodney had already seen and heard the length of the Himalayas, from here to Nepal and Arunachal Pradesh in the farthest east. The dancing which now began was more warlike and athletic than what he had watched in other places. The Mishmis had been athletic but there had been a sense of ritual posturing in many of their movements, and though there had been a strong rhythm it was not shaped by much grace. The Nepalese dancers had been all grace, only now and then strengthened by explosions of energy, and those minor and controlled – a Gorkha leaping up, half turning in air, crouching, leaping again, all the while his palms beating on the madal, sliding again into the rhythmic loops and swirls of the dance. The Khattaks here danced with bare daggers in their hands, and roses between their white teeth, or stuck into their bobbed hair. They danced with fierce warlike movements, full of grace and fire, repetitive but not hieratic. The music was wild and fast, rising now above the thunder of the river, and echoing back from the rock wall the farther side.

The lieutenant leaned back, clapping, and cried out in Pushtu. All the Khattacks, both those dancing and those watching, bounded to their feet and answered him with a shout, knives raised. The lieutenant shouted, 'Pakistan zindabad!', and the Khattaks answered, 'Pakistan zindabad!'

Long Live Pakistan, Rodney thought. And across the mountain enthusiastic Indian boys were shouting Bharat ki jai! It was a natural and healthy patriotism in both cases, but . . . he could not rid himself of the certainty that these shouts, too, were part of the orchestration now being written for the Himalayas.

He reached out for the whisky bottle and helped himself.

CHAPTER THIRTEEN

The major interrogating him was wearing uniform, but the pretty secretary who took down the questions and answers in shorthand was dressed in the typical narrow trousers, long *kurta* and cotton scarf of most young Pakistani women. The three of them sat in the shade of a large tree in the middle of the grass lawn outside a big official building. Rodney did not know what the building was since he had not been taken inside. He knew only that he had left the Kishenganga in an official staff car early this morning, under escort, after a warm handshake from Lieutenant Nawazish Malik and a salute from the taciturn Khattak havildar; had spent several hours coming down the big river valleys, and finally out on to the plains – it was very hot there as the sun neared the zenith of the May day; had spent an hour dozing under guard, in a small room in what 'he was told was Rawalpindi; had eaten a light lunch brought to him in the room; and now, near two-o'clock, had been brought to this place for interrogation.

The major was brusque but not personally hostile. He just spoke the way he had been taught to speak when getting intelligence information.

'You must have passed through Lundarwan before you started to cross the Balhom Tiger,' he said.

'No,' Rodney answered, 'I turned off short of that, a little beyond Darugmal on the Kharhom road.'

The major looked down at the map spread on the table beside him. 'I see. What military activity did you see at Darugmal, or on the road before you got there?'

'Nothing,' Rodney said, 'nothing at all. We didn't pass a single soldier, or convoy, or anything – once we left the main Baramula road.'

The major looked up, frowning. 'You are not telling the truth, Mr. Bateman!'

Rodney said patiently, 'I am.'

'We have definite information that there are a large number of Indian troops near and in Lundarwan. We even know who the commander is. The troops have only recently gone there, as a matter of fact. There are so many that signs of them must have been evident even in Darugmal – headquarters flags, sentries on large buildings, vehicle parks . . .'

'Nothing of the sort,' Rodney said. He realized that this was an outcome of the rumour that had been started in order to break the K.P.P. cipher. It would take the Pakistanis a litle longer to find out that there was no truth in it. He wouldn't be surprised to read of a clash between the two Air Forces over the northern part of the Vale of Kashmir any time now; that would denote that a Pakistani photo-reconnaissance mission had caused an aerial battle.

The major returned to his notes. 'Very well. . . . We have information that many Indian troops have recently been leaving Kashmir by the Banihal pass, including armoured units. Did you see any signs of that?'

Rodney shook his head. 'No.'

'What about the opposite direction, over the Zoji La toward Ladakh?'

Rodney said, 'A few days ago I was up the Sind valley, and there did seem to be a lot of activity there, as a matter of fact.'

The major said, 'Our sources tell us that that movement was false . . . the convoys would go up, come down, and go up again, to give the impression of heavy troop movements towards Ladakh when in fact there was none. Can you confirm that?'

Rodney said, 'It could be true. I can't say definitely, one way or the other.' Privately, he thought that the Pakistani intelligence jibed with what he himself had felt.

'Why did you do it?' the major snapped suddenly.

Rodney started, not exactly taken off guard but surprised by the vehemence of the question. 'Do what?' he said after a moment.

'Try to enter our territory secretly.'

He was ready now. He answered, 'I wanted to catch some trout in the lower Kishenganga. I was told that the Indian Army would not let me go downstream from Dhakki, so I went over the mountains.' He was tempted to ask the major how they knew where he was coming, but thought the man probably had no idea himself.

The major felt in the briefcase beside him on the grass,

and pulled out Rodney's musical notebook. He opened it and rifled through the pages. 'Musical annotation?' he asked inquiringly.

'Yes. I am a composer.'

The major looked carefully at a few pages. 'This could be a cipher, I suppose, the various notes representing letters or figures, depending on where they are placed?'

Rodney said, 'I have heard it can be done, but that is not a cipher. Those are my notes, musical memoranda, on themes, tunes, snatches of song I've heard. Look, these are the tunes the Khattaks were playing on that sort of pipe . . .'

'*Sarnai.*'

'. . . last night. I'll play it for you, if you like. Or you can get anyone who can sight-read music to play it, play any of them, for that matter.'

'I believe you,' the major said. 'You were very lucky to fall into the hands of our patrol when you did, you know. The Indians would have had no hesitation in shooting you. Then you would have lost your life just for a little fishing.'

'I know,' Rodney said, feigning contrition. 'It was foolish of me. I suppose I'm obstinate. I like getting my own way.'

'That can be dangerous,' the major said, half-smiling at last. 'I have orders, unless I found you had committed some crime, or are an enemy intelligence agent, to get you out of the country as soon as possible.'

'Can I go back to Kashmir? I am keeping a houseboat there all summer.'

The major said, 'Not directly. You have no Pakistani visa and the Indian officials at the border crossing might get suspicious and think you were one of *our* agents, ha ha! We will send you to Kabul. From there you can take a flight the same day to Delhi.'

'Right back over here!' Rodney murmured.

'Yes. You will leave tomorrow. . . . Do you know Mr. Ikramullah Khan?'

Rodney thought, then shook his head. The major said, 'He was in the Royal Vindhya Horse with your father during the war, but resigned immediately afterwards to enter the civil service of our country at its creation. He told me that your father was a good cricketer.'

Rodney said, 'He was. He hasn't played for some time

now, not even village cricket, but I know he was good. When he was at Sandhurst he got a trial for Surrey, and did very well. He would have played for them regularly before the war, only of course he was serving in India.'

'Quite. Mr. Ikramullah wanted me to ask whether you also played cricket.'

'A little. I played for my school, and university.'

The major said, 'Would you care to turn out for Mr. Ikramullah's side this afternoon? They are playing the Arsenal, starting at four p.m. Mr. Ikramullah himself no longer plays.'

Rodney laughed. 'You had orders not to invite me until I'd been cleared, I suppose?'

The major smiled. 'That is so. Mr. Ikramullah would not wish to have a spy in his team.'

It was hot sitting in the pavilion, the heat of the afternoon permeating under the roof into every nook and cranny of the room inside; and no breeze stirred on the open front verandah where Mr. Ikramullah's side sat in deck chairs, watching the play, fanning themselves with newspapers, now and then languidly clapping a good stroke. Rodney sat with his pads on, for two wickets were down and he was next man in. Beside him Mr. Ikramullah Khan, dressed in silk suit and Panama hat, droned on in a pleasant monotone about his days in the Royal Vindhya Horse, the British and Indian friends he had made, his two visits to England. Rodney moved his body sharply in the chair to keep himself awake. Mr. Ikramullah Khan was a dear old boy, but as good as a sleeping pill. . . .

Out on the field there was a sudden flurry of activity. The slip fielders dived this way and that, the bowler swung round fiercely on the umpire, arms raised in supplication, the wicket keeper leaped in the air, and all eleven men of the Arsenal team yelled '*Huzzat*?' at the tops of their voices. The umpire majestically raised one finger and the batsman started his walk back to the pavilion. Rodney stood up, pulling on his batting gloves.

'Good luck,' Mr. Ikramullah Khan said kindly. 'Watch that left-handed slow bowler. He mixes in a googly now and then.'

Rodney found that out with the first ball he received,

which broke savagely in from the leg, though as far as he could see it had been delivered with a spinner's standard finger action which, from a left-hander, should have made it an off break to him, a right-handed batsman. Behind him the wicket keeper muttered an Urdu imprecation as the ball missed his off stump by a coat of varnish. Rodney watched the next one on to the middle of his bat, and the next; and was heartily relieved when he reached the end of the over with only one more narrow squeak. A fast-medium right-hander was on at the other end, and he watched each delivery carefully, getting his eye in.

A few overs later he was facing the right-hander himself, and, finding that he had no other weapon but an obvious off break, the fast bowler's usual, he began to open his shoulders. The sweat ran down his face and neck and forearms, making his hands clammy inside the batting gloves; but it was much better out here than inside the stifling pavilion, even though the sun temperature must have been close to 110°. He ran a dangerous single and faced the slow bowler, hitting him so hard that he scored twenty in the over. Five minutes later, attempting a cover drive, the same man bowled him with a ball that looked like another googly, but wasn't. Thirty-three runs, in about twenty minutes – not too bad.

Mr. Ikramullah Khan received him with a smile, pushing himself up out of his chair. 'I told you he was a cunning fellow,' he said. 'Still, you have a beautiful style. I suppose your father taught you.'

He held out a glass of cold lime juice and soda, which Rodney took as soon as he had got out of his borrowed pads and turned the clammy batting gloves inside out to air. 'Phew, it feels close in here,' he said, gulping the drink.

'Let us walk outside a bit,' Mr. Ikramullah Khan said. 'Under the trees over there. That will be nice, eh?'

They strolled away together, Rodney thankful to be out of the pavilion. A few Pakistani spectators rimmed the ground, mostly apparently off-duty soldiers from the Arsenal, with a sprinkling of older men from the bazaar. Mr. Ikramullah Khan said, 'I believe you met another ex-RVH officer recently.'

Rodney said, 'I don't remember . . .?'

'Brigadier Gunturkala.'

167

Rodney said, 'Oh, yes, I'd forgotten.' He was thinking that, like the slow left-hander, Mr. Ikramullagh Khan was not as innocuous as he seemed. Ikramullah chattered on. 'Of course Gunturkala didn't join the regiment till after I'd left, but I know his name, the Officers' Association News Letter, you know. . . . What did you find in the Luhit Division of Arunachal Pradesh, Rodney?'

Rodney answered evenly, 'Nothing much. I met Tondrup . . . listened to a lot of music . . . met a couple of Chinese instructors.'

Mr. Ikramullah said, 'I can't really believe that anything serious will occur in that area, can you?'

Rodney said, 'What do you mean, serious?'

Mr. Ikramullah said patiently, 'I mean, such as a major Dafla, Mishmi, Naga and Abor rising, aided by the Chinese.'

'All that's rather out of my field,' Rodney said, 'I'm just a composer.'

'Quite so,' Mr. Ikramullah said gently, 'but you have eyes, and a brain, and you travel, you see all sorts of things. You must think, eh?'

Rodney said, 'Yes, I suppose I do . . . I agree with you.'

'Quite.' They walked on in silence. Mr. Ikramallah Khan was sixty or a year or two more; of medium height, with a very thin bony face, a high forehead; and thin grey hair. His hands were long and the fingers long. He said now, 'Did you pass through Bangladesh on your way to or from the Mishmi country?' Rodney shook his head. 'Well, I advise you to visit that country, if you are interested in the affairs of our sub-continent. Bangladesh has been in chaos since its foundation in '71. The Indians are working very hard there to foment a movement that would eventually unite the two parts of Bengal – their own State of West Bengal, and Bangladesh, which is little more than the old East Bengal. The new united Bengal would, of course, be a part of the Indian Union. They are supporting and financing groups whose task is to cause the collapse of the present government of Bangladesh. Then India would have to step in to prevent anarchy . . . and would see that people agreeable to their ideas were appointed to govern under them . . . people who could be trusted to eventually declare a reunion of Bangladesh with India. It's an old dream of

Bengali nationalists, except that to them, of course, the goal is still the independence of the united Bengal.'

'It's hard to believe,' Rodney murmured.

Mr. Ikramullah said, 'Easier than to believe in Mishmi risings, or Chinese invasions of Nepal. Those are the alleged reasons for the recent Indian troop movements.'

'I haven't heard anything about that,' Rodney said.

'Nobody has. These stories are not to dupe the public, but to mislead the lower echelons of their own government hierarchy. Under this cover plan, as we might call it, large numbers of troops are leaving, or will leave, Kashmir and our Punjab frontier – we know that this is so – and head east, ostensibly to deal with the Mishmi-Abor threat, or to protect Nepal from the Chinese. In fact they will position themselves ready to intervene in Bangladesh when the time is ripe.'

They turned at the far end of the ground, and strolled back. The trees gave some shade, but the sun beat down between the leaves and Rodney's battered old fishing hat with the flies hooked into the band hardly kept it out. Mr. Ikramullah was not perspiring and his clothes were still immaculate.

'It sounds rather far-fetched, if you don't mind my saying so,' Rodney said at last.

'Perhaps. But all our indications are that it is true. I wonder how we can make the Government of India understand what a very dangerous course they appear to have embarked on, and dissuade them from it?'

They turned again. Clapping from the pavilion signalled a boundary, and a moment later excitement on the field signalled that the boundary hitter was out. The scoreboard showed 89 – 6 – 6.

Rodney said carefully, 'It seems to me, as an outsider, that if India interfers in Bangladesh, China might decide to intervene too. She might take a Bangladesh revolutionary party under her wing, and after the collapse of the present regime, declare Bangladesh a protectorate of her own. That would give her direct access to the Indian Ocean.'

Mr. Ikramullah Khan said, 'Good heavens, what an idea! I'm quite sure you're wrong, dear boy.' His response was quick and sounded genuine; but Rodney thought that it had been rehearsed. Ikramullagh, and perhaps other

Pakistani officials in the know, were to react with just this mixture of outrage and disbelief if it were suggested to them by anyone that China might be considering intervention in Bangladesh.

Mr. Ikramullah continued, 'No, Rodney, we fear the Indians really do have a perilous venture in mind, and we do not think they will be able to control the course of events, or their allies, when it comes to the crucial points of self interest. That is why, if you have any influence with highly placed officials or politicians in India, do point out the dangers to them. . . . For instance, they are weakening their forces in the Kashmir-Ladakh areas, because they need the troops in the east. That would be dangerous, as it would give us an easier task if we decided to regain Kashmir . . . but we can spare no more troops than we already have up there, because we have had to move reserves toward our frontier with Afghanistan. Considerable unrest is brewing among our tribes there – demands for the immediate creation of a new Pushtu-speaking nation, for instance – trumped-up religious charges against us. We have evidence that these troubles are being fomented, and paid for, by Russia.'

'Rodney said, 'At the request of India, do you mean?'

Mr. Ikramullah nodded. 'Precisely! To free their hands in Bangladesh, they have asked the Russians to see that we are under continuous pressure here. But the Russians do not give anything away free. They will exact a price. What will it be? An Indian attack on Tibet to support a future offensive of their own against China along the Ussuri River? The conversion of India into a Communist state and adherence to an extended Warsaw Pact? I don't know . . . and I think the Indians don't know either, which could be much more dangerous for them as well as for us. You must realize how much India's nuclear capability threatens us . . . and how much her seizure of Sikkim and Bhutan alarms us.'

Rodney said nothing. What Mr. Ikramullah Khan had been pointing out was true enough. It was also true that just as India might have asked Russia to aid her in some venture by neutralizing Pakistan, it was also true that China might have asked Pakistan to neutralize India in some venture of *hers*. Nothing was as yet clear. He'd have to try

to sort out some of the tangles during his flights, before reporting to Ayesha; but he would definitely follow Mr.
Ikramullah's advice, and take a look at Bangladesh. It
wasn't in the Himalayas, but perhaps it was now carrying
the main theme; and if so, he'd have to find out why.

Mr. Ikramullah said, 'Dear me, three more wickets down.
We had better be getting back to the pavilion. It has been
most pleasant talking with you, Rodney. Do please give
my best regards to your father next time you write to him,
and you can always reach me care of the Club here, if you
wish.'

The F-27 climbed lazily out of Peshawar toward the west,
heaving and rolling in the heat waves. Looking down,
Rodney saw a fortress and stone walls and a winding road.
His neighbour leaned over and pointed. 'The famous
Khyber Pass.' Taking off from Rawalpindi on the first
leg of the flight the Friendship had risen, just like
this, heaving up through the dust haze into the brilliance
of the sun. And what he had seen then, looking out of a
right-hand window, was the glittering mass of Nanga
Parbat, the western anchor of the whole Himalayan range.
This below him now, where the tribes were causing trouble
for Mr. Ikramullah Khan and his superiors, was not
Himalayan. Harsh, barren and hostile though it was, it
wasn't big in the Himalayan scale – and the riddle he was
trying to solve, was. This frontier did not frighten him,
and nor did it really interest him, neither in itself nor any
role it might be playing. He heard no music in it.

He tilted back his seat and closed his eyes. Gunturkala,
Ikramullah, at the opposite ends of the sub-continent, holding different ends of the riddle, but linked by the Royal
Vindhya Horse . . . as indeed he himself was, through his
father. Would he solve the riddle more readily if the
Chinese and Russians had also served in the RVH? He
felt that the Indians and Pakistanis spoke the same
language as he did, not only literally but metaphorically.
The Chinese did not. Nor did the Russians.

The Fokker was taking his body west, but his thoughts
were flying east. Farther than Nepal, not as far as the
Mishmis in their uttermost corner of the great peninsula;
between the two, a land of waters – Bangladesh. He

171

frowned. Surely flood plains and mighty rivers could not conceal the answer to a Himalayan riddle? Well, time would tell.

The first shafts of day were shredding the night when the taxi deposited him outside the main gate of the Purana Qila. It was just after five a.m., and already he was sweating heavily. Getting on in May, the monsoon less than a month away and the heat building. Today was going to be a scorcher. He thought of the cool breeze playing over the Dal Lake, and the distant glimmer of snow, and sighed heavily.

Two horses were waiting under a big peepul, the syces standing ready to take their heads. Ayesha appeared out of the deeper shadow. She was dressed in western riding gear, white blouse, jodhpurs, and a quilted pith helmet. Rodney peered at her and started laughing. 'I'd never have recognized the *pakka memsahib*.'

She said, 'You know we can't ride properly in saris. Don't waste time, Rodney. That's your horse.'

He mounted, chuckling. Ayesha was not in a good temper this morning. She was already up, helped by a hefty push from one of the syces. She swung her pony's head round and started off at a brisk trot. The syces fell in behind, loping easily along. She called back over her shoulder, telling them to stay where they were and look after her car. The light spread fast, giving her skin a pale greenish glow.

'This is about the only part of Delhi you can ride in these days,' she said. 'And this will be built over soon. We'll keep on round the outside of the walls, then down to the railway line. . . . You got my message at the airport yesterday?'

'Obviously,' Rodney said. 'I do not normally go riding at this hour.'

She waved her crop imperiously. 'Tell me what happened.'

He told her as they slowed the horses to a walk, moved out across fields and waste land, over a railway crossing, and down a dusty lane. A steam locomotive whistled forlornly; behind them two trains passed; the sun burst through the horizon.

When he had finished she said, 'I can throw some light

172

on what happened. A message giving details of your intentions to pass over the Balhom Tiger and down to the Kishenganga went direct to Indian Army security headquarters in Kashmir through an old drop of Major Sanders. The message did not give your name, only that a foreign spy in the employment of Pakistan was escaping with vital military information. It gave your route, and said that every effort should be made to stop you, preferably by killing you, to avoid future questions or trouble with other governments. My people, including Braganza, were not informed of this till later . . . till it would have been too late, if the army had caught you. Patrols were sent out at once, but didn't find you. Now, who gave that message to the drop? It was passed to him on the telephone, by the way, a man's voice, speaking Kashmiri.'

Rodney said, 'I don't know who that was, but the only people who originally knew of my intention, and the route I was going to take were Kit Sanders and Chandra Gupta. Of course, either of them could have told any number of other people, though I asked Chandra not to tell anyone, and I don't think he would have. And Kit herself stressed that we must keep secret about it.'

Ayesha mused silently a while. The ponies' hooves clopped on a metalled road, then fell to a blanketed thudding as they rode out on to open ground. The sullen mass of the Purana Qila rose out of the pearly ground haze as they circled to the left. It was about 100°, and the sun climbing.

She said, 'The intention of whoever sent that information was to get you killed.'

'I think so.'

'Does Kit Sanders have any reason to want to kill you?'

'I didn't take her up on a proposition she made me . . . a bodily proposition. And I asked her where one could hire murderers in Srinagar. I also asked her partner Akbar Khan, later.'

Ayesha looked at him sharply. 'You think she had Mike killed?'

'It's possible. If she tried to get me killed, it becomes probable. That means that my question frightened her. . . . The original message to the drop might have been passed by Akbar Khan. He's a Kashmiri.'

173

'What about Chandra? Does he have any reason to want to kill you?'

'I can't believe it. He's a friend, a very close friend by now. It's more likely he sent the other message, the one to the Pakistanis that got me rescued by Nawazish's Khattaks before the Indian Army could run me down. It *was* a rescue, I'm beginning to be sure. Nawazish knew where to look for me, and no one in Pakistan seemed to want to hurt me.'

Ayesha said, 'How could Chandra have got any message to the Pakistanis in time? Telephones are censored, so are cables.'

'Perhaps he's a Pakistani secret agent and has his own radio transmitter, or knows where he can use one.'

'Nonsense!' she said vehemently. 'We've had him thoroughly checked, several times, because he does go into sensitive areas.'

'Is he an agent of yours, then?'

'No. When he comes back from somewhere like Nepal we always talk to him to find out if he's learned something we don't know, but that's all.'

Rodney reined in under a heavy-branched tree, took off his hat and mopped his dripping forehead. He said, 'One of those people was responsible for sending one of those messages. Logically, the other most probably sent the other. One of them at least knew about Mike Sanders' drop. I plump for Kit there – she was married to him for a long time. And I plump for Chandra as being the one who saved me.'

'You're accusing him of being a Pakistani agent, you realize that?'

'I'm not. I'm stating facts. I haven't made any deductions from them yet.'

She said, 'It has to be the other way round. . . . Chandra somehow learned about Mike's drop and sent the original message. Kit sent the second. So Kit is the Pakistani agent, or in touch with them. I'll put a good man on to a really thorough check on her.'

They rode out into the sunlight, which now struck with the force of a hammer blow across the eyes. Rodney thought that Ayesha was wrong, and being obstinate about it. Why? Perhaps Chandra was in fact an Indian agent,

174

and she couldn't bring herself to accept that he might also have some sort of arrangement with the Pakistanis. She had been in love with him once; was she still? He put the problem aside for the time being, and said, 'I saw some Pakistani troops along the Kishenganga, but they didn't seem enough to pose any threat to Kashmir from that direction.'

'I know. They're massing along the Punjab border, in the plains, ready to stab us in the back if we have trouble in the east.'

'Is it possible that you are going to create trouble in the east?'

'I suppose Ikramullah Khan told you that? It's not true.'

'Who is he?'

'Head of the security intelligence – opposite number to Bajwa. He's very clever.'

The walls of the fort loomed ahead. By now the road was thick with bicyclists pedalling to work, women carrying baskets slung from their shoulders, pedestrians hurrying along the verges, mini-cabs puttering through the bicyclists, horse-drawn carriages and an occasional rubber-tyred cart drawn by a buffalo.

She said, 'Come to my house tonight, after dinner.'

'Is that an order, madam?'

She leaned across and laid a hand on his. 'It's a hope. No shop.'

'Is your son with you?'

'Yes, but he'll be asleep, and his room's at the back. *You* know.'

He said, 'Eleven o'clock?'

The syces ran out to hold the reins and they dismounted. A circle of pipe-playing snake charmers, the cobras' heads waving rhythmically to the tunes, formed round them. Another day's work had begun at the Purana Qila.

She had the radio on softly in her drawing-room, the curtains pulled, and the only light making a pool of gold on the carpet behind the sofa. A whisky bottle, soda and glasses were set out. She was wearing an evening sari of white silk with a simple gold border.

She said, 'I've found a concert of Indian classical music, just for you.'

'Thank you,' he said. 'I know you'd prefer hard rock.'

'It's true,' she said, 'but I have to keep it secret from Bajwa. He thinks rock is unpatriotic.' She sank down on the sofa and indicated the whisky behind her. 'Help yourself. I don't want anything.'

He poured himself a small whisky and topped it with an ample quantity of cold soda. The room was air conditioned, the machine making a low purring hum under all other sounds. She had decided he should make love to her, or, in the parlance – screw her. It would be a more accurate word. He stood in front of her, and said, 'I'm going to Bangladesh.'

She frowned up at him. 'I thought we agreed – no shop.'

'I didn't agree to anything. *You* said – no shop.'

'Why do you want to go down there?'

He said, 'I think . . . feel . . . that the rhythm of the thing, what we're trying to track down, has swung there.'

'I want you to go back to Kashmir. There's plenty to be done there – help us find out more about Kit Sanders, trace what really happened to Mike – a message came in today from Braganza, by the way. It said to tell you that all the known murderers of Srinagar have alibis for the time Mike disappeared on November 10 last year.'

'They would,' Rodney said.

She went on as though he had not spoken. 'You can find out whether it was Akbar Khan who phoned that message to the drop. You can look into the KAM and the K.P.P.'

He said, 'I could, but I'm not going to. It's all secondary now. The lead theme is being played in Bangladesh. What's going on there? What might happen? What do you know?'

She stood up in her turn and walked up and down the carpet, her sari swishing at the turns. She said, 'President Reazuddin doesn't have the authority of his immediate predecessors, still less of Sheikh Mujib ur Rahman. He's weak, and indecisive. His party is split by dissension and jealousy. The country's been suffering from a food shortage for a long time and is now facing famine. Cyclones and floods and epidemics have made conditions worse. They've abolished parliamentary government and in effect made the president a dictator. Everyone's dissatisfied to some extent. Parties are being formed to overthrow the regime. Those parties are illegal.'

'Do any of these illegal parties support union with India?'

'One small one does, I believe. But we don't support it.'

'Supposing that this party, or others, do succeed in toppling the regime, or that it falls from its own troubles, is India planning to take any action?'

She turned on him. 'Why should we? Bangladesh is an independent state. You've been listening to Pakistani propaganda.'

'You have no troops down there – no more troops than usual?'

She said, 'There may be some. We have now detected considerable Chinese troop movements south from Lhasa, and Russian satellite photos have confirmed them.'

'Towards Nepal?'

'Farther east. Toward Sikkim and the passes into Bhutan.'

Rodney thought of the map. Due south of Sikkim it was only a very narrow neck of Indian territory that linked Assam, Meghalaya, and Arunachal Pradesh, isolated in the far north-east, with the rest of India. South of that narrow neck was Bangladesh, three hundred and fifty miles of it to the Indian Ocean. A Chinese attack there would cut off all the north-east and give them a good port – Chittagong – even if they did not extend their operations to West Bengal, which would give them Calcutta itself. Politically and for propaganda purposes the Chinese would say they were acting in support of Bangladesh independence . . . which would be the Indian claim, too.

He said, 'Are there any pro-Chinese movements operating in Bangladesh?'

She said, 'No. Some are anti-Indian, which means that they would call for Chinese intervention under certain circumstances. . . . The chief anti-Indian party there is a branch of the Naxalites. They believe in violence, Maoism, very dangerous people. Their head is Nazma Begum, a woman . . . but I'm not going to talk any more about this. If you feel you must go to Bangladesh, go. I'll give you the name of a drop there, another photographer. But let me warn you: keep your eyes on the job I've given you, and you've accepted. Don't go poking your nose into what *we're* doing or not doing. It's none of your business.'

177

'But it is,' Rodney said equably. He had a feeling that the evening was not going to end in love-making or even screwing, and decided he might as well probe more deeply into Ayesha's motivations while he was at it. He said, 'There are laws of action and reaction. I have to know whether what I observe is an original action by India, or China, or Russia for that matter – or a reaction to something someone else has done. I can't compose this Himalayan Concerto if I am hearing only the echoes of sounds. I have to find the original harmonies, and know who made them. So I'll go to Dacca in a day or two. Meantime, tell me more about your affair with Chandra.'

She stared at him. 'Who told you about that? Kit Sanders, I suppose. Jealous bitch!'

'It ended late in 1971 didn't it? Just in time for you to take me on. Did he end it?'

'No,' she snapped, 'I did.' She swung round. 'That's a lie, to save my self-respect. He did. Just told me it was over.'

'And you took up with me to make him jealous?'

'No. Yes. Have it any way you like. Why are you bringing this up now?'

'It might have a bearing. You're still in love with him.'

'Yes, damn you. But he doesn't give *that* for me.'

'He admires you . . . likes you.'

'What's the good of that?' She was weeping now, flung down on the sofa, her head in her hands.

'He had an affair with Kit once. Do you think Kit's still your rival?'

'Kit? Good God, no!' She looked up, her khol-rimmed eyes running black down her cheek. 'You are!'

'Me?' He laughed bitterly, for the exchange had made him jealous of Chandra. Everyone loved the bastard and everything came easy to him. If Chandra had been a composer, the Himalayan Concerto would have been written by now, the Himalayan riddle solved. 'I'm not a pansy, nor is he. There may be some other woman, though.'

She shook her head. 'No woman has anything for Chandra. They try, but it never works for long. He just doesn't need them.'

Her vulnerability moved him and he put his arm around

178

her shoulder, whispering, 'Don't cry, Ayesha.' She glared at him a moment, then grabbed a book off the table and hurled it at him as he backed off. 'Get out!' she snarled.

'Not until I get the name of the drop in Dacca.'

'Malik Shah. Mujib Avenue.'

CHAPTER FOURTEEN

The river seemed at least five miles wide, a turbid brown-green flood swirling ponderously toward the sea. Lateen-sailed boats, loaded to the gunwales with earthenware pots or sacks of grain, crabbed across from one intense green shore to the other. The sky was a coppery bowl, pressed down, exuding an invisible moisture which condensed on everything – shirts, clothes, skin, the ferry boat's wooden deck, the steel funnel and its stays, the painted railings. The fore deck was barely visible under the mass of animals and humans camped all over it under a dirty striped awning.

The young man standing beside Rodney, where he leaned over the forward rail of the upper deck, suddenly pointed and shouted, 'Look!'

There was no one else close, so Rodney asked, 'What at?'

The young man said excitedly, *'Mugger* . . . crocodile!'

Rodney followed the pointing finger and saw a long shape like a log stranded on the sandy point of a small reed-covered island in the river. Someone on the bridge had seen it too and a moment later a rifle cracked out. The 'log' slid with increasing speed toward the water and vanished with a swirl as another shot exploded, to die, echo-less, in the vast emptiness of the Padma.

'Rotten shooting,' the young man grumbled.

'I thought crocodiles were sacred,' Rodney said.

'Oh, some old-fashioned people think so,' the young man said, 'but that is all bloody nonsense. They eat the farmers' cows . . . and the farmers, and anyone else who falls into the river.' He leaned back over the rail, staring moodily down the great river. 'Are you American?' he asked after a while.

'English. Why?'

'I was going to ask, why does your country not support us more. President Reazuddin says we are too proud to ask. I say, really, he is frightened.'

'Frightened of whom . . . or what?'

'Everyone . . . China – India – Pakistan even. Only one of those is a real danger. The others are paper tigers. They are miles away. What can they do?'

'Are you afraid, yourself?'

He said, 'India means to have us. They will let us starve and everything go to bloody pot so that we will fall into their hands like a rotten apple.'

He was an excitable young man, his arms waving, his eyes popping. The blatant heat and damp had no effect on the outpouring of his energy and indignation except to make the sweat run faster down his cheeks, and drip off the end of his nose. He continued, 'I am a student, studying law at Dacca and just now returning after a visit to my uncle who is sick in Calcutta. . . . I know what is going on. Reazuddin and the Indians try to hush everything up, push it under the bed, you know? But there are underground newspapers, radios, sheets, which the political parties put out. Some are lies, but some tell the truth.'

'Do you belong to any political party yourself?' Rodney noticed the young man's sudden air of suspicion and added quickly, 'I am a musician, a composer, travelling round India gathering material for a concerto or some other piece with an Indian theme.'

'This is not India. This is Bangladesh.'

'Yes, yes. I mean Indian in the sense of pertaining to the Indian peninsula – the sub-continent, I think the geographers call it.'

The young man's animation returned. 'Jolly good! We have terrific music in Bangladesh. You must hear some.'

'I will . . .'

'Oh, my politics. I am a member of the Bangladesh Independence Party, which is legal, though Reazuddin hates us. . . . We want to remain free. We know we need help from somewhere but it is hard to know where to get it from without too many dangerous conditions tied to it, you understand? Not India, even if India was not nearly bankrupt herself. Not Russia. Or China. America perhaps, but that would upset India.' He looked round a little furtively. 'You know, there is going to be a big procession this evening, in Dacca, against the Indians. I am going home for it, a day early.'

'Will you be taking part?'

'Yes,' he said proudly, 'though Reazuddin's puppets will try to bash my head in with their *lathis. Everybody* will be there . . . us, the Farmers and Workers Progressive . . .'

'What are they?'

'Pro-Chinese Maoist. *We* think they are nearly as dangerous as the B.S.D.P. – Bangladesh Socialist Democratic Party – which is pro-Indian, but they'll be there. We can't stop them, nor can the police, and at least it'll show that we're not the only ones who fear India.'

Rodney said nothing, wondering why Ayesha had not bothered to tell him about the Farmers and Workers, and not said more about the B.S.D.P. He wondered what else she was holding back, not only about Bangladesh but about the whole range of his investigation.

He asked the young man, 'What about the Naxalites?'

The young man looked horrified. 'The Naxalites? My goodness, mister, they don't go in processions! They just appear and murder someone, or many people, like landlords, or policemen, or officials of government. They are very dangerous people . . . though sometimes I wish I could be a Naxalite. Sometimes everything seems so bad, so many people are crooked, fat, rich, selfish, and I can do nothing. . . . Then I would like to have a scythe blade in my hands.' He laughed. 'Though I know that if I did I could not cut anyone's throat with it. Perhaps nick his finger, to teach him a lesson.'

Rodney laughed too, for the young man hid an infectious gaiety under the surface of his pessimistic fury. He asked, 'Who can I talk to about Bangladesh – life, politics, music? A true Bengali.'

The young man didn't hesitate. 'Mr. Karam Ali. He is the Minister of Education in the present government, though he thinks nothing of President Reazuddin. I know, because he is a friend of my father's . . . but, he says, if good people don't try to help Reazuddin, then our fate will be left in the hands of nincompoops, criminals, and worse.'

'What could be worse?'

'Traitors,' the young man hissed. Recovering himself he pointed forward. 'There,' he said, 'just round those trees is Narayanganj. That's where the ferry steamer stops – then it's only ten miles by train to Dacca.'

182

The train was crowded, and Rodney found himself sharing his coupé with two large Bengalis whom he did not remember seeing on the long ferry journey down from Goalundo Ghat. 'You are come to see our beautiful capital city?' one of them asked heartily, popping a piece of betel nut into his wide mouth. He and his companion were squatting up barefoot on the seat, their *dhotis* tucked round their behinds, their chests covered by thin shirts, their slippers on the floor, where over the years errant gobs of betel juice had patched the composition with red stains.

'Yes,' he said, adding, 'I am a musician.'

'Ah. Our music is very different from yours,' one said. 'Older.'

'I have studied it,' Rodney said. The train ground to a halt, the locomotive whistling plaintively. The heat shimmered over the fields, not a thing moved, the carriage emanated heat of its own as well as taking it in from the sun now directly overhead.

'I hear there is going to be an anti-Indian procession this evening in Dacca,' Rodney said, intending to get some opinions out of these prosperous-looking men.

One spat betel juice accurately out of the open window. 'Rotters!' he said, 'India is our only hope. All this agitation is the work of agitators, no less.' His English grew more picturesque as his ire increased. 'Dashed Chinese scoundrels disguised secretly among us, spreading lies. Our Bangladesh will be province of China, they mean. You'll see!'

The other merchant said more equably, 'I do not know whether Chinese really wish to take us over, but it is certain that many people want our country to fall apart, so that they can pick up the pieces.'

'The Naxalites?' Rodney asked.

The other's thin eyebrows rose. 'Yes, indeed. And the Farmers and Workers Progressive Party. Our only hope is India. Only they can save us from falling into anarchy . . . anarchy first, then Communism, like China. No democracy. No freedom. No private property.' He shuddered, and like his friend, began chewing betel nut.

The engine whistled triumphantly and the train again jerked into motion. Rodney thought longingly of the Eastern Star Hotel, a cold bath, and sleep in an air-conditioned room.

The sun had set and the street lights shone out on the steamy streets. The pavements felt hot to his feet, even through his shoes. He wondered, not for the first time, how the many barefooted Bengalis could stand the hot stone and concrete. The big stores and shops, which would normally have still been open at this hour, were closed, and most of the plate-glass windows had been boarded up. He noted that the boarding was properly fitted to the windows, and firmly fastened with bars and locks. That implied that the protection had been necessary before, and that the shopowners thought it would be again.

Punctually at seven o'clock, standing on the steps of a bank building on the west side of a tree-lined avenue, he saw a flurry of movement far down to his right. Soon banners began to appear, flowing steadily into the avenue as various groups poured out from the side streets where they had been gathering. All cars had long since vanished and the groups coagulated without hindrance into a straggling procession and surged northward. There were men and women, mostly young, and dressed in everything from a simple *longyi* to coats and suits. They held aloft banners and huge photographs – of Chairman Mao, and of other figures whom Rodney did not recognize. There were several caricatures of the Indian Prime Minister shown reaching out with a ghoulish expression to tug Bangladesh out of its place on the map and into her own arms, where a gagged baby entitled 'Bhutan' already rested; behind was the gleam of bayonets.

Everyone was shouting. Trying to pick out words in the confusion Rodney thought they were all yelling, in Bengali, variations of a single theme – *India, hands off Bangladesh!* It was hard to count the number of people in the procession as a whole, but he thought it must be close to two thousand. Among the generally disorganized marchers were groups of ten to fifteen men armed with short clubs – the strong-arm men or 'guards' of the parties. The police, whom he had seen in considerable numbers earlier, had now vanished, like the motor traffic. The authorities had obviously decided that this demonstration should be left alone.

Rodney stepped down from his perch, pushed through the spectators ahead of him, and joined the procession, walking beside a pretty girl wearing shirt and slacks and waving a banner inscribed with another version of the Indian Prime Minister's seizure of Bangladesh. He fell into step beside her and, raising his voice to be heard, said, 'Do you really think the Indians are going to try to take Bangladesh?'

She nodded energetically and shouted, 'Yes! First cause chaos, then march in to restore order!'

'Do you think you can stop them, if Bangladesh really does collapse economically or politically? Don't you think that most Bengalis would welcome them, in that case?'

She said, 'Chairman Mao can stop them. We have his promise that . . .'

Without warning another stream of people surged out of a side street and into the procession. A squad of the club-wielding party guards turned to face them, but the new-comers were armed, too. The yelling of slogans turned to cries and screams as fighting became general. He saw daggers drawn from concealment, bicycle chains whirling, clubs rising and falling. The spectators who had been lining the avenue began to disperse. He thought he saw men running round the side of the bank building on whose steps he had originally taken up his position.

A man, stumbling backwards, hand to his head, sent the pretty girl sprawling. Rodney knelt, and helped her up. She was dazed and trembling, but not really hurt. He picked up her banner and walked to the side of the avenue, hold-ing her round the shoulders, and saying 'You'll be all right – but you should go home now.'

After a few minutes she shook the tears from her eyes, took back her banner, murmured, 'Thank you,' and walked away. Rodney surveyed the avenue. The front of the original procession was a long way off, probably unaware of what had happened at the back. The fighting was lessening, but half a dozen men and a couple of women were sitting or lying in the street, casualties of the violence. Smoke was pouring from the windows of the bank, and here, very close to it, he could distinctly smell kerosene. Police had suddenly appeared, two of them pointing at the smoke. Whistles shrilled. Rodney walked away, for the area would soon be full of fire engines, and in the mean-time he looked suspicious, almost the only person there, close to the bank.

Not quite the only one . . . a few men were bending over the dead and wounded in the street, more police were arriving, people were gathering in side streets; and, across the avenue, standing under a tree, a single man watched the burning bank much as he himself had been doing a few moments earlier. He walked over, studying the man as he did . . . medium height, hair long and dank under a round black cotton cap, dark pock-marked skin. The tree shaded him from the brightness of the streetlight, and Rodney knew he had seen him before, in another dim, unlighted place. Then he remembered – Jansingh Gharti, the mysterious buyer, the man he had talked to in the Kosi Palace Hotel in Kathmandu.

Jansingh watched the bank, his mouth downturned at the corners, his expression sullen. Already some glass was exploding, and tongues of flame licked out twenty feet from the windows. Somewhere to the east sirens wailed. Policemen were trying to break down the bank's front door.

Rodney stopped a few yards beyond Jansingh, thinking. He had given some information in Kathmandu. It could have been genuine, or it could have been part of the process of orchestration to which he felt that everyone was being subjected. He might have a valid reason for being in Dacca – as buyer for an import-export house he could have a valid reason for being almost anywhere; but it was odd that when the rhythm of the music was swinging towards Bangladesh, it should have swung him there, too – unless he was part of the music.

He made up his mind, put his right hand in his jacket pocket and walked up behind the man under the tree. 'Jansingh,' he said quietly in Hindi, 'don't turn round. I want to talk to you.'

Jansingh stiffened but did not turn. Rodney said, 'I have a pistol in my pocket and no one will hear a shot, the fire's too loud. . . . Walk away down the street. I shall be close on your left, and little behind. We will be talking.'

Jansingh moved away from the tree, and walked north. He did not look round, but said, 'Who are you?'

'You don't recognize me? I spoke with you in the Kosi Palace Hotel in Kathmandu in April about going to Lhasa to study music.'

'I remember. What do you want?'

186

'Information. Better than you gave me in Kathmandu . . . or shall I say not so one-sided? Here, turn right here.'

The roar of the fire at the bank had lessened but fire engines were passing, sirens screaming. The side street was long, the people in it were gathered in knots looking toward the red glare of the fire and the winking of fire engine and police lights reflected in the night sky. Rodney saw a parked car ahead and said, 'Try the door of that car.' The door opened and he said, 'Get in!'

Jansingh looked full at him then, his skin drawn taut with fear. Rodney said, 'I won't harm you, if you tell me what I want to know. Get over.' He followed in, Jansingh sitting behind the steering wheel on the right, Rodney beside him in the passenger's seat. The car was old and small and the interior smelled of sweat and over-ripe mangoes.

Rodney said, 'You are an agent. Who pays you?'

Jansingh did not answer for a while, then, 'So are you. Your name is Bateman, I remember. I am asking the same question.'

'Perhaps, but you do not have a gun to enforce an answer. You work for the Chinese, don't you?'

Jansingh said nothing and Rodney suddenly guessed that he was worried about his job. He said, 'I shall not tell your employers – Kapur & Katari, isn't it? You're too small to bother with, and anyway, it will help us to leave you where we can get at you again if we want to. How much do the Chinese pay you? It must be a lot to make you betray your country.'

Jansingh burst out vehemently, 'India is not my country! Nepal is. They paid me very little, because I was doing it for love . . . until now.'

'Love? It's a strange way to show your love for Nepal, isn't it? To help the Chinese do – whatever they are intending to do to it. What is that, by the way?'

'Nothing,' Jansingh said angrily, '*This* is where the Chinese will do it. All their promises to me are so many lies – worth nothing.'

Rodney thought back: Jansingh was a Gharti; perhaps a Shivbhagti Gharti. The 'feel' of him was quite different here than it had been in Kathmandu; then he had been

187

acting a part, and doing it well. Here and now he was surly, frustrated, angry.

He said, 'Your father was a slave?'

Jansingh started and said, 'How did you . . .? Not my father, my grandfather. He died, whipped to death. My father died when I was ten . . . starved to death. He could not find work, because he was Shivbghagti. My mother died of fever, my brothers and sister of fever, hunger, accidents. None of the rich in Nepal would help them.'

'And you decided to change the system . . . help make a revolution?'

'That's what the Chinese promised,' Jansingh said sullenly. 'They were going to overthrow the King and all the rich, like the Indians turned out the Ranas. They were going to make Communism there, everyone equal. I would give my life for that to avenge my grandfather, my father – all that my family has suffered.'

'And now they're not going to do it?'

Jansingh shook his head. 'I learned three, four days ago. All the work we were doing in Nepal, all preparations there, is pretence, to fool the Indians, see? *This* is what the Chinese are wanting—' he took his right hand off the steering wheel and waved it out at the street, its darkness puncuated by areas of light from street lamps – 'Bangladesh, not Nepal.'

Rodney sat back, thinking. The swell of the music was stronger, louder, more dominant – Bangladesh, Bangladesh . . . the eighth largest nation in the world, population seventy-nine million, excellent ports on the Bay of Bengal . . . a prize worth having and, once established, a centre from which India could be converted, or subverted.

But . . . Nepal had been 'betrayed' for the sake of what the Chinese leader regarded as a greater object in Bangladesh. Was it not possible, perhaps probable, that Bangladesh, in its turn, might be 'betrayed' for some prize which he valued still higher?

Jansingh said, 'I came here to see if it is true, about the Chinese plans for Bangladesh. I am sure now that it is.'

'What are you going to do?'

'Sell what I know,' he said. 'Names, times, dates, codes.'

'Do you know those for Bangladesh?'

'No, only for Nepal.'

'What does *Azad Shadhinata* mean?'

'I don't know. Something to do with freedom, I suppose. Why?'

'Is it a code word, or code name?'

'I don't know. It was never given to me. . . . Do you think the Indians will pay me much?'

'Not much, but something. . . . Tell me one thing. If you were acting for the Chinese, why did you tell me in Kathmandu that they were massing troops along the Nepal border? You believed that to be true, then, didn't you?'

Jansingh made a weary gesture. 'Yes. *I* would have lied to you. But my orders were very clear – to say what I did say, no more, no less, to anyone who enquired. I asked my superior why, and he said it was not my business to ask questions. But later he said it was a matter of timing. The liberation of Nepal was set for October, after the monsoon, so I thought that the Chinese wanted the Indians to get nervous and suspicious in May and June, then find they had been wrong, and not believe the same evidence when it came up again in October. I was a fool . . . I will go to Calcutta tomorrow.'

'Don't. Go to Delhi. Can you remember a telephone number?'

'Yes. I have much practice.'

'Six-three-one-zero-three-seven. Say you want to talk about the Himalayan Concerto.'

'Six-three-one-zero-three-seven. I want to talk about the Himalayan Concerto . . . What is a concerto?'

'A piece of music, usually for a solo instrument accompained by a full orchestra.'

He sat in a cheap restaurant, sweet tea in the cup beside him, a bowl of rice and vegetables in front of him. From a radio set on a shelf in the corner a female singer crooned a Bengali love song, accompanied by a drone and drums. He knew the song: Indreni had sung it to him when he was learning Bengali, and falling in love with her. It carried memories of her father's gracious house in Calcutta, the Hooghly flowing in the distance between other houses . . .

Jansingh would report to Ayesha, he was sure: but he must make a report himself. His musical notebook was

189

open on the table beside him and he began to jot down thoughts . . . the procession; the irruption of the Maoists; the fire at the bank which was certainly arson. Apparently it was an Indian-owned bank, the Bank of Kashi. It was rumoured that an Indian clerk working in the bank had been burned to death. It was said that the Indian Embassy had been attacked, that the police had opened fire on the crowd somewhere . . . but everyone had a different story as to where, and who had been fired on . . . rumour, rumour, rumour!

Assume that the main Chinese objective was Bangladesh, and everything else was deception. That music swelled loud and dominant, but it jarred. The notes were there, but they did not make the right harmonies. The counterpoint theme had become the point, the main theme; and it did not make musical sense.

Time to return to his hotel, and try to get some sleep; early in the morning, send off his report to Ayesha, and then find some more people to talk to.

He walked back to the hotel through empty streets, the smell of burning acrid in the night. At the door of the hotel, his mind still far away, he heard a familiar voice greet him. 'Rodney! I didn't expect to find you here . . . but I did, really, because wherever one of us goes, the other seems to follow, eh?'

It was Chandra Gupta, smiling, cool-seeming in the heat. Rodney said, 'The *Independent* sent you down?'

Chandra nodded. 'Rumours of trouble brewing, big trouble for Reazuddin. Look out for yourself if you're going to stay long. I'm off. There's a night ferry to Goalundo Ghat which I've got to catch. More snooping in the boondocks, as Kit would call them – the *mofussil* to your grandfather.'

Rodney said, 'Chandra, you know that trip I made, to the Kishenganga?'

'Yes. I want to hear about it some day, but not now, Geminus, I've got to . . .'

Rodney insisted. 'The Indian Army had been tipped off. There were patrols on the Balhom Tiger, trying to kill me.'

'Good God!'

'Fortunately a Pakistani patrol got me first, by chance. But who could have tipped off the Indians?'

190

'I'm damned if I know. It wasn't me. And now . . . taxi! taxi!' – and then in Bengali – 'Ferry dock at Narayanganj! Of course I can afford to pay, man. Look at that! How many *taka* do you want? Bye, bye, Geminus. See you in the mountains next time, eh?'

CHAPTER FIFTEEN

Mr. Karam Ali, the Minister of Education, was in his mid-forties, wore western clothes and horn-rimmed glasses and had the lawyer's sober, somewhat portentous manner. He must have had plenty to worry about in the state of his country, but seemed willing to talk to Rodney for as long as he liked. After some generalities and discussing the young student of the Goalundo ferry, Rodney asked, 'What about the rioting last night, sir, and the burning of the bank?'

Karam Ali spread his hands. 'Well planned, well executed. I expect the President has already received the official complaint from Delhi. If not, he soon will.'

'The paper this morning says that the Farmers and Workers Progressive Party was responsible for the riot . . . but they weren't! They were moving along quite peacefully when they were attacked from a side street. That was what caused the riot. I was there.'

'That newspaper is owned by interests friendly to the Indian connection,' Mr. Karam Ali said wearily. 'The same report claims that the Farmers and Workers set fire to the bank and killed the Indian clerk inside. Someone did. He wasn't burned to death, but stabbed.'

'I don't know who did that,' Rodney said. 'I saw men breaking in, but they weren't wearing any distinguishing badges. You don't think it was the Farmers and Workers?'

Mr. Karam Ali said, 'I have heard from a man who is close to that party – a man who has never told me false yet – that the Party vehemently denies having started the fire. They say the Socialist Democratic Party did it.'

'But they're pro-India!'

'Precisely. Someone has burned down Indian-owned property, yes. Another way of looking at it is that someone has provided India with one more excuse for interfering in our affairs. . . . You took the train from Delhi to Calcutta, I think you said? Did you notice anything out of the ordinary along the route?'

Rodney thought back. 'I saw a big airfield that seemed

over-full of jet fighters . . . and we passed a train of flat cars that were loaded with things covered by tarpaulins, but one of the tarpaulins had blown loose, revealing a heavy tank. But the Indians seem to be very paranoiac at the moment, with fear that the Chinese are going to try something in Nepal, or Sikkim. The eastward movement of fighters and tanks could be a precaution against that.'

'It could be,' Mr. Karam Ali said, 'but that paranoia, as you call it, could also be a cloak to cover other intentions – against us. Time is short for Bangladesh, I believe, Mr. Bateman, and . . .'

'How short?' Rodney interjected.

Karam Ali looked at him steadily. 'The monsoon is in full strength by mid-June. Before then.'

Twenty-eighth of May today, Rodney thought – say about eighteen days in hand. The Concerto was taking shape, but was there time?

He said, 'Could you put me in touch with the leader of the Farmers and Workers, sir?'

'Qureshi? We are enemies, of course. If they get into power, mine will be one of the first heads to fall, unless I am knifed in the street even earlier . . . but he trusts me in an oblique sort of way. He has been in hiding for nearly six months now, but he has let me know where he is, so that I can pass messages to him. The President will probably want me to get a message to him when he has studied the protest from Delhi.'

He took a sheet of paper and began to sketch on it. 'This is your hotel, the Eastern Star. This is Jinnah Street – we left that name after our revolution . . . here by the old Hindu temple it becomes unpaved. That's two miles from the Eastern Star. Then there are three crossroads; take the fourth, to the right. It has no name but there is a three-storey brick house on the corner. In a few yards it ceases to be a street and becomes a country lane, winding past the outskirts of the city through paddy and jute fields. Here are two shacks set among four palm trees. Qureshi will be in one or the other. Say you are from me. Now, have a good look, and memorize this, because in a minute I shall burn it.'

Rodney concentrated on the sketch, then said, 'All right, I've got it.'

Karam Ali set a match to the paper and ground up the ash in an ash tray. 'You will undertake not to reveal his whereabouts to the police, of course,' he said.

'Certainly, sir. I hope I can learn something from him – if he'll talk at all.'

'Oh, he'll talk, talk the hind leg off a donkey, especially to a journalist. You are a journalist, I suppose?'

'Not exactly,' Rodney said.

'Ah, an author. I hope events will not overtake your book. . . . You might care to know, when you talk to other ministers, which of them inclines to one side and which to the other, or shall I say another, for there are many sides to our problems.'

'It would be very useful, sir.'

'Well, most of them try, at least, to think only of what is best for Bangladesh. One or two honestly believe, for instance, that an Indian connection of some kind would be best for us. But some ministers, in my opinion, do not think of our interests, but of others'. Madame Bilkis Khatun is pro-Chinese, and a secret member of the Farmers and Workers. She is Minister without Portfolio. My colleague Chaudhri is the unacknowledged leader of the Bangladesh Socialist Democratic Party, which wants union with India. And the President has given him the portfolio best fitted to help him achieve his aim. He is Minister of Security.'

Rodney rose to leave, the Minister following suit. Rodney said, 'Thank you very much for your patience, and help, sir. . . . By the way, have you ever heard the phrase *Azad Shadhinata*?'

The Minister said, '*Shadhinata Dibash*, March the twenty-sixth, is our Bangladesh Independence Day . . . but I've never heard the word "shadhinata" coupled with "azad". That's an Urdu word meaning free . . . Sayyid Ghulam Mohammed's party up in Kashmir is called the Kashmir Azad Movement, isn't it?'

'Yes,' Rodney said, 'It's almost as if someone was trying to couple Bangladesh with Kashmir in some way.'

The artificial pond, of the sort called in India a tank, was about two hundred yards square, considerably larger than most village tanks. The earth retaining walls were six feet high and very wide, and on them stood a few shade trees,

for the tank was centuries old. Rodney stood under one of
the trees, his line stretched out taut into the brown-green
water, the float submerged. Perhaps the fish was another
catla, of which he had already caught two, of about ten
pounds each, on a bait of dough pellets. But this one was
fighting more energetically than the others, and it was
probably also bigger. His leader was light, and he had to
play the fish as carefully as any salmon or *mahseer*. After
ten minutes of give and take he eased it to the edge of
the tank. One of the dozen naked small boys and girls who
had been sitting with him ever since he arrived ran down
and took it off the hook. Rodney looked at it – about
twenty pounds, carp-shaped, silver tinged with bronze.

'What is it?' he asked the small boys.

'*Mirga, mirga,*' the eldest cried impatiently.

Rodney made a gesture of throwing it back into the
water, but the children all screamed and he gave it to the
smallest and dirtiest girl, who could barely carry it. 'Now
run along,' he said, waving in dismissal. The children went
away without argument. They must be tired, he thought,
and it was damned hot, even this late in the afternoon.

He took the Thermos from his haversack, drank some
cold lime juice, then felt in his pocket for the letter he had
picked up at the drop this morning. He opened it and re-
read it carefully.

*Further confirmation of Chinese troop concentrations
south of Lhasa. Ground reconnaissance being carried out
on Sikkim front and along parts of the Bhutan frontier.
Mishmi area – patrol activity.* No word of what India herself was doing to counter all this, though he needed to
know.

*Kashmir: body of known professional assassin Lall Khan
found in Jhelum below Srinagar, stabbed to death. Corpse
clothed, in inner pocket found Rolex gold chronometer
watch valued Rs.4000. Serial number erased. Lall Khan's
known associates being closely interrogated.*

*Also Kashmir: increase in K.P.P. radio activity and
passage of illegal arms into Kashmir. All being allowed in
without hindrance, but recipients being noted.*

*Report progress, if any, in your task in Bangladesh. Re-
peat, keep out of involvement with Bangladesh politics.*

He tore the letter into quarters, took out a match, burned the quarters and scattered the crushed ash on the surface of the tank. After he had filled and lighted his pipe he re-baited the hook, adjusted the leader so that the hook would be about two inches above the floor of the tank, and cast it out. Then he sat down.

Expensive gold watch . . . serial number erased; therefore stolen. Might have belonged to anyone. Might have been stolen anywhere, come to that. But most probably in Kashmir. Loss so valuable would have been reported to the police . . . unless the owner was killed in the theft. Or vanished. The Kashmir police would have checked their files on reports of stolen watches. But they should go to Mike Sanders' insurance agents – hadn't Kit said some time that it was Cox's and King's – and ask to inspect the insurance policies of the late Major Mike Sanders. He suspected that a gold Rolex chronometer, with serial number, would be listed among the individually insured items.

As for the K.P.P. . . . the activity meant nothing, at least nothing definite. It probably pointed to forthcoming action, but then so did everything else he had come across. What it did not prove, though they would think so up in Kashmir, was that Kashmir was to be the focus of the forthcoming events. At the moment, all indications pointed to Bengal, especially the eastern part of it, which had become Bangladesh, as being the focus. He didn't like it, but that was the fact. At present.

He glanced at his watch. He'd stay another half hour and then walk back into the city. Everyone who saw him, clearly had thought him mad, striding out after lunch in shirt sleeves, wearing his old fishing hat, and carrying his haversack and telescopic rod; but he had felt the need for exercise, and solitude, and had walked north-west on Jinnah Street until it died away in cart tracks and little villages on a branch of the Buriganga. And on the way he had noted the old Hindu temple and the tall brick house where the turn-off led to Qureshi's hiding place.

He reeled in, moved along the bank, and cast again, the float splashing heavily on to the water. He sat down, waiting . . . waiting . . . The Girwan torrent appeared in place of the murky tank; the air was fresh and sharp, instead of as from a damp oven; the trees were pines and towering deodars and the horizon was jagged with ice peaks. Surely the heart of the music *must* be there – not necessarily in Kashmir, but somewhere in the Himalayas, not in these waterlogged delta lands of lower Bengal? And there, in the white water of the Girwan he had rescued Chandra Gupta from death. He glanced at the ring on his finger, and closed his eyes. Now, at a distance of several weeks, the event became diamond sharp in his mind, far clearer than at the time or since. There *had* been men running away into the woods across the stream. He *had* interrupted a murder, not come across an accident. Chandra had said nothing of the attempt. It might be something personal, but on balance it was much more likely to be political. Ayesha had assured him that Chandra was not an Indian agent. She might be lying, to protect him, but if she was not, for whom was Chandra acting? And who would have tried to kill him?

Coming farther forward in time, he was sure that it was Kit Sanders, using information she had somehow got from her husband, who had tried to get the Indian Army to kill him on his trip across the Balhom Tiger. And therefore it was Chandra who had got the Pakistanis to save him. *And who therefore had means of secret communication with the Pakistani Government.*

Assume that Chandra was a Pakistani agent. Every normal political factor would have led him to ensure that he, Rodney, learned nothing during his Balhom-Kishenganga jaunt; the best way to ensure that would be to see that he was shot. Therefore, thinking politically, Chandra would have sent a message similar to Kit's – *There's a dangerous spy loose* – *get him*! . . . Unless he *wanted* Rodney to see what there was to see on the Kishenganga; because it was a false trail . . . Or unless he was not acting politically, but personally, trying to save a friend's life.

He must talk to him, soon, and as he had said, in the mountains. For personal reasons, because they were Gemini, yesterday's meeting had emphasized the loneliness he felt away from him. And Chandra heard the music more clearly than Rodney did. Why? Because he was playing in the orchestra? Or at least turning the pages for the musicians?

CHAPTER SIXTEEN

The trilling of the telephone almost in his ear brought him awake with a jerk. He fumbled for the light switch and turned it on as the ringing continued. His watch read a few minutes after twelve, midnight. The air conditioning must have failed, for his pyjamas were wet with sweat and he seemed to be breathing invisible steam rather than air.

'Rodney Bateman here,' he said into the phone.

The voice at the other end was urgent. 'The police are coming for you.'

'What on earth for?' he asked, still not fully alert.

'You were carrying an inflammatory banner in the procession, and took part in the rioting, is the accusation. If you get out at once you should be able to reach the British High Commission in time. Then you'd be safe. I can warn them you're coming.'

He recognized the voice now – Karam Ali, the Minister of Education. He thought quickly, by now shocked into full wakefulness. 'Who's responsible for this?' he asked.

'You can guess. . . . You haven't much time, you know.'

Rodney thought, it must be Chaudhri, the pro-Indian Minister of Security who was behind this; and he probably just wanted to get him out of Bangladesh during the critical days to come. He doubted if the hunt for him would extend beyond Dacca. Into the telephone he said, 'Don't call the High Commission. I'll get away somehow.'

'Don't resist arrest,' the voice urged, 'they'd welcome an excuse to shoot. Good luck.'

Rodney hung up, leaped out of bed and dressed as quickly as he could. He stuffed his wallet, notebook and passport into his pockets, took a long swig of cold water from the jug and ran out and down the stairs, bareheaded and empty-handed. At the foot of the stairs he broke into a walk. The lobby was empty, the night clerk working at a ledger behind his glass screen. The clerk glanced up, said nothing, and looked down again. Rodney went out through the double glass front door. A car was parked just down the street and he began to turn round to go in the opposite direction, thinking he saw people inside; but there was no one, only a trick of the reflections from the street lamps. He walked back toward the car, glanced in, and saw the keys hanging in the ignition. He stepped in. It was a Fiat, so probably belonged to some foreigner. He turned the key and the engine kicked into life. He drove off, heading east.

Looking in the rear view mirror he did not think he was being followed. There was quite a bit of traffic – more than he had expected at this hour – taxis, private cars, a few bicycles. There was no one on duty under any of the awnings set up at intersections to protect the traffic police from the thrusts of the daytime sun, and the cars hooted and honked at each other, but did not bother to reduce speed or take any other precautions. He did not know this part of the city but drove on toward the east, having a hazy feeling that his eventual route of escape must be in the direction that he did know, towards the country where he had been fishing, north and west.

What on earth did they mean about him carrying an inflammatory banner? Ah, the girl who had been knocked down. He had picked up her banner. Chaudhri must have had agents and secret watchers stationed along the route of the procession. But this accusation of the banner was only an excuse, obviously. Why was he to be arrested? Why was he thought important enought to bother with? What had he learned or done? He had no leisure for extended speculation now. Later, later . . . now his only task was to get away. It was good of Karam Ali to suggest that he take sanctuary in the British High Commission, but even if the High Commissioner was willing to accept him, he would be shut in until Chaudhri undertook not to arrest him, and that would not be until after the coup or plot or whatever had come off: then he and his ideas or information would no longer matter.

He was almost out in the country now, a good three miles from the centre of Dacca. There were few lights in the houses, the street lamps had ended far back, and the houses, ramshackle and crumbling in the hazy moonlight were separated by open spaces, dung heaps, sleeping cows, and scattered palm trees.

He slowed, drove the car on to one of these open spaces and stopped it under a banyan tree. An old man wrapped in a white sheet rose in surprise from where he had been sleeping on a stone platform round the base of the tree, and a pariah dog scuttled off, barking tremendously.

Rodney said, 'Go back to sleep, grandfather'; carefully shut the car door, leaving the key in the ignition, and walked away, still toward the east. The old man was watching him as he looked back over his shoulder from twenty paces off; soon after that the light was not strong enough to show any details, nor could he see the car or the banyan tree. After five more minutes he turned north, and walked across a field, and along an alley with hovels on one side and open fields on the other. Twenty minutes later again he turned west, being now certain that he was nearly a mile to the north of the route he had taken coming east in the car. He walked steadily, his light-weight jacket unbuttoned, his arms swinging.

His mind had settled, without any act of decision on his part that he could remember, where he was going; he was going to join Qureshi, the head of the Farmers and Workers Progressive Party, in his hiding-place. If the pro-Indian faction was after him, the pro-Chinese faction would probably help him. He thought it likely, with the country in turmoil and the police obviously suffering from the general malaise, that he would not then find it difficult to move about the country, or get out of it, especially with the aid of Qureshi's people.

Qureshi's hiding place was beyond the north-western outskirts of the city, about four miles away from where he now was. If he kept on in his present direction, but taking what opportunities presented themselves to work farther north, he would hit Jinnah Street well below the old Hindu temple and the brick building that marked the turn-off to Qureshi's two huts.

He had re-entered the zone lighted by street lights, and almost at once he saw something gleaming under one of them. He paused, easing back against the wall of a house. It was uncomfortably hot to his back and he stood a fraction away from it, still staring. He made out two policemen leaning against the lamp post, brass-bound *lathis* on their shoulders. It was the brass tip of one of the *lathis* that had caught the light. He edged back pace by pace along the house wall, and at the next street turned north.

By now the police would certainly have got to the hotel and learned of his escape. The theft of the car might also have been reported. The police he had seen did not seem to have walkie talkies, but it was important that no one should see him heading west.

The moon was partly obscured and it was nearly two o'clock. The street lights had again ended and he was in a thick semi-darkness, what light there was apparently coming from star glow behind the murky sky, and haphazard yellow lights and flames from burning rubbish. There was a vile smell, or rather, a mixture of several smells – human ordure predominating, then stagnant water, rotting vegetation, drift of burning cowdung. He was crossing an open space, eyes of red and green watching him from ahead and to the side, metal gleaming. The open space was not empty, but covered with straw and grass hovels, bodies sleeping out in the open by the banks of deep ditches filled with stinking black water and dead dogs.

Something brushed past his side, white teeth snapped as he jumped, eyes flashed . . . a dog or a jackal. He kicked out at it, but missed. The animal backed off, its teeth bared, and began to howl, pointing its sharp muzzle to the dark sky, an insanely mournful wail pulsing from its throat. One by one a dozen others took up the howling, at first from all over the waste land and under the red and green eyes and in the darkness beyond, but quickly concentrating, gathering towards him.

He shivered in fear as the jackals massed round the one which had tried to bite him. Jackals were not supposed to attack human beings, unless they were rabid. Were all these rabid? Even the first one had not seemed mad, only hungry and cunning. They were swirling round now, moving this way and that, three or four slinking off, half trotting, to get behind him. The howling had changed to a high shrilling cackle. He hurried on westward. The jackals followed. He walked faster, his eyes desperately searching the gloom for a weapon. Two jackals leaped at his ankles from behind, and as he kicked, jumped back again, making no real attempt to reach him . . . they mean to wear me out, he thought: they will keep on attacking, jumping in, and I will keep on lashing out at them, and missing, and the sweat will keep running into my eyes, and . . .

He nearly tripped over a steel rail, then another . . . close together, metre-gauge: the red and green eyes shone toward him, painting the rails with red and green bars; dark shapes of wagons stood on a siding. The far side of the rails a pair of handlebars broken off a bicycle lay by the near edge of the ballast. He stopped and grabbed them up. They made an awkward weapon, but better than nothing – much better, he saw as he took an unexpected swing at a jackal sidling up to him, and hit it on the head. The animal's cackling broke into an agonized howl . . . but the pack came on, more distant now, and suddenly silent, as though at the wave of an invisible conductor. Rodney's nerve broke and he began to run. The jackals closed fast, rushing, still silent but he heard their panting and the lapping tongues of the closest. Something tripped him, hitting him across the shin, and he fell headlong, ploughing into the filth, unmindful of his pain or the dirt smearing him, blind with panic. He turned and swung even before he had finished falling. One of the jackals was close and by chance he hit it precisely in one eye with the end of the handlebar. The jackal sprang back, screaming, scratching frantically at its dangling eyeball with one front paw. The other jackals closed in on it with the same un-rehearsed unison with which they had fallen silent a few minutes before.

Rodney scrambled to his feet and backed away, the handlebar ready. He felt his nerve and commonsense flow-ing back into him as palpably as though they had been draughts of a cold drink. He turned and moved faster, but looking carefully for his footing all the time. The wounded jackal's sobbing howl was cut off with a choke. He heard worrying and snarling, and walked faster. The smells now were ordinary smells of city slums at night, not pleasant but not the infamous foulness of the area he had just escaped from. The darkness seemed to thicken, and when he looked back he could see nothing of the hovels or the pack of jackals, or even the railway signal lights; nor could he hear anything.

Soon after three o'clock he reached a road running north and south across his path which he recognized as the con-tinuation of Jinnah Street. Yesterday he had walked up here with his fishing rod. The village with its big tank was two miles north – to his right. The turning to Qureshi's hideout was about half that distance. The road was black-topped here, with wide dusty verges and a line of heavy trees on the east side. He turned up it, heading north in the dust under the trees.

He realized that the bicycle handlebars still swung from his hand as he walked. He thought, I'll keep them, God knows what else I might run into. But surely there'd be no more jackals, and if anyone saw him swinging them, he'd remember . . . best to get rid of them.

As he was making up his mind, a figure stepped out from behind a tree a few paces in front of him and said in Bengali, 'Stop! Give me your money.'

He turned, clutching the handlebars. Another man was closing up behind him, having appeared from a tree he had passed. They were ordinary *goondas*, waiting for the chance to steal five or ten rupees from peasants going home from the city after perhaps visiting a brothel or a session in an opium house. He ran at the first man, swinging the handlebars. He hit him on the shoulder as the man ducked, knocking a big knife, like a kitchen carving knife, from his hand. Rodney ran past. He could not see their faces well in the darkness under the trees, but he had an impression that neither was particularly big, nor young. He ought to be able to outrun them; and they probably would not chase him very far, thinking it better to go back and wait for easier game.

Hearing nothing as he ran he glanced back over his shoulder. No sign of them . . . he eased his pace a fraction, then again pushed his muscles to their full effort, for he had caught the glint of metal down the road and heard a whirring of tyres. Then he saw them, on bicycles, gaining on him fast. He swore. They must have realized that he was a European, and expected that he would have a lot of money on him. And he did – at least five hundred Bangladesh *taka*, as well as Indian rupees.

It was no good trying to run away from men on bicycles down a flat road. He could try the open country, but in the darkness he would not have much chance there; and first he'd have to get across a deep wide ditch, which had been flooded yesterday afternoon, and presumably still was, that ran parallel with the road.

The *goondas* were level with him now, one holding back, the other pedalling faster to get ahead. He made a sharp turn to his right, behind a tree, and allowed the front man a full two seconds to turn after him; then he ran out at him. Again, the surprise of the attack served him. The flailing handlebars hit the man in the face, sweeping him out of the saddle onto the ground. He screamed in pain as Rodney turned on the other, but the second man wrenched his bicycle round and pedalled off fast, body bent low as a bow. Rodney turned back, to find the man he had hit on his knees, pulling out a knife from the belt where he had tucked it. Rodney hit him on the head as hard as he could with the handlebars, and as he fell stamped on his knife hand with his heavy shoes. As the *goonda* screamed again, Rodney grabbed the knife, threw away the handlebars, picked up the fallen bike, jumped on it, and pedalled on up the dark road.

He slowed a little to gain his breath. The Hindu temple was not far ahead. The *goondas* wouldn't bother him any more, but he'd certainly keep the knife. Here was the ruined wall of the Hindu temple, the broken dome, the fallen stones, the entwining fig tree. A little farther, here was the tall brick house. He turned right along deeply worn ruts on the earth road. It became next to impossible to stay on the bicycle for he could not go fast enough to maintain the bike's equilibrium; even if the surface had allowed it, he could not see where he was going. After running into a broken cart wheel that had been abandoned in the middle of the lane, he dismounted, threw the bicycle into the scrubby bushes at the side of the path and continued on foot. He was among tall crops, probably jute. He'd been going twenty minutes since the brick house. The clouds had lifted and the stars were visible, lightly hazed over, the heat oppressive. He was dripping with sweat, his clothes wet and filthy where dust had caked on to them. The knife gleamed in his hand.

Palm trees stirred in feathery silhouette against the stars . . . two . . . three . . . ah, there was the fourth lower and to one side . . . and two huts, no light in either . . .

Cold sharp metal pricked the back of his neck and a voice said in Bengali, 'Don't move. Drop that knife.'

204

Rodney did so, then froze, answering in the same language, 'I mean no harm.' A light shone in his face and was instantly extinguished. Another voice said, 'A European. This must be the man.'

The first man said in halting English, 'Who are you? Why you coming here?'

Rodney answered, also in English, 'My name is Rodney Bateman. I am English. The police are trying to arrest me and I have come to ask Mr. Qureshi to hide me.'

'Who sending you, how you knowing?'

'Karam Ali, the Minister of Education, told me where Mr. Qureshi could be reached. Originally, I wanted to talk to him about his party and the future of Bangladesh. Now, I just want to be hidden, and later helped to escape from Bangladesh.'

Neither of the others spoke for some time. The point of the knife pressed more sharply into Rodney's flesh. He could be killed in a moment, without a sound, and in this city of dreadful night, full of such terrors, who would ever know – or care? He tensed himself for a desperation lunge.

He felt hands patting him; then, 'Go forward to that hut. I am just behind you . . . up three steps. Stop there.'

He was facing a low door; the man came up level with him and knocked quietly, a rhythmic pattern, then spoke close to the hinge in Bengali. 'Rahim, the man who attacked the watchers on the road has come here. He's an Englishman, and is asking for help. He says Karam Ali told him where to come.'

A deep voice from inside said, 'Bring him in.'

The man with the knife said in English, 'Open door. Go in.'

Rodney went in carefully, for it was quite dark. The new voice spoke in English, 'Wait. Shut the door.' A match scratched and soon a pale yellow glow spread from a hurricane lantern set on the earth floor of the hut, shining up under the thin lips, deep socketed eyes and domed forehead of the man squatting behind it. He was short and barrel-chested, about thirty-five, with a golden brown skin. The hut contained no chairs or tables, only a heap of white ash in one corner and a few pots nearby; but there was a red book set on a precariously pinned shelf on the opposite wall. Overhead the lantern light struggled and died in a maze of small beams, dirty straw, empty sacks, cobwebs, and dust; there were no windows.

The squatting man was looking at him with a neutral expression, waiting. He wasn't committing himself to hostility or friendship, yet. Rodney said, 'Mr. Qureshi?'

The man said 'Yes. Who are you?' The voice was deep and resonant in the barrel chest. Rodney took out his passport and gave it to Qureshi, repeating the story he had told outside. When he had heard him out, Qureshi spoke a word to the man with the knife, who went out, leaving them alone.

Qureshi said, 'Why do the police want to arrest you?'

Rodney said, 'Carrying an inflammatory banner is the official reason, but there must be something else.'

'Did you take part in the procession?'

'In a way. It was well organized . . . by your people, I presume.' Qureshi nodded. Rodney continued, 'And the attack on it was well organized, too.'

'So I have been told. And the burning of the Bank of Kashi. We did not do that – Chaudhri's secret agents did. So why is he after you?'

Rodney said, 'I don't know. I'm not a journalist, I'm a musician, a composer . . . but in order to experience India, the sub-continent, deeply – which I must do before I can create music about it – I must go beneath the surface. I must see not only what appears to be happening, but what is really happening, deep down, and what is being felt. If you know about, oh, for instance, polyandry in the Himalayas, the hill folk dances take on a different tone. . . . I have been all over the north of India – Kashmir, Nepal, Darjeeling, as far east as the Mishmis, looking, listening, leaning, making notes. Here . . .'

He handed his notebook to Qureshi, who flipped over a few pages and gave it back. His tone carried a hint of respect in it, as he said, 'You're not just another western tourist, at least. Why did you attack my outposts on the road?'

'The two men? I didn't attack them. They tried to rob me.'

Qureshi said, 'I don't pay them. They have to live somehow. The police must come that way to get me, and there's a direct path here from their post. The one you didn't

nearly kill was here ten minutes before you arrived . . .'
He stroked his chin thoughtfully. 'You may be a spy, but
if so, I don't know for whom.'

Rodney said nothing: denials would carry no weight
against concrete evidence, but there was no evidence,
merely some mysteries – which were as mystifying to him
as to Qureshi.

'What do you want me to do?' Qureshi said.

'Can you help me get out of Bangladesh?'

Qureshi considered. 'Probably. You are much more con-
spicuous than a Bengali would be, of course, and we can't
use any of our normal methods, but I think we can do it.
It'll cost you money, for our funds.'

'I have five hundred odd *taka* on me. And rupees, which
I'll need when I get to India.'

'We'll leave you what you need,' Qureshi said, half
smiling. 'Did anyone see you coming this way, do you
think?'

'I don't think so. I hope the police think I escaped eastward.'

Qureshi stretched. 'Good. You should sleep an hour or
so now. Be prepared to move quickly if I wake you. I will
think what is best to do.'

He leaned back against the mud wall of the hut, closed
his eyes and in a moment seemed to be asleep. Rodney
examined the hut more carefully. It was an amazingly
barren headquarters for the leader of an important political
party; not that man could not exist in even more meagre
surroundings, but Qureshi did far more than exist; from
here he was in touch with his lieutenants all over Bangladesh, from here he organized processions, and protests,
negotiated with other parties. The red book caught his eye
and he craned forward to look at its title.

Qureshi's deep voice said, *'The Thoughts of Chairman
Mao.* Now blow out the lantern and sleep.'

The hand on his shoulder shook firmly but gently. The
voice whispered, 'Wake up! The police are coming.'

Rodney sat up with a jerk. Thin light pervaded the room
and he saw that the door was open. Outside, it was the
first minute of another hot clammy day. His shirt was
damp, his mouth furry and his eyes gummed. He took up

207

his rolled jacket and slipped into it. 'This way,' Qureshi said, and led out of the door. Two men standing there eyed Rodney stolidly as Qureshi whispered something to them. They nodded and ran off up the lane. Another man appeared out of the crops that surrounded the little enclave of two huts and four palm trees, and went into the hut which Rodney and Qureshi had just left.

Qureshi hurried across the beaten earth towards the farthest, smallest palm tree. Near the base there was the wooden winch of a wellhead, and a simple brick platform surrounding it. Qureshi leaned out, took hold of the rope dangling into the well and, sliding down it, disappeared from sight. Peering into the gloom Rodney could see him for about fifteen feet, then he vanished. He stared down, shading his eyes; not a sign of him, only a faint shimmer reflected from the surface of the water still farther down.

A thin voice echoed up. 'Come on. Hurry!'

Rodney seized the rope and slid carefully down. After a few seconds a hand caught him round the waist and Qureshi's voice muttered close to his ear, 'Swing . . . reach out your foot . . . this one.' Qureshi pulled hard as Rodney stretched out his foot. It touched a flat surface and he stepped off, abandoning the rope. He was in a small alcove, like a vertical coffin space, about six and a half feet high and four feet square, cut out of the earth wall. The air was much cooler than on the surface above. The light falling down the well shaft became partly obscured and the rope began to pass, water splashing, and Qureshi murmured, 'It looks more natural if the bucket's up on top, and the rope hanging short.'

They waited. After ten minutes they heard voices. The voices went farther; five minutes later, came close. Again the light pouring down the shaft was partly obscured Rodney began to feel an impulse to sneeze, for the comparative chill of the air in the shaft had brought him to the edge of shivering. He gasped and opened his mouth, and tried to yawn. Qureshi must have understood the danger, for he seized his nose and pressed his nostrils sharply together, at the same time grabbing him by the throat and squeezing.

Voices in Bengali echoed clearly down the shaft. A woman whined. 'There's no one there, great presence'; a man said, 'I don't see any Englishman climbing down into a well, do you?'; and again the woman, 'It's dangerous, presence . . . twice we have had to repair it, for the earth crumbles and falls in.'

The voices moved away, but not before Rodney had heard the man say, 'All right. If you see anyone who seems to be hiding, you . . .' The voice faded into silence.

The sneeze would not be suppressed and came out, but was mostly smothered with Qureshi's hand. They waited tensely, the two pressed together into the tiny space. Rodney muttered, 'They're only after me. If they come back, I'll call up and surrender.'

'Quiet!' Qureshi snarled into his ear.

Ten minutes passed, then twenty. The bucket came down, then the rope. The woman called down, 'Ready?'

'Wait. You go first. Hold tight. They'll pull you up.' Rodney stepped out, grabbed the rope with arms and twined legs, and at once began to rise up the shaft. A minute later he was on the brick platform; soon Qureshi joined him and the two men and a woman already there.

Qureshi said, 'When did you last have anything to eat?'

Rodney thought and answered, 'Dinner at the hotel last night. I didn't eat very much. It was too hot.'

Qureshi said, 'We'll give you something now. I don't know when you'll be eating again.'

He led into the same hovel where they had been before, throwing some words over his shoulder to the others. The woman went toward the other hut, the men turned back along the lane through the crops and soon disappeared.

Inside the hut Qureshi squatted against the wall and Rodney sat on the floor facing him. Qureshi said, 'Give me your wallet.'

Rodney handed it over. Qureshi looked through it, took some money, and gave it back. 'I've left you a hundred *taka* and a hundred rupees. Some of my people will come for you this evening. You will be in India two days later. Then . . .'

He paused, cocking an ear; then got up and went to the door, which was half open. Rodney, peering through behind him, saw one of the men who had gone off along the lane returning at a jog trot. He ran up the steps and whispered in Qureshi's ear so that Rodney could not hear.

Qureshi turned to him. 'Visitors. I know who they are but it's best if they do not see you.'

'Back into the well?'

'Not this time. Up into the roof here.'

He pointed, and snapped an order to the other man. 'Climb on to his back, Bateman. Catch that beam. Swing yourself up.'

Rodney swung up a leg and scrambled in among the beams. Dust and bat droppings were everywhere. From below Qureshi called, 'To your right! There's a thatched section. You won't be seen there.' He crawled crouching on all fours from one beam to another. The corner opposite the one where the ashes of the fire were had been strengthened by putting a layer of thatch on top of the lower beams, making a little house within a house. Someone seemed to have slept here at some time, he thought. Perhaps it was often in use as a hiding place, though it offered no real protection and would easily be discovered by a determined searcher.

He lay down, hoping the dust that tickled his nostrils would not make him sneeze again, and made himself as comfortable as he could.

Five minutes later the door of the hut was opened wide and two men and a woman came in, escorted by one of Qureshi's personal guards.

The woman spoke first, in Bengali. 'Greetings, comrade Qureshi.'

'Greetings, comrade Nazma,' Qureshi answered. Rodney thought he spoke with some reserve, though he could not see his face. 'It is always good to see you, though I was not expecting you for another week or two.'

The woman said, 'We were told to come at once. *Azad Shadhinata* is to be June the thirteenth. The monsoon will not be at full strength, but it will have started. The date serves. You may expect our allies from the north to reach Dacca by the end of June. So we will have to operate without support for seventeen days. The Messenger has already told our people in West Bengal and Bihar.'

CHAPTER SEVENTEEN

Trying to catch all the rapid Bengali, it took Rodney a few seconds to understand what he had heard. A date had been given: June 13. But for what? . . . *Azad Shadhinata*! He gave a start that caused the twisted beams under him to creak and would have given him away if the woman below had not raised her voice. Today was . . . May 29. He listened tensely as she spoke: 'We have five thousand comrades ready, all with some sort of firearm. They have been smuggled to us through our comrades in Bihar who get them from Nepal.'

'From Jansingh Gharti?' Qureshi asked, and the woman said, 'Yes.'

'He supplies my people, too. He must be getting fat.' They didn't know Jansingh had defected, Rodney thought. That could be useful.

'He does good work,' the woman said briefly. 'How many can you muster?'

'Throughout Bangladesh, twenty thousand,' Qureshi said, 'Here in Dacca, about five thousand, many of them students. Only about half have firearms . . . but we will get more from the police. We are strong enough to raid police barracks, and many police are secretly on our side.'

'Good. But do not act before *Azad Shadhinata*.'

'Do you have written instructions on this?' Qureshi asked, his voice polite. 'I am sure you are correct, but as you know, our parties are independent of each other.'

The woman said 'Here.' Peering down Rodney saw her give Qureshi a small wellfolded piece of paper. No one spoke while Qureshi unfolded it and read the contents, which must have been brief for in a few seconds he produced a match, and set fire to the paper, saying, 'That seems to be in order.'

'Have you remembered the new wave-lengths that will go into effect two days before *Azad Shadhinata*?'

'I have. How did this reach you?'

'The Messenger. I and the comrade chairman of our party in Bihar met him in Ranchi a few days ago. We spent many hours going over our plans . . . and it was at that time that he wrote out those instructions I have just given you.'

Qureshi said, 'Do you know why I was not invited to that meeting in Ranchi?'

The woman said, 'I don't know, comrade. Perhaps our friends do not consider your party hard enough – you have made some public references to the need to avoid violence, you know. Or perhaps he considered it too dangerous for you to make the journey, or for him to come to you. The activities of Indian secret agents have much increased in the last month.'

Qureshi said, 'Are there any real changes in the plan anywhere? There is none in mine.'

The woman said, 'The role of the Bihar Naxalites has been changed. They must not now try to prevent the Indian Army moving eastward into Bangladesh if they should try to. Nor must they make any moves aimed at driving them back westward.'

'Why not?' Qureshi asked. 'The only time I discussed the operations with the Messenger he told me that it was everyone's task – including the Bihar Naxalites' – to do all we could to prevent Indian forces moving into Bangladesh, thus making it easier for our friends from the north.'

The woman said, 'When was that? About six months ago? Ah . . . The plan at that time was for our friends to occupy Bangladesh as quickly as possible, and then defy the Indians to turn them out. It was thought that in such circumstances India would have to accept the conditions as it found them. That has been changed. The plan now is to lure as many Indian forces as possible into Bangladesh, and see that they do not, cannot, move back to the west. The aim is not to keep them *out* of Bangladesh, but to destroy them *in* Bangladesh. If our friends can annihilate a sizable proportion of the Indian Army here, everything will be much easier afterwards, not only in our own political negotiations – we think there will be very little resistance to the secession of West Bengal to join our new country – but it will be easier for Pakistan to improve its situation, by force or negotiation, along India's western border.'

Qureshi said slowly, 'I see. . . . My party has no wish to

help Pakistan . . . not after what their armies did to us Bengalis when they ruled here, but I can see that it will be an unavoidable by-product of our actions. This is a better plan than the original one. On *Azad Shadhinata* we all rise and cause the collapse of the government, and of all law, order, and communication. The pro-Indians will force Reazuddin to ask for Indian help. They come in; we see that they don't get out. The Naxalites in Bihar destroy their communications back to the west. Our friends come down from the north, and destroy them. Very good!'

Silence. A match scratched. The acrid smell of *bidi* tobacco smoke drifted up through the rafters and Rodney covered his mouth with his hand. He had heard the core of a large-scale plan that would, if it were successful, unite Bangladesh and West Bengal into a new Bengali-speaking nation, a puppet of Red China, with either Qureshi or this Nazma Begum as its nominal head, probably the latter.

Another of Qureshi's guards came in. Qureshi was talking to the Naxalite men. 'I have an Englishman here, whom I have undertaken to get out of Bangladesh. The police are after him, on behalf of Chaudhri. Perhaps you can help me.'

'Where is he?' a man asked.

'Above us, in the rafters.'

The woman's voice was sharp. 'Has he heard what we have been saying?'

Qureshi said, 'I suppose so, but he doesn't speak Bengali, so . . .'

The guard said, 'Rahim, you are wrong. He speaks Bengali. When I first challenged him last night, it was in our language, and he answered me in the same.'

Rodney felt the stab of urgency as though it had been a literal thrust from a knife into his flesh. He sprang down between the beams, landing on top of one of the Naxalites. Swinging a fist at the guard, who fell over with total astonishment registered like a photographic negative on his face, he burst through the door and, running as fast as he could, dived into the tall crops and kept running.

Behind him he heard shouted commands whose meaning he could not make out, and they did not last long. Qureshi has to be careful, he thought, since he too is in hiding. But this would be resolved one way or another very soon. The

213

village where he had fished was about two miles straight ahead of him through the crops. The jute was high enough to hide him, except that his progress would be given away, especially if one of his pursuers climbed a tree, by the waving of the plants where he parted them. To his right he saw a patch of jungle and headed for it. A drainage ditch appeared, and he jumped with all his might, trying to cross it; but it was too wide and he landed a foot short in noisome black ooze, splashing himself from head to toe; then scrambled up the bank, his hands full of earth and grass. It must be about seven in the morning, another in the succession of pre-monsoon days, building up to an insufferable heat and humidity. The sweat poured out of him and his throat was dry and aching.

Just before he reached the jungle patch he crossed a narrow path in the jute, and there two men wearing only loin cloths leaped on him from hiding and bore him to the ground. A knife gleamed and a voice snarled, 'Still! Quiet!'

He relaxed. Qureshi's people knew the country and he didn't. They had guessed that the jungle patch would seem to offer a special haven for him; and they'd got there before him.

Now what would they do? Stab him and leave him? It depended. He was half a mile from Qureshi's huts, perhaps more. The villagers here probably did not know about Qureshi, so would report a body found in their fields, especially the body of an Englishman obviously murdered, to protect themselves from a charge that they had done it.

'Into the jungle!' one of the men muttered. 'Crawl!'

They crawled forward on hands and knees. This is to keep our heads below the crop level, Rodney thought; they suspect or know, that there are some peasants about who could see them. So perhaps they'd hold him in the jungle patch until dark, then take him back to Qureshi for orders as to his disposal . . . or perhaps they'd kill him in the jungle. There was certainly no chance now that Qureshi would let him go, knowing what he knew. And little that he would risk keeping him alive. The only question for Qureshi was how to kill him without causing investigations, and perhaps the loss of his hiding place and what amounted to a fixed headquarters. It would be important not to jeopardize that at this stage in their plans.

Walking upright now, they penetrated farther into the jungle, Rodney in the centre, Qureshi's men in front and behind. In the treetops a troop of small brown monkeys swung and gibbered, and the man behind Rodney swore under his breath. Parrots screamed and a kite took off with a sough of wings and a thin high whistle.

They stopped, as near as Rodney could guess, in the centre of the jungle patch, which was about four hundred yards square. The men began to jabber in low voices, in a dialect of which he could not make out more than a word or two; but one of the words he did understand was 'kill', and another was 'rope'. They were debating whether to kill him or tie him up; and they didn't have any rope except what they could manufacture from the vines trailing from the trees. It was now or never for in a few moments they'd have made up their minds. He'd either be securely tied ... or dead.

He raised his right foot in its stout shoe and jammed it down on the kneecape of the guard nearest him, driving the kneecap down on to the man's shin. The man fell sideways, screaming, and Rodney dived for the knife that had fallen from his hand. He got it just as the second man came at him, knife cocked, blade up. in an upward slashing movement. Rodney kicked at it hard, missed the blade but hit the man's wrist. He did not drop the knife but spun round, half right, his hand down, offering a perfect target for another kick. Rodney stepped in and kicked as hard as he could into the testicles. The guard doubled over. Rodney snatched the knife from his hand, and ran westward, bent low, forcing his way through the undergrowth. For a few seconds he could hear the moans of the two men, but then the denseness of the jungle foliage smothered them.

At the edge of the jungle he paused a moment. West and north lay the tank and the village, but there was no escape there. There was the road, too, but it ended just beyond the village at a ferry over the river. Eastward there would be a main road out of Dacca, and a railway. In his flight through the city – how long ago? only last night? – he had crossed a railway. It was there that he had fought off the jackal pack, beside the lines, watched by the red and green

215

eyes of signal lights. The metals had been running due north.

He glanced over his clothes. He looked pretty bad. It couldn't be helped. He ran his fingers through his hair, brushed the worst of the dirt off his clothes, and set off walking east, along lanes where he could find them, breaking into crops sometimes to avoid a hut. Several times he passed men and women working in their fields, but they barely looked up; it was eight o'clock, the sun climbing, the temperature nearly 100° and the humidity close to a hundred per cent. No one cared for anything except his own immediate business.

An hour later he came to the line. A pair of steel ribbons arrowed into the heat haze to the north, coming up seemingly over the curve of the earth from the south, tall jute crops dense on both sides. As he had remembered, it was metre-gauge, and God knows where it would take him – if he could catch a train. He began walking north, away from Dacca, and keeping off the railway right of way, for he suspected that train crews would report him at their next stop if they thought he might be trespassing on their precious preserve.

A mile on, when he was beginning to feel that he would faint if he could not find shade and a cool place to rest, he saw buildings ahead, and by the line the distinctive masts of semaphore signals: a station. He paused, leaning against the bole of a thorn tree, and considered. The country was in disorder. The station staff had more to do than report to the police the presence of unkempt-looking foreigners. But it would be wise not to hang around the station premises too long. That would give the station-master time to think things over, to wonder, to speculate. He had no idea when a northbound train would come. Suppose it were six hours? He'd just have to be patient. His best plan was to hide up in the crops, but closer to the station, and wait. When he heard or saw a passenger train coming up from Dacca, northbound, he would walk to the station and board the train with or wihout a ticket. Where should he buy a ticket to? He had no idea where the line led . . .

Then what? Suppose the train reached the border between Bangladesh and India. There would be inspection of

216

passports. He had his, but perhaps Chaudhri had notified frontier posts everywhere to arrest him. Perhaps not, as his aim appeared to be to get him out of Bangladesh.

He remembered something he had seen on a train, in 1971, in south India. A young American hippie had been sitting in a crowded third class carriage when a murmuring and chattering among the Indian passengers indicated that the ticket inspector was coming through the train. The hippie had watched his neighbour, squatting on the bench beside him, produce a ticket, and had said in English, 'Man, I don't have a ticket,' and opened his palm in the universal gesture. 'I don't have it.'

The people round him had instantly understood; and as instantly formed themselves into a band of conspirators against their natural enemies – authority, the government, in this instance embodied in the ticket inspector. They had seized the hippie and rolled him under the bench among peanut shells, betel juice stains, spilled milk and curry, and old leaves that had been used as plates. On both sides of him they had put bedding rolls, battered cardboard cases, and sacks of vegetables, all the while gesticulating, moving about, waving their arms and their own tickets and generally obstructing the inspector's view of the carriage. He had suspected nothing; and when the coast was clear, the beaming Indians had pulled the hippie out of his hiding place, with expressions that clearly said without words, 'We showed the bastard that time, eh?'

Not knowing where the line led, nor whether a frontier would be crossed, he decided not to buy a ticket. He could do no better than pray for a crowded train and the same help that had been given to the hippie in Madras. He moved forward until he was barely two hundred yards from the station. The jute was tall and thick. He crept in, lay down, pulled some leaves to cover his head, and dozed off.

The hours crawled by, in sleeping, waking, yawning. The heat was fierce, his stomach empty, his throat dry. No one passed.

Then, near half past three a man and a woman passed, walking along the tracks toward the station. Soon, another pair. Rodney crept closer and watched. People were gathering at the station. Ten or fifteen were already there, and obviously waiting for a train. Now, would it be going away from Dacca, or back towards it?

At four o'clock a diesel horn blared from the south. Rodney sighed with relief and then gathered himself for action. The train was coming, rumbling up between the crops. He rose from his hiding place and walked along the edge of the fields to the station. The train passed him when he still had fifty yards to go. There were no gates, no doors. He walked onto the gritty, levelled surface of the 'platform', climbed up the steps of a third-class carriage near the back of the train, and squeezed inside seconds before the diesel horns blared again and, with a jerk, the train started off. He didn't think any railway official had even seen him. Nor, yet, had his fellow passengers realized that there was anything strange about him; for they were all too busy settling themselves and their bags and boxes for the journey and squeezing themselves into the available places, which were too few by a quarter for everyone to be able to sit down.

What now, he thought? He had enough money to buy a ticket from the conductor-guard, once he found out where the train was going to; but would it be wise to reveal himself so close to Dacca? It was not very likely that the police had already alerted all railway employees to be on the lookout for a runaway Englishman, but it was possible, and the information that he carried was so important that he decided not to risk it.

He turned to the grizzled old man squeezed into a corner by the window next to him, and said in Bengali. 'Where is this train going, uncle?' The old man looked at him in amazement, not understanding the plain Bengali because he could not believe the white man in the dirty jacket could have spoken that language. Rodney repeated his question, and the old man exclaimed, 'But you're speaking Bengali!'

'Yes, uncle, I am. Where is this train going, please?'

'Akhaura, and then to Silchar,' the old man said. 'It gets there near midday tomorrow.'

'Silchar is in Bangladesh?'

'Of course it is not! You are a Bengali and you don't . . .?'

'I am not a Bengali,' Rodney interrupted. 'I am an Englishman. My wife is a Bengali – from Calcutta.'

'Ah, an Indian . . . The train crosses our frontier at Karimganj and goes on to Silchar.'

Rodney decided to try to get to Silchar. He knew the name and had an idea it was a fairly big place. As for crossing the frontier, he had to do it somewhere, and it was probable that in that remote north-east corner of Bangladesh the authorities would have had no message about him. To the old man he said, 'I have no money and consequently no ticket, uncle, yet I want to go to Silchar.'

The old man's expression changed, 'You, an Englishman with a coat and trousers, and no money! What misfortunes must have befallen you! Don't worry, we have ways of arranging these things. I don't suppose you've ever travelled third class before?'

'No,' Rodney said untruthfully.

'Well, we'll look after you. No Englishman is going to say a Bengali from Bangladesh failed him in hospitality. Here, squeeze in here. When the inspector comes – under the seat with you, understand?'

Half the carriage had heard the conversation and knew the situation by now, and Rodney was surrounded by smiling gesticulating men and women, all pointing under the seat and saying in various accents, 'When the inspector comes, under there, understand . . . understand . . . understand?'

'Yes,' Rodney said, 'I understand. Thank you, thank you.'

He lay on his stomach under the wooden slatted bench, face down, his nose an inch from the floor. It smelled of dust and feet and the contents of the cardboard carton that had been pushed in after him, which seemed to be tobacco leaves or the leaves of some other plant used as a drug. He felt that time had run backward, and he was not Rodney Bateman, but an anonymous American hippie. This was his third time under the seat, and it was near dawn. The old man had gone, but handed the care of him over to another. The passengers were mainly Khasi now. He recognized the placid beauty of the women from his time in

219

Tinsukia, which couldn't be too far north of where he was now.

He had learned a lot these past few days, so much that he had made a quantum leap toward a statement of the mystery which Ayesha had asked him to isolate. The Chinese had gained control over certain underground parties in this area, and had supplied them with arms through Jansingh Gharti, the traveller of Kathmandu. Jansingh presumably had also been supplying similar groups in Nepal, for the prime force which moved him was not money but desire to see the overthrow of the regime in that country. Now he had defected, feeling betrayed; but by now everyone had the arms they needed.

Another man, called the Messenger, brought instructions to the underground groups from somewhere, perhaps the Chinese Embassy in Delhi; and the Messenger had passed through Ranchi, the capital of Bihar, a few days ago. He was considerably higher in the chain of command than Jansingh, for he not only passed orders, but he co-ordinated. Where was he now? Calcutta perhaps?

The Chinese plan seemed quite clear: on June 13, *Azad Shadhinata*, the underground groups in Bangladesh would rise. The government would fall, law and order vanish. The Indian Army would move in, ostensibly to restore order and protect Indian lives and property, which would be specially attacked. Once they were in, the undergrounds would rise behind them in Bihar and West Bengal: the Chinese would come south from Tibet in force, probably through Sikkim, and destroy them *in situ*. Pakistan might be able to take advantage of this situation by retaking Kashmir twelve hundred miles to the north-west.

Now, the Indians . . . what was their plan, for he was morally certain that they were not merely reacting to the Chinese, but had intentions of their own. . . . Well, Chaudhri and his pro-Indian underground inside Bangladesh would originally have precisely the same objectives as the pro-Chinese parties: they would rise to overthrow the present government and destroy law and order. Then they'd call for India to step in to protect Indian lives and property. But there the scenarios changed, for India obviously did not know, or did not believe, that the Chinese were going to attack in force; they believed that they would be able to

220

set up a puppet government, and probably run a plebiscite which would show that the people of Bangladesh wanted to be reunited with the other Bengali speakers in West Bengal, and rejoin the Indian Union. All these moves and actions had to be done in secrecy and with speed, not to give time to Pakistan to act in the north-west before the bulk of the Indian Army was back there, and not to allow protests in the United Nations or from China to gather force.

He shook his head, trying to blot out the picture he saw, of war and famine and pestilence in this land, already on the verge of universal starvation: then remembered where he was and lay very still.

Who was the Messenger? He gave out instructions from the top, he settled disputes, he made alterations at the local level without having to consult back to his own superiors. Who fitted all the requirements, who was always where the music was strongest, like a conductor facing that part of his orchestra then carrying the theme? He could not continue his logical questioning, feeling a peculiar sense of vertigo and near nausea.

'You can come out now,' his new friend said. 'The inspector's gone.'

Rodney struggled out and sat down. His friend said, 'You'd better try to sleep. You look very tired, and it's still nearly two hours to Karimganj, and two more to Silchar.'

'Is there much formality at the border? I have a passport, but, if it can be avoided . . .'

He didn't have to finish his sentence, for his friend exclaimed, 'They try, the police, the officials, but there are only two or three of them, and all they do is look in at the train windows and everyone waves a piece of paper, or cries that he is only visiting his aunt at the first town in India. What can they do? We will get you back under the seat. There will be no trouble.'

Rodney sighed with relief. His sigh turned into a deep yawn, as he said, 'Is there an airport in Silchar?'

'Yes,' the man said, eyebrows raised.

'Does it have flights to Calcutta or anywhere out of Bangladesh?'

'I think there is a flight to Calcutta every day, but . . . *I* could not afford such a luxury.'

Rodney said, 'My wife has rich relatives there. They will be glad to pay my fare, to get rid of me.'

His friend said, 'Ah, it is like that, is it? Marriage is not always a bed of jasmine flowers, is it?'

'No, it is not,' Rodney said.

He closed his eyes. He could use his credit card to pay his air fare. Pray there was a plane he could get onto. Send a telegram to Ayesha's cover address, if he had time, incorporating the word '*Azad*' and the date . . . something like 'Azad due to arrive June 13 will confirm in writing'; then to Calcutta. Indian security paranoia being what it was he'd certainly have to show his passport to board the plane, but the Indians had nothing against him. He went to sleep.

He awoke, a thought as strong and unpleasant as a nightmare seething in his brain – that the most significant fact about his visit to the Mishmis was that Chandra Gupta had also been there. The Mishmis had only played a little tune, a curlicue designed to distract attention from the main theme – but in that moment it had been important, and the conductor would have been looking at the men and women playing it, his baton poised over them . . .

It was only seven o'clock, the early sun bright, tea gardens stretching away to infinity on both sides of the rumbling rocking little train, but he could not get back to sleep.

CHAPTER EIGHTEEN

'No suitcase?' the Sikh taxi driver asked, eyebrows raised, black beard curling. He eyed Rodney's dirty clothes and unshaven face suspiciously.

'Nothing,' Rodney said. 'The Maurya Hotel, please.'

He got into the taxi, which was in rather better condition than the others massed outside Dum Dum Airport, and the Sikh accelerated away, his horn blaring.

Rodney sat back fanning his face ineffectually with his hand. It was a foul afternoon, oppressively damp and hot, the sky heavy with burnished masses of cloud. It had been a bumpy flight down from Silchar through pre-monsoon turbulence, but at least it had been cool in the Friendship. Now, already his shirt was wet again.

He felt very tired, but tried to concentrate on what he must do before he could go to sleep. The telegram to Ayesha had been sent off from Silchar. He'd got to get some money. Buy a toothbrush, toothpaste and razor, at least. It might be worth writing a letter to the Dacca hotel asking them to pack his belongings into the suitcase he had also left, and send it to the Kashmir houseboat address. He couldn't lose anything by trying, and he'd like that rod back, if at all possible.

'Very hot day,' the driver threw conversationally over his shoulder.

As Rodney opened his mouth to agree, a peculiarly loud rattling interrupted him. The driver glanced to his right, shouted something unintelligible, and swung the taxi fiercely left toward the edge of the road, at the same time jamming on the brakes. Rodney picked himself off the floor as the driver yelled, 'They're firing at us . . . that car!'

Rodney saw, ahead and to the right, a dark grey car, probably one of the larger Austin models. It had no rear number plate. A hand and arm and half a head were sticking out of the left rear window, and the muzzle of a sub-machine gun. Over the sound of the engine the gun stuttered, and three bullet holes appeared in the windshield.

The Sikh swore and pressed his foot hard down on the

accelerator. The taxi, which had almost stopped, bounded forward, passing the Austin on the inside. The Sikh bent low over his wheel. A single shot was fired from the other car then they were past . . . no front plate either. Rodney saw . . . three men in it, a driver and two others, one with the tommy gun and another with an automatic pistol.

The Sikh cornered on two wheels into a narrow street leading left, and accelerated again. Looking out of the back window Rodney saw the Austin make the same turn, followed immediately by a black Mercedes coming from the opposite direction, that is, from the centre of Calcutta. Then the tarmac ended, the street degenerated into a wide lane and dust began to billow out from the taxi's wheels, hiding the two pursuing cars.

'It's me they're after,' he said urgently to the driver. 'Next time you get to a house, any place where I can hide, slow down so that I can jump out. They won't see. Go on a mile at least to give me time to get away.'

'I can't stop or slow,' the driver said. 'They're too close.' Fainter now, but definite, Rodney heard the bark of the machine gun, and a hole appeared near his head above the back seat.

The driver muttered something in Punjabi and slewed the taxi across the lane in a skidding stop. The gates of a railway crossing barred the road, and a steam engine was whistling in the distance. Rodney leaped out before the taxi had come to a full stop and ran for a mud hut beside the gates. An old man standing there, presumably the gate keeper, stared at the taxi in dumb astonishment. By now the Austin had stopped and all three men in it were out. The black Mercedes arrived as Rodney reached the shelter of the back of the hut. A burst of automatic fire chipped pieces of mud off the hut, and he heard the old man's quavering shriek of terror.

The hut was his only protection, and all they had to do was come at him round it, from both sides. Perhaps they thought he was armed . . . the railway lines were close, but there was no cover there, no ditch, nothing, only the steel rails under the sun. The engine whistled again, closer.

He heard more firing, but the bullets were not coming towards him. He hesitated, crouched behind the hut. What the hell was going on? More shots, a burst from the tommy gun, several single shots, fast . . . he ran toward the tracks, keeping the hut between him and the cars, then stepped sideways until he could see what was happening. The Mercedes was blocking the road, back the way they had come, the taxi was by the level crossing gate, no sign of the Sikh driver. Someone was firing from behind the Mercedes, and one of his original assailants was clutching his shoulder and bleeding heavily. As he watched, the other two jumped into the Austin, and dragged the wounded man in after them. The engine raced and the Austin bounded through a hedge of prickly pears bordering the lane and charged across the field toward the railway line. The engine shrieked again, a long continuous whistle, very close. The Austin raced up on to the ballast, stones flying. The whistle hurt Rodney's ear, continuing its wail over a fearful crunch as the big freight engine hit the Austin square, rolled it over and ground it into a tortured mess of shrieking metal and broken glass, all three men being rolled along in it, falling out, chopped under the wheels.

A man was hurrying toward him from the Mercedes, and he began to run away, back along the track beside the shrieking brakes of the freight wagons. A voice yelled, 'Geminus! Come back!'

Blue smoke and the smell of white hot steel acrid in his nostrils, he stopped and turned. It was Chandra, an automatic in his hand. He called again, 'Come with me! Hurry!'

Rodney ran toward him and as he came Chandra raced ahead, leaped into the Mercedes and began to turn it. Rodney jumped in as the turn was completed. The Mercedes gathered speed back down the lane. The locomotive, half a mile beyond now, stopped whistling.

Rodney gasped, 'What happened to the taxi driver?'

'Ran over the railway and hid the other side. They weren't after him.'

'Those men were all killed, weren't they?'

'Yes . . . I've got to put the proper plates on this car now.'

He slowed, stopped and jumped out, carrying two number plates. When he got back with two others, Rodney said, 'How did you get here, there . . . here?'

'Tell you later.'

225

'Who were those men?'

'Tell you later.'

Rodney awoke to the trill of the bedside telephone and reached out groggily. Chandra's voice said, 'Half past eight. You've slept fourteen hours, and I'm Prince Charming. Get up.'

'I've got to buy some things,' Rodney said. 'I had to leave everything in Dacca.'

'Why don't we have breakfast in your room? Then you won't have to worry about how you look. And afterwards you can slip out in a taxi to some suitable emporium.'

'Good idea.'

'I'll order. I know what you like.'

Rodney hung up and after waiting a moment to pull himself together climbed out of bed. He was wearing his underpants and undershirt, both stained with sweat and dirt, but the room had been too cold for him to be comfortable naked, even in bed. The Maurya Hotel was new and efficient, in the case of the air conditioning over-efficient. It was one thing to be protected from Calcutta's ghastly heat, humidity, and general stench; it was another to run the system so furiously that a man could only be at ease in his room wearing woollen underwear and a tweed suit.

He went into the bathroom and began to wash himself. The stubble on his chin looked very uninviting. His eyes were bloodshot . . . not surprising. May 31 . . . thirteen days to *Azad Shadhinata*. . . . What would the police make of the three men killed by the goods train near Dum Dum? The train crew would not have seen the pistols or, perhaps, heard the shooting. The bodies would be so badly mangled that the one man's wounded shoulder might go undetected . . . three fools try to beat a train over a crossing, and lose. Their weapons would be found. Their car might have been – probably was – stolen; and they themselves probably had criminal records. So the police would write it down as an accident, or a gangland killing, depending on what the old crossing guard told them. And Chandra had been forewarned of the attack. Fortunately for himself.

He dressed, shaking his head at the state of his clothes, and waited for Chandra and the breakfast to come. They came almost simultaneously, and as soon as the waiter had gone, leaving them to tackle the grilled kidneys and scrambled eggs on their own, Chandra said, 'Geminus, I owe you an explanation – not an apology, because I've only been obeying orders. I am a secret agent of the Government of India. Don't worry, I know this room's not bugged. And you are an agent too, for the moment, eh?'

Rodney looked steadily at his friend. 'I have been asked to look into a problem and tell the Indian security people what I make of it, yes.'

Chandra said, 'Ayesha told me. She thought I needed to know, and she was quite right. I and certain others would have become quite suspicious of you, the way you were wandering about, appearing at all the likely trouble spots, if we hadn't known you were on the same task as ourselves . . . you being the brilliant amateur, Lord Peter Wimsey, while we play the pedestrian professional, Chief Inspector Parker.'

Rodney smiled then, and put out his hand across the table. 'Greetings, comrade. I'm glad that's out. Ayesha should have told me the truth. What are you doing here, if I may ask?'

'Something's going on in Bengal and Bangladesh, and it's being backed by the Chinese,' Chandra said. 'I don't think it's very important – probably just to divert our attention and efforts from the main thrust, which will be towards Kashmir, but several political parties are involved, mostly underground or prohibited ones . . . like the Naxalites, and other Maoist groups. When the time comes, they are planning to rise in guerilla warfare – we are sure of that and we know they are well armed. They have a schedule worked out for all this – the date of the rising, and so on – but we don't know what it is.'

'I do,' Rodney said.

'I thought you must,' Chandra said, 'that, or something equally important, because the people here were very sure they had to kill you, and in a hurry.'

'They would have been too late,' Rodney said. 'I cabled the information to Ayesha from Silchar.' He was glad that Chandra did not ask him what the date was. That was the professional attitude, and of course Chandra was a professional at this work and must have been for a long time.

Chandra said, 'We have planted one of our men right in the heart of the Maoist Revolutionary Guard here. Yesterday – no, the day before yesterday – he told me that his leader had got a phone call from Dacca about the escape of an Englishman, Rodney Bateman, who had vital information about the plan, and must be got rid of.'

The caller would have been one of Qureshi's men, Rodney thought, sent into Dacca after they were sure he'd got away.

Chandra continued. 'Qureshi has a big organization all over Bangladesh and neighbouring Indian territory, ready for intelligence or guerilla action, and he put it into high gear. Yesterday morning one of his men phoned in from Silchar saying he'd seen you at the airport there, and that you were buying a ticket for Calcutta on the Indian Airlines flight.'

Rodney said musingly, 'That might have been anyone. The place was full. Anyone could have come up close to me and heard me give my name to the clerk, while I was buying a ticket, or showing them my passport.'

'Well, the Maoist chief here then told our man to get three killers – hit men, I think they're called, aren't they? – and have you killed before you reached your hotel. Our man did what he was told and then got hold of me – that's a fairly complicated business, too, as you can imagine, and it takes time. By the time I got the news you were close to landing. I rushed out, jumped into the car I've hired while I'm in Calcutta and drove out to Dum Dum as fast as I could . . . I didn't see your face in that taxi as it turned off the main road, but I saw the Austin swing after it, and saw that a man in the back seat had a tommy gun. That was enough. I followed.'

'Saving my life,' Rodney said. 'Not to mention that Sikh taxi driver's. They would have killed him too, as a witness.'

Chandra nodded. He finished a piece of toast and marmalade and said, smiling, 'Now we are quits?'

Rodney said, 'You mean, my pulling you out of the Girwan?'

'What else?'

Rodney did not answer the question, but after a time said, 'I thought I saw some men running away into the forest just before I found you that time.'

Chandra said, 'You did. That was the K.P.P.'s work.'

Rodney said, 'Braganza told me they did their own strong-arm stuff, usually.'

'It was so in my case. . . . You know Zulfikr's head of the K.P.P.? Well, he thought I had got some vital information about him and was going to the security people with it. I really don't think that he knew or guessed that I am a security agent myself – just that I might betray him to them. So he dressed up some of his members as *gujjars* and they tried to kill me. They failed, thanks to you. Afterwards nothing happened – I mean, the Indian security people never arrested Zulfikr, or even questioned him, so he apparently decided that I hadn't learned anything about him after all, and has not made another attempt against me.'

Rodney sipped his coffee. It was pretty awful, but he had never liked tea for breakfast so he'd have to put up with it. Chandra said, 'What do you make of the situation, in general, Geminus? I have my own conclusions, but I'd like to know yours.'

Rodney said, slowly, 'Everyone seems to be gearing up for a big day . . . *the* big event, the star turn, the grand finale. Everyone is pointing this way – at Bengal, Bangladesh. Though you don't agree, it could be true. If it is, the outcome will depend more on tactics than strategy, it seems to me. As you know well, India has its plans too. All the armies and guerillas and agents and weapons and plans are almost ready. It is who executes best that will decide the issue.'

'We have an enormous advantage, knowing the date, thanks to you,' Chandra said.

'*If* this is the big event. It it's a feint, as you think, then we'll be in worse shape than even if we knew nothing.'

'What do *you* think?' Chandra asked. His face was peculiarly intent, pale in the shuttered light. By chance their left hands were both on the table, and the Gemini rings gleamed side by side.

Rodney said, 'I agree with you. I can't accept it. I have tried, I am still trying . . . the decision to kill me yesterday *ought* to mean that the information I had was real, true, vital. Yet still I can't swallow it. The rhythm's wrong,

229

the country's wrong – flat lands, flood plains, dense greenery. The music's wrong.'

'It's only you who are writing a Himalayan Concerto,' Chandra said, 'The Chinese – or whoever – may be writing a Bengal Symphony.'

'It's possible, but again, I don't think so. *I* have been involved in this music from the beginning, as a lover of mountains and above all of the Himalayas. I think . . . I *know* . . . that we are hearing an overture, a prelude, not the main work.'

Chandra seemed to be frozen in concentration. His eyes, wide in the dim light, stared deep into Rodney's. He breathed, otherwise not a muscle moved. At last he whispered, 'My God, if you're right!'

Rodney picked his way carefully among the white-sheeted bodies, looking like corpses, settling down on the sidewalks. Perhaps some of them *were* corpses, he thought. No one would know the difference until they began to reek, then they'd be thrown into the Hooghly to join the bodies which the crocodiles and fishes had not fully eaten of the hundreds floating down the river. On the beaten earth of a big open space more people were gathered in their thousands, some smoking, some asleep in the twilight, some doing absolutely nothing, all separate, all entirely unaware of each other. There a woman squatted in the open, relieving herself, there another fed her baby from her bared breast, there five boys were beating a pariah puppy to death with rude clubs, there a man had stolen some small object belonging to another and was running away through the crowd. There were no police in sight, no aura of authority, just people at the bottom of the human pyramid – existing.

He had done a lot – got some money, bought pyjamas and another lightweight suit, and toilet articles sufficient to get him back to Kashmir. He had shaved and bathed. Ayesha had not contacted him, though he had phoned her cover number to tell her where he was. He knew the name and address of the drop in Calcutta, but he did not expect instructions by that route. Time was getting short. Messages would come by telephone, or cryptic telegram, or by messenger.

He wished he could rid his mind of all personal feelings

230

and think clear and cold . . . but he couldn't. He could not compose music like that, and this riddle was a form of composition. Human emotions entered it – love, hate, jealousy, patriotism, lust, ambition.

'What else?' Chandra had asked, referring to Rodney's saving his life on the Girwan. But there was a big 'else' – Chandra's saving of Rodney on the Balhom Tiger. Only Chandra could have done that, he was sure; and to be able to do it he had to have a quick secret means of communication with the highest authorities in Pakistan – men themselves able to get in touch with remote frontier outposts, and command action in a twinkling. Suppose he had said, in reply to that 'What else?' – 'What about the Balhom Tiger?' – what would Chandra have answered?

And the reference to Zulfikr as the head of the K.P.P. Zulfikr wasn't the head – Dr. Jaffar was. Ayesha knew that, Braganza knew that; but Chandra apparently didn't. Ayesha and her superiors, believing that he was only an agent of theirs, had not told him. Why? General principles? Suspicion? He couldn't answer . . . but he could say that if Chandra had instant communication links to high-ups in Pakistan, he *must* know who the head of the K.P.P. was. The lesson of the recent conversation was that he did not know that Rodney knew, and was not going to tell him.

And the Messenger? His mind had approached the idea that Chandra was the Messenger, and had shied away from it as something too obscene to contemplate. Now he didn't have to, for Chandra had come out in his true colours, an agent of his motherland, Bharat-India . . . with intimate links to the Pakistan high command.

He had been thinking that attempts to kill him made the information he had gathered more valuable because if it weren't, why should the 'enemy' bother? Supposedly the purpose of yesterday's attempt near Dum Dum Airport was to ensure that information he had learned in Dacca should not be passed to his employers, that is – the Indian government. But Ayesha already knew the one vital fact he had been able to gather – the date of *Azad Shadhinata*. And the enemy knew that she knew. One of their agents had spotted him in the Silchar airport, buying a ticket; *after* that he had gone off to send the cable to

231

Ayesha. Any good agent would have followed him from the airport, watched him write and send the cable, and one way or another found out what was in it. So the real purpose of the Dum Dum attack was not to kill him, but to give weight to information he had already passed . . . and if it is your enemy who is doing this, then the information must be wholly or partly false.

But this was familiar terrain. It had happened in Nepal, certainly once, perhaps twice – orchestrated attempts to make him believe that information he had gleaned was true and important, while at the same time ensuring that the information did in fact reach the Indian authorities. He had had a feeling that the *Yeti* surveyors never fired at Chandra and himself at the same time – only one at a time; then, if they had killed one, they would have let the other get away with the news, but not realizing that he had been *allowed* to get away – it certainly hadn't felt like that at the time, for under the press of fear and exhaustion, the calculation of the enemy's firing had not been noticed . . . so the hardly gathered information went to Delhi – Chinese surveying the Rasua Bhanjyang, and determined to let no one find out more.

Then, the attack on him in the Kathmandu street. He was sure now, thinking back, that the *goondas* could have killed him if they had wanted to . . . but they didn't. Why? Because they wanted the information he had gathered from the Chinese Lieutenant to reach his superiors. The Lieutenant might have been a plant, he might not – it made no difference, as long as 'they' knew what information he was in a position to give.

Orchestration, orchestration: complex, subtle, but becoming clearer to him every hour. . . . And what about India's own composition? The strains he was picking up of that were interfering with the ones he was hearing from the Chinese, and he could not sort them out unless he had the Indian score in his hand. Why in hell couldn't Chandra and Ayesha tell him the whole truth instead of leaving him to find out bits and pieces from their enemies?

Oh, damn Chandra! It was Chandra who had been the cause of his love affair with Ayesha really for she had taken him just to forget Chandra . . . and the same with Kit Sanders, surely, trying to use him only to bring Chandra

232

back to her. He felt a slow anger at Chandra's facility with women, compared to his own. Scorned by his wife, used by others simply to arouse jealousy in their true loves. It wasn't fair that a man should be born with such advantages. *He* had not been born able to compose music, it had taken him years of study, hard work, concentration, love. He had devoted all that to women, too, and the result? Dust and ashes.

He was back at the hotel, running up the steps, full of resentment. The cold inside congealed the perspiration on him and he swore aloud. He hurried to the elevators, up to his room, tore off his clothes, shivered, bathed, redressed, flung himself down in the easy chair, lit his pipe and drew deep. The telephone rang.

It was Ayesha. Her voice was remote and the connection bad, with faint whisperings and unintelligible rustlings on the line. She said, 'Is this line bugged?'

'I've been told not.'

'It doesn't matter. If anyone's doing it, it will be my Calcutta people. Remember your friend in Kashmir, the one you went fishing with?'

'Yes.'

Have you seen him? He may be in Calcutta, perhaps even at your hotel.'

'He's here. Not with me now.'

'We have to dispose of him, finally.'

Rodney stared disbelievingly at the receiver. 'Did I hear you properly?'

'Yes. I've just learned that he's the top man for the other side.'

'Which?'

'China. Our ambassador in Peking heard something by chance which put us on to the trail. . . . Do you have a gun?'

'No. He does.'

'It doesn't matter. He trusts you . . . loves you, for God's sake! Go to him in his room. Hit him with a lamp, an ashtray, a chair leg – kill him. You will be totally protected. Just go back to your room, wash up, and carry on normally. Nothing will be discovered till the maid goes to his room in the morning. As soon as you hang up I'm calling our head man in Calcutta, and he'll fix everything with the I.G. of Police. Then, in a day or two, come back here.'

'I don't think . . .' he began.

Her voice was hard and viciously determined. 'A hundred thousand rupees into your pocket and all the other stuff finished, done with. You can leave India whenever you want.'

'Ayesha, I don't . . .'

She interrupted. 'The alternative is arrest for espionage on behalf of a foreign power. What we don't already have, to prove that against you, we can easily make up. Our prisons are not luxurious. You may not survive.'

He hung up quietly. He had meant to advise her not to throw all India's resources into the *Azad Shadhinata* basket, but her vehemence, and the mission she had given him, had driven it out of his head. She probably wouldn't have listened, anyway.

Kill Chandra? He wasn't surprised, somehow, nor particularly shocked. People who accepted the sort of job he had taken were expected to do such things, even to their girls or best friends. But, suppose he did kill Chandra, what then? If there was anything beyond *Azad Shadhinata*, Chandra might be the only person who could lead him to it. The Chinese had used Jansingh Gharti's fervour for a new Nepal as a cover for their plans in Bangladesh. Suppose they were going to use the fervour of Qureshi and the Naxalites and all Bengali Nationalists as cover for their plans somewhere else? Where did Chandra stand in that situation? One of the deceivers, or one of the deceived? The great day was approaching. What would Chandra do now? Go to the top, surely, in either case. If he was one of the deceivers – to play his part in the final phase, wherever it was to take place; if he was one of the deceived – to protest against the betrayal.

He needed time to think this over. The bar was the place to think in.

He had been at the bar, a cold beer in his hand, for twenty minutes, and had reached no conclusion. Someone sat down at the stool next to him but he did not look up, still deep in his thoughts. A hand fell on his shoulder and a hearty voice cried, 'By God, if it isn't Rodney Bateman!'

He looked up. Air Vice-Marshal Nawal Contractor was beaming down at him, hand extended. The Air Marshal called to the barman. 'Another beer for this gentleman, or would you like something stronger?'

Rodney said, 'No . . . wait, I think I will.'

'Two *bara pegs,* Johnny. What's the matter? Been having a rough time, music hunting?'

Rodney said, 'Sort of. I hate this weather, too. . . . I've just come down from Bangladesh, analysing their music.'

The music's the same as ours in West Bengal,' the airman said, 'But everything else . . .' He lowered his voice – 'Bangladesh is a mess. Riots, strikes, famine. Very explosive situation.'

'You seem to be getting ready to deal with it.' Rodney said.

The Air Marshal lowered his voice still further. 'You aren't supposed to say things like that . . . but we have reason, you know. The Chinese are moving a lot more troops down to the Tibet-Sikkim border. Why?'

Rodney said, 'You tell me.'

'Because they might – just might, I say – decide to intervene in the internal affairs of Bangladesh. And we couldn't allow that, could we?'

'No . . . and I suppose some Chinese general could be telling some Vietnamese visitor that the Indians are proposing to interfere in Bangladesh, and *we* couldn't allow that, could we?'

The Air Marshal laughed, brushing up his luxurious moustaches. 'I suppose that's true. Thank God it's the bloody politicians who have to think up the lies to explain away what they want us to do. We only have to do.'

'Or die.'

'Have another drink. You look . . . strained.'

'I am. Bangladesh worries me, too.'

'Yes.' Long pause. 'Oh, I saw a friend of yours – that writer fellow Chandra Gupta. Saw him in a taxi with another man I know quite well, as a matter of fact – Dr. Jaffar, the best radiologist in Kashmir . . . saved our eldest girl's life five, six years ago.'

'When was this?'

'This morning.'

'What would Dr. Jaffar be doing here?'

'Haven't the foggiest.'

Rodney thought a moment. He must clear as much clutter out of his mind as possible. Nepal was out. The Mishmis were out, except for one small niggle in his mind. He asked the Air Marshal. 'I've wondered why you gave me a ride in your plane up to Dambuk that day.'

Contractor said, 'Do you remember a lady leaving your houseboat the day after you came down from the Girwan?'

Rodney thought back – Ayesha, after recruiting him for this job. He said, 'Yes.'

Contractor said, 'I was in a *shikara*, passing, with my wife. I saw her. I know what she is and does . . . and how she operates. I was in Air Intelligence, for a time.'

Rodney drained his glass. 'Thanks, anyway . . . and for the drink. See you in Kashmir?'

'When I can get away again.'

'Which shouldn't be too long?'

'No comment.'

Rodney went out and to the lift. Room 1145. What was he going to do when he got there? Just pick up the desk chair and break Chandra's head with it? Say, I've been told to kill you but I'm not going to, if you talk? But Chandra carried a gun, so that was out. He had no choice but to attack at once . . . or not at all. To stand outside in the corridor, as he now was, like Macbeth, indecisive, was the worst of all. Chandra was his Geminus. The ring on his finger had given him a shared mother with Chandra, a shared blood. Ayesha's threats did not frighten him, but . . . as much as he loved Chandra, he hated him too. His hands were clenched, the nails biting into the palms.

He took a step forward, his hand out. The door opened and a maid came out, loaded with linen in a basket.

Rodney stared at her dully. 'Is the sahib in?'

'The sahib? Oh no, he left earlier.'

'When?'

'One, two o'clock.'

'Took his bags and left? Checked out of the hotel?'

'Yes, sir.'

He leaned back against the wall, covered his face with his hands and felt a heavy oppression of tears, burning his eyeballs like acid.

CHAPTER NINETEEN

The room in New Delhi's luxurious Ashoka Hotel did not have a number, and was tucked away round a corner on the fourth floor, seeming to be part of a servants' cleaning and storage area. The view would have been out over the swimming pool and gardens at the back of the hotel, but the blinds were always kept drawn, for this was a room used only by Ayesha Bakr's department. She had been waiting for him when he knocked on the door; that was inevitable, for only she and her superior in the department held the keys. She opened it, he walked in, she closed and locked it behind him. The lights were on, though it was ten o'clock of a burning June morning. Indian music clanged softly from a hi-fi set-up along one wall, and Rodney knew that the set was also a tape recorder with extremely sensitive microphones hidden about the room.

Her first words were, 'Why did you stay an extra day in Calcutta? And then crawl up by train?'

He sighed. She was looking her best, though viperish, her colour heightened, her eyes flashing, the heart-shaped face full of animation, her ample breasts heaving under the plain white sari.

He said, 'I like trains. Also, I needed a rest. My time in Bangladesh was anything but peaceful, and Calcutta wasn't much better.'

'If you'd told us at once that Chandra had left, we'd have had a better chance of getting him.'

He said, I don't think it would be a good idea if you "got" him, yet.'

'Because you're in love with him!' she said furiously. 'You're just a filthy pansy! No wonder your marriage has failed. That's why you didn't kill him when I ordered you to.'

He thought, the mikes are not switched on, or she wouldn't let herself go to this extent. She would never make Nixon's mistake and bug herself into a trap.

He said, 'Chandra had already left when I went to his room.'

237

'But you would have killed him?' Her tone was a sneer.

'I don't know. At that moment I was feeling jealous. It's possible.' He wondered whether he was speaking the truth. If Chandra had been there, what would he have done? He didn't know, and it was that doubt about himself which had caused the breakdown that the cleaning woman had witnessed with such astonishment.

'Where could he have gone to? Do you have any idea?' she asked.

A memory of the Air Marshal stirred him and he said, 'I haven't the foggiest.' He smiled at the memory.

She snapped, 'There's nothing to smile about, Rodney. I warned you of the consequences of failing to do what I ordered.'

'Don't be ridiculous, Ayesha,' he said, his anger rising. 'If he'd gone, he'd gone.'

She sat down in a hard chair by the desk, pushing it round to face him. Her expression had altered, from anger to harassment, apprehension. She said, 'Oh God, I wish I knew where he was. Until a couple of days ago I would have sworn he'd be somewhere in the north – Kashmir, Ladakh. Because that's where he's been telling us the main Chinese effort was going to come. But now that we know about him, he must have been lying. He'll be in Bangladesh or Bengal.'

'You think so?'

'Of course I do! All the hard evidence points that way.' She rummaged in her briefcase and pulled out half a dozen large glossy photographs. 'Satellite photos along the Sikkim-Tibet border . . . south of Lhasa on the road to the Natu La . . . columns of tanks . . . ammunition and supply dumps under urgent construction. . . . And the evidence of our own people . . . daily overflights by Chinese jets well inside India photographing. Heightened patrol activity where troops are in contact. Then the reports from our security network in Bengal and agents in Bangladesh – great activity among all political parties and underground movements. Then what that Nepali, Jansingh Gharti, told us. Arms cache unearthed at Ranchi. A man caught making technical sketches of the Howrah Bridge over the Hooghly in Calcutta. Your own information that the date's been set – June the thirteenth. *Azad Shadhinata*, Independence!

How on earth can you *not* believe that this is the main thrust?'

He said, 'This is a mountain symphony. And *Azad* points west just as much as *Shadhinata* points east.'

She said, 'You talk nonsense, Rodney! What evidence do you have to set against all we – and you – have uncovered that points to Bengal?'

He was silent, wishing that he could open the blinds and see the wall of the Himalayas two hundred miles away, wishing the air was sharp with the freshness of ten thousand feet, not this laundered and artificially chilled air of the plains. He said at last, 'I think I'm right.'

She said, 'Everyone else in the department is sure that the centre's going to be in West Bengal and Bangladesh. Till now I've been arguing against them, on the strength of what you and Chandra felt. God, what's the good of mystical feelings – and the advice of a traitor – against hard evidence?'

He said, 'I believe I have a feeling for rightness or wrongness in affairs like this. I feel the centre is going to be Ladakh and Kashmir.'

'You are wrong,' she said. 'That's all there is to it. And you have made me back your wrongness to the limit. Do you realize that this is going to give Bajwa the opportunity he's been looking for for years to downgrade me, shunt me into some backwater, where there's no hope of getting to the top?'

'That would be awful,' he said sarcastically. 'Muslim wonder woman of the I.A.S. fails to make the top grade after all.'

'It's not only for me,' she stormed. 'It's for all women in the service. Bajwa hates women to have ideas of their own.'

He said, 'Why do you have so many troops and aircraft in Bihar and West Bengal?'

'That's obvious, isn't it?' she said. 'Anyway, it's none of your business what *we* do, only what foreign countries or our own traitors do.'

He said, 'You should have told me at the beginning that Chandra was an agent of ours.'

'I didn't think it was necessary for you to know.'

239

'I suppose you're sure of what your ambassador picked up in Peking?'

She said, 'Yes. And we have independent proof, too. Yesterday evening, early, someone met secretly for two hours with Lau Chung – he's the head of the Chinese intelligence and espionage group in their embassy here. This morning we learned who the man was – Chandra Gupta. If you'd told us at once that he'd left Calcutta we would have got him.'

'And never solved the big riddle,' Rodney said. 'Chandra has the key.'

'And he's vanished.'

'Taking the key with him. . . . Why would he have a close relationship with Dr. Jaffar?'

'The Kashmir radiologist? Head of the K.P.P.?'

'Yes. They were together in Calcutta two, three days ago. And Chandra doesn't know that anyone else knows that Jaffar is the real head of the K.P.P.'

She said slowly, 'Chandra's either a triple agent – acting for Pakistan as well as for us and China – or he is the man who co-ordinates action between the Chinese and the K.P.P.'

'The latter,' Rodney said. 'That's what he does with the Naxalites and other groups. . . . You told me about Nehru easing Chandra's father out of the Civil Service for advocating Bengali Nationalism. Do you know if Chandra ever felt the same as his father?'

'We looked into it when we took him on. Incidentally, it was Panditji himself who told Bajwa's predecessor to do everything he could for Chandra.'

'Guilty conscience?'

'Perhaps. All I know is that we never unearthed anything of the sort, and we went closely into Chandra's background at the university, interrogated his friends, everything. We were especially careful because his twin brother *was* involved in a Bengali Nationalist group. In fact, he was killed in a car crash when arranging a terrorist attack for them.'

Rodney looked thoughtfully at the ring on his hand. It had belonged to that brother, whom Chandra had loved. He said, 'Jansingh Gharti defected from the Chinese because he found that their plan to foment a revolution in

Nepal was mere cover for action in Bangladesh and Bengal.'

'Yes.'

'Suppose Chandra was secretly an ardent Bengali Nationalist. Suppose he discovered that the Chinese plan to unify both Bengals into a new independent nation was mere cover for action in Kashmir? What would he do?'

'God, I don't know. *I'm* not his boy friend.'

'I think he'd go to his top Chinese contact and complain. Or he'd take some action against them.'

'He might . . . but how *can* it be Kashmir or Ladakh?' she said with exasperation. 'We've had regular satellite photo coverage and they haven't done anything important since that scare a few weeks ago . . . a small new road here, work on the old turquoise mines there, an unimportant airfield somewhere else – no sign of troop increases, and some evidence of the opposite. An infantry regiment from Ladakh has been identified on the Sikkim front.'

'How long did that take – for them to move the regiment?'

'Not more than six days.'

'About twelve hundred miles,' he said. 'Mostly over thirteen thousand feet, on a macadam but not asphalt road. Fast work.'

'It has been improved, over the past two years,' she said, 'just for operations like this, apparently. And of course the move might be a fake. The identification was from radio call signs.'

'Which can be switched without moving the unit,' he said. 'Now, what about Kit Sanders?'

Ayesha shrugged. 'Braganza looked into the insurance policy. The watch did belong to Mike Sanders. Or at least he had one exactly like it. Then the police interrogated Kit again, and she simply denied knowing anything, as she has always done. Yes, she said, it probably was her husband's watch, it looked just like it, and as far as she knew he was wearing it when he set off that day – he always did wear it – but about the murder or the murderer, nothing. We haven't got enough evidence to arrest her.'

'I don't think we should. We've got to find out what she is, though. First, is she one of yours? The truth, please.'

'No,' Ayesha said sullenly.

He said, 'I've come to the conclusion that it was Chandra who got the Pakistanis to save me on the Balhom Tiger, acting through Jaffar's K.P.P. radio, with a cipher we haven't cracked yet.'

'Why would he want to do that?'

'Personal friendship, I think. What you call love. He saved my life again in Calcutta. He gave me a story about learning of the attempt on me through an Indian agent in the enemy's councils, but now it is clear that he himself was in the enemy's councils, but just wasn't going to allow me to be killed. Personal relations matter more than business or duty, or patriotism, to some people.'

'Like you?'

'I'm not sure – yet. I'm finding out. . . . But to get back to the Balhom Tiger episode – if Chandra warned the Pakistans it must have been Kit Sanders who passed information of my plan to the Indian Army in such a way that I was likely to get shot on the Balhom Tiger. Therefore it was she who used that old contact of her husband's to get the message through.'

'You know it was a man, speaking good Kashmiri.'

'I still think it originated with Kit. It has to. The man was Akbar Khan, her partner, perhaps. You swear she's not one of yours?'

'She's not, and never has been.'

'Then if she doesn't work for China, like Chandra, and she doesn't work for India, like her husband, who does she work for?'

Ayesha said slowly. 'The only other possibility is Russia.'

'I have come to the same conclusion.'

'But Russia is our friend. Why should she spy on us?'

'Russia is a great power and she would want to have her own observers in important spots, to check up on the accuracy and completeness of what you tell her. Kashmir is important. Russia has no common border with India, but she has a common border with China just north of Kashmir, in the Pamirs. She's vitally concerned with what the Chinese might be planning to do in that area – far more directly so than she is with Bengal. . . . I should think there are at least a dozen Russian agents in India, besides Kit Sanders, who took the job for ideological reasons, I imagine. You could find out about her early years easily

242

enough. And being in the business herself, she soon realized her husband was, too. She was probably aware of everything he did or said or sent to you.'

Ayesha said, 'All that is possible, but why would she want to kill you? And why did she kill Mike, if she did?'

Rodney said, 'Again, probably personal. Perhaps she had come to hate Mike, because she wanted Chandra. Me . . . I was getting on to her track, not as a Russian agent, but as a murderess.'

Ayesha said, 'She's in Delhi now, you know.'

He shook his head. 'I didn't.'

'We've been keeping a check on her since the watch turned up. The police have a theory, which would fit Kit as well as anyone else, but they have never come up with a motive . . . The man who was found with the watch was called Lall Khan and he was a professional *badmash* and killer for hire. His usual partner was a man called Anwar Rashid. The Kashmir police think that someone hired those two to kill Mike Sanders. That someone knew Sanders was going to visit his mistress that morning on his way to the airport. They killed him and got rid of his body somewhere, somehow – that's not difficult in India. And although they must have sworn not to take anything or do anything that would incriminate them, Lall Khan couldn't resist taking the watch. He didn't wear it, but carried it in his pocket, where it was found when they took his corpse out of the Jhelum.'

'Why was Lall Khan killed, then?'

'The police think it was jealousy. Anwar Rashid swears it's not true, but they've heard rumours that Lall Khan had been having an affair with Anwar Rashid's wife . . . but the police have no idea who hired them. They've interrogated Anwar Rashid within an inch of his life, but he just swears he had nothing to do with it, and they can't prove that he did. Anwar's wife has been frightened by the murder of Lall Khan and says she knows nothing, either. Lall Khan was unmarried . . .'

'Personal, again,' Rodney said, 'personal feelings, personal emotions, personal insights are just as important in this affair as high political strategy . . . and that's why I'm going north.'

'You think Chandra's up there?' she asked, her lips tight.

'I don't know. I feel he *ought* to be.'

She looked very alone then, small and indomitable. She wanted to be a woman and she wanted to be a senior official and sometimes the two wouldn't lie down together. She was in love with Chandra, and he had been jealous of Chandra because of that.

He said, 'Chandra doesn't love Kit. She'll never get him.'

'Nor will I,' she said, 'because you have him. Anyway, he's a traitor.'

He was silent. Now it was her turn to be jealous. It was true that he and Chandra had a special relationship and understanding, and perhaps no woman could believe the truth – that there was nothing homosexual in it. Chandra was a human being apart, and he had gone. He and Ayesha, deserted, were left with each other.

He said, 'Last time we met, we fought. Can't we go back to how it was in the *shikara*?'

He slid his hand inside her sari and cupped her breast. She never wore a bra and the breast was cool and round and heavy in his hand. 'Is it *lèse-majesté* now to make love to the Joint Secretary?'

Her voice broke. 'Oh God, I feel so miserable.'

'Because Chandra's gone – for good?' he said.

She was already sprawling back on the bed, tears welling from her eyes. They made love, he bathed in her tears, unable to tell which of the spasmodic movements of her body were sobs and which the thrusts of passion. Afterwards, she looked so soft, her skin damp and rosy, her expression tender and relaxed, that a wave of love spread through him, as uncontrollable as the previous lust. He whispered, 'Ayesha . . . Indreni and I are washed up, and have been for years. So are you and Ali. . . . Why don't we get married?'

She rose slowly from the pillows. Her expression changed, the fulfilled womanly softness freezing first into astonishment, then anger. She said, 'Marry you?'

'Why not?'

Her voice rose. 'But you're a foreigner!'

'So what?' he said, aggrieved. 'Surely you're not against mixed marriages?'

She almost screamed, her hands out like claws. 'How

244

could I ever get to the top in the department with a foreign husband?'

She was hurling herself into her clothes, while he lay back on the bed, naked. She said, 'I have to go. Here is a report from Braganza you might find interesting. Burn it when read. Wait here at least ten minutes after I've left. The door is self-locking.'

She threw her papers together into her briefcase, locked it, and after a final quick glance round the room, went to the door. There, she paused, looking at Rodney. When she spoke her voice was a little softer. 'If you love me, find Chandra. Kill him if you have to – but bring back the secret of the Chinese plans.'

'The master theme of the Himalayan Concerto,' he said. Then she was gone.

The radio in his own room was not a hi-fi, but it was adequate. While a garish movie tune was being blared out he could not concentrate, but a programme of music from Spiti, Lahoul and Rupshu followed, and he sank back with a sigh in the easy chair, notebook and pencil ready. This was music from the very heart of the Himalayas. After forty minutes he had jotted down half a dozen new tunes, and his head was vibrating to the deep, often repeated throbbing boom of the great brass and copper temple horns : a diapason of two notes, the first being held for a count of six, then sliding down to the second, a count of three, pause for breath, up again, count of six, down deep . . . north, south . . . east, west . . . man, woman . . . love, hate . . . life, death . . .

He turned the volume down and closed his eyes. There was nothing important in Braganza's report and not much even interesting, except the information that two professional assassins from Bombay had arrived in Kashmir and were enjoying the amenities of Srinagar, especially the whores, with apparently not a care in the world. The men were Hindus, which would be expected from Bombay; and there was circumstantial evidence that they had been hired by or through Lau Chung, the Chinese Embassy secretary. Why would he want assassins in Kashmir? And weren't there plenty of good ones available in Srinagar, good Muslims too, and therefore less likely to be remarked on?

The two men were being watched, but they were doing nothing suspicious, and had made no contacts – except, of course, with the whores.

Kashmir, the vale famed down history and throughout the world for its beauty . . . trout and *mahseer* fishing . . . chenar and lotus . . . trekking and mountaineering . . . pale hands, slim bodies, for hire. . . . How did Kashmir figure in the master plan? A great many human beings lived there, but they were passive. Jaffar's K.P.P. was well organised, well armed – but very small in numbers. How could it hope to survive if it came out into the open against the Indian Army? Or, being relatively unknown and unattractive to Kashmiris, how could it hope to ignite the mass of the people to act with it, under its expert direction? *That* would be very dangerous, but how could it be brought about?

He lit his pipe and in the familiar mechanical process slowly swung his mind in another direction. The pipe puffing well, he thought of *Azad Shadhinata*. It was a code phrase and it denoted the day of insurrection against authority in Bangladesh, West Bengal, and neighbouring parts, notably Bihar. It was known as such to the leaders of all the parties and subterranean groups who were going to rise there; but it was not known apparently, to anyone in Kashmir or the west, or to the Mishmis. Where had Ayesha's people first heard it? It was possible that someone had been careless. It was also possible that the 'slip' had been intentional – that the code phrase had been fed to Ayesha's branch, who then naturally set out to learn what it meant; and in the process gave it vital significance . . . once again, orchestration. If there was another phase of the Chinese plan beyond the Bangladesh operation – real or feint – then that too would have its own code name. Or perhaps it would go into effect automatically so many days before – or after – *Azad Shadhinata*.

The problem was by no means solved but on thing was obvious; the fact that *Azad Shadhinata* seemed to affect only Bangladesh and Bengal did *not* mean that there was no other facet to the overall plan.

He swung himself round in his chair and turned the radio off, for it was some politician talking in Hindi and saying nothing. . . . Chandra Gupta. Geminus. Genius. Lover of all the world. Especially Bengal. He had the key, the real key. Had he always had it, or had they palmed him off with a false one, as they had done with Jansingh Gharti?

He was sure, and growing increasingly more sure, that only Chandra could lead him to the heart of the riddle, the finale of the concerto. That was why he had given him time to get clear of Calcutta, and in fact clear of Delhi, too, after his long interview with Lau Chung. What had that interview been about? Final instructions, or bitter protests? In any case, the time had come for Chandra to go to the Chinese command post. And where was that going to be? Kashmir? Very possible, but Braganza would be on the look out for him. Nepal? Too far east, too close to the false 'heart' in Bangladesh. Spiti, Lahoul, over the Rohtang Jot? Possible, but that area was a little too far from Ladakh to be vital . . . that left Ravi. Ravi or Kashmir. Chandra wouldn't have flown north because it was too easy for Ayesha's people to cover the airports. Railhead for both Kashmir and Ravi was Pathankot; but he wouldn't have taken the train, for the same reason. He would have driven there, an overnight journey. . . . To Pathankot then, to pick up Chandra's tracks. It was his only bet now, and not so slim a chance as it seemed.

He picked up the phone and dialled. Ayesha answered. He said, 'I'm going to Pathankot by the night train, to-night.' He hung up.

There was a knock on the door. A man in simple Indian clothes stood outside. He salaamed briefly and said in Hindi, 'I am Mr. Gupta's servant. He left this message for you, sir.' He pulled a piece of paper out of his shirt pocket, handed it over, and turned to go.

Rodney said, 'Wait, please.'

'Sorry, sir, the police are looking for me. I had to give you the message before they catch me.'

Rodney watched him go along the passage toward the lifts, and disappear. Inside his room he read the note – GEMINUS – that word was spelled out in capitals; the rest in a pencilled script: *Au revoir. Do not look for me now. We will meet again somewhere some time. Your Geminus.*

247

CHAPTER TWENTY

Rodney got out the bottle of Black Knight and poured a stiff drink into his tooth glass. The train was rumbling over the Jamuna bridge, and if he looked out he would be able to see the lights of the city reflected in the many streams of the great river. But the blinds were down and he felt too lazy to pull them up. This was air-conditioned class, and inside this steel box he was insulated from the stifling heat of the night. He found one of the bottles of cold soda he'd bought on Delhi Junction station for the journey, opened it and poured some into the glass. Soon there'd be the stop at Ghaziabad, and the attendant would tap on the door and ask if he wanted anything more; then – the rhythm of the rails, cradling sway and rock of the train, hours sliding by in sleep and in the freshness of morning, Pathankot, and perhaps a distant view of snow – thě Himalayas.

He sat back in the chair, consciously enjoying his aloneness. If someone else had been sharing the coupé with him, he could not have relaxed, though perhaps he would have gone to bed sooner, if only to emphasize his desire to be alone. But here he was really alone, turning the glass in his hand, sipping, his mind running along familiar rails . . . gradually curving away . . . snow . . . he had been too long away from the mountains. The thought of snow, the silent repetition of the word, brought mental canvases before him, only these moved; cloud shadow in heavy masses sailing across the face of Langtang, over Kathmandu . . . the changeful light on the Pir Panjal, mirrored in the Dal Lake among floating lotus blossoms. . . . Now there was music in his head, too, his own, striving to move on up . . . up . . . but the theme began to repeat itself. He had run into a dead end; no way out, except to climb higher.

Another theme entered his mind. This was one he had developed after meeting the Sayyid, and going to the Kashmiri concert with him. It was a nobly calm tune, and for some reason he had delegated it to secondary status – no more than a bridge between more turbulent statements.

248

But now he saw its importance. It could be, ought to be, the centre of the whole work.

So, the Sayyid was the centre. He had long thought that, or rather felt it in some deeper part of himself, but it didn't make logical sense. The Sayyid was a pacifist and would allow no violence; yet, whatever was being planned would involve violence on a large scale and over a large area – not just blind hitting and killing, but carefully orchestrated to a purpose; but the Sayyid would never play in that orchestra.

But if the Sayyid was the key, then he should go to Kashmir. From Pathankot he could easily get up there. Pathankot was the normal railhead, and there would be fleets of buses, and cars he could hire. But the Sayyid, by definition, would not be taking any active part in the violence to come. It would not serve to go to Kashmir and sit staring at him until something happened. By then it would be too late. For the Sayyid might be the centre, the key, the fulcrum – but it was Chandra who would lead him to the brain that would somehow use that fulcrum. And where was Chandra, and where was he going? All the evidence pointed to Bengal and Bangladesh. He couldn't believe it, simply because his Himalayan Concerto couldn't accept it; but in logic he had no case. No wonder Ayesha was furious with him. Well, he'd committed himself to the north now.

The train stopped at Ghaziabad. The attendant tapped on the door. Rodney wanted nothing. The train began to move. He prepared for bed, yawning and stretching. The whisky would help him to get to sleep, perhaps. If only he could clean his mind of all that filled it . . . or perhaps of all except the core of the problem.

He turned out all the lights except the blue night bulb and stared at the ceiling. The diesel locomotive far in front blared faintly, the sound driven back in the hurrying dark. The wheels clattered daderum daderum daderum . . .

He awoke to a certainty. Till this instant it had only been an inchoate feeling, almost an emotion: before this concerto worked itself to its conclusion, either he or Chandra would die. He wondered idly, he or I? Did it matter?

He did not hear the breathing first, but a slight sound on

249

the floor, as of a bare foot turning. His ears, suddenly sharpened to pick up small sounds under the continuing subdued roar of the train's passage, now heard the breathing. Then, before he had time to move, a hand was laid over his mouth, and something dark obscured the night light. A cold sharp point pricked his side and a voice by his ear said softly, 'Don't move, don't make a sound.'

The hand over his mouth was not soft, but it wasn't a working man's hand either. It was firm, smooth, strong – a woman's. And that had been a woman's voice whispering. She muttered in Hindustani, 'Turn on the light.' After a moment a switch clicked.

Kit Sanders was leaning over him, her hand over his mouth. Next to her Akbar Khan was crouched beside the berth, a short knife in his hand, the point under Rodney's ribs. Kit said, 'Remember, quiet.' She produced a big bandana which had been tucked into her waist and tied it round Rodney's mouth and head, making an efficient gag. That done she spoke in a normal voice, but softly, 'Akbar, you come here.'

She went to his suitcase, opened it and began to search through it, while Akbar sat in the chair by Rodney's head, the knife well in view. Rodney watched as best he could, for his head was not propped up. She looked carefully through the suitcase, examining the only paper she found, which was his musical notebook. She studied this, made an exclamation of annoyance, and put it aside. Then she searched his clothes, where they hung. When she found his wallet she took out all his money and gave it to Akbar Khan.

Rodney's mind which had seemed to function in glue, so that everything passed in slow motion, jerked into activity. If they were stealing his money, it could only mean that they meant to kill him; and the empty wallet would show the motive. But they were really looking for something else . . . information, obviously. Perhaps he could trade something of what he had learned for what they knew. His recent intuition about death had also told him it would not come till after the concerto was resolved . . . both concertos, the one written in notes of music, and the one written in maps and military orders.

She came over to him, the musical notebook in hand. 'I

know you're a composer, but is there a code in these?' She looked into his eyes, saw that he knew her intention and said, 'I'll see that it doesn't hurt. But it won't help you to keep quiet. Come on, what's in here?' He shook his head. She said, 'Nothing? Or, you won't talk?'

He made a motion of writing and she said, 'I'll loosen the gag a bit, but remember, any sound and you get it. Your life's not important to what's in the balance.' She loosened the knot so that the bandana hung just under his mouth. Akbar slid the knife close to his right eyeball.

Rodney said quietly, 'None of our lives are important to those who employ us.'

She said, 'I want to know what the Chinese intend to do. I *must* know, now.'

Rodney said, 'I can tell you what I think they are going to do, but it's only my guess, so far, and . . .'

'Don't waste my time,' she said coldly. 'You *know* what they're going to do, and you're going to tell me.'

He stared at her with his amazement slowly abating, as understanding came to him. He said, 'You think I'm an agent for some government?'

'Of course you are,' she said impatiently.

'What government?'

'China,' she said, 'And I don't think it. I know it. My people have one of their men in Ayesha's department and he saw a top secret paper from Bajwa to the Prime Minister, listing you as one of the leading Chinese agents in India.'

Rodney was silent a minute. At length he said, 'The truth is that I am an agent for India. Ayesha Bakr employed me. Bajwa hates her and has secretly had me listed as an enemy agent to make my work more difficult, and because he thinks I am giving Ayesha wrong information. If he denounces me now, he will get the kudos later when my information is shown to be false . . . and then he can get rid of Ayesha.'

Kit Sanders said coldly, 'You must think I'm a god-damned idiot. Why should Ayesha employ you?'

Rodney said, 'Because I found out something useful to her, by chance, in the Darjeeling-Sikkim area seven years ago. Later she used me to look into a group of radical conspirators at Calcutta University. I never told her I was coming back to India, but she found out and came to my houseboat to tell me she wanted me for another job.'

'Who's your contact in Srinagar?' she snapped.

'Braganza.'

'Message drop?'

'Firoz Ali, on the Bund.'

'Mike used him, too. . . . What were you doing in Nepal?'

Rodney felt the sweat cold in his palms and at the back of his neck. It was a duel, but her life was not at stake – only his own. Akbar's knife point hovered under his eye. He said 'To find out what the Chinese were up to along the Nepal-Tibet border.'

'Whom did you see there?'

'A man called Jansingh Gharti, and a Chinese deserter, a lieutenant.'

'Liar! He's not a deserter, but a Chinese plant.'

'Is that what the Russians think? They may be right. I don't know. He fed me the same story that Jansingh had, and I didn't believe him, or disbelieve him. He was just part of the orchestration . . .'

'And Bangladesh?'

'Same thing. Listening. Looking.'

'You went to see Qureshi and we *know* he's working for China. I don't have any time to waste, Rodney. I . . .'

Rodney said desperately, 'I went to Qureshi because Chaudhri was out to get me.'

'The Minister of Security?'

'Yes.'

'He's an Indian agent, I know.'

'Yes. Well, God knows whom he thought I was working for, but the police came for me in the middle of the night and I just ran for the only place I could think of – Qureshi's hideout. I learned a lot there, but then Qureshi decided he had to kill me. It's a long story.'

She leaned back as though resting the point of an invisible sword on the floor. The grey eyes were still cold and steady on him, but she said, 'Tell me what you know.'

He tried to control his breathing. He must not show fear or doubt. He said, 'I don't know much. I'll tell you what I suspect. . . . The Chinese are planning to invade West Bengal and Bangladesh, or Kashmir. The main thrust will either be over the Natu La, directed at Bengal and Bangladesh, or over the Zoji La, directed at Kashmir . . . and beyond. Whichever is not the main thrust will be used as a feint. June the thirteenth is the date set for concerted action by pro-Chinese guerillas against the governments of Bangladesh, West Bengal, and Bihar.'

'And you don't know which thrust is the real one?'

He shook his head, the knife point following his eyeball. 'I don't think anyone outside China does, yet – and only two or three there.'

'And what about India? What are their plans?'

'All I can say is that they are concentrating troops and aircraft in or towards West Bengal. So either they think that's where the Chinese thrust is going to come or that's where they intend to make a move of their own.'

She said, half to herself, 'My people are really worked up. I've never had such messages. They don't care what I do, what cover I blow, as long as I find out. This is going to be my last job, the end of my life in India . . . perhaps of my life, period. So, you see, I'm desperate. I shall kill you without any compunction at all, if that's what I need to do.'

'Murdering me might land you in jail before you've found out the truth,' he said, trying to sound light; but his chest was tight and he felt cold. He didn't have much more to give and she didn't seem ready to bargain.

She said, 'You'll be found dead. *Goondas* did it – it's not uncommon – for the sake of your money, and there are no clues. That'll be that.'

Rodney said, 'Why did you try to kill me before? When you sent that message to the Indian Army security people about my going over to the Kishenganga – using one of your husband's drops?'

'Oh, you worked that one out, did you? I did it because you were getting too close to the truth about Mike's death.'

'Which is that you killed him out of jealousy, because he had an Indian mistress in the bazaar?'

'Nonsense. I wasn't jealous. I never loved him.'

'Then you did it because he was on the verge of discovering that you were a spy for the Soviet Union.'

He had been wrong about her, he thought, when he had guessed that her reasons might be personal. She was without deep emotions, a ruthless person, who happened to be born female. It was in her eyes and the carriage of her body, the way she flew her planes. She had no soft spots, except perhaps one.

She said, 'About that episode, how did you escape?'

'The Pakistanis rescued me, before the Indians could get me.'

'How did they know your route?'

'I have no idea,' he said.

'You didn't tell anyone else but me of your plans, did you?'

'No,' he lied; of course actually he had told Chandra but Chandra would have done nothing until he heard about Kit's message to the Indian Army security people. So the drop Kit had used was probably a double agent, who had acted for the K.P.P. as well as for Mike Sanders; and on receiving the message from Kit through Akbar he had passed it on to Dr. Jaffar – who had told Chandra.

Kit said now, 'Well, I've got to have the whole truth, now. If I don't get it, Akbar will push that little knife into the back of your head and you'll feel no pain, ever. Don't you understand, it's you or me?'

He knew she meant it. He said, 'I can tell you no more, because it is not I who am the chief Chinese agent in India. It's Chandra Gupta.'

She cried aloud – *'What?'* She sprang away from the rocking wall of the compartment, put her face low to his and hissed. 'I don't believe it! What the hell are you saying? Chandra's an *Indian* agent. I've known that ever since I've known him. He's an honest man, an Indian patriot.'

'A Bengali patriot,' Rodney interrupted quietly.

'You're a liar!'

Akbar Khan said in Hindustani. 'Speak more softly, memsahib. What Mr. Bateman says is possible. I believe him.'

Rodney said, 'The Indian ambassador got confirmation, by chance, in Peking.'

Kit straightened, she turned away, looking toward the window and the drawn blind. She swung back, snarling, 'Are you still in love with him, and he with you?'

'It's not like that,' Rodney said patiently. He had been right: Chandra was Kit Sanders' weak spot. Like Ayesha, she was deeply in love with him; more than that – he possessed her, none the less wholly for not wanting to. So she was jealous of the relation between the two men, the Gemini, hating Rodney because he enjoyed an intimacy with Chandra that would always be denied her.

'I wish to God I could kill you,' she said at last, '. . . but instead I have to believe you. Why didn't I see it long since?'

Rodney said nothing for it was a rhetorical question. Kit Sanders knew well why she had not seen anything in Chandra except what she wanted to see.

Rodney drew a slow breath. The time had come to take his gamble. It would precipitate matters one way or another. If things went badly he might just save hmself, anyway; he was strong and Akbar was not young, though he looked as though he knew how to handle the little knife.

He said, 'We ought to help each other, Kit. India's an ally of Russia and all I'm trying to find out is what is going on. So are you.'

She said, 'India is *supposed* to be our friend, at least, but we don't get told everything, particularly when it's as shady as this might be. The Politburo isn't going to be pleased if India is cited in the U.N. as an aggressor against Bangladesh. And of course, we need to make our own plans, both political and military. . . . Where's Chandra now?'

He said, 'Where the music is loudest . . . no, not loudest – truest.'

'What do you mean?'

He shrugged. 'I can't explain. You would say, where the principal action is, or is going to be.'

She said 'Surely that will be Bengal? I can't believe they're really going to come into Kashmir. What would they get out of it? Nothing, except to harass India. Kashmir's the feint, Bengal's the real thing . . . militarily it doesn't matter whether India's going to start it or merely react to the Chinese. It's the ultimate intention that we have to know.'

Akbar Khan said gently, 'I do not agree, memsahib. The Chinese want to free us Kashmiris from the Indian yoke. That is enough justification. They will pretend to attack Bengal only to force the Indians to keep their soldiers down there. Once they have freed us, they will return to China. After that, when there will be Pakistani troops in Kashmir to help us, the Indians will never be able to re-conquer us.'

Rodney said, 'I have a feeling that the Sayyid Ghulam Mohammed is important – central, perhaps.'

'To what?' Kit said quickly. 'To the situation in Kashmir, or over all?'

He shrugged again. 'If we knew the answer to that, we'd have solved the riddle.'

She sat on the foot of the bed, her chin cupped in one hand. Her lips were pursed and she was staring past him, unseeing. At last she said, 'Where are you going now?'

'Trying to find Chandra. For many reasons, few of them logical, I believe the centre of the mystery is in the Himalayas, not in Bengal or Bangladesh. I hope I can get on his tracks.'

'By intuition?'

'If you like – that and good luck. We *do* think alike you know, he and I.'

'The Gemini,' she said. She made up her mind. 'All right, I have to trust you. We'll work together. Put away the knife, Akbar.'

Rodney tried to speak but found he could not, the sudden relief was too great. She looked at him dispassionately, the grey eyes steady, while he swallowed and finally got out the words, 'Thank you. . . . Where are you going?'

'I have to get to Kashmir and send out the message telling them what I have learned or suspect so far. You'll come to me in Srinagar as soon as you can?'

'*If* I can,' he said.

'We'll go back to our room, then.' Akbar Khan stood up, giving Rodney a small bow. The door closed behind them.

After a time he got up and examined the lock. It was quite undamaged. They'd had a master key. He poured himself another drink and filled the glass with now tepid soda water. It was half past three in the morning of June 4th, nine days before *Azad Shadhinata*.

On Pathankot station even the chill of early morning could not freshen the damp blanket of the approaching monsoon

256

season. The air was heavy with the powerful smell of mangoes being sold by vendors, cut open, and eaten by travellers just off the train. Porters crowded round the upper-class compartments grabbing at baggage, hundreds of passengers swirled slowly toward the exit, staggering under bags and boxes and rolled carpets containing God knew what.

Rodney saw Kit, Akbar Khan now a respectful two paces behind her, with two porters. He wondered for a moment whether he should not greet her; but of course, he should. They had known each other well enough in Kashmir.

'Good morning, Kit,' he said.

She looked up, then smiled, 'Oh, I didn't know you were on the train. We could have had a meal or something in Delhi. Going up to Srinagar?'

He shook his head. 'I think I'll go to Basohli. I've been told that Ravi's a very typical *pahari* state – or was, before the states were abolished. I would like to hear some *pahari* music from this part of the world. There must be something to match the Basohli school of painting.'

She nodded. 'The whole of Ravi was very picturesque while Rajah Krishna ruled. He would hardly allow any westerners in, and certainly no innovations, though he fought in France with the British in the first war and I believe got some sort of a medal. But he was one of the old school. I think he's still alive, though he must be about a hundred. I know he succeeded to the *gaddi* in 1917 and he wasn't a child then. . . . It's part of Himachal Pradesh state now. You wouldn't have had a hope of getting into the high country when he was ruling – I know, because Upper Ravi borders Kashmir and soon after Mike started his business he tried to organize trekking between the two. Nothing doing, Rajah Krishna said – he wouldn't have any corrupting influences in Ravi. Are you going to trek up there?'

Her eyes were sharp on him. He said, 'I think I'll try to get over into the Chenab valley at least, perhaps farther north. There must be some passes over into Ladakh from that area.'

'There are,' she said, 'but they're high and difficult.'

'All right for one man travelling light,' he said.

They were out now and a large car with a driver whose face Rodney thought he recognized was waiting. The driver, standing beside the door, saluted Kit Sanders. She said, 'Give me a call when you come to Kashmir. I'll *kill* you if you use anyone else's houseboat.'

'I still have a lien on *Dilkhusha III*,' he said, 'and most of my clothes are there. I'll be back, one way or another – perhaps coming in over a pass from Zaskar.' He turned away, waving.

His new Calcutta-bought suitcase suddenly felt heavy in his hand and he put it down. The sun was up, throwing down hot rays between scattered heavy clouds . . . two, three weeks at the most before the monsoon reached here.

'Taxi, sahib? Taxi?' a voice importuned in his ear. He turned and looked at the man – a tall young Sikh – and his vehicle. This one was in good condition, for its age, which was considerable. Sikhs were good mechanics, and careful with their belongings.

'All right, sirdar-ji,' he said in Hindustani, 'I want to go to Basohli.'

'Basohli?' the Sikh said in obvious surprise, 'Not going Kashmir?'

'Basohli,' Rodney repeated.

The Sikh opened the door and he slung his suitcase in, followed, and sat back. The tax started. The young Sikh began to talk over his shoulder, giving him a history of Pathankot, of the various Indo-Pakistani wars and skirmishes that had taken place nearby, and of the Khalsa. He closed his eyes, and after a time the Sikh realized he was not listening, and concentrated on driving.

After two hours they entered the outskirts of a town, the Sewaliks rising in a green backdrop, and a river to the left, running in several distinct channels in a wide bed. White temples and heavy shade trees broke up the patterns of the low houses. The streets were irregular and curving, and there were many open spaces small and large. Basohli, at least, had never suffered the attentions of western town planners.

He said to the driver, 'I want to hire porters to go into Upper Ravi. Take me to a good contractor, please.'

'There is only one,' the Sikh said. 'Hari Chand. Here.' He swung round a wide plain of beaten earth and pulled up outside one of a row of white-washed offices and stores on the far side. As Rodney got out, he said, 'Do you want me to wait? You may not get any porters. And there's no Europe-hotel in Ravi. The old Rajah wouldn't allow it. The government want to build one but they daren't while he's still alive.'

Rodney counted out the money, plus a good tip. 'Thank you, sirdar-ji, but I'll take my chances. I can always come down again by bus if I have to.'

He went into the office. Punkahs whirred, files of paper stirred on three desks, where two clerks worked with pen and ink and one with an ancient typewriter.

A man in a western shirt and trousers stood in the door of an inner office and Rodney walked toward him, carrying his suitcase. 'Mr. Hari Chand?' he asked.

The other nodded, adding, 'Contractor and General Merchant. What can I do for you?' He led back into his office and sat down, indicating another chair for Rodney.

Rodney said, 'I want to go trekking up in the Chenab valley and beyond.'

'For how long?' the other asked.

'I don't know. About two weeks.'

'The monsoon will have broken by then.'

'It won't be too bad the other side of the passes.'

'Ah, you know India?' His English was good and he had a sharp, intelligent eye.

'A little,' Rodney said. 'I am a composer of music, and I want to hear *pahari* music. I have been told that Upper Ravi is a good place for it.'

Hari Chand nodded. 'That is true. There is good music up there—' he jerked his head toward the north – 'in the villages, in the temples, too.'

Rodney said, 'I'll need a dozen porters, and lightweight tents for all of us. And suitable clothes and an ice axe for me. I have boots. And dehydrated food, with some normal stuff, like rice.'

'No rice, it's too high up there. It won't cook. You want *atta*.'

'All right. Are the porters here or at roadhead?'

'All my porters live here in Ravi. You will have to hire a lorry to take them and yourself and the baggage to road-head.'

'Where's that?'

'Alwas.'

'And you can provide the lorry?'

'Yes. When do you want to start?'

'Tomorrow. Or get as far as roadhead today, if possible. I presume, there's a *dak* bungalow or inspection bungalow or circuit house of some kind in Alwas?'

'There is a *dak* bungalow there – but it would not be possible to get the porters collected until tomorrow . . .' He paused.

Rodney said, 'What do you mean, would not?'

Hari Chand said, 'I mean, even if there were porters available.'

Rodney sat back and eased his shoulders. He said patiently, 'There are no porters?'

'Only three I could rely on. We have just twenty-four working porters left here now that so many motor roads have been built in the hills. Of those, six are working this week in Kashmir, four are sick with fever . . . and twelve went away yesterday, trekking into Upper Ravi, the Chenab valley, and Ravi-Lahoul. That only leaves three. Not enough for you.'

Rodney said, 'So there's another European trekking in the Chenab?'

'I did not say he is European, did I? He is Indian. A gentleman of your age.'

Rodney said, 'I wonder if he's a friend of mine who said he might be coming up here – Chandra Gupta.'

The contractor shook his head. 'This gentleman's name is Domel Singh.' He picked up a heavy account book and said, 'I am sorry, but I would not be able to help you . . .'

Rodney waited: Hari Chand finally finished the sentence – 'even if you had a permit to trek in Upper Ravi.'

Rodney said, 'Where does one get such a permit?'

'From the Himachal Pradesh Government office. It is the other side of the *maidan* – this big square used to be the *maidan*, where our Ravi Lancers used to parade and play polo, but that was a long time ago. It's that building there, with the flag of India flying. The man who gives permits is Mr. Sohan Lall.'

'Security department?'

'Oh, no!' Mr. Hari Chand looked shocked. 'He is just

a state government representative, here to help the travel and tourism industry. . . . What is your name?'

'Bateman, Rodney Bateman.'

'Mr. Bateman, sir, to save you time, I must tell you that since yesterday no passes are being given for Upper Ravi.'

'How did Mr. Domel Singh get one, then?'

Hari Chand looked nonplussed. 'I don't know. He got pass, from Mr. Sohan Lall. I saw it and checked it carefully myself . . . but how he got it, I do not understand. Ah, it was immediately afterwards that Mr. Sohan Lall informed me that no further permits would be issued.'

'Well, I'll try. Can't lose anything by trying.'

'You had better hurry. Mr. Sohan Lall will shortly be leaving his office for his lunch, and will not return till tomorrow.'

He came out of the temple into strong light, and stood a moment in the shade of a convoluted tower, to let his eyes adjust. It had been cool in there, and very quiet – no sound at all from inside the building, only some muted chanting from outside, in the great adjoining building perhaps, which someone had told him was the palace of the rajahs. There had been no person in the temple, either, except one pale figure squatting in an alcove, whom he had hardly been able to see, for his eyes had not then grown accustomed to the gloom. Later he had seen clearly enough – the statues embedded in the walls, the laughing *maithunas*, the twined bodies; and the always impressive giant phallus, alone, black in the marble, its crest powdered with turmeric.

He leaned back against the stone, found his pipe, and lit it. He'd caught Mr. Sohan Lall, the government's tourism-promoter, just putting on his coat ready to leave his office, and obviously in a hurry. At first he had tried to tell Rodney to come back tomorrow, but when Rodney had insisted, and explained what he wanted, Sohan Lall regretted that he could not issue a pass for Upper Ravi for the time being.

'Why not?' Rodney said. 'The area's been opened to travel for five years, I've been told. It was opened at the same time as Leh, in 1974.'

Mr. Sohan Lall was narrow-eyed, short, and tight-lipped.

He said, 'The government is under no obligation to explain why passes are not issued at any time or place.'

Rodney said patiently, 'I understand, but I do read the big advertisements begging foreigners to come to friendly India, and it's discouraging to find some departments run like a Fascist state.'

Sohan Lall said, 'There is cholera in Upper Ravi.'

'And Mr. Domel Singh can't get it, or spread it?' Rodney said tartly, his patience wearing thin.

'Who? Oh, Mr. Domel Singh. Yes. He is a doctor, and is sent up under orders of the Government of Himachal Pradesh.'

'I see. But . . .'

'I am sorry, Mr. Bateman, but there are no permits being issued. None. If you want to trek, go to Kashmir, or Kulu. Now, if you will kindly excuse me . . .' He walked past and out, Rodney following.

That had been an hour ago. Since then he had eaten a little at a stall, sat under the trees by the river, walked through the bustling bazaar, admired the many costumes, and noted the obvious influence of Tibet, Lahoul, and Ladakh in the homespun woollen clothes of the men, the bronzed skin tint of many of the people, and the turquoise and silver ornaments of the women.

Thunder had been rumbling round the city for some time, and now he realized that it had begun to rain. He stood away from the wall and looked round, wondering where to seek shelter. Nearly opposite, the outer gates of the palace were covered by an arch, lanterns in alcoves on either side. He broke into a run across the front entrance of the temple. Too late, his head bowed against the rain, he saw that someone was coming out. He ran into him, and would have sent him sprawling to the ground, only he had foreseen the encounter just in time to put out an arm and save the other from a heavy fall.

He gasped, in Hindi, 'I am sorry!'

Three men appeared from nowhere. One shouted at Rodney, 'Fool! Clumsy idiot! Can't you look where you are going?'

Another made obeisance to the man Rodney had run into. This latter was very old, and was wearing the national dress of India, in pale tan. The speaker said, 'Highness, lord, are you all right?'

The old man was recovering his breath and composure. After a time he said, 'I am not hurt.'

The rain fell harder and Rodney said, 'Can I help you anywhere?'

One of the newcomers said, 'His Highness can help himself, or if he can't, we, his subjects, can.'

Rodney said, 'I am sorry, sir.' The old man's eyes were deep brown, the face had been handsome and still showed comparatively few stigmas of great age. He stood almost upright and had no cane in the thin-boned hands.

He said to Rodney, 'You were in the temple, I think. You are a student of our religion?'

'No, sir. I am a musician, a composer. I always go into temples when I can. Even if there is no music, they give me a better sense of India, and so help me in my composition. One of my pieces is about a temple.'

'I see. What is it called?'

'*Konarak*, sir.'

Rodney wished the old man would lead out of the rain, but he seemed to be impervious to it, or unaware of it, standing stock still, staring now at Rodney, the face as impassive as it had been from the beginning, but the eyes stirring, light moving in their depths.

He said, 'Then you are Rodney Bateman.'

'Yes, sir. Do you know my music?'

'I do. . . . What are you doing in Basohli?'

'Trying to get a permit and porters to trek in Upper Ravi. I haven't had any luck so far.'

'Have you been to Hari Chand?'

'He has, lord,' one of the gathering bystanders said, 'One of the clerks told me there are only three porters left here, and this man wants twelve.'

The Rajah said, 'And permits? Will Sohan Lall not issue you a permit?'

'No, sir.'

'Why not?'

'He said there was cholera in Upper Ravi.'

The old man stood, saying nothing, looking at Rodney. He said at last, 'You have a family?'

'Yes, sir. Two children. But my wife and I are separated. She is a Bengali.'

'I see. Your father is alive?'

'Yes, sir.'

'What is his name?'

'Rodney Bateman, sir – the same as mine. He was in the Royal Vindhya Horse. . . . We are an Indian Army family. My grandfather was 44th Bengal Lancers.'

'Did your grandfather leave any brothers or sisters?'

Rodney thought, and said, 'The only one I met was my great-aunt Diana, his sister. She died about seven years ago.'

'I see.'

The rain fell. The Rajah had spoken throughout in Hindi. He continued to look at Rodney and Rodney could have sworn that tears were forming in the corners of his eyes and running down the side of his nose; but it must have been the rain.

At length he said, 'Why do you want to go to Upper Ravi?'

Rodney began to say that he was hunting out local tunes and hill music for his Concerto: but something in the sadness of the Rajah's face made him tell the truth. He said, 'I think that a great friend of mine is there. I have to see him, to learn something that is very important for both of us, and for India.'

Again the Rajah said, 'I see.' He stood silent, the rain falling. Everyone was soaked, no one moved away. The Rajah turned to one of the bystanders. 'Take the sahib to Ram Chandra's hotel. It is Indian style, but clean and the food is good. . . . Tomorrow morning at seven o'clock a lorry will come with twelve porters and a driver to take you to Alwas, where the motor road ends.'

'And the permit, sir?'

The Rajah said, 'You will need no permit as long as you are in the territories which used to belong to the lords of Ravi. The porters I send will not leave Ravi, either, but that should give you plenty of space.'

He suddenly held out his hand and said in English, 'Goodbye. God bless you.' The crowd parted, salaaming respectfully, as he walked slowly across the square in the rain and passed under the arch of the gate into his palace.

Rodney sat in the room's only chair, listening with half an ear to the strumming of a *sitar* down the street. The rain had stopped and the wind was off the snows. It would not be cold tonight, but even at this low altitude, it would not be hot, either.

The old Rajah *had* been weeping. He ought to find out more about him, but that would be mere idle inquisitiveness. He had obviously been much revered when he ruled – he still was. Though he had no official status his word carried more force than the permits of Mr. Sohan Lall and the orders of the governments of Himachal Pradesh and of India.

Domel Singh must be Chandra. Probably he had shown Sohan Lall his Indian secret service identification, and said he needed a permit under a false name. And that no more permits were to be issued, for a time . . . time enough to enable himself to get clear away and into the heart of the great tangle of the Himalayas . . . above and beyond this welling green valley, above the hanging forests of pine, above the grass, into the silent vastness of the great valleys, the plains where the wild ass roamed, the frozen streams, the snow-draped monasteries.

The *sitar* music had ended, replaced by a different simpler rhythm. He did not know whether it was live or from the radio, but the tune was stirring and lifting, a lilting dance tune, and with it, coming now on the night wind, the steady blare of the bronze horns from the high country.

CHAPTER TWENTY-ONE

It was a small old truck, its tyres worn, its wooden sides
decorated with busty dancing girls. It climbed at five miles
an hour in bottom gear and when the road sloped down
it trailed a pall of stinking blue smoke; but it was taking
him north. From every ridge now he could see snow ahead,
and in the body of the truck behind him the porters sang
in plainsong, an untuneful but oddly compelling melody.
He jotted it down as best he could, wedging himself against
the sway of the truck into the corner of the front seat,
where he sat beside the driver.

A khaki-uniformed policeman stepped out into the road
from a hut on the verge and raised his arm magisterially.
The driver slowed. From behind Rodney the head porter
Sita Mull stuck his head over the side and called, 'Order
of His Highness, friend!' The policeman stepped back at
once, saluting smartly.

Rodney glanced at his watch. Eleven o'clock and still
sixty miles to go. It would hardly be worth loading and
making a march by the time they reached Alwas; yet he
should insist, for it was important to get the loads allotted
and properly packed, even if only a couple of miles were
covered. Otherwise it would all have to be done tomorrow,
and the best part of that day would be lost, too. They
ought to be in by three, with luck. He got out a sandwich
and began to eat. *Azad Shadhinata* was eight days away.

Next day they moved out of camp, a field two miles beyond
Alwas, at half past eight o'clock in the morning, and
Rodney had had to threaten the porters with the Rajah's
displeasure to achieve even that modest a start. 'Tomorrow,' he said to Sita Mull with all the force he could
muster, 'we get up with the first light – five o'clock in the
morning, understand? And move off at six. Nor will we
stop on the trail to cook – we will eat the *chupattis* we
cooked the night before.'

'Very well,' Sita Mull said, 'but if this sahib we are trying to catch has gold, and we catch him, it will be proper to give all us porters some extra reward.'

'He has no gold,' Rodney said shortly.

He strode out now ahead of the porters on the steep path, his pipe in his mouth, hired ice axe and fishing rod strapped to his pack, feeling confident of at least one thing, and that the most important – Chandra was ahead of him on this trail. There were two other minor roadheads for Upper Ravi, and from them, too, footpaths led north to passes over the Great Himalayan Range; but the merchants of Alwas had confirmed that an Indian traveller had gone through there two days earlier, heading for the Arau Jot. Arau must be a common word in these parts, for it was the same as the name of the village on the Girwan where he'd first met Chandra.

The sun was hot, and the woods tinder dry. The air smelled of hot pine needles, and resin seeping out of the pine bark under the steady heat. Whatever rains had fallen in Basohli and in the lower country had not reached the higher ranges. Clouds were banked to the south, but here the air was clear and the sun untrammelled. The sweat soon stained his shirt and from the porters, leaning into the sixty-pound loads each carried on a headband, sweat dripped on to the stones by the path.

On the Arau Jot, thirteen thousand feet above sea level, the air came thin into his lungs and he was glad to sit down under a tree and wait for the porters to come up. This was the first ridge of the Himalayas. To the north, the way he faced, the Chenab River flowed east to west below him in the mile deep trench of its valley. Farther west it would cut south, break through this first chain and flow out to the plains close under the walls of the Kashmir rampart. Beyond the Chenab, the mountains rose again, to the true centre ridge of the Himalayas. Beyond the lines of snow which he saw thirty miles to the north, the rivers flowed north again, eventually reaching the Indus. It was easy to think of it in diagrammatic terms in his mind – but it was hard to equate the diagram with that fierce glittering tangle ahead there. And somewhere in that forest of peaks and shimmer of light, that wilderness of high desert and hidden tarn, he had to find his Geminus.

And then what? Sita Mull was carrying a .22 repeating

267

rifle with a telescopic sight, which Rodney had asked the contractor in Basohli to supply in case he found himself on his own, which he thought quite likely when he reached the borders of Ravi State; but he could not imagine himself using it against Chandra. And Chandra would be armed. Well, he'd have to wait for the circumstances of the moment to solve that problem.

The porters came up. Each man carefully lowered himself to a squatting position in front of a rock or tree stump; then straightened his back until his load was resting on the rock; then loosed the tump line and at last, free of the load, lit a *bidi* and puffed contentedly.

After quarter of an hour, '*Chalen, chalen*!' Sita Mull cried. The porters adjusted their headbands and took the strain of the loads. Rodney started on down the path at a fast pace. There ought to be some decent sized fish in the Chenab: grilled trout tonight . . .

An hour later he stopped, sniffing the air. Had he smelled burning? The wind had been blowing from the north, out of the valley of the Chenab and up the slope into his face. It had been clean and fresh, scented only with hot pine bark and resin. But there had been a swirl, and surely . . .? It was back in the north and clean. Shaking his head he went on down.

Ten minutes later he smelled it again, this time unmistakable, for the wind had veered and was now blowing steadily down the long slope. Burning wood, a forest fire! The condition of the forest certainly explained it. But where was it? How far behind him? His porters would be about a mile back now. He saw a rise to the right of the path, and ran to it. It did not give him enough height to see over the trees, but between the ranks of the pines he saw, up the hill, a drifting curtain of smoke. My God, he thought, I was coming down through there less than quarter of an hour ago. How could the fire have got started, and established, so quickly? He ran back to the path and up the steep slope, as fast as his lungs could supply the necessary oxygen.

After twenty minutes of hard work he reached the fire. Flames were spread across the mountain side for two hundred yards on either side of the path. The thick carpet of pine needles was burning everywhere, sending columns of sparks bounding and twisting into the air, where they ignited the tinder dry needles and the smaller twigs on the trees. The barks of several trees had caught fire at ground level, and all the bushes that were scattered about trying to grow under the pines were blazing furiously.

He ran as close to the fire as he could and shouted through it, 'Sita Mull! Are you all right?'

The roaring of the flames drowned his voice. What on earth had happened? Had one of the porters been idiot enough to throw down a *bidi*? Surely not, for he had watched them being most careful to stub out the remains after their smokes on the Arau Jot back up there; and stuff whatever was left of the rolled tobacco leaf back into their *dhotis* or shirt pockets. They were men from these same mountains – they knew what a forest fire could do; and they never smoked while actually carrying a load.

He looked left and right, chose the right side of the fire and hurried panting along the hillside until he was opposite the limit of the flames in that direction. Then he started on up the hill. After five minutes he saw that he was keeping pace with the fire, and a few minutes later realized why – the wind was still blowing down the mountain towards the Chenab; the flames were being blown back on to already burned pine needles, trees, and scrub. It was risky running in toward the centre line of the fire, for if the wind changed, it would again start up the hill, fast, and he might not be able to keep in front of it; but his porters were somewhere in there and they surely faced the same danger. He turned in and ran hard. Almost at once he saw a porter, struggling up the mountain away from the fire, bent under his load; and then another, and another. He counted quickly . . . ten, eleven, twelve, including Sita Mull over there with the rifle; but three of them were without loads.

He shouted, 'Sita Mull! This way! I've come round the fire.'

Sita Mull nodded and shouted to the others; they turned and came towards Rodney along the slope, with occasional apprehensive sideways glances downhill toward the yellow and red flames that seemed to be trying to climb the trees there; but the wind held, and in five minutes the porters had all passed the western limit of the fire. Fifteen minutes later, they were gathered on the path a quarter of a mile below the lower limit of the fire. The wind was backing to its original uphill direction and the fire spreading. A huge irregular and growing patch of black and yellow smoke stained the blue sky.

The porters were free of their loads, all standing round, chattering excitedly. Sita Mull said, 'Those three had to drop their loads, sahib, to save their lives. They were a hundred yards ahead of us, and were almost trapped.'

'It doesn't matter,' Rodney said, 'What were they carrying?'

'One of their tents, some bedding, fresh vegetables.'

'We'll have to do without. What caused the fire?'

'Man,' Sita Mull said decisively.

'How do you know?'

'There was no lightning. There is no dew on the ground to catch the sun's rays. And it began and spread too quickly. And I smelled kerosene when I was in the area of the actual fire.'

He moved a little aside, motioning for Rodney to follow. When they were a few paces from the porters, who had again lit *bidis*, he said in a low voice, 'Sahib, I am under His Highness's orders to take you where you wish to go, in his kingdom. But I am also responsible for the lives of these men. They have families. . . . His Highness told me that you are following a man, for some important purpose. Is this man dangerous? I must know.'

Rodney looked at him. He was about forty-five, tall, very thin, the face almost cadaverous, the dark eyes deepset. He wore a flat round cap in the Kulu style, of red cloth and green velveteen. Rodney said, 'I do not think he will hurt anyone, if he can avoid it. He is my friend.'

'But he would not let you catch him?'

'He would try to prevent it, yes. He too is on important affairs. But I think he would be very sad if he could see no alternative but to kill or wound us.'

'We also,' Sita Mull said with a touch of sarcasm. He thought a while, eyeing Rodney; then said, 'We will complete the task His Highness laid on us, but remember, we are not men of war.'

'I hope there'll be no more trouble,' Rodney said. 'Let's go on, now.'

He walked on, thinking. If the fire had been man made
– and there didn't seem to be any other explanation – it
was too much of a coincidence to imagine it was done by
anyone except Chandra. But how did Chandra know that
he was being followed, for when he passed the last telegraph office, at Alwas, two days ago, Rodney had not left
Delhi?

Suppose Chandra had hung back on this mountain to
see whether anyone was on his trail. . . . No, he wouldn't
do that, because he'd lose his time advantage. But he had
obviously thought it likely that *someone* would follow . . .
probably, that the someone would be himself . . . and had
left one of his men behind. The man would have been well
paid; the importance of the matter emphasized, and secrecy
sworn, with a flashing of Chandra's Indian secret service
credentials, perhaps. At all events, the message was clear:
I have come this way: do not follow: or, follow at your
peril.

He swung down faster and three hours later walked
into the scattered houses of Dharwas, where a young
woman led him to the headman. Rodney asked whether
an Indian traveller had passed through, and which way
he had gone. 'Oh yes, sahib,' the old man assured him, 'he
passed through at just this hour the day before yesterday.'

'With porters?'

'He had twelve, from Basohli, when he came, but one
was sick and turned back from here.'

'Which way did this traveller go?'

The old man pointed east. 'Up the Tiaso Nala, sahib.
I told him, myself, that the track was bad and the Sersank
Jot, at the top, worse – but he only laughed and said there
was good fishing on the other side.'

Rodney thanked him, and glanced at the sun. They must
do at least two more hours. He'd wait here and see that
Sita Mull got the porters through Dharwas with no more
delay than necessary. It wasn't exactly a hub of commerce
and industry but they might be able to buy some fresh
vegetables to replace those lost in the fire.

He got them away from camp on the Tiaso an hour earlier
than the day before and thought that by the time the
porters left him at the borders of the state they'd be ready

271

and willing to make their daily start soon after first light. He wondered idly what he would do when the time for parting did come. He might be able to persuade them to come farther . . . he might have caught up with Chandra . . . there might be other villagers, who could be bribed to come at least a day with him, or to the next *gompa*.

According to the maps which the Rajah had sent along to him by the hand of Sita Mull, here they were barely fifteen miles from the source of the Tiaso under the Sersank Jot, but it was hard to believe, for the river was thirty feet wide, and running fast and deep in its torrential course. At the camp, close to Dharwas, there were narrow strips of flat land along both banks, planted with potatoes or rye; but he did not think that would last for long, for ahead he could see the ridges closing in on either side. Dharwas had been about seven thousand feet above sea level; the camp had been over nine thousand. They'd certainly have to make another stage before crossing the Sersank's 17,635 feet, for the porters could not climb more than eight thousand feet in a day, and he didn't think he could, either.

The fields ended and the path became a narrow stony trail pinned on to cliff walls. The river boiled noisily down on his right: the sun climbed with them toward the notched snow of the pass far ahead – now visible, gleaming like a pendant at the neck of the sky, now hidden in the bosoming folds of closer side spurs. He hitched up his pack straps and climbed steadily.

By four in the afternoon he was within four miles of the pass, and close to fourteen thousand feet above sea level. The air felt tight in his lungs and his head light. Pausing on a high place where the path rounded a point of rock a hundred feet above the stream he examined the way ahead. The porters would do no more today. There was an open meadow a little distance ahead, the land rising in bands and plaques of snow behind it to the pass. That would do well for the camp, and with luck he might be able to get a few more trout.

The meadow was on the other side of the river, and he could clearly see the path trailing across it; so there must be a bridge somewhere close by. He went on, the path sloped down, and five minutes later he came to the explanation: this true right bank of the river became a cliff reaching three hundred feet straight up out of the water. Faced with this grim barrier the Lahouli shepherds who were the only inhabitants of these far reaches of Ravi-Lahoul had made a rope bridge across the Tiaso. The river had shrunk to fifteen feet wide here, but seemed to be correspondingly deeper, running for once silent between black rock walls. The bridge swung from iron posts hammered deep into the rock fifteen feet above water level on this side, to similar posts set in a lower rock, near the river's edge on the far side, thus sloping down sharply from where Rodney stood. There were three ropes – one heavy double strand for the feet, and a single strand each side of the hands, the side ropes being loosely connected by a continuous V pattern of cord to the foot rope.

The bridge swayed in the cold wind that blew downriver and Rodney shivered. He thanked God it wasn't set high up, at least. He checked that his rod and ice axe were secured, and his bootlaces tight, and took a first step out on to the bridge.

It swayed jerkily under his weight, and he took another step, holding grimly to the side ropes, his boots set at an angle on the foot rope to afford him some security. It didn't feel quite as bad as he had expected and he took another step; before the bridge had begun to sway leftward in response to that, he took another, and the swing was countered. . . . Ah, that was it, a continuous quick shuffling motion, rather than deliberate steps. He shuffled on, the ropes creaked once, and the foot rope parted with a low crack. For a fraction of a second he hung to the hand ropes but his arms could not support the weight, and he fell into the river, drawing in a last big gulp of breath before disappearing.

For a second all was darkness, with a sense of motion, swirling, fast moving, then a buffet on the shoulder, now down, now up, his face broke surface and he gulped in more air, down again and now the predominant sense was cold, cold cutting through his skin, deep, deeper into his flesh, numbing him. He struck out blindly to prevent paralysis rather than with any idea of swimming. Again his head broke surface, and he saw the bank very close and lunged for it, but the racing water pulled him back

273

and pushed him under . . . down, round, the cold an aching agony in his bone marrow now . . . up again, rock close, and on the rock, on the path, Sita Mull. He croaked wordlessly, saw Sita Mull drop the .22 rifle, saw the incredulous expression on his face, even as he sprang down the rock and reached out. Their hands met . . . slipped . . . Sita Mull braced himself a step farther down and got a new grip, one foot in the edge of the water. The grip held. Slowly he heaved. Rodney could do nothing, every muscle in him crying out only for relief from the cold, unable to move. Gradually Sita Mull pulled him out, a foot at a time, scraping him up the rock. After five minutes he lay in the path, among the sharp stones and sheep droppings, gasping. Sita Mull was on his knees, slapping, kneading, tugging. His shirt was off, the sun touched his bare body. The other porters were around, blocking out the sun, Sita Mull was yelling at them, they moved back, let down their loads. Men worked on his feet, on his arms, his neck. Feeling came back in sharp stabs of pain, as though bayonets were being eased into his flesh at every point. Sita Mull gave him a mug with three inches of the fiery hill rum in it.

He sat up, feeling very tired. 'Don't move for half an hour,' Sita Mull said. 'Just rest there. You, you, see that the sahib gets rest. I'll be back in ten minutes.' Rodney closed his eyes.

He had first met Chandra drowning in the Girwan, under the towers of Kolahoi. Now he had all but drowned himself. He would not have lasted much longer in that water, and it was pure chance that the current had swept him within reach of a rescuer; he might have gone on down stream for five minutes before touching the bank. After that, he'd have drifted a long long way farther, but sodden, dead, eternally cold.

Sita Mull's voice brought him back to the present. 'The rope had been cut, sahib – almost through, but not quite, on the underside, where it would be impossible to see before getting on to the bridge.'

Rodney struggled to his feet. A porter had wrung out his shirt and he put it back on. There was enough sunlight left in the day to dry it on his back, the same with his trousers. He said, 'We can't get past that cliff. We've got to cross somehow.'

Sita Mull said, 'Are you sure you want to go on, sahib?'

'I must.'

'Very well. Do you remember seeing two huts the other side of the river a mile back, where there was a sheep pen and a little grazing space and two fields?' Rodney nodded. 'The place is called Ruhar. There's a ford there that is usually passable at this time – not last month, from the melting snow, not next month, from the rains . . . but now, perhaps.'

'We'll go back there, and try that,' Rodney said.

'And if the river is after all unfordable?'

'We'll come back here and remake the bridge.'

'I don't think it will be necessary. We will cross at Ruhar and the woman shall make a fire to dry your clothes. Tomorrow we can go up the other bank. It is not easy, but it can be done.'

Rodney sat hunched over the smoky fire, his hands out to the glowing mass of fibres. There were a few stunted bushes here at Ruhar but it was so near the vegetation limit that nothing grew easily and the sheep and goats had eaten most of the seedlings, before they had struggled to maturity. The Woman of Ruhar was taller than most *paharis*, and strong-faced, but not beautiful. Sita Mull told him she had four husbands, though Rodney saw only three. Everyone had eaten and the three brothers, the woman's husbands, were asleep on a shelf above some penned goats at the far end of the hut. The porters were asleep in the other hut, with the sheep.

The wick burned low in its bowl of animal fat. The woman was standing beside him. She said, 'Are you following the man who went up the river two days ago?' She spoke Hindustani with considerable difficulty, hunting for the right words.

He said, 'I want to speak with him, yes.'

'He is Indian . . . I saw him across the river and called to him to come and spend the night with me. He laughed and would not come.'

Rodney looked up at her. She was staring into his eyes, close. Her fingers were ringed with heavy turquoise and silver, and her hair was plaited with butter, shiny black

275

in the flickering light. The goats stirred, her husbands snored.

He said quietly, 'Your husbands are not men enough for you?'

She said, 'They are animals, to pull the plough, that is all. In fifteen years they have given me no children.'

'Perhaps it is you who are barren.'

'Not I.'

Sheepskins and bright-coloured felt rugs were spread in front of the fire. It was her bed where, when she wanted, she beckoned one of her husbands to join her. But she had not been able to entice Chandra. Chandra was the master of women. She put her hand over the flaming wick and it was dark, all but the glowing embers. Rodney felt her slipping down beside him, her hands reaching out for him, taking his hand, guiding it through the folds of her dress. She sighed and spread herself beneath him.

She was a dark figure in the door of the hovel, smoke seeping out around her, when they left in the dawn. One of her husbands was sitting on the roof playing a pipe, an extraordinarily joyful little tune, as though in celebration of the woman's night of love.

Rodney turned from the crest of the first ridge and waved in farewell; but she did not respond. She had whispered words of passion to him all through the night, but she had not asked him to stay. She was no Woman of Shamlegh, to beg for the impossible; and he was no Kim, a seventeen-year-old boy to be seduced into seeing a new vision of life through her eyes. His visions were already formed, and leading him on, on and up. He tried to dismiss her from his mind as, he knew, she was dismissing him – how otherwise could she live her life here?

After two hours of hard scrambling, having come down now to the meadow beyond the broken bridge, he had succeeded: of his night in Ruhar only the husband's tune remained. He had it in his head, and now he took out his notebook and jotted it down, noting beneath – *Ruhar, Ravi-Lahoul, June 7, 1979.*

They began the climb to the Sersank Jot, still more than three thousand feet above them. The minutes dragged into hours, the hours strung together, the sun rose and climbed, circling by their right hand, for here they were temporarily heading due east. At half past twelve Rodney and Sita Mull, tramping one behind the other across a snowfield, reached the flat saddle that was the Sersank Jot. There were marks in the snow showing where others had crossed before, but not today nor yesterday; for the hot suns of the days had enlarged the tracks and made them almost shapeless, mere blurs in the snow.

Sita Mull stopped and said, 'This is the Sersank Jot, sahib.'

'I know,' Rodney said, 'It's beautiful.' The sky was full of high-sailing cottonwool clouds; the wind blew from the north, edged with ice, but here and now the sun shone. Beyond a deep trench ahead, cloud shadows moved in stately procession across another snowfield, rising to another pass.

Rodney said, 'That must be the Poat La.'

'It is,' Sita Mull said. 'The valley between here and there belonged to the Maharajahs of Kashmir. Beyond the Poat La is Ladakh, which also belonged to Kashmir.'

'And there the rivers run to the Indus,' Rodney said dreamily.

Sita Mull said, 'Yes . . . but here, where we stand, is the northern limit of the domain of our Lord Krishna, Rajah of Ravi.'

Rodney said, 'Turn back then. You have done what your lord ordered you to. I will give you a letter telling him so.'

'The men are already far from their homes.'

'I have said, turn back. I will go on alone.'

'But what will you do? How will you live?'

'I have my fishing rod. I don't want the gun. You take it back. There will be *gompas*, places like Ruhar, every three or four days at least. The summer is young.'

'The monsoon is almost upon us.'

'But it does not bring much, except clouds, beyond Himachal, beyond the Poat La there.' He stood, absorbing the magnificence spread before him. The music was pouring out, so that he felt that he was himself a full orchestra. His being was filled with sounds that had become music – rushing water, shepherds' pipes, wind in deodars, the screaming of eagles.

When Sita Mull spoke it took him a long time to realize

277

that he had been spoken to, and to grasp the content of what had been said to him. 'We will go as far as the river the other side of the Poat La – the Choshirok.'

'It is good of you, Sita Mull, but I have said, you may return to your homes.'

'We cannot leave you. You are not like any other sahib, any other man, I have met. As long as there is no danger to my men, I . . .'

A sharp crack in the air nearby made Rodney start. What on earth was that? He remembered suddenly the sound of the Chinese surveyors' bullets by the Rasua Bhanjhyang. They were being fired at. Sita Mull knew already and had thrown himself flat on the snow. Rodney said, 'Give me that rifle! Go back and see that the porters don't come up on to the pass.' Another bullet smacked by. 'Run man!'

He grabbed the rifle and stumbled forward, running diagonally across to present a difficult target. Two more bullets passed. The shooter was firing from the left side of the pass, where the mountain rose in snow-mantled crags to wider snowfields. Rodney ran to the right side, found a sheltering rock and sprawled behind it, gasping for breath. When he had recovered he began a systematic scanning of the other side. Nothing stirred. A lammergeier quartered the sky above, seeming to drift in and out of the moving clouds, so high was it. A score of men might be hiding in those rocks, two hundred yards away across the snow saddle, and he would never see them unless they moved. How many were there? And who would it be, what sort of person? It was not likely to be Chandra himself, for the same reasons that it was not Chandra who had set the forest fire below the Arau Jot. So it had to be one or more of his porters, probably with only one weapon between them. If that were the case, the man or men would be doing this for a reward and nothing more. Their hearts would not be in it.

He took careful aim at a rock with snow on one side and deep shadow on the other, and fired. Nothing. He took aim again, but an idea struck him and he lowered the rifle without firing. Why had he not thought of this before? The man could not spend the nights up here on the Jot: so he slept lower down, and in the morning came up,

278

tramped off to his ambush place, and settled in for the day's vigil. His tracks ought to be visible . . . and they were – an unmistakable series of shadow blobs on the snow, leading up the shallow slope away from the centre of the saddle and disappearing into the base of the far rocks. The man would have gone up a bit from there . . . not too far because he'd want to be able to come down fast; probably ten feet up. He picked a likely looking crag, aimed at the shadow to the right of it, and fired.

Almost at once, two men stumbled out into the sunlight and he heard their thin shouting. 'Don't shoot, don't shoot! We are friends!'

They ran down across the snow, one carrying a rifle over his head. At the low point he dropped the rifle into the snow, then both stood with hands raised. Rodney thought briefly that it might be a trap to lure him into the open, but they'd had him in the open at the beginning. He walked out and down the snow toward them, calling, 'Sita Mull, come up. There is no more danger.'

The men were typical *paharis,* of the sort he'd seen all along the route and in the villages and *gompas* they'd passed through. Both were dressed in the same way, in baggy breeches and jerkins of homespun wool, a woven goathair rope wound round their waists, and in it slung a porter's headband. Over one shoulder, suspended on a broad cloth band each carried a heavy scrip.

Rodney said, 'Now explain yourselves. Why were you shooting at me?'

One of the men whined. 'I was not trying to hurt you, sahib. The bullets did not pass near, I swear. They were only to frighten.'

Sita Mull's voice was high and angry. 'Ram Dass, in the name of Vishnu, what are you doing?'

The other said, 'It is the sahib's order – the other sahib, the Bengali sahib. He gave us the gun and two hundred rupees each, and said, go back to your homes, but first, hide on the Sersank Jot and frighten the sahib and his porters so that they will not come any further. That is all we did, I swear.'

Sita Mull said, 'Worthless grandson of a dog!' He stepped forward and smacked Ram Dass hard across the

279

face, then gave the other a swinging backhander. They knelt, crying for mercy.

'Do you want to punish these men, sahib? We can take them back to Basohli and they will be charged with attempted murder, in the new courts. In the old days His Highness would have dealt with such scum himself, and in an hour, not a year.'

Rodney said, 'No, send them back. But first take that money off them, and keep it for yourself and our porters. And the gun. That is a fair punishment . . . Ram Dass, where is the Bengali sahib now?'

'He sent us back from the Choshirok, yesterday morning,' Ram Dass answered eagerly.

'And he has nine porters still with him?'

'Yes, sahib. One went back from . . .'

'I know. What weapons?'

'A rifle. Some think he carries a pistol as well, but I have seen the rifle. Also a fishing rod. And a radio set which will send out messages as well as receive them. It is no larger than a small suitcase, a marvel.'

'Where is he going to?'

'He did not tell us, lord, although we asked, for we wanted to know when we would be turning back toward our homes.'

'Where would he get to if he went on down the Choshirok?'

Sita Mull cut in. 'To the Zaskar River, sahib, and so to the Indus a little below Leh. But that would be twelve days march, or more.'

'He was carrying only twelve more days' supplies,' Ram Dass said.

Rodney thought, so he is either planning to restock in Leh, the capital of Ladakh, or go on say four days and back eight, to roadhead at Alwas. But he wouldn't be heading for any place in Indian control, with Ayesha's people after him.

Ram Dass said, 'He takes a tin of tomato soup every day.'

'I know,' Rodney said, smiling at the memory.

Encouraged by the smile, Ram Dass said eagerly, 'And he only bought eight tins from Hari Chand in Basohli. I know, they were in my load. He has three left today.'

'Anything else give you an idea of what he was doing or where he was going?'

Both men shook their heads. 'Nothing, sahib, nothing. He was usually cheerful, though when he sat apart in the evenings with his radio and the things on his head, then he looked very sad. But he told us nothing, and we could learn nothing by other means.'

'Though you searched his belongings when on the road, I don't doubt?'

'There was nothing except some money and we are not thieves.'

'Are you finished with them, sahib?' Sita Mull asked. 'Go then, owls' pizzles, and when you get back to Basohli, find other work. I shall see that you are never again employed as porters. Go, go!' He swept up snow and hurled it after their running figures.

Alone on the pass again Rodney said, 'Where are our men?'

'A hundred yards down the hill. We must turn back, sahib. I was saying, when those scoundrels fired at us, that as long as there was no danger, we would go on. But the Bengali sahib has a rifle and perhaps a pistol, and heaven knows what else he will order his porters to do. I cannot risk my men's lives any more. They will bring the loads up here, and you shall choose what you want to take out of them. Do not carry too much, sahib. Between here and the Zaskar there are a few small *gompas* – miserable places of one or two houses, but you will be able to buy barley flour and sheep milk, at least. For four days' march beyond the Poat La there are such places. Beyond that, for seven days down the Zaskar to the Indus, there is nothing. Do not venture beyond the last settlement unless you are well stocked, or have other porters.'

'I doubt if I'll be going much farther north,' Rodney said, 'Thank you for everything, Sita Mull. I told you, I don't want the rifle. . . . Goodbye.'

The old campfire had been made of juniper roots beside the Dhariang River. He had come down more than five thousand feet from the Sersank Jot behind him : ahead the ground rose steeply even farther to the Poat La, 18,752 feet above the sea. Here he really stood on the edge of the

Tibetan world, and the names of the passes showed it: *Jot* was a pass in the language of the hill people to the south, essentially Hindu and Aryan in spite of an admixture of Sino-Tibetan blood and habits. *La* meant pass in Tibetan: and Ladakh's other name was Little Tibet. Not very far to the east an unmarked boundary defined the eastern limit of the Republic of India, the western limit of what had for so long been the Hidden Kingdom of Tibet, now a conquered subject province of Communist China.

This fire, which he had rebuilt and relit, had been made by Chandra two days ago. But what was he doing now? Sita Mull said there were four days of inhabited terrain north of the Poat La. Very sparsely inhabited, true, but what could Chandra do among people, where his actions might be observed, and reported? The new Indian strategic road from Kulu to Leh was not far to the east, and was well used: word could be got to the authorities without much delay. . . .

He got out his map and studied it. Tomorrow he'd go over the Poat La and down the Tema to the Choshirok River – perhaps twelve miles from this campfire, but an enormous climb. Then the *gompas* began – Burduna Gompa, Padam, Ukti – these last two with caravanserais: then more – Thonde, Zangla, Naerung. . . . By then Chandra would have used up his remaining tins of tomato soup. He smiled again: it was really ridiculous how something so mundane and petty had suddenly become a vital piece in a jigsaw puzzle, for if Chandra had taken a certain number of tins only, he expected to be trekking less than that number of days. He would run out before reaching Leh if he went forward. So he wasn't going much farther – no more than three days from today. Then how was he getting out? Levitation?

By God, yes, levitation, twentieth century style! A helicopter! His destination was somewhere close to where he now was: to that place someone would come in a helicopter and fly him out – presumably back to the place where the helicopter had come from. But that could be a hundred and fifty miles away, or more. Modern helicopters had a long radius of action.

Now, quick, as the twilight thickened and the cold bit

sharper – where could the rendezvous be? Not down the Zaskar, because of the number of *gompas*. Back up the Choshirok then? He peered at the map – no, that stream was just as dotted with settlements southwards as it was to the north, towards the Zaskar. Ah, nine miles below the point where he would reach the Choshirok tomorrow, a valley came in from the left, the west – the Doda . . . but on the Doda, too, *gompas* were marked for thirty miles, up to its sources under Nun Ser. Two rivers came into the Doda from the south. The first one, the Seni, reached it only five miles above the Doda's junction with the Choshirok: and no *gompas* were marked in the Seni for its fifteen-mile length. The next river was the Bardur – too far, and it looked to be steeply inclined. The Seni was the best bet.

But Chandra was either already there, or would be to-morrow. To reach the same place Rodney had to traverse an inverted U – cross the Poat La, go north for twenty miles, west for five, then back south until he found Chandra . . . but Chandra wouldn't be there by then. He would have made his rendezvous with the helicopter, and gone.

He had to cut the corner somehow. He got out his flash-light and switched it on. The little circle of light wandered over the map's surface. He had two possibilities . . . no, three. First, he could cut out the Poat La altogether by going down this stream for ten miles, then tackling the mountain wall which separated it from the Seni. But he had looked at that wall as he came down from the Sersank, and it was a monster of rock and ice, the top four or five thousand feet very severe.

Secondly, he could go up to the Poat La but, instead of passing on over it and down the Tema, he could head west-ward along the ridge until he was above the Seni, then drop down into it; but traversing along the top of that mountain wall was going to be just as difficult as crossing it.

Thirdly, he could cross the Poat La, go down the Tema to the first settlement in it, called Kanjur, and from there cross the intervening ridge to the Seni. It couldn't be as high as the wall he was looking at, and there was at least the chance of finding someone in Kanjur to indicate the best route, or perhaps even guide him.

283

The Poat La and Kanjur it would be. He switched off the flashlight and it was dark, light gleaming high in the night from the ice walls on three sides of his little fire. He arranged himself for sleep, humming a new theme that had come into his consciousness at that instant, a lifting theme as massive as the mountains, as evocative as the starlight on the high snow.

CHAPTER TWENTY-TWO

There had been a man in Kanjur, three in fact, husbands of a woman who owned two fields and a borax pit there, sent up by her to plant seed and do some mining while she stayed behind in Padam with her other husband, apparently her favourite. One of the men had volunteered to guide Rodney up the ridge separating the Tema and Seni valleys, and had refused payment. Rodney thought he welcomed the chance of finding an opportunity to escape from doing something his wife had told him to do. He was a few years older than Rodney but his legs and lungs were used to these tremendous slopes and Rodney had to keep telling him to slow down. Not only was he not as fit as the Kanjuri, but he had risen at four a.m., eaten as much as he could and set off at five, crossed the Poat La four hours later, and reached Kanjur before noon. When he had explained that he wanted to cross over the ridge into the Seni the men there had looked at the sun, gesticulated, and said he should wait till the next day – they had a place for him to sleep – and pointed out the usual spread of sheepskins and Ladakhi goathair blankets by the aromatic fire. It was late, they said – the wall of rock and snow was high – he could not reach the crest line within four hours, and then – there was the long way down.

Rodney had said, 'I must go,' dearly wishing he did not have to. His night would be cold at best, at worst – fatal.

A glacier descended into the Tema valley a short distance below the three hovels that constituted Kanjur, and Rodney's guide crossed the base of it, where a line of gravel marked the terminal moraine, and then led up the mountain on the glacier's left side. For an hour the climbing was hard but not difficult, and Rodney thought they had ascended about fourteen hundred feet. The next hour was steeper still, and now plaques of snow began to appear, and had to be crossed with care, for it was impossible to tell how deep they were. His boots were good, with deep-cleated soles, and now he climbed with the ice axe in hand.

In the third hour the snow grew deeper, but the moment

of most danger came when the Kanjuri, a few yards in front and higher up, suddenly called out a word that Rodney did not recognize, and stopped in his tracks, holding on to a steep rock face beside him. Rodney too stopped, balanced himself and looked up, for he heard a hurried clattering . . . an ibex, with a magnificent pair of horns, was galloping at full tilt diagonally up and across the rock fall immediately above them. Already it was fifty, eighty, a hundred feet up. The Kanjuri was shouting with excitement, but neither man was armed and the leaping goat was in no danger. But Rodney saw, before the Kanjuri, that they themselves were – the ibex had started a rockslide. Small stones were bounding down the fall far above, larger rocks beginning to move, grey dust rising across the face of the mountain, and under foot a rising rumble and roar.

They were both near the edge of the rock fall and now the guide too saw the danger and, a second after Rodney, began to run for the shelter of the cliffs close by. A stone the size of a tennis ball whizzed at Rodney's head; he saw it coming and ducked so that it missed, close. A bigger rock bounded off a ledge in the slide twenty feet above and crashed into his left arm, swinging him round. A moment later he reached the cliff and pressed himself flat against the under side. The Kanjuri was not so lucky: another rock bounding down from above hit him square on the left temple. He went down without a sound, rolling over and over on the steep slope. Rodney sprang after him and, with rocks crashing past, the stones moving like a wave under his feet, smaller stones hitting him in the back and head, he grabbed the Kanjuri's homespun coat, pulled him to a stop, and, hit twice again, dragged him off the rock fall to the side. There he held him, lying on top of him to protect him from the stones.

Gradually the noise subsided. Fewer and fewer stones rattled down. The Kanjuri groaned, mumbled a word, and put his hand to his head. Rodney examined a big bump, with a clean cut in it; nothing broken, but the man was bleeding and looked ill. He knelt beside him and said, 'How are you?'

The man muttered, 'My head aches . . . I will be well in an hour or two.' He leaned over and vomited.

Rodney said, 'I must go on. Thank you for what you have done. Go back to the village when you feel better, not before.'

The man nodded, wincing. He said, 'Wait, sahib . . . Go on up this line to the top. There will be snow. On the top, go north till you see bare rock – then down into the Seni. Before that bare place the snow will be blown out far on that side, but without support.'

Hidden cornices, Rodney thought: that was to be expected. He shook the man's hand and started on up the slope.

He reached the crest line at half past four, having climbed four thousand feet from Kanjur. The altitude must be about nineteen thousand feet and he was on hard-packed snow. His thigh muscles ached and his calves had turned to jelly. His head was light, and his lungs burning from the long effort. Afternoon clouds were crowding the sky. If they sank down on to this ridge before he reached the place to turn down toward the Seni. . . .

North now, the Kanjuri had said. He moved off over the snow, rolling, glissading, sliding, twice falling through soft patches to his knees, struggling up, twice cutting steps on icy stretches. How far was that damned bare place? His eyes must be failing behind the dark glasses, for he could see nothing; but it was the clouds, lowering ever closer, the darkness suddenly split by a blinding glare of lightning farther down the ridge in the direction he was going. Forty minutes, fifty . . . seventy . . . a big place, the snow always blown off by the perpetual wind.

He staggered to the western edge of the ridge and looked down. Thick veils of cloud drifted across the mountain face below him, so that he could only see the distant valley floor in brief cameos. Down there sometimes the land was indigo in the shadow, sometimes glistening silver-grey in the light. But at his feet the rock fell away, and he started down, from ledge to ledge, always on the knife edge of a westward-descending ridge line. Sometimes there was angled snow on the ledges, and he had to sweep it away with his hand or boot to make a secure place to stand for the next drop. Sometimes he had to go out on the snow to bypass a drop too long to be taken without a rope. Once, on such a snow traverse, he began to slide, and fetched up twenty feet lower, ice axe dug in as a brake, spread-eagled against the rock and bruised again, this time on the other arm. Now both arms ached, but those pains were nothing in the rising ocean of fatigue which was beginning to engulf him and all his capacities . . . the light was fading fast . . . how far down was he? Two thousand, three thousand from the top? Two thousand, no more than that . . . so, at about seventeen thousand feet. A moment later, finding himself flat on his face on the ground, his left hand clutching a handful of snow, he realized that he had passed out.

This must be his bed. Only the height was bad, for there had been much worse places. Whatever its faults, it would have to do. He needed the last remaining atoms of strength to secure himself for the night. He sat with his back against a rock face, facing out over the slope which began again a foot past the toes of his boots. He pulled the extra wool sweater out of the pack and put it on, the windjacket over that again. The hood of the windjacket was already raised and his gloves and goggles on; there was nothing more he could do, except, when he felt stronger, eat something. His eyes closed.

He awoke with a deep chill permeating him and tried to move but could not. The stars were out and there was no wind. If I live, he thought, it will be because of that. He tried again, concentrating his whole attention on his left hand. Come up! he commanded, forcing his will out from his brain, into his shoulder, down the arm. . . . Slowly the arm moved, the hand rose. He put the wrist close to his face and read his watch: two o'clock.

He spent the next fifteen minutes moving each part of his body, one after the other, with infinite slowness, and with pain that steadily increased until edged streams of agony ran from every extremity and from all the pores of his skin into the centre, where it seemed to concentrate in the middle of his chest. But he knew he was alive, and in the end he managed to drag himself upright against the rock face behind him. Then he raised one foot, painfully lowered it, raised the other, then again the first . . . left, right, left, right. At the same time he began to sing, at first a miserable croak, then a recognizable tune. As his feet moved faster up down up down, his singing strengthened.

288

He was singing the theme that had come to him on the Sersank Jot on the main range of the Himalayas, and it would be the master theme of the last movement of the Himalayan Concerto; and he was alive and would finish the work.

Half an hour later, the chill retreated from him, the pain no longer agony but a dull ache, and something that almost approximated warmth in his belly, he ate some of the mixed butter and barley flour, called *tsampa,* which the Kanjuris had given him, and swallowed a mouthful of whisky from his flask. Three o'clock: he would not go to sleep again, but stay here, stamping and singing on his ledge till the brightness of the stars began to fade in the coming of day.

He reached the floor of the Seni valley at ten o'clock in the morning, the sky clear in all directions. He seemed to be at the head of the flat lower section, for to the south-west, uphill, the land rose rapidly to make a huge cirque, striated by many glaciers coming down from the main Himalayan crest, and from the subsidiary ridges to right and left. In the other direction the Seni floor sloped gradually. Twelve or thirteen miles down there, a wall of mountains closed the V of the Seni. That wall marked the far side of the Doda, where there were *gompas.* If Chandra had indeed turned up this valley, he would be somewhere between the wall and where Rodney now stood. He ate another handful of *tsampa* and started down the valley, the ice axe again strapped to his pack. The first clouds of the day were beginning to peer over the rim of the south-western crests.

An hour later, when he had covered a cautious two miles, he heard a distant humming throb. He stopped, moving automatically to the shelter of a great rock beside the small but strongly flowing Seni, and looked round. It did not sound like a truck or an agricultural machine. The sound grew louder . . . it wasn't a helicopter. The sound suddenly increased to the unmistakable whine of a turbo-prop aircraft. Then he saw it, sunlight on its wings, a high-wing monoplane with fixed tricycle undercarriage. It was Kit Sanders' Saab. It had come in over the wall of the cirque and was now dropping sharply, flying close to the ridge that he had crossed from Kanjur, tilting its wings, spilling air . . . it was down to less than a thousand feet above the valley floor now. It stood on its left wing, turned 90°, and came up the valley toward him. It passed over him at two hundred feet, its flaps fully extended, its engine whistling eerily, and landed on the tamarisk-dotted gravel of the valley floor three hundred yards behind him.

He stayed crouched by the rock, thinking. Kit was behind him and Chandra in front. How had Kit known to come to this particular valley, at this particular time? Why had she come? To murder him . . . or Chandra? He must warn Chandra.

He left the shelter of the rock and hurried, crouched, down the bed of the Seni away from the plane, which he could clearly see on the gravel behind him. It had made a perfect landing. Two people were beside it, and one of them had a rifle in his hands. A second later a bullet cracked close over him. A woman' voice called faintly, borne down on the wind, a single word – 'Stop!'

He began to run, but after a few paces he stopped as another bullet smacked overhead. It was not the bullet that made him stop, for he was thinking – Kit Sanders and I need each other's help, and we both need Chandra's. Surely she could be made to undertand that. We three have been thinking and acting as though we are merely agents of nations pitted against each other, but we are also brothers and sisters trying to uncover truths which our masters are concealing from us. We are not trying to make war, but forewarn of catastrophe. In that endeavour we are a single team and must act as one. He turned and started back toward the plane.

It was Kit who had fired, though Akbar Khan also carried a .300 rifle slung over one shoulder. She was wearing flying overalls and heavy gloves slung round her neck. 'It's cold up there,' she said, 'even with the cabin heating on. We were seven thousand feet higher than I'm supposed to go without oxygen . . . Rodney, give us a hand here.' She climbed up on to the step of the Saab and began to hand out four-gallon cans of aviation fuel. 'Put them over there, by the bank of the stream . . . There, that's enough to get us to where we're going.'

'Who's we?'

'Akbar, myself, and Chandra. We're a hundred plus air

miles from Srinagar, and rather closer to Pakistani territory near Sialkot. And you presumably can find your own way out of here as you found your way in? Where are your porters?'

'They went back from the Sersank Jot.'

She whistled, and said, 'Well, perhaps I can leave you some stores, but I can't take off with more than three on board, at this altitude, and on this surface. And now, we've got no time to waste. Are you going to promise to sit quiet here till we come back, or do we have to tie you up – or take some more final means of immobilizing you?'

'You're going to get Chandra?'

She nodded, her grey eyes on his. He said, 'I'll come with you. I want to talk to him, too. I was thinking, when you fired at me just now, that we're all ready going the same way – you, me, Chandra – perhaps Akbar, too. Don't hurt Chandra, will you?'

She said, 'Of course not, if I can help it. Look, Chandra spent last night in Padam.'

'On the Choshirok!' Rodney exclaimed, 'He hasn't turned up here yet?'

'Not as of ten a.m., when I took off from Srinagar. Well, actually my last message contained information received at five-thirty a.m.'

They were walking down the valley now, rocks in place under the Saab's wheels, the sun warm on their necks, and snow glittering along the ridges on either hand. The clouds were thicker and higher behind them.

Rodney said, 'What kind of information? How do you know exactly where he is? I have been just guessing where he might be, and what he's doing, but you seem to know.'

She said, 'We don't know what he's doing, but we do know exactly where he is. I might as well tell you. He's using a radio transmitter and we have satellites that can pick up any such signals and by computerized cross-bearings pinpoint the location of the transmitter. If he stops sending, we'll be in the dark, but so far he's been sending quite long messages mornings and evenings, when the transmission is clearest.'

'Who's receiving them?'

'A Chinese station at Kokche Gompa. It's on the Indus, about a hundred miles above Leh. Our satellite has taken

291

a photo of the spot, and it's been processed and interpreted – nothing to see, a *gompa*, half a dozen mud huts, the remains of an old mine, an unimproved airstrip.'

'And, of course, the Chinese military road down the Indus valley?'

'Yes. It passes close – but there are no signs of unusual traffic on it.'

They strode on abreast, sharp scents rising from the herbal weeds that they crushed under their boots.

After half an hour the valley narrowed, and the Seni stream curved through a narrower place, not severe enough to be called a gorge. Here the banks were of rock, and steep.

Kit glanced back and said, 'Can't see the plane. This will do. Akbar, please climb up a bit and keep a lookout down the valley. Don't show yourself.'

They settled themselves to wait. After an hour Kit began to fidget, muttering, 'What the hell's keeping him?' She kept looking at the sky, and when Rodney asked her what was the matter she said, 'Look at those clouds. I hoped to be out of here by one at the latest. . . . It's past that now, and no sign of him. I'll have the hell of a job finding my way through those clouds under twenty-two thousand and that's the absolute ceiling, even if I use the little personal emergency oxygen tank I carry. It's the plane's ceiling – I've tested it.'

'You could get out to the north or north east,' Rodney said, gesturing at the clear skies and brilliant pale sunshine in that direction.

'And run into a Chinese fighter,' she said sarcastically; then grudgingly, 'We might, I suppose . . . go out that way till we hit the Indus valley then fly down it. But there's a close radar watch on the Indus and you're very likely to be picked up by a fighter. No, if it comes to it, I'd rather wait till tomorrow early, then sneak out low over the ranges and down into Srinagar or Sialkot before they know what we are or where we're heading.'

Another hour passed. Forty minutes more. Near three o'clock a small stone landed beside them. They looked up. Akbar was on his way down to them. When he reached them he said, 'He is coming. About half a mile away now.'

'Alone?' she asked quickly.

'Yes.'

'Armed?'

'I think he has a rifle slung.'

She thought a moment. 'You two wait there' – she pointed at a rock near the stream – 'I'll be behind you. When he gets close, but before he reaches you, I'll step out, and tell him to stop. If he does anything silly, I'll shoot him in the foot, and you overpower him.'

They went to the place she had pointed out. Old Akbar, beside him, smelled of garlic and aviation fuel, and now burped quietly. The henna was fading from his hair, leaving the white predominant. An eagle was examining them from a mile straight up in the sky, under heavy slow moving clouds. They waited. The eagle widened its circles.

Behind him he heard Kit's sharp voice. 'Stand still, Chandra! Hands up!' Rodney stepped out of his concealment, Akbar beside him. Akbar's rifle was raised and pointed.

Chandra was wearing rough homespun grey-brown breeches such as the *paharis* wore, with a bright yellow windjacket, on his head a flat topped Tibetan cap with much gold braid, one flap down over his left ear; and dark glasses. He had a rifle slung, a pack on his back and in his right hand an object that looked like a small black plastic suitcase.

Akbar Khan stepped up to him, unslung his rifle, and opened the breech: but there were no cartridges in the chamber or the magazine.

'I was hoping perhaps to eat wild ass some time,' Chandra said apologetically, 'but I haven't seen any. Nor any other big game. A few hares.'

'What have you done with your porters?' Kit asked abruptly.

'They're in my last camp in Padam,' Chandra said. 'I didn't need them to come up here and look for *kiang*.'

'You didn't need that, either,' she said, pointing at the suitcase.

'That's my dinner jacket,' Chandra said, his face straight. 'My father was I.C.S., don't forget. We were never allowed any of your American slovenliness.'

'It's no joking matter,' Kit snapped. 'And your porters aren't in Padam, either, are they? You've sent them back.'

'As you will, Kit,' Chandra said. 'You were always wiser than I in the ways of the world.'

'Well,' Kit said, 'I don't know what you've come to this Godforsaken place for, but you're leaving it with us. I'd take off now, but I can't in this weather.'

'You may not be able to tomorrow, either,' Chandra said. He jerked his chin at the indigo clouds lowering across the southern and western horizons.

'We'll get out at dawn,' she said impatiently. 'The question is, where shall we take you? India, where you may spend the rest of your life in prison? Or Pakistan, where you will be sharply questioned, but nothing worse, particularly if Akbar here vouches for your efforts on behalf of Kashmir's independence? Think about it. We have all evening to talk it over.'

She turned and started walking back up the valley towards the place where they had left the Saab and the cached fuel.

It was five o'clock. They were sitting under the wing of the plane, Kit, Chandra and Rodney. A little distance away Akbar Khan crouched over an empty can filled with sand, doused with aviation fuel and set alight, a 'desert cooker', boiling water for coffee and heating a large tin of beef and vegetable stew.

'Now,' Kit said, 'what are the Chinese up to? Rodney has given me the alternatives, but which is the right one?'

Chandra said, 'I don't know, Kit. I wish I did.'

He really doesn't, Rodney thought; that's why he has come here, to find out. Kit doesn't understand that, she just thinks he's on the run, perhaps hoping to slip through Indian controlled territory into Tibet proper.

She said, 'You *do* know, Chandra. You *must*!'

'I don't.'

She said angrily, 'Look Chandra, I love you. You know it. But I have a duty to what I believe in . . . Russia. The Soviet system. Revolution. The masses. If you won't talk, I'm going to hand you over to the Indians.'

Chandra stayed silent, his face immobile and calm.

Rodney leaned forward. 'You're on your way to find out the truth, Geminus, aren't you?'

Chandra nodded.

Rodney continued. 'To learn whether you have been duped, as Jansingh Gharti was.'

Chandra nodded again.

Rodney said, 'And to learn whether it is Bangladesh or Pakistan that is to be duped in the same way, but on a national instead of a personal scale . . . because one of them is certainly going to aid in its own destruction.'

'Shhh!' Kit Sanders said sharply. A faint thrashing sound filled the air.

'Somewhere close,' Rodney said.

Akbar stood up, spoon in hand. 'In this valley,' he said.

Kit leaped to her feet and seized her rifle. Akbar dropped the spoon and grabbed his. A big dark-green helicopter came roaring up the Seni valley toward them, less than twenty feet above the thin tamarisk. A second followed close behind the first, and a third followed, behind again and a hundred feet higher. Kit climbed into the cabin of the light plane and pressed the starter. Akbar ran to remove the rocks from under the wheels. Rodney watched the helicopters idly – Indian or Chinese? Perhaps even Pakistani. . . .

The Saab's engine coughed and fired. Blue smoke poured from the tail pipe and the propeller whirled. The nearest helicopter clattered directly overhead, and a stream of machine gun bullets kicked up gravel all around them. Rodney moved away from the plane, hands raised, as the second chopper landed fifty feet off, its rotors raising a whirling spray of gravel and whipping the water of the Seni stream into froth. Soldiers in the unmistakable quilted uniforms of the People's Republic of China poured out of it. Rodney counted fifteen, as the third 'copter landed and fifteen more men climbed out of that. He was surrounded, rifles and sub-machine guns poking into his ribs. The chopper that had been on guard above now landed and two men, obviously officers, jumped down and walked briskly towards them.

The propeller of Kit's plane slowed and stopped. The engine whined into silence. She climbed out and down, menaced by bayonets. One of the approaching officers said in excellent English, 'Which of you is Mr. Chandra Gupta?'

Chandra said, 'I am.'

The officer saluted, saying. 'Captain Wong Tien San. Who are these others?'

'Agents of India and Russia.'

'Do you wish them killed?'

'No. They will have much to tell us, if they are willing. And in a few days what they know or suspect about our plans will be of no value, anyway. Take them with us, please.'

The captain glanced at his watch. 'We shall board at once. Shall I destroy the light aircraft?'

Chandra shook his head. 'Leave it, please, captain. It may be that I shall use it to return to India, after our meeting at headquarters.'

'It is yours?'

'Yes.'

'Follow me then, please.' He barked orders in Chinese and the soldiers began tumbling back into the helicopters. Five minutes later the three choppers rose and with their turbo engines roaring, hurried low back down the valley; then, as the land rose again, climbed steeply eastward towards the serrated snow ridges of the Zaskar Range. Beyond lay the Indus.

CHAPTER TWENTY-THREE

To the south the monsoon clouds towered over the mountain wall in ever higher masses, their lower parts deep indigo and seemingly as solid as the rock and ice bastions occasionally seen between them, their upper curves glowing in the late sun. Below, the land ran away to the north and north-west in a series of tremendous ridges, separated by narrow valleys. A few minutes after climbing out of the Seni valley Rodney had seen a square building to the north, which he thought might be the old fort marked on the map at Padam. After that, as the choppers climbed higher, he saw no sign of human habitation in all the widening circle of Zaskar – only snow, rock and ribbons of grey shale and gravel in the deep cut trenches of the valleys. The choppers flogged on eastward, the two troop carriers to the left and a little ahead of the captain's command 'copter with Chandra and the prisoners.

Chandra sat on a folding seat behind the pilot, taking to Captain Wong, who was in the co-pilot's place. There was no co-pilot. Two Chinese soldiers with AK47 submachine guns unslung sat opposite the three prisoners. The 'copter was of the same size as the two troop carriers, so there was a great deal of empty space between the prisoners and their guards at the rear, and Wong, Chandra and the pilot up front.

Rodney, watching the savage land rise and fall below, felt that some vital electrical contact had been disconnected in him. He had expected to meet Chandra in the Seni valley, and it had really come as no surprise to him to meet Kit Sanders there, too; nor had the sequence of events seemed out of the ordinary; he had subconsciously expected to become Chandra's prisoner, or Kit's, before too many days had passed, for *Azad Shadhinata* was very close now. Through music he had found where the water was, so to speak, rushing toward the lip of a fall, and had launched himself into that current. The fall was near, but he was not fully self-involved . . . not yet.

Why had Chandra told Captain Wong that the light

plane was his? It was risky, seeing that Wong might know that he had been walking for several days to reach the rendezvous. Obviously Chandra was counting on it that Wong had merely been told to take some soldiers, go to such and such a place and pick up an agent called Chandra Gupta. Yet it was a risk, and Chandra had taken it – for what? To save the light plane, for the Chinese would probably have destroyed it, if he had not spoken up – the plane and the extra fuel cached in full view nearby? So Chandra thought he might need to use that plane: but as he was not a pilot, he expected to have a pilot with him. Kit . . . ?

Far below a snake of darker colour winding through occasional snow across a high plateau caught his eye. He pushed his head against the plexiglass and peered down . . . a road, vehicles crawling northwards along it, casting long shadows in the sunset. It could only be the Rohtang-Leh road. The choppers were in full view. Any observer on that road would be able to report them. So what? They were past now, over the next range, and they'd be out of Indian-controlled territory in a few more minutes.

He turned to Kit. 'Did you see the road down there?'

A gun muzzle was pushed into his stomach and the soldier opposite shouted angrily at him in Chinese. He sat back.

Chandra came down, holding on to one of the overhead aluminium hand rails, for the chopper was lifting and swaying in the turbulent air over the great ridges. From the front Captain Wong shouted a few words and the soldier answered, putting his gun back at his side.

Chandra said, 'I've told the captain I want to interrogate you.' He stood in the centre of the chopper, a little forward of them all so that he did not obstruct the soldiers' view of them. His face was grim and his voice sharp, but low. He said to Rodney, 'Any questions you want to ask?'

Rodney shook his head.

'Kit?'

'Can Wong hear us?'

'Not if you mumble, as though you're frightened.'

'Why were you using your radio so much? Didn't you arrange a rendezvous through Lau Chung in the Chinese Embassy before you left New Delhi?'

Chandra frowned. 'I did. The old rendezvous was north of the Rohtang, in Spiti . . . but I thought one of Ayesha's men was on my tail. I gave the man the slip – whoever he was – in Chandigarh, and went on up to Pathankot and Basohli, but then I had to use the radio to tell them where I was and fix a new rendezvous, and they had to confirm that they could get a 'copter there without being intercepted by Indian fighters. Anything more?'

Kit shook her head. Akbar Khan said, 'What is to happen to my country, Kashmir?'

'I don't know. I expect to learn very soon. Do any of you have a concealed weapon?'

There was a brief silence. Rodney felt that the other two were making up their minds whether to trust Chandra. Finally Akbar said, 'I have a knife, in my shoe.'

'Keep it hidden if you can.' Captain Wong slipped out of his seat back toward them. Chandra said, 'Well, if you won't talk here, you'll have plenty more opportunities later. You will find the Chinese generous – if you help them. If not – no one will ever know where you went, or what happened to you.'

Wong nodded, adding sententiously, 'The People reward, the People punish.'

Chandra turned and went forward. Wong stood over them a few moments longer, swaying with the motion of the 'copter, his long pale yellow face glowing deeper red in the afterglow of the sunset.

Fifteen minutes later the note of the thrashing rotors above changed and the nose of the 'copter tilted down. The land rose, they passed low over a snowy ridge, then the rate of descent increased. Water gleamed ahead, running diagonally across their front; a narrow ribbon of road followed the course of the river. It was the Indus – it could be no other. They were coming down somewhere in Chinese-controlled Ladakh or extreme western Tibet, on the road that linked Lhasa with the troops facing the Indians above Leh. Something flashed across the near horizon and Rodney turned his head quickly . . . a jet fighter . . . two, flying close, circling close above the descending helicopters. He could see the red star markings . . . Chinese. Now directly to the side he saw the clear shape of an airstrip on the plain to the north of the big river. There was only one runway, parallel to the river line. It was long, but not all-weather, simply a mile and a half of earth and rock levelled and beaten down. There was no control tower, but two camouflaged tents had been set up near one end of the runway, and another jet fighter was parked to one side of them. It was apparently an auxiliary airfield, only used when operations were expected in the Ladakh area. Well, it was being used now, though three fighters would hardly cause Indian or Russian interpreters of their satellite photos to reach any startling conclusions about the Chinese plans.

North of the airstrip the land rose sharply to mountains that were already towering far above the level of the descending choppers. A mile or so upstream the mountains pressed close to the river and there he saw the marks of quarrying or mining, a few mud houses built against the quarry's outer slopes, and others between the road and the river bank.

His ears buzzed and he swallowed hard to equalize the pressure. Two minutes later the helicopter settled gently on the open plain. Overhead the rotors still whirled as Chandra flung open the doors and Captain Wong came back toward them, shouting, 'Out now, quickly!'

Rodney jumped down on a hard natural surface of gravel. The parked fighter and the airstrip were half a mile to the north-west. The other two fighters were landing in twilight. The quarried hill and mud houses were close. Kit jumped down beside him, and a moment later Akbar Khan, too, stumbling and falling as he landed. One of the soldiers jabbed him in the back with the muzzle of his gun, and snarled in Chinese. The troop-carrying helicopters came down close by, and the soldiers tumbled out of them, shook out into spread formation, and ran toward the mountain.

Wong said, 'Follow them – not one behind the other, in a line.'

The mountain was barely a hundred yards away here. Rodney thought, why is everyone spread out? Ah, so that they would not make a track visible in air photographs.

He heard Kit gasp and looked up. Close ahead he saw a man, a Chinese soldier, on guard, weapon raised: but the man was in shadow, in the mountain itself. The soldiers were closing in now toward a fissure in the face of the rock, beside the old quarry. It was twelve feet or more in height, six feet or so wide – not wide enough to take a vehicle, except perhaps a jeep.

At Wong's heels he passed in, from the dusk and the swirling wind into a cool passage lit by spaced neon tube lights. He checked in wonder, and a gun muzzle was poked into his back. He hurried forward. This passage was man-made, for he saw the dynamite shafts.

It opened up and he entered a large cave, part natural and part enlarged by man, he thought. The ceiling height varied from twelve to thirty feet. Light came from more neon tubes placed on natural pillars supporting the ceiling. The whole cave was about a hundred and fifty feet wide, and twice that length. The space inside it had been neatly divided by painted lines to mark passages and corridors Between these there were complete offices, with tables, desks and typewriters, sleeping accommodation with tiered bunks, a mess hall to feed two or three hundred people, and a kitchen – even then something was cooking, smoke swirling out towards the roof.

Wong turned and said, 'Wait here.' The three prisoners stopped where they were, their guards behind them. The soldiers from the other helicopters had been swallowed up among the people in the cave. Wong and Chandra threaded their way forward to a spot near the centre where an officer was sitting at a table, others flanking him. Wong saluted and a moment later Chandra stepped forward. They all talked for ten minutes, Wong apparently acting as interpreter. Rodney could not see their expressions, for they were too far, and his view of them was often obscured by soldiers passing to and fro immediately in front of him. He wondered what exactly this place was. It felt like a headquarters of some kind, rather than an arsenal or depot, for he could see no signs of storage of food, ammunition or fuel; but perhaps there was more that he had not seen. And, if this was a headquarters, where were the troops?

Wong came back toward them, and signalled to them to follow him. He led on through the cave to the far end, and there turned right and opened a door apparently in the wall of the cave. They entered a short passage, well lit, and the guards closed the door behind. At once Rodney heard the throb of motors and a moment later, after passing another door, he followed Wong into a second cave. This was larger in all dimensions than the first, and it was man-made – a huge chamber divided by pillars and marked out by yellow lines. And this was a depot, for he saw cans of fuel oil stacked to the even sixteen-foot ceiling; open-sided ammunition crates, the shells clearly visible inside; sacks of grain, set up on duck-boards to protect against ground damp. The cave was clean and cool and fresh smelling, and resonant with the subdued drone of ventilator fans.

He felt now that they were again heading toward the front of the mountain and would soon come out into the open, the other side of the quarry, close to the houses of the little *gompa* he had seen from the helicopter. But large double doors, closed, blocked the way, and were guarded by sentries. Many soldiers were lying in cots asleep, others playing cards; this must be the guard house. Tucked into bays in the network, he saw half a dozen jeep-like vehicles, and a few larger trucks.

Another Chinese officer came forward, saluting, and Wong spoke briefly to him. The officer led to the side of the cave, beyond the parked jeeps, and indicated a square of floor, clearly demarcated, which contained cots, blankets, and wooden pillow bolsters. Wong said, 'You will stay here until the general has decided what to do with you. The latrines are through that door, marked with green letters.'

He turned away with a curt word to the two guards, who followed him. The younger officer went about his business, and the three were alone, standing in their 'cell'. No Chinese were nearer than thirty feet, and no one was taking any notice of them.

Kit Sanders said in a low voice, 'They haven't even searched us.'

Rodney said, "They don't have to worry. We're in the middle of hundreds of them, and all the doors are guarded. And if we do get out of here, we are . . . where?'

'Somewhere in the Indus valley,' she said. 'From the speed and direction the helicopters were flying, I'd guess we're about a hundred miles above Leh. And that's where the satellite direction finders placed the radio that was answering Chandra . . . at Kokche Gompa. It's been a small headquarters ever since the Chinese invaded Ladakh in '62 – we thought a company – but this!' She waved a hand at the humming complex about them, and shook her head in wonder.

She sat down slowly on a cot, and fumbling in a pocket of her flying overalls, found a pack of cigarettes and lit one. Rodney followed her example, sitting down and lighting his pipe. Akbar Khan went off to the latrines. Rodney noticed that no one glanced up as he passed. He came back saying, 'It flushes with grey water.'

'Snow melt from the Indus, or a side stream,' Kit said, 'and flushed back into the Indus. We must be very close to the river.'

'Under the quarry, behind the houses of Kokche Gompa, I think,' Rodney said.

'Very likely.' She drew impatiently on her cigarette, and said, 'I can't see the Chinese making all these preparations just for a feint, can you?'

Rodney thought for a while and said, 'Not unless we, or someone, is *supposed* to discover it in time for the information to influence India's reactions.'

She said, 'It's almost too late for that already, and they're still keeping this very secret . . . just the fighters, and the helicopters temporarily parked at what has been an auxiliary airfield for a long time. But there aren't enough troops here to make any serious dent in the Indian positions farther down the Indus.'

'They'll be on their way soon, from Lhasa,' Rodney said. 'It's about eight hundred miles from there to here. By the time the satellites have discovered they've moved . . . and made sure they haven't gone over the central passes into Sikkim or Nepal, they'll be here . . . with much of the ammunition and fuel they'll need to reach the Pir Panjal.'

'And then?'

Rodney shrugged. All three were silent. After a long time, so long that Rodney thought she had gone to sleep, Kit said, 'You said in the train that you felt the Sayyid was central, but I don't see . . .'

Old Akbar Khan apparently had been dozing, for he sat up with a jerk, and said, 'Sayyid Ghulam Mohammed?

303

Let them touch a hair of his head and every Indian in Kashmir will die like a dog.'

'Yes, but . . .' Kit said.

A sudden flame burned in Rodney's head and the circuit of his thoughts was completed with an electric jolt. 'That's it!' he exclaimed.

'What?'

'We haven't been able to make out how the Sayyid can be used to make the Kashmiris rise and help the Chinese invasion. For one thing, he doesn't approve of and will not take part in any use of force, and even if he were not a pacifist he doesn't want the Chinese to take over – he wants Kashmir to be independent. But the Chinese have worked out a way to get the Kashmiris to rise for them, against the Indians . . . all Kashmiris everywhere, the shepherds in the high country, the slum people of Srinagar and Jammu, the road labourers, lorry drivers, everyone. They'd have their roads cut, their convoys ambushed, information of their every move given to the Chinese . . .'

But how?

'Kill the Sayyid!' he said vehemently. 'Have him murdered by Indians! . . . And it's going to be done. Braganza reported some time ago that two professional murderers – Hindus – from Bombay had come to Kashmir. They were being watched, but no one could find out what they were up to. Well, it's clear now. Their job is to murder the Sayyid, and there'll be some plan to hide them until the Chinese army reaches the Vale. But there will also be a plan to make sure every Kashmiri knows that the Sayyid was murdered by Hindu Indians, on the orders of the Government of India.'

Kit expelled her breath in a tuneless whistle. Akbar Khan was sitting bolt upright, staring at Rodney with a look of horror, his hands clenched. Kit said, 'Three days to *Azad Shadhinata*.'

'But that's only the signal for the start of guerilla operations and a general rising in Bengal, Bangladesh and Bihar. They don't want Kashmir to blow up until the Indian Army's been committed in the east, and they themselves are ready to invade at this end. I think the Sayyid will be killed about the time the main Chinese forces pass here.'

'Suppose they leave Lhasa ten days after *Azad Shad-hinata*. It will take them ...?'

'Three days. They'll be ready to attack the Indians in Ladakh about two weeks from now. The Sayyid will be murdered that day or the day before.'

Akbar Khan broke in. 'But, this is the act of savages ... to murder our most respected man, a saint, just for ... I cannot believe it.'

'You had better,' Kit Sanders said grimly, 'and accept that we can do nothing to save him.' She lit another cigarette, seeming to dismiss the Sayyid and his fate from her mind. 'How in hell did they make this place without anyone knowing?' she asked.

Rodney said, 'I've been thinking. ... This was a turquoise mine, or a quarry. The stuff is both mined and quarried. That would give good cover.'

Kit said, 'And for the last five years the Chinese have been exporting more and more turquoise to help their foreign exchange position ... and to explain any activity at this and other mines in this part of Tibet. They have thought of everything.'

Rodney said, 'The main problem would normally be disposal of the spoil ... but they've got the Indus outside the door, and perhaps other old shafts or potholes in the back where they could dump what they blasted out. The truck traffic to bring all this material forward must have been at night, and spread over a long period, to avoid attracting attention. And they've been able to conceal the trucks by day – perhaps in other caves, perhaps in *gompas* or monasteries, where they've evacuated the inhabitants, cleaned out the insides of the buildings and used them as garages. ... There must be far more radio traffic than would be normal for a company headquarters, which is what the Indians and Russians think there is at Kokche Gompa. I don't know how they've worked that out, but they obviously have. This complex won't solve all their problems, by any means – but it will enable them to hit the Indians above Leh with far more than Indian intelligence will believe possible. That, and the Bengal feint, should get them over the Zoji La into the Vale of Kashmir. The murder of the Sayyid will get them over the Pir Panjal, using Indian supplies they'll expect to capture in the arsenals and depots in the Vale. After that . . . well, my guess is that they'll make Pakistan a Communist puppet, under Chinese military protection, of course – that'll be to guarantee Pakistan's independence against attack from India, they'll say. And they'll have Pakistanis all trained and lined up to be the figureheads of the new government.'

Kit shook her head and said, 'And the Soviets won't be able to do a thing to stop it because they won't *know* till too late! God, they'll kill me!'

Rodney said, 'It seems probable that someone's going to kill all of us.' He looked at his watch. 'I'm going to try to get some sleep.'

He lay back, closed his eyes and tried to relax his brain. But he was alert and fine-tuned now, and found it hard to accept that there was nothing he could do. He must somehow save the Sayyid's life; more, save the thousands who were fated to be the victims of the vast strategic plans now taking form before him. His head was filling with the same lifting theme that had come to him on the Sersank Jot. Left hand, right hand, now moving together, the single instrument rising above the mass, leading the orchestra on and up, into battle across the roof of the world, the wind blowing and the bare bones of earth sticking up among scattered flowers and running water.

'Chow,' Kit said. Chinese soldiers had brought them rice and soup in plastic bowls. Soon after, they all three went to sleep.

Rodney awoke several times during the night. The lights were always on and Chinese soldiers and technicians always at work. Akbar Khan was awake from midnight on, squatting on his cot, his eyes open and seeming to gleam red, though the light was the brilliant white of neon tubing. Kit Sanders slept heavily on her back, head lolling, knees drawn up, arms outspread. During the periods when he was awake Rodney's mind returned to the concerto, and while its developing themes filled his inner ear, his inner vision contemplated this war in High Asia that he was watching the orchestras of power prepare for. The cacophony of tuning up the instruments was almost over. The conductor was walking on, the house lights dimming . . . now there'd be a brief pause, then the baton would jerk

306

down, and the first crashing bars would launch Death – unrecallable.

At seven in the morning, they were fed again. Then they waited, hardly speaking now. At noon they were fed once more. At half past four in the afternoon – the light in the cave unchangingly bright through night, dawn, day – Captain Wong came, with Chandra, followed by the same two soldiers who had guarded them on the flight here from the Seni valley.

'Up!' Wong barked. 'Stand up! Raise your hands above your heads!' They did so. The soldiers searched them vigorously, patting their bodies, jabbing their hands into their groins, and under their armpits. Rodney waited anxiously for a command to take off their shoes, but none came. Akbar Khan still had his dagger.

The captain handed three pieces of rope to the soldiers who started to tie their hands behind their backs. When that was done, Wong said, 'The general was in favour of disposing of you here as spies and enemies of the people, but Chandra Gupta persuaded him to let him take you back to main headquarters for further interrogation. Your lives will depend on how much, and how accurate is the information you can give there. You are being tied because we can spare no more men to guard you. The first stage will only be a hundred and fifty miles, then you will all proceed by truck as far as is necessary. Go now with Chandra Gupta. Remember, these soldiers have orders to shoot to kill at the first sign of trouble from any of you. Chandra, the helicopter has just landed.' He turned and walked briskly back through the pillared cave.

Chandra snapped, 'Follow me.' He motioned to the two soldiers to bring up the rear, adding a single word of Chinese. They nodded and obeyed, sub-machine guns unslung. The lieutenant was waiting at the double doors; at his command one of the two sentries standing there opened a small single door at the side, and Chandra led through.

Rodney, at Chandra's heels, walked out into a world pale brown, brilliant under an afternoon sun beyond the shadowed rocks immediately around them, snow mantling all the horizons. He had come out of what looked like a battered old wooden door in a tumbledown mud hovel. The hovel was built against a quarried rock face, and to his left, under the overhang of the rock, was the outward side of the double doors so efficiently guarded inside by the Chinese soldiers. Three or four other hovels lined the cliffside and the dusty white road led past them. Two paces ahead of him Chandra was walking down the road. A hundred yards away, on the remains of a barley field, a big helicopter stood, churning up the dust with its slowly thrashing rotors. The wind blew up the valley into their faces, and beyond the barley field the land tilted down sharply to the grey and white waters of a powerful river – the Indus.

Chandra turned and barked angrily at Rodney. 'Drop back! Make the soldiers push you. Delay them.'

Rodney's ears heard the words, and a moment later he acted, for his mental connections were working perfectly now. He knew where he was and what he was doing. He deliberately turned his ankle over and stopped with a cry of pain, his left foot raised. Akbar and Kit passed him, then the soldiers came up. They shouted at him in Chinese, and he grimaced at his foot. One seized him by the elbow and made a shooing motion – get on! The other waved the muzzle of his gun at his belly and made a fierce face. Ahead, Rodney had seen Akbar stumble and fall, a shoe come off, Chandra stooping into the dust, a quick sweep of the hand and an upward cut, then he was cuffing the old man, and shouting angrily in Hindustani. Then Chandra ran up the steps and vanished into the machine's capacious belly. And Rodney had a hard time hiding the mixed excitement, fear and joy that surged through him: for what Chandra had shouted to Akbar was, 'When you board, take back your knife, which I will have plunged into the pilot's neck, and cut Mrs. Sanders free'; and Akbar was only holding the rope that had bound him; it had been cut and his arms were free.

By now one soldier was dragging Rodney forward by his arm, and a gun muzzle was in his back. He hobbled forward, dragging his foot and groaning with imaginary pain. The chopper was big, the pilot not visible. Chandra reappeared in the doorway and pulled up Akbar, who at once vanished forward. Kit followed and Rodney heard Chandra snap at her, 'Akbar will cut you free. Get it ready for take off.'

As she disappeared she said, 'It's your funeral, too. I've never flown one.'

The soldier pulling Rodney's arm let go and began to scramble up the steps ahead of him. Chandra leaned down and helped him in. Something the soldier saw made him turn his head and open his mouth to shout. Chandra cried 'Jump in!' and Rodney hurled himself up the steps and into the 'copter. The first soldier was on the floor by then, the thin knife in his throat. Chandra was yelling, 'Take off! Take off!' With a fierce jerk the 'copter jumped forward, then backward, lifting fast. The second Chinese soldier was on the steps, his arms coming up, the AK swinging round towards them. Chandra leaned out and, hanging on to the overhead bar with both hands, kicked him in the face. A spray of machine gun bullets crackled into the cabin and through the fuselage as the soldier fell, twisting spreadeagled the hundred feet to the ground, where his body landed on top of one of the mud houses close to the river. Chandra cut Rodney free, then took the first soldier's body and, after unslinging the AK from his shoulder, pushed it out.

'Give me a hand with the pilot,' he said.

Akbar was there already, trying to release the pilot from his place in the left-hand seat. Kit was flying the plane from the right-hand seat, for today, as before, there was no co-pilot. Between the three of them they got the pilot's corpse free of his harness and pulled him over the back of the seat without letting his dangling feet or legs touch the controls. A small spot of blood marked the back of his seat, and there was another in his neck, where Chandra's thrust had entered at the base of the skull, killing him instantly, without a sound.

When they returned, having thrown out the pilot's body to follow the others, Kit asked, 'Where are we going?'

'I don't care,' Chandra said, 'I'm finished everywhere. You decide.'

Rodney said, 'Back to the Seni.'

The 'copter lurched viciously, throwing them to the floor. 'Sorry about that,' Kit muttered between clenched teeth. 'Touch these controls with a feather and it turns somersaults on you.' The 'copter levelled, and she said, 'I'm heading west. . . . There's the chart, Chandra. Show me where we've just been, and give me a bearing for the Seni.'

Chandra said, 'That place is Kokche Gompa.'

'We guessed that. Course is about due west, isn't it?'

'Yes.'

She eased the 'copter a little to the right until the gyro compass indicated 270. She said, 'I have no idea what the wind will do to us, but I think I'll recognize the course as long as we get there before we run into that lot.' She gestured toward the line of monsoon clouds far ahead.

The rotors thrashed steadily. Chandra stood motionless behind Kit, staring moodily forward. The sun was low to their left front, and sinking fast into the distant clouds. Akbar had gone to the rear of the 'copter and was seated, cleaning the blade of his knife.

Kit said, 'Why don't the Russian DF satellites, or ordinary Indian radio monitorings, pick up more traffic into and out of Kokche?'

'Because it sends very little by radio . . . no more than it did seven, eight years ago. There's a multiple-channel land line, laid across-country from Gartok, which *is* big enough to explain the radio traffic it gets.'

They were silent. Rodney, looking at Chandra, could feel his friend's desolation. He said at last, softly, 'Geminus, what happened?'

Chandra said, 'Betrayal. . . . I came out to give my final information, and take my place in the provisional government of the new Bengal – as far as the Chinese knew. But ever since Calcutta my own purpose has been different – to find the truth, the real truth.'

'The bottom line,' Kit said.

'Yes. . . . I found out, last night. The whole Bengal plan is a fake.'

'I know,' Rodney said.

'I've been working half my life to one end . . . a free, united Bengali nation. For the last six years I've had it in my grasp, an attainable reality. I was going to be what my father was prevented from being – a creator of it. . . . And now – ashes and bitter fruit. And for this I risked the life of the only human being I've ever loved. Did the rope bridge go?'

'Yes. Don't think about it.'

Chandra laughed grimly. 'And of course that leak about me in Peking was no accident. To Ayesha and Bajwa I've all along been stressing the importance of Kashmir and Ladakh. So, as soon as it is revealed that I am working for China, all my evidence is discounted. Obviously I must have been concealing the true target – Bengal!'

He grasped Rodney's hand and kneaded it. 'Geminus, what are we going to do? *What are we going to do?*'

'Pray,' Kit said succinctly. 'Look!'

A towering wall of cumulo-nimbus cloud blocked the view ahead, lightning flashing in its centre, the anvil head gleaming ten thousand feet above them. 'Strap yourselves in,' she said, 'this will be rough.'

Rodney slipped into the pilot's seat and strapped himself in. Chandra joined Akbar Khan in the body of the 'copter. The helicopter began to buck and heave. It grew dark, the sun disappeared, swirling grey cloud boiled past, hail hissed and crackled on the perspex, flashes of lightning filled the cabin with sudden fierce glares. The helicopter dropped two hundred feet and Rodney's stomach rose, pressing against his throat till he was ready to vomit. Then it shot up, his stomach now pressing down into the seat . . . lurched sideways, the safety belt creaking. Akbar vomited, groaning and crying out in Kashmiri. Kit's hands were white and bloodless on the controls, the sound of the whirling blades only fitfully heard in the thunder. A bolt of lightning struck the nose of the craft close in front of her and she reared back, her hands in front of her face, the cabin full of unearthly light, an orange ball of fire slowly rolling down the floor toward the tail. Her hands off the controls, the 'copter side-slipped and plummeted downwards. She struggled, the rotor thrashing, and gradually the helicopter righted itself, snow now shining close below.

They burst out into the sun. 'Wipe my face,' Kit said through tight-clenched teeth. 'We've got a few minutes of peace . . . but we'd better be close. This is snow falling, not hail.'

Rodney leaned over and with his handkerchief wiped the sweat off her face. Her shirt and overalls were drenched with it. The snow thickened outside. He felt the nose go down. 'I think the Seni's over the ridge,' she said. 'I'm going down anyway. We're done for once the snow builds

311

up on the rotors.' Below, the undercarriage seemed to scrape over a snow ridge with less than six feet to spare; a final heave and lurch and they were descending fast, the snow thinning. Now they were under the cloud base, dropping faster yet. Rodney said, 'There's your Saab! Left, about two miles.'

Heaving, dipping, buffeted by the turbulent winds below the banked snow clouds, the helicopter sank towards earth. Fifty feet from the ground a wind shear sent it lurching violently upward. Kit swore, pushing the stick forward and shouting, 'Hold tight!' Without warning the wind changed and the helicopter dived toward the stony bed of the Seni. 'She's got away from me!' Kit cried; then they struck, landing with a crash on the right wheels of the under-carriage. Metal splintered and twisted and Rodney felt something fly up and hit him hard on the cheek. The heli-copter tilted and fell on its right side, the whirling rotor blades breaking off one by one as they struck the ground. The engine raced, louder and more crazily, until Kit leaned over and pushed the throttles forward.

In the silence Rodney heard the wind howling through the broken plexiglass and the flapping side door, its open-ing now pointed to the sky. Tiny snow flakes, driven by the wind, raced down the valley like an army of demented demons. Kit Sanders leaned forward and began to cry.

CHAPTER TWENTY-FOUR

The snow had stopped and the skies were clearing from the south-west. Stars appeared, at first only toward the north and east, peering shyly over the glimmering white crest of the ridge on that side, then filling all the depths of the sky. Chandra and Rodney had collected roots of tamarisk and other scrub and made a fire, and Akbar had heated another large can of beef stew taken out of the Saab. As they ate Kit said, 'This is it. There's no more food in the Saab.'

'We're not proposing to stay, are we?' Chandra asked, ladling the hot stew down his throat.

'Some of us must,' she said. 'The Saab can't take off from here with four. Anyone volunteer?'

No one spoke, all busy eating. Rodney finished his stew and said, 'Before we discuss that, we have something else to settle. What are we going to do about what we've learned?'

Kit Sanders said, 'I must send a message. I have the cipher.'

Akbar Khan said, 'The Sayyid must be warned at once of his danger.'

Rodney said, 'I should send a message, too. And I have my cipher.'

Chandra said, 'I do not need to send a message, but I have our cipher if you want to send anything secretly to the Chinese.'

Rodney made up his mind what he must say and wondered whether the other three were thinking the same thing: or deciding who among them must be killed.

Kit put down her bowl and said, 'I have a bottle of Old Crow in the Saab.' She walked over and came back with the bourbon. 'Just paper cups, I'm afraid. Lots of water behind us.'

They washed out their bowls in the stream, and Akbar filled the paper cups with whisky and ice-cold water from the Seni. They returned to the fire and arranged themselves on seats unscrewed from the wrecked helicopter.

Rodney filled his pipe with the last of his tobacco, Kit lit a cigarette.

Rodney said, 'We all have messages to send . . . and they're all the same message.'

Kit drew on her cigarette and blew the smoke slowly up in a ring. She said, 'I think I get you.'

Rodney said, 'We are each of us agents of a different party. You, Akbar, are in the Kashmir People's Party, aren't you?'

'I am,' Akbar said. 'Also in the Sayyid's Kashmir Azad Movement.'

'I didn't know that,' Kit said. 'I've been getting careless . . . and unobservant.'

Akbar said, 'It was I who saved Mr. Bateman's life on the Balhom Tiger, for after I had passed your message to the Indian drop, I at once passed the same information to Dr. Jaffar . . . whence it quickly reached Mr. Gupta here.'

Rodney said, 'Thank you. . . . Look, we are in one sense representatives of mutually hostile powers . . . but we are also representatives of humanity, or, if you prefer, we represent the peoples of India and China and Russia and Kashmir, as well as their governments. And the governments of India and China, at least, are bent on courses which will cause the deaths of thousands, perhaps millions of their own people, besides Pakistanis, Bengalis, and probably Russians and others before it all settles down — which may take twenty or thirty years. These plans will not end in little skirmishes, but will make fundamental changes in the condition of Asia. It may or may not improve the condition of China to have an outlet on the Indian Ocean close to the oil centres . . . but Russia certainly will not think so. It may or may not be good for the Bengali-speaking peoples to form a union and a new country . . . but India certainly will not think so. And we are the only ones who can prevent the gathered forces from being released. Once they move, as we know from experience, sheer momentum will carry them onward . . .'

'We can't stop them,' Kit said.

'Yes, we can. By publicity. No one *knows*, except us . . . the Chinese don't know, the Indians don't know. *We* know. . . . I am going to compose a brief message to the world, describing what we know to be the plans of India,

314

Russia and China. I propose to submit it to you all for your approval. And then we will send it out, on the Saab radio, in clear, on different wavelengths, all night. By dawn it will be on the desks of all the presidents concerned. By dusk orders will have gone out to cancel everything, revert to the status quo.'

He fumbled in his pocket, found the musical notebook and pencil he always carried with him and began to write by the light of the fire. After half an hour he re-wrote at half the length; they were not, after all, very complicated plans, once the real intention was separated from the deceptive measures, and the shorter the message the stronger would be its impact.

After an hour, while the others sat silent, smoking, wrapped in their own thoughts, he passed round the notebook.

Kit read it quickly and said, 'I agree with that.'

Akbar Khan said, 'Put in that the Indian police must protect the Sayyid, sahib.'

'All right.'

Chandra Gupta read it, then looked up, the notebook in his hand. 'You were born in Lucknow on June 12, 1942. Whereabouts in Lucknow?'

'In the British Military Hospital, I believe.'

'I was born at home, in Lucknow, on the same day, as you know. Our home's about fifty yards from the hospital. What time of day?'

'I think I remember my mother saying she had a hard time. She went in the evening before, but I wasn't born till dawn.'

'About 4.30 a.m. in Lucknow on June 12. That is the moment of my birth. We, of course, noted it exactly so that the Brahmins could prepare my horoscope . . . which says that I will not see my thirty-seventh birthday, as I told you at Arau, remember?'

'But that's tomorrow!' Rodney exclaimed.

'For you too,' Chandra said, smiling. 'But we don't believe that superstitious tommy rot, do we?' And Rodney realized that if he had been born at the same time and place as Chandra, he would have the same horoscope.

Chandra said, tapping the notebook. 'I agree entirely

315

with this message. Let's start sending it. Who'll take the first spell?'

Kit said, 'I will. I'll send it five times, signing off with all our names, and ask for acknowledgements from any station or ham operator that gets it.'

She walked over to the Saab, climbed in and switched on the cabin lights.

Rodney turned to Chandra. 'Where are you going to go? How can I help?'

'Back to India, Geminus. Ayesha's people think I betrayed India when I became an agent for China, but now I'm telling them all they want to know, so they won't be so thirsty for my blood. Anyway, I am an Indian. Perhaps we can unite Bengal without force, some day.'

Rodney said, 'Ayesha's going to be just as furious with me, for letting out the true Indian plans.'

Chandra laughed, 'So we're in the same boat! Twins in adversity, twins to the end, in sunshine and rain. Have some more of Kit's whisky' – he poured – 'and I think I'll break a lifelong rule . . . a rule my father asked me to make, and I have kept for his sake and in the name of a united Bengali people. I shall have a drink.' He filled another paper cup and raised it. 'To the Gemini!'

They drank, then both relapsed into silence, staring into the fire. After a long time Chandra said softly, 'What are you going to do about your marriage, Geminus?'

Rodney did not look up. Indreni and the children had come into his mind during the terrible helicopter flight, and he wondered why. He said, 'Look back, into myself, try to find out what went wrong, why. Then try again, I suppose.'

Akbar Khan said, 'It is nearly ten o'clock, sahib. Can we make the radio in the helicopter work, to pick up the news from Srinagar?'

Chandra got up. 'I am sure we could. It may have been damaged, but they make those things pretty tough.'

They walked together to the chopper, lying on its side like a huge dead green beetle and clambered up and inside. Akbar's torch flashed, and Chandra crouched over the radio, turning knobs. Sound flooded the cabin and Rodney said, 'We won't jam Kit, will we?'

'No. She's sending on short wave and this is on the medium band. . . . Wait a minute. That sounds like Urdu.'

'That is from Lahore,' Akbar Khan said. 'It is an educational programme that ends at ten o'clock. Srinagar is a little to the right.'

Strains of Indian classical music ended and a voice said, 'This is All India Radio, from Srinagar. . . . Here is the ten o'clock news, on Monday, June 11, 1979. We regret to announce the tragic death of the Sayyid Ghulam Mohammed, prominent Kashmiri statesman, at the age . . .'

Akbar cried, 'In the name of Allah the Merciful!' His arm flashed and Chandra Gupta fell forward on to the tilted radio dials.

The voice continued, 'The Sayyid was accidentally run over by a car driven by his son outside his residence in Awantipura late this afternoon. He was killed instantly. The burial will be . . .'

Akbar turned a dial and the voice was cut off. He said, 'I thought the Chinese had killed him.'

Rodney bent over Chandra and turned up his face. Akbar's torch showed the eyes open, the generous mouth smiling. Akbar Khan had killed him with the same short murderous stroke with which Chandra had killed the helicopter pilot, in this place, a few hours ago. He was stone dead, no mark except the narrow knife entry in the nape of the neck, and a drop or two of blood there.

Akbar Khan said, 'I am not sorry, sahib. He knew they were going to kill the Sayyid. He would not have saved him, if the Chinese had not deceived him over Bengal.'

Rodney eased the Gemini ring off Chandra's finger, and put it on his own, opposite the other. Then he climbed out of the helicopter and walked away up the valley. By the starlight he began to collect roots. His Geminus had been a Hindu and should be burned before the following sunset. The available wood was not enough, by itself, but there was plenty of aircraft fuel in the helicopter. A man's eldest son should light his father's funeral pyre. Chandra had no son, so he, his Geminus would do so, and pray.

The Concerto, to the coda of the last movement, was complete in his mind now, and only remained to be written down, and the parts for all the separate instruments orchestrated. And it would be dedicated to the Gemini.

THE MAN WHO WILL BE KING

H.R.H.

BY TIM HEALD AND MAYO MOHS
(ILLUSTRATED)

H.R.H. Prince Charles is currently the world's most eligible bachelor and heir to the greatest institution left on earth: the British throne.

In this in-depth portrait of the monarch-to-be, the man behind the official figure comes vividly to life. His childhood in Buckingham Palace; his years at Cambridge as the first Prince of Wales to earn a university degree; his stunts flying helicopters and diving under the ice for the Royal Navy; his 3,000 acre estate in Kent, which he calls 'the most desirable bachelor pad in Europe'; his royal tours to Africa, Asia and the Americas; and his rarely disclosed insights into the peculiarities of his office.

Here also is the private story of his real and rumoured romances – Lady Jane Wellesley, Lady Sarah Spencer, Princess Marie-Astrid of Luxembourg, Davina Sheffield – and his comments on marriage.

Now, after three decades of elaborate preparation for kingship, Prince Charles emerges as the most engaging member of the Royal Family, the world's most dashing bachelor and an impressive future monarch in
THE MAN WHO WOULD BE KING.

'By far the frankest, most revealing book about British royalty in years'
JOHN BARKHAM REVIEWS

BIOGRAPHY   0 7221 4495 4   £1.50